UNDEVELOPED

A Pine County Mystery

Dean L. Hovey

ISBN: 1938382056
ISBN 13: 9781938382055

Other books by Dean Hovey

The Pine County mysteries
    Where Evil Hides
    Hooker
    Unforgettable

The Two Harbors "cozies"
    Whistling Pines
    Whistling Sousa

For Charity, Heather, and Garret

DECEMBER 1998

Aaron Roberts was chilled to the bone yet somehow felt oddly giddy as he trudged through the snow. When he arrived at the house he tried to lift the flower pot but his frozen fingers couldn't grip the terra cotta. It fell aside, sinking into the snow. The key he expected to find under the flowerpot was gone. He let out a sob and fell to his knees. In desperation he twisted the doorknob and to his surprise the door opened and he struggled to his feet.

The warmth of the house engulfed him as he pushed the door closed. He fell back against the door and slid to the floor. He used his teeth to pull off the thin work gloves, letting them fall to the floor. The warmth seeped into his clothes and skin as he sat on the mat embossed with the greeting "Welcome to the Boonies."

Strong arms lifted him and with assistance he stumbled to a kitchen chair on numb feet. Someone stripped off the wool jacket he'd taken from the cabin where he'd spent the night and a warm blanket was wrapped around his shoulders. Sitting upright was too much effort so he put his arms on the table and rested his head on them.

A conversation in hushed voices mixed with the clattering of pots and cups as he drifted in and out of consciousness. Someone pushed him upright and wrapped his fingers around a ceramic cup.

"Drink this."

The warm liquid felt heavenly. Suddenly shivering, he tried to set the cup on the table but slopped the coffee. He tried to take a deep breath, but searing pain stopped him. Looking down, he saw blood oozing through his shirt and around the edges of the bib overalls and he blacked out.

He felt someone open his fingers and press something into his palm. "Take these."

Lifting his head, he stared at two white tablets. He pushed the pills into his mouth and washed them down with lukewarm coffee that dribbled from his numb lips. Next to the puddle of spilled coffee sat a brown prescription bottle. With great effort he mumbled, "Thanks," and then lowered his head to the table.

After a few minutes he felt the oxycodone numbing his pain and he drifted off to sleep.

Cold air rushed in as the door opened. "What the hell is going on?" An argument ensued and he felt another blast of cold air as footsteps faded away, followed by the slamming door.

A hand roughly lifted his shoulder and he turned, finding himself staring into a hazy male face. "You should be dead by now."

CHAPTER 1

"The flower business swings wildly and half the time my cash flow is stretched. I get a couple of weddings or funerals and the money comes in, and the checkbook looks great. A week later I get a wholesale flower delivery, no one dies, I have to pay the girls, and suddenly I'm tapping into my savings to pay the bills." Mary Jungers sighed as she spread butter on a caramel roll at Tobies Restaurant and Bakery, known as the halfway stop for Twin Cities' travelers driving to Duluth. Generations of families have exited I-35 at Hinckley to stretch, use the restrooms, and stock up on Tobies famous baked goods.

Sergeant Floyd Swenson, of the Pine County Sheriff's Department, was sitting across the table from Mary sipping coffee and watching cars moving through the parking lot. He'd occasionally make a supportive noise and smile at her, but he was obviously focused on the people in the parking lot and at the bakery counter.

"The problem with Tobies caramel rolls is that they're so sticky," Mary said, licking caramel from her fingers. "They stick to your fingers, they stick to your teeth, and they stick to your hips." The last comment was directed to Floyd's inattention.

His eyes came back from the window and he saw her teasing smile. "A little padding wouldn't hurt your hips," he replied, taking the hint and focusing back on Mary.

"Why Floyd, I didn't know that you'd ever noticed my hips."

"I notice lots of things," he replied. "I'm a trained observer." It was obvious that Mary was self-conscious about her body. He'd rarely seen her in anything but a sweatshirt that drooped below her hips or a blouse covered by a blazer of the same length, both of which obscured her figure. She wasn't full-figured, but compared to Floyd's very slender build, she was padded like Floyd expected a middle-aged woman to be.

"I was thinking I'd stock Department 56 products and move the big cooler—it takes up so much of the front of the shop—into the back room where I'm storing boxes. I talked to Robbie Peterson and he said he could move the cooler, update the décor, and put in new shelving for twenty-two thousand dollars. I think I could recoup that in profits in a year. What do you think?" Mary asked as she ate the piece of roll she'd buttered.

Floyd refocused on the front window. He set his coffee cup down and slid his chair to the right so he had a better view of the front counter, now lined three-deep with people waiting to buy baked goods.

"Floyd, did you hear me?" Mary asked sharply.

"Hold that thought for a second," Floyd replied as he stood and walked quickly to the front door. His walk turned to a trot once he eased past the free-standing rack of artisan breads and the people lined up at the cash register. He surprised the young woman who was unlocking her car door by putting a hand on her shoulder. Mary watched the animated conversation. Floyd spoke to her with emphatic gestures, then led the sullen girl by the elbow back into the store and guided her to the cash register. The girl pulled crumpled bills from her pocket and paid the clerk who bagged the loaf of bread the teen had tucked inside her leather vest.

When he returned to the table Mary asked, "What was that all about?"

"A shoplifter took a loaf of bread from the display and walked out."

"And?" Mary asked.

"And I encouraged her to come back inside and pay for it."

"You're not going to arrest her or give her a ticket or something?"

"I didn't see much point. The bread's only worth a couple of bucks and she paid for it."

"Won't she do it again?"

"I've got her name and if she shows up on the arrest docket I'll call Tobies and ask the manager to press charges. The girl knows that and I suspect she'll be reluctant to shoplift here again. Besides, the county attorney and the courts don't have time to deal with somebody who's lifted a loaf of bread."

"And you gave her a little fatherly advice too?"

"I didn't have to."

"Why not?"

"She peed her pants when she saw my uniform. I think the message was received."

"Do you mean that she literally wet her pants?"

"Yup. She's wearing shorts and there was a puddle on the ground around her flip-flops. I almost laughed, but managed to keep up the 'bad cop' façade."

Mary put her hand over her mouth and laughed. "My big, tough deputy, who weighs maybe one hundred and fifty pounds, scared the pee out of somebody."

Floyd shifted in his chair, uncomfortably. "I weigh one-sixty."

"Right. You might weigh that if you include your handcuffs and gun."

"Weren't you talking about moving your cooler to the back room?" Floyd asked, redirecting the conversation. "It sounds to me like the estimate you got from Robbie Peterson is pretty reasonable. Construction is a little slow and it sounds like he's given you a fair bid. I think you should do it."

Mary took a deep breath and broke another piece off her roll. "I'm trying to decide how to put it to the bank. They know the checkbook is looking a little light at the end of the month. I don't know if they'll be excited about adding a loan payment to my cash flow drain."

"Call Robbie and tell him to do it. I'll write him a check."

Mary's hand stopped halfway to her mouth. "You can't do that."

"Sure I can. I've got the money sitting in a savings account that's earning no interest. I might as well give it to you as have the banker make money off it."

"It will have to be a loan that I'll repay," Mary said after a moment of thought.

"If that's what you'd prefer, we'll call it a loan. Otherwise, I can just give it to you." Floyd leaned to the side to watch a young couple arguing in the parking lot. Satisfied that the argument wasn't escalating, he leaned back and looked at Mary. "It's not like I need the money."

"We'd have to write up some sort of partnership agreement and then agree on what percent of the flower shop value twenty-two thousand dollars represents."

"I won't pay lawyers for busywork. Can't we just make it a handshake deal between us?"

Mary reached across the table and touched Floyd's hand. "You are either the sweetest or most naïve person I know."

He took her hand in his and kissed her knuckles. "I might have something other than a business partnership in mind."

"If anyone else said that to me, I'd think he was trying to get into my panties."

"Maybe when I was younger," Floyd said as he let go of Mary's hand and stood. "My interests have matured. Now I'd rather get a seat at your table for supper." He pulled a ten dollar bill from his wallet and threw it on the table. From his other pocket he took out a keychain and snapped a key loose. "Here's a key for my house," he said. After searching for words he blurted, "In case I get tied up and can't get home, I thought I could give you a call and you'd let the dog out. Now, I have to get back on the road."

Mary palmed the key and smiled. "Sure, I can let the dog out. I'll pick up some pork chops after I close up. Come over when you can."

"Are you making brown gravy?"

"I'm making brown gravy and mashed potatoes."

"I may use the siren and flashing lights," Floyd said with a smile.

CHAPTER 2

"Is there a deputy in Pine City," the female voice asked softly. The enhanced 911 system display showed that the call originated from Gordy's Drugstore in downtown Pine City.

"What's the nature of your problem?" the dispatcher asked as she noted that Floyd was back on duty and probably closest to Pine City, near the southern edge of Pine County's twelve hundred square miles.

"I think I'd better speak directly to a deputy about this," the woman replied. Then she added, "It's regarding some pictures that were dropped off for processing." The voice was soft, and the words came out so slowly that the dispatcher wondered if the caller was mentally challenged.

"I'll page Sergeant Swenson."

"Well," the woman said, "I've got a customer right now. Leave a message for him to stop at the photo counter at Gordy's Drugstore." As an afterthought the caller added, "Tell him Barb Dupre called. Tell him to come over within the hour if he possibly can."

Floyd was driving south on I-35 when the dispatcher radioed him.

"Floyd, I had a call from Gordy's Drugstore. Barb Dupre requested you stop over at the photo counter within the hour."

"The call wasn't an emergency?" Floyd asked.

"It didn't sound terribly urgent, but she wants to talk to someone about pictures and she emphacized that it had to be within the hour." The dispatcher paused. "If that's not convenient, I could see if one of the investigators is in the office."

Floyd smiled. Barb was Deputy Sandy Maki's girlfriend. "He's on the night shift, so I'm sure she thought of calling for a different investigator as second choice," he said to himself.

"I'll take the call," Floyd responded. "I should be there in about fifteen minutes."

Floyd parked the car on Main Street. He greeted the pedestrians enjoying the sunny July morning as he walked to the only pharmacy in Pine City. Gordy's was a small drugstore, with an owner who had been able to fend off the pressures of the new Super Walmart only because of his loyal customers and his low overhead in the hundred year-old building. Gordon (Gordy) Hall, the pharmacist, had remodeled the store, opening a door between two defunct businesses and installing a digital photo-processing center so he could develop and print photos on site from either film or digital cameras. Near the photo center he built an expanded gift shop that catered to the tourists who came to enjoy the surrounding lakes during the summer months.

Floyd wound his way through the aisles, past the photo supplies that ranged from telephoto lenses to batteries and displays of custom-printed photo T-shirts and mugs. He passed a rack of gray T-shirts with giant mosquitoes printed on their fronts, each with the logo, "Minnesota State Bird" and a rack of kelly green hooded sweatshirts with *Pine City Dragons* printed in white.

Floyd spotted Barb Dupre in the far corner of the photo center workspace, looking at a computer screen. Her blonde hair had been recently touched up—the dark brown roots barely noticeable. The white gloves she wore to keep from getting fingerprints on the photos covered the unusual tattoos Floyd had seen on her fingers, but her white blouse allowed a large blue starburst tattoo on her shoulder to faintly show through.

"Hey Barb, the dispatcher said you wanted to talk to me," Floyd said.

Startled by Floyd's voice, she turned and then quickly scanned the store to see if anyone was in earshot. Carefully clearing the computer monitor, Barb walked to the counter.

"I don't know that it's a big deal," she said with her usual slow verbal gait, "but I wanted someone else to look at these pictures before I gave them to the customer." Barb reached under the counter and took out an envelope. She opened the outer envelope and pulled out the inner sleeve of pictures and was about to hand the first photos to Floyd when a deep voice interrupted.

"Hi, Floyd," the pharmacist said from the doorway. "Is there some problem?"

"I called the sheriff's department because of some pictures I developed," Barb replied.

"Well," Gordy said gruffly, "I don't know that we can show our customers' private pictures to anyone without a release or a search warrant. I think they're private property. The only reason we look at them is to make sure the color balance and exposure are correct. I've always told you that anything you see in private photos is private. We *do not* make copies for our own use and we don't discuss what people choose for photographic subject matter."

The pharmacist was slightly over six feet tall, a few inches taller than Floyd, with a full head of gray hair. He wore a white smock with his name embroidered on the chest. Floyd knew he was past retirement age, but stayed on because he enjoyed the customer interaction.

Barb nodded emphatically. "I haven't said a word when people take pictures of themselves in the nude or having sex," Barb said indignantly. "But these are different."

Floyd took the five photos that Barb offered and spread them on the countertop so all three could view them. The pharmacist moved closer to get a look but the expression on his face said he was very uncomfortable.

The first images looked foreign, reminding Floyd of someone's vacation photos. The scenes were of people on a busy street lined with signs written in Asian characters. The fourth picture was apparently taken in a bar with two young men sitting at a table with young women on their laps and a lone woman in the third chair. There were beer bottles and glasses on the table, and the silly laughing expressions on four of the five faces led Floyd to believe that they were all intoxicated. All the pictures were slightly faded and tinted yellow. He recognized one woman because he'd arrested her for a DWI and he'd seen at least two of the others around town, although he didn't recall their names.

The fifth picture was underexposed, as though it had been taken in subdued light too far from the flash. It showed a man sitting against a tree with his hands tied behind the tree. The victim appeared to be nude, with the exception of white underwear. His head lolled forward so his face wasn't visible behind long blonde locks, but there was blood on his bare chest. In appearance, the subject was probably a skinny man who was either unconscious or dead.

"What do the rest of the pictures on the roll of film look like?" Floyd asked.

Gordy removed them from the envelope, his earlier reluctance suddenly gone, and spread them across the table. All of the rest appeared to be vacationers playing at a resort. The subjects included adults and children in activities from water skiing to cooking marshmallows around a campfire. Floyd looked quickly between the first five pictures and the later pictures and didn't note any resemblance in the faces or locations. Even the color definition was different. The later pictures were brighter, without the yellow cast.

"Are you sure these are all from the same roll of film?" Floyd asked. "The color balance looks so different between the first five and the rest."

"They all came through the developer together in one strip," Barb replied. "As a matter of fact, the first six pictures are still on the same strip of film. I noticed the difference, too, so I checked that right away. I called the Kodak help line and they told me that exposed film ages faster than unexposed film. I gave them the lot number from the film canister and they said that film was manufactured in 1997. They said that after a few years the exposed images start to lose color balance and the yellow would be more prominent, like we're seeing in the first five pictures."

Gordy picked up the outer envelope and looked at the name. "The name and address aren't local," he said, turning the envelope so Floyd could read the information. "Are these from that young woman who came in here Monday looking for camera batteries?"

"I think so," Barb replied. "You waited on her because I was busy, but I think she was the same woman who dropped off the film."

"She came in with an old Yashica camera," Gordy explained. "The batteries were dead and corroded so I helped her find some new batteries and then we cleaned up the battery contacts inside the camera to get it working. She'd purchased the camera at a garage sale as an alternative to replacing a digital camera she'd forgotten at home. The person at the garage sale sold it as-is but she hoped that it worked. I assured her that it was a fine piece of camera equipment — they don't make 'em like that anymore. When we got the thing cleaned up and working she bought a roll of 35-millimeter film and was ready to put it in when I realized there was already a roll of film in the camera."

Floyd picked up the outer envelope and noted the name and address written there. "Have either of you ever seen this Martha Rolfes before this summer?" he asked.

Both Gordy and Barb shook their heads. "I would guess she's a seasonal renter," Gordy replied. "I may have seen her in the past but I really don't recall her face."

"She dropped the film off," Barb said, "then said she was going to pick up some groceries. I told her they'd be ready in an hour. That was about forty-five minutes ago."

CHAPTER 3

Floyd and the pharmacist went behind the pharmacy counter where Gordy poured coffee into two Styrofoam cups.

Floyd savored a sip of coffee like fine wine and asked, "When did Barb start working for you?"

"That's quite a story," Gordy said, easing onto a stool. "I put a "Help Wanted" sign in the window and she walked in, asking about the job. My first take on her, with her bleached hair, tattoos, and slow speech, was that she had some lingering mental problems from drug use. We talked a little and she started telling me about photography classes she'd taken at the University of Minnesota before getting mixed up with bikers. The whole biker thing was a little concerning, but she made it clear that part of her life was over, and her knowledge of the photo chemistry and photo equipment was a little dated, but really sharp. Since we still get a few rolls of film coming in and there's not a lot of return on teaching someone new how to run the developer, I thought she might be a good job prospect if she was all she claimed to be.

"She promised to bring me some pictures and I figured I'd never see her again. She was back in a half hour with a portfolio of fine photographic work. She showed me how she adjusts the f-stop to get depth of field and special effects, and then she showed me some nature pictures she'd taken. They could easily equal a lot of shots I've seen in the major magazines. She took me to the computer and pulled out a CD of digital images she'd taken, then showed me how she used multiple exposures of the same shot to layer a close-up photo so that all the layers were in focus. She showed me a print of a flower on a lichen covered rock she'd taken on the North Shore. Everything was in perfect focus, from the stamens in the flower to the lichens on the rock and the grain of the rock itself. Then she showed me the dozen individual digital photos that she'd layered to produce the final print. It was incredible and far better than anyone else in the shop could achieve."

Gordy paused and looked to make sure Barb was out of earshot. "The truth is, even all that wasn't enough to make me overlook her dress and demeanor. She came in wearing a tank top that was a size too small and shorts that barely covered her bottom. I was afraid she'd scare off business with a look like that. I think she sensed my concern and told me that she knew how to dress for business. To top that off, she added that she was rooming with your deputy, Sandy Maki, and that told me she must be trustworthy if she was living with one of the deputies. I hired her on the spot and I've never regretted it."

"She helped us solve the murders down in Henriette a couple of years ago," Floyd explained. "She got to know Sandy then and they've been together ever since."

"What do you think is up with the pictures?" Gordy asked.

"When I got the message from dispatch, I assumed that there'd be some pornographic photos, or maybe something even darker than that," Floyd replied. "There's been a lot of talk about kiddy porn on the news lately, although that seems to have thankfully passed us by. I was expecting that maybe we'd got our first taste of something like that."

"The first three pictures look like they were taken someplace in the Far East," Gordy said. "They looked like some scenes I saw in Viet Nam. I guess most of those Far Eastern cities look a lot alike to me with lots of people on bikes and not many cars. The fourth picture looks like something my buddies and I would have taken of ourselves when we were stationed somewhere. You know — the guy's night out — have a few beers, talk to a local girl, and then back to the base before leave was over. It must've been taken in the States or Australia because the girls are Caucasian."

Floyd nodded in agreement. "The last one is the kicker. It doesn't look like the rest of them. The tree is more like an oak than something in Asia. It looks like the picture was taken after sunset. His chest has cut marks that were obviously inflicted while he was alive, because they're bleeding. On the other hand, I can't tell if the guy was dead or alive at the time the picture was taken."

"Are you sure it's a guy?" Gordy asked. "It might be a skinny woman or young girl."

"That's possible, but when someone is cut up like that it's an act of hatred and that kind of violence is usually directed at a man." Floyd paused, then asked, "How many shots had been taken on the camera before you replaced the batteries?"

"A few," Gordy replied. "I think it was like four or five, but I don't remember exactly. There's a display on top that tells how many pictures had been taken. I just noticed that the number wasn't zero.

Floyd helped himself to a coffee refill, and looked through the pictures again.

"I've heard we have better coffee than the courthouse," Gordy said.

"Most people don't call the brew at the courthouse coffee," Floyd replied. "It's closer to coal oil. The only thing it's got going for itself is the high caffeine concentration." Floyd turned the picture of the man against the tree a different direction and shook his head. "I wish there was a little more definition to this print. We might be able to see some distinguishing mark that could tell us who it is."

The sound of footsteps preceded Barb appearance at the end of the pharmacy counter. "Ms. Rolfes is here for her pictures. I assume one of you would like to talk to her."

Martha Rolfes was wearing a one-piece swimsuit covered by an unbuttoned pink blouse and a pair of running shorts. Floyd guessed her to be in her middle thirties. She had a deep tan and short brown hair that was sun-bleached almost blonde. She looked at Floyd with curiosity as he approached the counter.

"Is there a problem?" she asked, obviously concerned at the sight of Floyd's uniform. Martha Rolfes's eyes went to the badge and then grew wide as her hand covered her mouth. "My god, who's hurt? I only left them a couple hours ago to shop."

"Your family is fine. I need to ask you about some of the pictures you had developed."

Martha let out a deep breath and composed herself. "You nearly scared me to death. I left my husband and the kids at the lake to water-ski. I thought something had happened to them."

"You dropped these pictures off for developing," Floyd said as he laid out all the pictures except the first five. "Are these all the pictures you took?"

The woman looked through the pictures briefly. "I guess . . . I'm not the photographer in the family, but these are all pictures of Bill and me with the kids. Is there some problem with them?"

Floyd set the first four pictures down, and held the bloody picture back. "Are any of these familiar to you?"

She looked through them quickly and shook her head. "I don't recognize any of the people or the places. Should they look familiar?"

"They were the first four pictures on the roll of film you had developed."

A wave of revelation appeared on the woman's face. "Of course! The pharmacist helped me get that old garage-sale camera operating. He said the roll of film in the camera was partially used, so I just told the kids to finish off the rest of the film and we'd all be surprised by what might be on the first part of the roll." She looked through the pictures again. "So the mystery is solved! Somebody was taking pictures while they were in Japan."

"Did you notice how many pictures had been taken on that old roll of film before you started using it?"

"I think five had been taken," she said before pausing to visualize the camera in her mind. "Yes, I'm pretty sure it was five." She looked at the four pictures on the counter and then looked at Floyd, "I guess that one of them must not have come out."

"I guess one didn't," Floyd said. "You said you got the camera at a garage sale. Where was the sale?"

"Well, it was last weekend, over the Fourth of July. We got it from a house a few blocks back toward the interstate and south of here. I don't know the address, but I could point it out to you if it you wanted."

"Would it be okay if I kept these old pictures?"

"They don't mean anything to me," Martha said with a shrug.

"I parked a couple blocks from here," Floyd said. "Give me a second to get my car and I'll follow you there." He leaned close to Barb and whispered, "Blow up numbers four and five. I'd like to see them in greater detail."

Floyd followed Martha Rolfes's red Chevy Yukon down a road running parallel to Pine City's Main Street. She stopped in front of an older bungalow with green siding and white trim. Floyd knew the owners — Alex Solstad had played football with him in high school and now worked at the feed mill. His wife Karen was a few years younger, but also a graduate of Pine City High School. Staring at the house, Floyd had a sinking feeling. The last time he'd been at their door was to tell the Solstads their son, Ken, had been killed in a car accident.

Martha Rolfes met Floyd at her rear bumper. "It was this house. They had the garage open and the driveway was full of tables. I bought the camera and a couple of sweatshirts to keep at the cabin."

"Where are you staying?"

"We bought a cabin on Cross Lake a couple years ago. Some schoolteachers owned it, but when their daughters grew up they decided to put it on the market. The sign in the driveway still says Plauda. We planned to change it this week, but we've been too busy having fun."

"I've seen the sign," Floyd said, having driven the road hundreds of times. "Do you have a phone?"

"No," Martha said, shaking her head. "We decided that we'd just use our cellphones when we're up here. I'm afraid I don't even know the numbers."

"I know where I can find you, but I don't think we'll need anything more. Have a great vacation."

Martha looked nervously at the house. "There was another picture, wasn't there? Otherwise you wouldn't be so interested."

Floyd smiled. "You should've been a detective." He walked to the house and knocked on the door. When he looked back, Martha Rolfes was sitting in her car watching him.

Karen Solstad opened the door, her expression quickly changing from blank to surprise. "Floyd! I didn't expect to see you here." She wiped her hands on a towel and opened the door. "C'mon in." Floyd followed her into the living room where she motioned for him to sit in a chair with carved wooden arms and a brocade-covered cushion. The living room was cozy and overfilled with older, well-kept furniture. There was a slight scent of cigarette smoke in the air, but the ashtrays were empty.

Karen was a big-boned woman with hair dyed the color of redwood. It was tied in a short ponytail. She wore an oversized Minnesota Twins T-shirt that was almost as long as her denim shorts. Her sturdy legs ended in a pair of tattered tennis shoes.

"I heard I missed the big garage sale last weekend," Floyd said as he sat down. "Did you do well?"

"We sold over two-hundred-dollars worth of stuff, and cleaned out a whole lot of old crap that was collecting dust." She sat back in the chair and studied Floyd's face. "You don't care how the garage sale went. What's up?"

"I did want to talk about the garage sale. Did you run it all by yourself, or did you get together with a couple of families?"

"Sue, from next door, brought over a few things, but most of it was just stuff Alex and I accumulated over the years. I decided it was time to clean house. I can't say Alex was too excited about having all his crap sitting out on tables for the neighbors to see, but I gave him a chance to throw any of it in the garbage before the sale started."

"Do you remember selling a camera?" Floyd asked.

"Sure," Karen said with a confused look. "Was it broken or something? If it doesn't work I'll refund their money."

"They put new batteries in and it worked fine. Who owned it?"

Karen's eyes darted around the room nervously, like she was trying to avoid the question. Her eyes settled on the dark wood fireplace mantle where a picture of a young man in uniform stood. "It was in Kenny's stuff. I figured we'd been hanging onto it long enough now. I cleaned it all out and sold it."

Floyd took out the four pictures from the roll of film. "There was a partially exposed roll of film in the camera when you sold it. The new owners just had it developed and these were the first four pictures."

Karen took the pictures reluctantly and flipped through them one by one. "Ken was stationed in Korea, and I assume that's where he took these." When she got to the fourth picture her eyes welled with tears and she held her hand over her mouth.

"Oh God, this brings back so many memories," she said, holding the fourth picture by a corner and staring at it. "Kenny came home on leave but the Army called him here like two weeks later and ordered him to Missouri where they were staging his unit for service in Iraq. He left a bunch of stuff behind with us and we never saw him again." "Excuse me," she said as tears rolled down her cheeks and she went into the kitchen.

Drying her eyes she said, "I'm sure you remember the story. It was you who knocked on the door to tell us that Kenny had been killed in a car accident. You said it appeared that Kenny had fallen asleep at the wheel and ran into a semi." She paused to compose herself and then added, "It was really so stupid. He'd been out drinking with his buddies the night before he left. I think he came home at like five in the morning. He only slept until nine and then said he had to get going or he'd be in trouble for showing up late at the Army base." She looked at the picture again and said, "I suppose he took this picture the night before he left."

CHAPTER 4

"Do you recognize the people in the picture?" Floyd asked, pointing to the photo of the three men and two women.

"They're Kenny's friends from high school." Karen pointed as she put names to the faces. That's Aaron Roberts with his girlfriend, Kathy. That's Mike Nelson, with his girlfriend, Betsy. And the lone girl is Kenny's girlfriend, Melissa. They broke up while Kenny was in Korea, but when he came home on leave she was still at loose ends and they got back together again.

"Were there any other people Ken was hanging around with when he came home on leave?" Floyd asked.

Karen pointed at the picture. "These were his drinking buddies," she replied. "Other than Aaron and Mike, Ken didn't hang around with many other people." She paused, looking deep in thought, then added, "There was a kid from Finalyson who had a stupid nickname I can't remember. Anyway, he didn't hang out with Ken's other friends much. He'd just show up once in a while to sit in his car and talk with Kenny."

Karen handled the picture gently and was lost in her thoughts for nearly a minute. She took a deep breath and let out a sigh. "Of course you remember Aaron," she said, pointing to the skinny blonde man with a raven-haired girl on his lap. "He disappeared the same day Kenny died. Some people thought he ran away out of grief."

"We found Aaron's car out by the rest stop on the interstate," Floyd said as his memories started to flow. "We figured he caught a ride with a trucker some-where," Floyd paused and added, "The boys were a hard-drinking bunch. I think we've picked Mike up at least twice for DUI. Kenny drank with them too."

Karen nodded. "They started partying in high school and never quit. Kenny tried to hide it at first. He'd sneak home after he knew we were in bed so we couldn't smell it on his breath, but I knew he was drinking. I could smell the stale beer and cigarette smoke on his clothes when I put them in the wash. Actually," Karen said. "That was why Kenny went into the Army. He'd been arrested for public intoxication and assaulting a guy at the casino in Hinckley. When he showed up at the hearing with the Army recruiter the judge agreed to dismiss the charges if he signed the enlistment papers and left for the first available basic training opening. We had high hopes that the Army would turn him around.

"In some respects, we were pleased with what the Army did for him. When he got leave after basic training he came home clean-cut and polite, like I'd never seen him before, but within two days he'd gotten in touch with Aaron and Mike, and the three of them were running around just like it was high school." She paused, "There was one big difference — Kenny had more money than he'd ever seen in his life and he had a big chip on his shoulder. It was like the Army had molded him into some sort of self-confident bully who thought he was better than most everyone. You should've seen the look in his eyes when I asked where he was going that last night. I was afraid of him."

"Do you remember anything else about his last trip home?"

"Not really anything special. He'd been in Korea for a year and I think that really opened his eyes to the world. He was a little disappointed with the boredom in the Army, and he was talking about getting out when his enlistment was up. I asked him what he thought he'd do, and he told me that he might apply to be a guard at the state prison in Rush City. I think he liked the idea of being a tough guy in the big house."

"How did you feel about that?" Floyd asked.

"It made me sick, but where else is a kid going to get a good paying job with decent benefits around here? I think half the people in the county work at the Hinckley casino or the prison, and that's the only reason they have jobs at all. Pine County is not booming."

"You mentioned Kathy and Betsy," Floyd said, "Do you remember their last names?"

"I don't. I imagine they've both probably married and moved out of town by now. I think your best bet would be to talk Mike Nelson. He's still around town and I'm sure he could give you names and maybe even help you track them down." Karen paused, then asked, "Why are you interested in this now? It's been years since these pictures were taken."

"I'm just following up on some loose ends. Things were slow and the pictures seemed like an interesting mystery since this seems to be the last picture anyone has of Aaron Roberts."

"Can I keep these?" Karen asked, clutching the four pictures in her hand.

"Sure," Floyd said. Then he asked, "You said that you were selling off Kenny's old stuff at the garage sale. Did you happen to have the clothes he wore the last night before he left for Missouri?"

"You know, it was really strange. The week after Kenny's funeral my sister came over and we took all his stuff and threw it into garbage bags. She set them in the garage but I didn't have the heart to put them in the garbage. A couple weeks later, the Army shipped his footlocker to us and I put that next to the bags of clothes without ever opening it. When we decided to have the garage sale, Sue, from next door, and I took everything out of the footlocker and sorted through it, putting prices on the stuff she thought would sell.

"The Army footlocker and the uniform stuff went right away. I guess we probably underpriced it but I wanted it out of my life. I opened the bags of clothes and lots of them were still neatly folded like we'd just taken them out of the drawers. Sue just set them out on the tables and put tags on them. There were a few pieces of rumpled clothing in the bag, and they must have been dirty things that we'd picked off the floor and just threw in the bag. Not many of the clothes were sold, so I donated them to the Goodwill. But the dirty ones I just threw into the garbage. They're still there."

Karen led Floyd to a pair of galvanized garbage cans next to the garage. They were brimming with black plastic bags. Karen pulled a few heavy bags off the top, and then retrieved a smaller white bag. When she opened it, the smell of a locker room mingled with garbage arose.

"Phew!" She said. "I don't think you want to dig around in here."

Floyd folded back the top and set it on the ground. He pushed the three or four shirts aside with the tip of a pencil and noted a few rust-colored specs on a pair of sneakers that were jammed in alongside the shirts.

"Can I keep this bag of clothing?"

"It's garbage," Karen replied with a shrug. "But why would you want it?"

"Let's just say I'm a pack rat," he replied as he pulled the bag closed and tied the top shut. "Do you recall when Kenny drove back to Missouri?"

"How could I forget? It was December, 1998, and the President had just announced there was going to be a troop surge in Iraq. I hoped they wouldn't call Kenny so soon after his return from Korea. He'd only been home two weeks when he got the call."

CHAPTER 5

Floyd drove back to the drugstore and parked a half block away. The mild morning temperatures had given way to a hot, humid afternoon. He overheard a white-haired couple standing next to their Cadillac complaining about the heat and humidity, then grinned when he noticed the Florida license plate. After hearing about the sub-zero Minnesota winters, people from the South didn't anticipate the sauna-like heat of summers.

Barb Dupre was examining a negative under a magnifying glass until she saw Floyd walk up to the counter. She reached to the side of the processing machine and picked up a large envelope.

"You've been a lot of bother," Barb said as she opened the envelope and slid out some enlargements. "I hope Gordy doesn't know how much time I'm putting into this project for you." She spread the three 8x10-inch photos on the counter and leaned over them to look more closely. "I studied these on the computer screen and I think the guy sitting on the far left in the fourth picture might be the same guy who's tied to the tree. Any idea who he is?"

"His name is Aaron Roberts, and he was reported missing the day after this picture was taken and hasn't been seen since. I'm reopening the case and chasing down all the leads I can find."

As Barb leaned over, Floyd was startled by the large amount of cleavage exposed. "How do the little old ladies feel about you showing so much flesh?" he asked.

Barb looked up without straightening up. "I don't lean over the counter for the little old ladies, just for the men." Then she cracked a smile. "I don't get the tips I used to make as a waitress, but they sure like to hang around and talk. It makes the days go by more quickly."

Floyd shook his head and looked at the photos. "What did you do to get the pictures to look so different? This first one looks like the original small print you made up, but these other enlargements have a lot more color and definition."

"I called up a photo lab in Colorado. Rocky Mountain Film specializes in handling old film and they are one of the few places in the U.S. that have the equipment to develop some odd types of film. They said I should have developed the film differently, but since it was already developed, they suggested some tricks using the computer. It doesn't help the color balance much, but makes everything a little darker. I'd show you on the computer screen," she said, looking around the store, "but I don't want to scare the customers."

"This picture looks like a still from the *Blair Witch Project*," Floyd said. "It's dark and grainy."

"It was obviously taken outside with a flash," Barb said. "You can see how the penetration of the flash diminishes as you get past the tree he's tied to. Look at this second one," she said, pushing it closer to Floyd. "I tried to adjust the colors to get more blues. This probably is the most realistic color balance. It looks like the blood on his chest is fresh, and you can see the cuts more clearly."

"It's hard to make out," Floyd said, picking up the photo and trying to get the light to hit from different angles. "But, I think the cuts might have a pattern. The last one seems to be an 'O.'"

"I thought so, too," Barb said as she stepped away from the counter. "So I made a blowup of just the chest. It just came out of the printer."

She set the new print on the counter. "This captures the area from his chin to his waist. You can see some of his hair dangling into the bottom of the print."

"It's awfully grainy," Floyd said, studying the print. "The blood dribbling down from the cuts makes it hard to see if there's a pattern." Floyd took the picture and held it at an angle to the overhead lights, reducing the glare.

"Biker's cut members who fall out of good standing with their gangs. You get the club tattoo when you're accepted, and they cut it off if you piss them off or try to quit." Barb's words were a statement made without judgment. Floyd looked at Barb and realized that in the tougher part of her life she might have witnessed things more gruesome than he would've guessed.

"I hear," she added, "that some Asian gangs cut people up to extract information from them. I read that in the old days Chinese emperors had this punishment they called the death of a thousand cuts. The executioner made long slashes on a guy's body. They weren't very deep, but they must've hurt like hell. They'd slice and dice the guy until he looked like hamburger. Eventually the guy would die of blood loss or shock, but not until he'd endured hours of agony. I guess the really good imperial cutters could make the punishment last for half a day while the emperor watched his revenge being exacted on the prisoner."

"I saw that in the movie *The Sand Pebbles,*" Floyd said, "but it sounds like you did a lot deeper research on it."

"I went through a 'torture is interesting' phase of my life. Living with Butch, the biker, kinda took the glamour out of it." Barb turned somber, apparently recalling the abusive relationship with her ex-boyfriend.

"Cutting somebody up is tough punishment," Floyd said as he slipped all the photos into the envelope. "Even if you were crazy enough to do it, why would you take a picture of it?"

"You don't have to be crazy," Barb said, "just high or drunk. Sometimes guys get off on it because it really sends a message about how 'bad' they are."

"You talk like it's matter-of-fact," Floyd said. "It's hard to believe that your life was that hard before, yet you turned it around and rejoined society."

"Hey, you meet a nice guy who treats you well and you learn to live with the boredom," she said with a shrug.

"Your life is boring now?"

Barb hesitated. "It's not an adrenaline high every night," she said. "On the other hand, I've got a feeling of security now and regular meals. A girl can get used to those after a while, especially when you're never experienced them before."

"But you still miss the adrenaline."

"There's hardly any rush that matches the feeling you get when you think you're going to die." Sensing disapproval, she added, "You know, like racing a cycle down a wet highway at a hundred-miles-an-hour without a helmet."

"That speed scares the hell out of me when I'm in a police car with the seat belt buckled."

"Sandy loves it. Don't you?"

"I guess I'll miss it when I retire someday."

"Sandy said that you're dating the woman from Pine Brook Floral. He thinks that she's really nice."

Floyd smiled. "She is really nice, but I don't know that we're dating."

Barb studied his face. "You were so sad after your wife died, I was worried about you," she said. "You have a sparkle in your eye again. I think she's good for you."

"I think so too." Floyd took the envelope under his arm and added. "Thanks for all the work you did to improve these. You will bill the department."

From around the corner, Gordy interjected an emphatic, "Yes! She will!"

CHAPTER 6

Deputy Pam Ryan was sitting at a desk in the sheriff's department bullpen when Floyd came back from the drugstore. She was the youngest deputy in the department and with her short blonde hair and small frame she could still be mistaken for the high school cheerleader she once was. Many people were deceived by her youthful appearance and mistook it for a lack of maturity and professionalism. On a few occasions, Pam's calming influence had defused tense situations that might have led to violence had a male deputy responded. At other times, men had underestimated her training, quickness, and strength, resulting in them lying face down on the floor before they realized what had happened.

"More reports?" Floyd asked as he walked to the coffee pot.

"Yeah," Pam said, leaning back and rubbing her hands over her eyes. "The last guy I served with a summons refused it, so I had to arrest him. I was just writing up the gory details so the judge can throw the book at him."

"Who was it?" Floyd asked as he pulled a chair next to Pam's desk.

"Larry Morton. He was late on his child support again so Angie's attorney filed papers to have his driver's license revoked and to garnish his wages."

Dan Williams, the undersheriff, walked in, catching the end of the conversation. He was carrying a Pine City Dragons coffee cup and wore his usual uniform, a white golf shirt with a gold sheriff's department badge embroidered on the chest and khakis. His physique had changed as he passed the fifty-year mark, but it was still evident that he'd been a star football player before joining the sheriff's department.

"There's an awful lot of guys out there," Dan said, "who think it's the woman's fault that they're having all these kids. They don't seem to feel any responsibility for child support payments."

"It's like they never heard of birth control," Pam replied.

"Or self control," Floyd added.

Pam looked at the envelope Floyd had set next to his coffee cup. "What's in the package?"

"Pictures," he said as he opened the flap and slipped out the enlargements. He separated them and set them out for Pam and Dan to examine.

"Bloody mess," she said. "Where's this crime scene?"

"I don't know. A woman bought the camera at a garage sale and it had a partial roll of exposed film. When she got it developed, this was the fifth picture on the roll."

"I'll bet she was shocked."

"Luckily," Floyd said, "Barb Dupre caught it at the drugstore when she developed the film. She had me come over to look at the pictures before the customer came back to pick up the prints."

"You're sure the customer wasn't the one who took these?" Dan asked.

"Yup. The batteries were dead in the camera when she bought it. Gordy helped her replace the batteries and clean the camera up. He said there were exposed pictures on the roll of film when the camera showed up at the drugstore."

"So," Pam said, "who took the pictures?"

"Ken Solstad owned the camera. It's been in his mother's basement since he died in a car accident in 1998."

"You really can't see the victim's face," Pam said, examining the pictures again. "I don't suppose you know who this unlucky fellow is?"

"Actually, I think it's a guy who disappeared at the same time Ken Solstad died. His name is Aaron Roberts but I don't know if he's dead or alive." Floyd took the close-up of the chest from the pile and handed it to Pam. "It looks like some pattern is cut into his chest. Can you make out what it is?"

"I can see the cuts, but the dribbles of blood make it hard to tell if there's a pattern to the cuts," Dan observed.

"He might be dead," Pam said, looking at the pictures again.

Dan took the remaining pictures from the envelope and leafed through them. "These were in Ken Solstad's camera when he died?"

"That's what we believe," Floyd replied. "That picture was probably taken by Ken the night before he died."

Dan set the pictures down and poured himself a cup of coffee. He returned to the desk and stared at the pictures, obviously mulling something.

"Floyd, what are you going to do next?"

"I'd planned to hand the pictures over to you, Dan, and then I thought that I'd finish my shift patrolling the northern part of the county, take a shower, and then go to Mary Jungers' house for pork chops."

Dan set his coffee cup on the desk and pulled a roll of Tums from his pocket. He thumbed a Tums off the end of the roll and popped it into his mouth, chewing while he stared at the pictures.

"I think you did such a good job solving that cold case with the girl missing from the summer camp that you should spend a couple days digging into this to see if something pops up."

"Hey," Pam exclaimed. "I was the one who identified the murderer in that case."

"Good point," Dan said. "You were a great team. Get to it," he said as he walked away.

Pam took a breath and was ready to fire back a witty retort, but hesitated as memories of the hours spent digging through computer and paper files during the missing girl's investigation flashed past her.

"Be careful what you wish for," Floyd said. "Your wish may come true, but not in the way you expected."

CHAPTER 7

Sandy Maki was in the shower when Barb Dupre got home. Their apartment was in a four-plex in southern Pine City that was shared with two retired couples on the lower level and a young schoolteacher on the other half of the upper level. The neighbors were quiet, a prime requirement for a deputy who rotates shifts and sometimes has to sleep days. They were quite happy that a deputy lived in the building and the perceived security that brought. They were less pleased about the deputy's roommate, the tattooed former waitress driving the purple Camaro with the *PRTYGRL* vanity license plates.

Hearing the door close and commotion in the living room, Sandy stuck his wet head out of the bathroom door. "Hey, babe, you're home early today."

Barb kicked her shoes off next to the door and started unbuttoning her blouse as she walked across the living room. "It was a more interesting day than normal," she said in her slow style. "I had Floyd Swenson come over to see some pictures a woman brought in for developing. I think there was a dead guy in one of them."

Sandy wrapped a towel around his waist and followed her into the bedroom. His light brown hair was combed but still wet from the shower. At age twenty-five he managed to maintain a moderately muscular physique despite spending most of his working hours riding in a county police cruiser or writing reports in the courthouse.

"There was a dead guy tied to a tree," Barb explained as she threw her blouse toward a hamper set in the corner and stripped off her khaki slacks, leaving them on the floor where they fell. After living together for over a year, they treated each other like a married couple. "It looked like someone had tied him up and carved on his chest." Barb made the observations as casually as another person might have described what they'd had for lunch.

Sandy took a carefully pressed uniform shirt from the closet while Barb slipped a pair of tattered denim shorts over her thong underwear. "What did Floyd say?" he asked.

"He said it was probably some guy who disappeared." Barb sorted through a pile of clothes near the bed until she found a Hooters T-shirt. She sniffed the armpits and then put it on over her Wonderbra. "I guess the guy left his car at a rest stop and disappeared. They never figured out what happened to him."

Sitting on the edge of the bed, Barb asked, "Have you got plans, or can we go out for something to eat before your shift? I'm starving."

"We can go out to eat," Sandy said. He took a pair of pants from a hanger and slipped them on. "So, how could you tell the guy in the picture was dead?"

"I could tell," Barb replied with a shrug. "He was really pale and his head was hung way down. I guess it looked like all his muscles had quit working and he was tied to a tree with his hands behind his back. I saw a guy Butch beat up once and he looked kinda like that, too. Except his head didn't fall that far down and he lived through it." Barb hesitated, and then added, "Sorry. I forgot that you don't like when I talk about being with Butch."

"Did Floyd think the guy looked dead?" Sandy asked, ignoring the comments about Barb's former biker boyfriend. "I mean, without someone actually being there I don't think you can say a guy in a picture is definitely dead."

"He was toast. Someone tied him to a tree, cut up his chest, his car was abandoned, and he hasn't been seen for like twenty years. I think he's dead."

Sandy pulled his holster and gun belt off the closet shelf. "The truck stop serves breakfast all day. Follow me over there and I'll buy before I go on duty."

CHAPTER 8

It was mid-afternoon and the diner at the Highway 70 truck stop was empty except for three truck drivers sitting in a booth drinking coffee. The man facing the door nodded for the others to look as Barb and Sandy entered. Barb smiled and put a little extra swing in her step as she passed the truckers' booth. Merle Haggard was singing about a lost girlfriend on a radio in the kitchen.

"I wish you wouldn't do that," Sandy said as he slid into the booth across the table from Barb.

"Do what?" Barb asked with a sly grin.

"You know exactly what I mean. I'll bet they'd be plotting how to get you into their sleeper cabs if you hadn't walked in with a cop." Sandy turned over the cup on the table and signaled to the owner for coffee.

"I'm with you whether you're in uniform or not," Barb said. She reached across the table and slid her hand onto Sandy's. "Are you feeling a little insecure today?"

Feeling Barb's toe raising his pant's cuff, Sandy scowled. "You know how silly this is. At home you ignore your sexuality and parade around naked like no one cares. As soon as you're around strange men it's like you have to put on a show."

"But you're the one I go to bed with."

Bud Merton, rotund, sweaty, and bald, set a large glass of Coke in front of Barb and poured coffee into Sandy's cup. He wore a stained white apron over his white T-shirt and jeans. "Yeah, you're the one she goes to bed with," Bud said with a grin. "Why don't you just make an honest woman of her?"

"She doesn't want to get married," Sandy replied as he poured cream into the cup. "Bring me a short stack with bacon and Barb wants her usual burger and fries."

Bud reached out and touched Barb's chin, getting a swat on the hand in return. "Oh, Barb, dump the cop and run off with a real man."

"If you're a real man, I'd hate to see what eunuchs look like," Barb said, rubbing the spot on her chin where Bud's hand had touched her as if she were trying to remove his fingerprint.

"Ooh, pretty and she knows big words, too!" The closest trucker said to his friends.

"All right, guys," Sandy said, turning in his seat to face the three truckers. "If you guys give me any more grief I'll have to do a safety inspection and check your log books."

With Bud gone and the truckers quiet, Sandy asked, "Did Floyd know the name of the guy in the picture?"

"It was Aaron something. I guess he disappeared the same day the guy who owned the camera died. At least that's what I understood."

"Tell me about the other guy," Sandy said, "the one who died."

"I don't know any more. Floyd's investigating and that's all." Barb stirred the Coke with a straw and then changed the topic. "I saw a pair of hooded mergansers with ducklings on Passenger Lake yesterday. The drake's plumage was incredibly iridescent. I'm going to set up a blind to see if I can get some pictures. The wind has been calm and I'd like to see if I can get a picture with the whole family mirrored on the water this evening."

"The mosquitoes will eat you alive if you sit out dressed like that," Sandy said as Bud set a stack of platter-sized pancakes in front of him.

"Haven't you ever heard of Ultrathon insect repellent?" Barb asked. "It's effective for twelve hours."

CHAPTER 9

Floyd plucked a scribbled note from a stack of files piled on his desk and handed Mike Nelson's name and address to Sandy Maki. He held up an eight-by-ten inch picture of the five friends sitting at the table.

"Mike is the guy with darker hair," Floyd explained before handing Sandy the photo of the man with his hands bound behind the tree. "The blonde guy at the table is Aaron Roberts, and it's likely that he's the person in this second picture."

Sandy studied the two pictures for a few seconds. "Barb said she thought the lone guy is dead. It's hard to tell from this, isn't it?"

"I think it's impossible to tell from the picture. He was obviously alive when he was cut or else there wouldn't have been so much blood. He was assaulted here or the blood would've smeared when he was moved. It's likely he's dead based on the fact that he's been missing for years. Anyway, I'd like you to talk to Mike Nelson. Ask him what he remembers about the night before Kenny Solstad died in the car accident, and have him identify the girls in the picture. The girl by herself is Melissa Smith, who was Kenny's date the night this picture was probably taken, and the girl on Aaron's lap looks like Kathy Tucker. I don't recognize the other girl, and that may mean that she wasn't in trouble quite as often as the others. I want Mike to tell us who they are, if they're married, what their married names are, where they live, and I want to question all three women to see what they remember about that night."

"You didn't say when these pictures were taken."

"I spoke with Karen Solstad, Kenny's mother. She said he was home on leave from the service between a Korean deployment and being called up for Iraq. The pictures were taken in December, 1998."

"All these people are like forty years old now," Sandy said, looking back at the group photo again. "Do you think that any of them will remember what happened on a specific night that long ago?"

"Unless I miss my guess, one or more of them will have very vivid memories of that night. Not many people forget the last night they spent with a friend who died . . . or participating in a murder."

Mike Nelson's address led Sandy to a new housing development on the western fringe of Pine City. The houses were different colors, but were built with the same design. The Nelson's house was gray with white trim. An aging Ford pickup sat on the asphalt driveway in front of the double garage. The garage door was open, exposing a riding lawnmower and several bicycles in a variety of sizes.

"Are you Mike Nelson?" Sandy asked the man who answered the door. The aroma of roasting ham wafted out the door around the man with a slight paunch and a few crumbs on the front of his white T-shirt. Behind Nelson, Sandy could hear the voices of several children and a woman. An air conditioner hummed from somewhere behind the house. Compared to the picture, the man at the door looked like Mike Nelson's father, with graying temples and a receding hairline.

"I'm Mike. What's up?"

"I need help identifying the other people in this photo," Sandy said, holding the photo out for Nelson to see.

Nelson stood staring at the picture for several seconds. "Wow," he said, flipping the photo over to see if there were any markings on the back.

"That's you with the dark hair, isn't it?"

Nelson stared at the picture as if he couldn't believe the image. "Where did you find this? I've never seen it before."

"Someone bought a garage sale camera and this was on the film."

"Well, yeah, that's me. The skinny guy is Aaron Roberts. The girls are Betsy Ring, Kathy Tucker, and

Melissa Smith. Of course they're all married now with different last names, except for Kathy."

"The picture was probably taken the night before Ken Solstad was killed in a car accident. Tell me what happened that night?"

Nelson's eyes shot up and locked on Sandy's. "The last night before Kenny died?"

Sandy nodded. "The picture was taken in December while Ken was home on leave. It looks like a group of you went out drinking together. What happened that night?"

"Kenny died the next day."

"I know, but what happened between the time this picture was taken and when Kenny drove away the next morning?"

"We partied all night. It seems like all we did was drink and get stupid back then. Kenny was leaving the next day for his Army base and all he wanted to do was get wasted and talk about how macho he was. He was like arm wrestling everyone he could find and he tried to pick a fight at a bar with some guy about something stupid." Nelson stared at the photo again. "I guess that's about all we did," he said, shrugging his shoulders and handing the picture back.

"Were you with Kenny that whole night?"

Nelson looked over his shoulder nervously, then stepped onto the front step, closing the door behind him. "Not exactly. Betsy and I left the others at the bar."

"The others stayed together, or did the whole group break up and go their own way?"

"I don't know," Nelson said curtly. "Betsy was pretty drunk and not resisting much, so I didn't hang around to see who went where with whoever else. We kinda left to, um, park." He ended with an embarrassed shrug.

"Where did you go parking?" Maki asked as he took out a notebook and made notes.

Nelson hesitated, looking past Sandy toward a spot on the lawn. "There's a road that runs out to Mink Lake that doesn't have any traffic that time of year."

"Were you out by Mink Lake a long time, and did you see any of the others after that?"

"We woke up in the car the next morning, and I never saw Kenny again. That's why I was so surprised to see this picture. I'd never seen it before and it's kinda strange that it'd show up now. Who took it?"

"It was on an old roll of film in Ken's camera that just got developed. It looks like Ken probably took it himself."

"That's spooky," Nelson said. "It kinda gives me the creeps."

"Were other people hanging around with you six that night?"

"Nah, we mostly were just by ourselves except for people we met in the bars."

"What happened to Aaron that night?"

"He was with Kathy," Nelson said, pointing to the raven-haired girl with a trim build sitting on Aaron's lap in the photo. "They were partying like the rest of us."

"Did you see him again after you left for Mink Lake?"

Nelson frowned, studying the picture again. His eyes suddenly went wide with recognition. "Is that what this is all about? Has Aaron shown up?"

"What happened to Aaron that night?" Sandy asked again.

"Whew! That was like half a lifetime ago." Nelson paused to collect his thoughts. "I don't remember anything special about Aaron that night. I mean he was there, but I don't remember him doing or saying anything special. He was with Kathy, but that's about all I remember about him." Nelson paused, looking at the photo. "I'm remembering more. Something *was* different about Aaron that night. He was quiet and wasn't drinking like he had. I suppose he might've been intimidated by Kenny's stupid macho shit or maybe he was pissed about something, but it just seemed like he wasn't into the party scene like he'd been other times. I guess that's all I can remember about Aaron."

"Do you know how I can find the three women?" Sandy asked, making notes.

"Well, I still see Betsy once a month when I pick up Alyssa. She's married to a guy in the Cities who's a truck dispatcher."

"Who's Alyssa?"

"She's my daughter. Betsy and I were married for a couple years."

"Can you give me her married name and her phone number? We'd like to ask about her memories of that night, too."

"Sure, it's Betsy Webb, and she lives in Brooklyn Center." Nelson repeated the phone number from memory. "I haven't stayed in contact with the other women, although I know that Melissa got married and moved off. Kathy Tucker still lives in Hinckley and runs the garden center with her parents. You can see it from the interstate, just off the highway 23 exit. She never got married as far as I know."

After dispatching Sandy to do interviews, Floyd drove to the supermarket and bought a strawberry-rhubard pie. The pictures of Ken Solstad's group were disturbing, but they quickly passed from his mind when he pulled into Mary Junger's driveway and saw the light in the kitchen window. He took the pie from the front seat and walked to the door, feeling like a high school kid going on a date. His heart was racing and he couldn't help but smile.

Mary lived in a clapboard house a few blocks off highway 23 in the town of Pine Brook. The town it-self had never been large in its heyday and when I-35 bypassed it a few miles to the east, and people migrated to other, larger towns and to the Twin Cities, many of the houses had fallen into disrepair. Mary's house had flower boxes on the windows and the yard was neatly trimmed, although the siding looked like it was about a year past due for a new coat of paint. Floyd rang the doorbell and waited on the top step.

When the door opened he held up the bakery box. "I brought pie for dessert."

Mary smiled and took the box. "You know, if I eat half of each pie you bring, I'll be as round as I am tall." She pushed the door open and stepped back. "You, on the other hand, never seem to gain an ounce of weight."

"So, don't eat any," Floyd said, stepping into the kitchen and slipping off his shoes. He was engulfed with the aroma of frying pork chops and boiling potatoes. He pecked Mary on the cheek and sat in a kitchen chair.

"Right. Like that's going to happen," Mary replied as she took the pie from Floyd and set it on the counter. Again she was dressed in an embroidered sweatshirt and baggy bluejeans, both effectively hiding her figure. She quickly went to the stove and started stirring vigorously. "You almost distracted me long enough to scorch the gravy."

Mary's kitchen was in need of new floors and the cabinets needed refinishing. The floor, cabinets, and counters had been cleaned so many times the paint

and linoleum had worn thin, but everything was spot-
less. Lace curtains hung in the windows, and the counters were pristine. The appliances were faded harvest
gold, hinting at their origins in the '70s.

Floyd watched contentedly as she hustled from
stirring gravy to draining potatoes, to uncovering the
plate of pork chops. She handed him a pot of potatoes
and a potato masher then strained the lumps from the
gravy. He was mashing potatoes when Mary poured
the gravy into a serving dish and looked up.

"Why are you smiling?" she asked.

Floyd shrugged. "You move like you're conducting
an orchestra."

"And why does that make you smile?"

"I guess because you're going to all that trouble
just for me."

Mary put the gravy on the table and said, "I like to
cook for people. There's no joy in cooking for myself.
And you really seem to enjoy a home-cooked meal."

As Mary set the table Floyd thought but couldn't
bring himself to say, "I enjoy your company even more
than the meal."

CHAPTER 10

The next morning Floyd sat on the one clear spot on his desk and read through Sandy's report while sipping coffee, both from the overnight shift. After re-reading the report he decided to drive to Tucker's Garden Center to interview Kathy Tucker. The morning traffic on I-35 was moderate, consisting mostly of semi-trailers originating in the Twin Cities and Chicago bound for Duluth and the Iron Range towns beyond. The flag hung limp at the post office and the cars parked along Main Street were covered in dew. Next to the interstate, four golfers were putting on the third green of the Pine City Country Club, their golf balls leaving trails in the dew.

Floyd took the first highway 23 exit and turned onto old highway 61, a road made famous by Bob Dylan. Tucker's Garden Center was housed in a pole building barely a hundred yards from the interstate exit. The metal gate hung open in front of a parking lot filled with potted annuals in a kaleidoscope of colors. Virginia Tucker stood in the gravel parking lot spraying water on the potted plants with a hose. Floyd and Ginny had been two years apart in high school, and they'd met several times after that when he'd arrested her daughter, Kathy, for drunken driving.

"Hi, Ginny," Floyd said as he climbed out of the car. "I suppose keeping all these plants moist is a real problem in this heat."

"Actually, it's not so bad. The high humidity really slows down the evaporation. Now if we get a wind and this humidity drops, then we'll be in trouble." Ginny stopped the spray and walked to Floyd's unmarked car. "Is that dwarf cherry tree leafing out for you? I warned your wife that it was a little late in the season to be planting. On the other hand, it had to go into the ground or it'd be dead in last summer's heat. I gave her quite a bargain just to save its life."

Floyd diverted his eyes to the gravel in the parking lot. "The cherry tree leafed out but it died after her funeral. I let a few things slip."

"Oh, Floyd, I forgot that your wife passed away." Ginny leaned into Floyd's shoulder and hugged him. "I'm so sorry."

"I came by to talk to Kathy," he said, patting her back. "Is she around this morning?"

"Kathy and Brian are in the back rearranging the bushes. Is something wrong?" Ginny searched Floyd's face for a hint about his inquiry, then added, "As far as I know she's still on the wagon and attending the AA meetings."

"I need to talk to her about some friends from years ago," Floyd said with a weak smile. "She's still on the wagon as far as I know, too."

Kathy was in the back loading five-gallon pots of arborvitae bushes into a wagon. Floyd had forgotten that the former all-conference women's basketball player was nearly six feet tall. She had been a lanky high school athlete who had stayed in shape doing the heavy lifting at the garden center. Her dark hair was tied back tightly in a short ponytail. She wore a bright green T-shirt over a pair of flowered shorts and it appeared that she had smeared potting soil on her limbs and clothing in the few minutes the nursery had been open.

"Hi, Kathy. Do you have a few minutes to talk?"

She hadn't noticed Floyd approach in her concentration on the loading project. She pushed a stray lock of hair back from her face with a wipe from her bicep. "Sure, Floyd," she said, pulling the work gloves from her hands. "What can I do for you?" Her body language showed discomfort, possibly the result of the time he'd taken her to jail for a DWI.

"I've got a picture to show you," he said, holding the group photo out for her. "I hope you can help me clear up the mystery that goes with it."

Kathy wiped her hands on her shorts. She took the picture, carefully holding it by the corners. Floyd saw her eyes go wide for the briefest fraction of a second before she gathered her composure. "Looks like I'd had a few too many drinks, doesn't it?" She handed the photo back.

"Do you remember the night this was taken?"

"I was drinking pretty heavily back then. I don't remember a lot of nights." Kathy blotted perspiration from her forehead with the neck of her shirt. "People tell me that I used to be a lot of fun."

"Do you recognize the other people in the picture?" Floyd asked.

"Yeah, there's Mike, Aaron, Melissa, Betsy, and me."

"You don't seem very happy about seeing the picture. I thought it might bring back some happy memories."

She took a deep breath. "I was drinking, partying, and making a fool of myself. As you know, I was picked up for driving drunk a couple times and after I lost my license I had to rely on Mom and Dad to drive me to work and the grocery store. Those weren't the happiest days of my life."

"Do you remember the night this picture was taken?"

"Not really. I ran around with those guys a lot back then. I suppose it might've been almost any Friday or Saturday. Does it make a difference?"

"I think Ken Solstad took it the night before he died."

Kathy frowned and nodded her head. "I remember. He probably hadn't sobered up before he took off for Missouri. He fell asleep at the wheel. Sometimes I'm surprised we all weren't killed back then." Her comments were made without emotion.

"You're sitting on Aaron Roberts' lap. Do you remember what happened with him that night?"

"You know, Floyd, I was delivered home falling-down drunk without any panties so many times that they all run together. I'm surprised I haven't got eight kids and that I've got enough brain cells left to function." Kathy tipped her head back and closed her eyes. "On that particular night, I remember sitting in the bar, and I remember waking up on my parents' front doorstep. A deputy stopped by that afternoon and I almost peed my pants, figuring that someone had reported something that I couldn't remember doing. I ran to answer the door before my dad got it. The deputy asked if I knew where Aaron was. He told me Aaron had never shown up at home. I told him Aaron had dropped me off at home and that was the last I'd seen of him." She paused and closed her eyes. "That was partially a lie. I was too embarrassed to admit that I didn't know who'd dropped me off. I assumed that Aaron had because he'd picked me up."

"Seems like I opened an old sore," Floyd said. "Sorry."

"Hey, I've got my life together. I'm thankful every day for the Carlton County deputy who arrested me for the DWI and for the judge that threw the book at me. If either had fallen for my fake tears I'd still be out there trying to keep my car on the road by straddling the centerline. It took me awhile to get here mentally, but it's a much better place."

"Hey, Floyd," Brian Tucker called as he walked toward them. "What brings you out so early in the morning?" Brian was wiry and a few inches shorter than Kathy. He wore a John Deere cap and a dirt-stained white T-shirt over bluejeans.

"Kathy and I were reminiscing about old times."

Brian threw Kathy a curious look and asked, "What old times?"

"Floyd wanted to know what I remembered about the night before Ken Solstad was killed in the car accident."

"Oh," Brian said. His pained expression said more than a million words.

Floyd found Dolores "Dottie" Smith, Melissa's mother, working at the Postal Credit Union in downtown Pine City. She was the teller, looking professional in her pink rayon blouse and dark slacks. Her carefully applied makeup and trim figure made her look younger than her age. She and Floyd had been classmates in high school, and Dolores had dated Floyd's best friend junior year. He waited in line behind two customers for a few minutes. The manager gave him a questioning look from the office, and Floyd motioned that everything was all right.

"Hi, Floyd," Dolores said, looking for the transaction he might have prepared.

"I need to find Melissa," he said, passing the photo to Dolores. "I'd like to see if she remembers these people and what happened the night before Ken Solstad died in the car accident. Mike Nelson said she married and moved away."

Dolores Smith set the picture on the marble counter and looked at Floyd with anger. "Is this some sort of joke?" she asked.

"Not at all. Some things happened that night that we need to clear up. I hoped that talking with Melissa might shed some light on things."

Dolores made sure no one was within earshot. "Listen," she hissed, "there is nothing that happened that night that Melissa wants to talk about. Let sleeping dogs lie." She pushed the picture back to Floyd, turned her back, and walked away from the counter.

Hearing the heated words, the manager emerged from his office. "Is everything okay?" he asked Dolores.

"Just fine," she replied tersely, as she counted checks at a table facing away from the customer counter.

Floyd was shaking his head. "Brad, can you give Dottie a break for a few minutes? We need to talk."

"We do *not* need to talk," Dolores said without turning.

Floyd took her by the elbow. "We'll borrow Brad's office for a few minutes."

Floyd closed the office door and stood blocking it. "What was that all about?"

"Kenny's dead. There's no need to hash it all over again, and there's certainly no need to dredge up those memories with Melissa. She's married with a new life and a great husband. Let Ken Solstad rot in his grave and let the memories lie with him."

"What happened that night?"

"Nothing!"

"Bull. You and I have known each other most of our lives, and I can see through your façade. Give it to me straight."

"I'll give it to you straight. Where in hell were you that night? Why didn't you stop those kids from drinking and driving?" Dolores suddenly broke into tears and ran to Floyd's arms. "Why didn't you stop Kenny from raping Melissa?"

Floyd took a deep breath and held Dolores tight until she stopped sobbing. The door clicked open and Brad stuck his head in. "Is everything okay?"

Dolores recoiled from Floyd's embrace and wiped at her cheeks with her palms. Her mascara was running and her make-up was smeared "It's fine, Brad. Can I have a few more minutes to get myself together?"

The manager looked at the scene with surprise. "Sure, take whatever time you need. There's a box of tissues in the top left desk drawer. Help yourself." He closed the door quietly and left.

"Tell me what happened," Floyd said as he opened the desk drawer and handed the entire box of tissues to Dolores.

"Those idiots went out drinking like usual. Melissa and Kenny had broken up by mail while he was in Korea, but then he started calling her in the middle of the night to apologize about whatever set her off. She hung up on him at first, but then they'd talk for longer and longer times. I can't imagine what he must've paid for all those international calls.

"Anyway, when Kenny got leave back in the States he showed up on our front steps with a big bunch of red roses. Melissa was still mad at him about something, but the roses and the uniform did her in and she let him in the house. He was really respectful toward us, which was a big turnaround from the jerk he'd been before he enlisted. I was kind of hopeful that he'd turned a new leaf, but my husband, Jeff, said that a tiger never changes his stripes. As it turned out, Jeff was right. Within a few days the old Kenny was back. He hooked up with Mike Nelson and they were drinking, driving drunk, swearing, and carousing just like before Kenny went in the Army. The big difference was that Kenny had muscles to go with his big mouth, and we saw him intimidating people.

"Kenny told us he was supposed to get a month of leave, but the end of the second week he called and demanded to talk to Melissa. Something had been brewing between the two of them. She'd gone out with Kenny a couple times the first week, but by the second week she was driven home early by someone else two nights in a row and she started checking the caller ID on her cellphone and if Kenny called she didn't answer. Then one night he called on our home phone and asked me if he could talk to Melissa. She spoke with him, and afterward told me that he'd been called back to Missouri because of the Iraq thing. She told him that she wouldn't go out with him alone again, so he promised to pick her up with at least one other couple. He showed up with Aaron Roberts and Kathy Tucker, promising that he'd bring Melissa home early. He said he had to start driving to Fort Leonard Wood early the next day so they couldn't be out late.

"I was pretty upset at midnight when there was no sign of Melissa, but she was twenty-one, and I decided I had to get some sleep. I heard car doors and looked at the clock — I think it was like two in the morning. I poked Jeff in the ribs and was getting out of bed when the front door slammed. I met Melissa in the hall. It was December and she was falling down drunk and had lost her coat and one shoe somewhere. I remember her bawling like a calf, but I couldn't get her to stop crying long enough to tell me what had happened. When I got her to the kitchen I saw that her face and arms were bruised, and her blouse was torn. I thought she'd been in a car accident—I always expected that when she hung out with that bunch.

"Jeff brought a warm washcloth and I started wiping her face while he put on some coffee to try and sober her up. At first we tried to get her to tell us about the accident, and we asked her if anyone else had been hurt. Then her blouse fell open and I saw that her bra was gone and that there was a big bruise on her breast. When she realized what I'd seen, she staggered for the bathroom and locked the door. I could hear the shower running and her sobbing the whole time she was in there.

"Did you call the police?" Floyd asked.

"No, we were stupid back then. Melissa said she and Kenny had a fight, and I didn't want to believe anything else had happened. When I picked up her clothes from the bathroom floor there were no panties, and the inside of her jeans was smeared with . . . well you can guess."

Floyd sat in the guest chair and put his hand over his eyes. "Oh, Dottie, I'm so sorry. You should've called me."

"Melissa said it was partially her fault. She said she led Kenny on, and said 'no' too late to stop things. I know better than that now, but back then it seemed almost believable."

"Let me guess," Floyd said, "Ken left for the Army and everyone said you might as well let it all pass. If

Melissa wasn't pregnant it would just be a bad lesson learned, and if she was. . ."

"She didn't get pregnant, and Doctor Bergstrom examined her and said there was no permanent damage. When Kenny died the next day we all figured there wasn't any point in airing the dirty laundry."

"What happened to Melissa after that?"

"She signed up for a nursing program and started spring semester. In two years she was a registered nurse and she'd met a nice radiology technician while she was doing her clinical work. She married Bob Schotten a year later and now they're living in Redwood Falls where they both work at the hospital. We've got three grandchildren, and we don't ever talk about Kenny Solstad."

"I assume you remember that Aaron Roberts disappeared that night?" Floyd asked.

"We knew that, but we were so wrapped up in Melissa's situation we didn't get too involved. A deputy stopped by and asked Melissa a few questions, but I don't think she had anything to tell him. To be perfectly honest, I think she might've been too drunk to know what else happened that night."

"Do you think she was too drunk to say 'no?'"

Dolores pondered the question. "If she didn't said no, why did Kenny beat the hell out of her?"

CHAPTER 11

No one answered the phone at the Schotten house and Floyd hung up when the answering machine beeped. He called the Redwood Falls hospital and asked to speak with Melissa Schotten. After being transferred twice, and cut off once, he got the nurses' station on the maternity floor.

"This is Melissa. How may I help you?"

"This is Floyd Swenson from the Pine County Sheriff's Department. I'd like to ask you about a picture that showed up in an old camera. Do you have a moment?"

"Hang on," she said. In the background were the sounds of a busy nursing station in the middle of the day. "I'm back. You said something about an old picture?"

"That's right," Floyd said. "An old camera was purchased at a garage sale and when the film was developed there was a picture of a group of people, including you." Floyd weighed his next words carefully. "It was taken the night before Aaron Roberts disappeared.

I was hoping you might remember something from that night that might help us."

Floyd stopped when he realized that he was speaking to a dial tone. He redialed and was quickly connected to the maternity ward. When he asked for Melissa Schotten he was told that she had left with a sudden illness.

Rather than risking another sudden phone-related illness, Floyd decided to drive two hours to Brooklyn Center where Betsy Webb and her husband lived in a townhouse development. As Floyd wandered the meandering streets with British sounding names he was struck by the feeling that this would be a drunken homeowner's worst nightmare. Each house was absolutely identical to the next, and the addresses repeated on every street. "How would someone with significant alcohol impairment ever find their way to the right house?" he muttered.

As expected, the Webb's townhouse was unremarkable. The beige exterior was accented with white trim and shutters. Enough driveway was provided outside each double garage so two cars could be parked off the pavement because the street was so narrow that cars parked opposite each other would block the road. Floyd pulled into the driveway and checked to make sure his cruiser was completely out of the roadway when the front bumper was against the garage door.

A teenaged girl trying to look twenty met him at the door. Her skintight jeans were low on her hips, exposing about ten inches of flat belly between the jeans and a cropped top. The gap exposed a silver navel ring. Her hair was in blonde cornrows and each ear was adorned with at least eight earrings.

"Is your mother home?" Floyd asked.

The girl's eyes narrowed. "You know," she said, looking at Floyd's badge, "this isn't Pine County.

"You know, young girls shouldn't open the door without looking to see who is on the other side. I might've been a kidnapper."

"MOM, there's a cop here to see you!" The girl walked away from the door with obvious contempt.

A harried woman appeared behind the screen door. "I'm sorry, but my daughter thinks her smart mouth is cute sometimes. What is it that you wanted?"

"I'm an investigator from Pine County. Could we talk for a few minutes?"

Betsy Webb opened the screen door. "Please come inside where it's air conditioned. It must be close to ninety out there."

Betsy was short, dressed in wind pants and a floppy shirt that hid her slightly heavy figure. Her hair was as blonde as her daughter's, but worn in a short cut that accentuated the roundness of her face. Betsy led Floyd into the small living room and shooed a cat off a chair to make a place for him to sit. She picked up a laundry basket from the couch and plopped where it had been. Her collapse seemed almost theatrical.

"We found a picture in an old camera that had been sold at a garage sale. You're one of the people in the picture. Could identify the others for me?"

Floyd handed the picture across the laundry basket just as the teen appeared at the door. "Hey, Mom, I don't have a clean pair of socks."

Betsy reached into the basket and rummaged for two that matched. Holding them out she said, "You know, I'm not the only person in this house who can match socks and fold towels."

The girl rolled her eyes and took the socks. She sat on the floor and pulled them on as Betsy looked at the picture. Betsy's eyes grew wide as she recognized the faces.

"Where'd you find this?"

"The woman who bought the camera had the film developed. That picture was already in the camera."

The girl got up and pushed next to her mother on the couch, trying to see what had captured her mother's attention. "Eeeww," the girl exclaimed. "You and daddy look wasted!"

"Go put the rest of these clothes away," Betsy said sternly. "And I wasn't wasted," she said to the girl's back.

"You look kind of wasted to me, too," Floyd said quietly.

"Shh. Alyssa doesn't need to know that."

"Do you remember when this picture was taken?"

"It's got to be back after we graduated from high school. It looks like we're in a bar somewhere, and Aaron Roberts was still around."

"The film was in Ken Solstad's camera. This picture was taken the night before Aaron disappeared."

Betsy's mouth dropped open. "Then," she took a deep breath, "Kenny took this picture the day before he was killed in the car accident." She took a deep breath and tears welled in her eyes.

"What do you remember about that night?"

"The six of us went out drinking. Kenny had just gotten orders to report for deployment to Iraq. It was his last night with us so we went out and partied hard."

"Do you remember what happened to any of the other people that night? Were you all together for the whole night or did Aaron leave early?"

Betsy continued to stare at the picture. "I guess I don't recall. I was with Mike, my ex-husband, that night, and Aaron was with Kathy Tucker. Melissa Smith was Kenny's date. I remember that there was something going on between them. All night Kenny was edgy and bitchy. Melissa told me she didn't want to be there when we went to the bathroom."

"Was Kenny's bitchiness directed at anyone in particular, like Aaron?"

"Oh, no. He was being bitchy to everyone. He acted like he was pissed at Mike and I because we were happy together. He was trying to pick fights with guys in the bar who he thought were looking at Melissa wrong. He was arm wrestling with everyone to prove how strong he was. Like I said, he was just generally bitchy."

"Do you remember if Aaron and Kathy left together?"

Betsy blushed. "Actually, Mike and I got tired of Kenny's antics and we left."

"Did you know you blushed when you told me that?" Floyd asked. "Is there something else wrapped up in that memory?"

"Sometimes I hate having a fair complexion," Betsy said. "I, um. . ." She hung her head. Floyd's experience said she was either carefully weighing her words or composing a plausible lie. "Mike told Kenny that I was horny and that he was going to help me take care of it. He figured that was about the only excuse Kenny would accept for us to duck out of the party. Even at that he called us short hitters and party-poopers."

"Did you see Aaron or Kenny after that?"

"I wish you'd stop asking embarrassing questions," Betsy said with another blush. "Mike and I drove out to a country road and parked for a couple hours. We never went back to the bar."

Alyssa spun around the corner. "You and daddy did it in a car? Really?"

Betsy's crimson blush answered the question. "Of course not, and that's not an appropriate thing for people to do on a date! We fell asleep and got in big trouble with our parents."

"Give me a break!" Alyssa said, again rolling her eyes. "Like I could believe that you and daddy could fall asleep in a car and not be doing it."

Betsy's arms dropped on the couch as she let out a deep sigh. "They watch this reality television crap and then they think every couple in the world has sex every time the lights go out. I was a virgin until I was twenty, and I'll be lucky to get Alyssa through school without a pregnancy."

"Bottom line, you didn't ever see Aaron or Kenny after you left the bar," Floyd summarized.

"I never saw them again, but three weeks later Mike and I were making wedding plans."

"Pregnant?"

"Don't you hate it when the kids can see right through you? Let's just say that Alyssa might almost be able to remember that night because she was there."

CHAPTER 12

Floyd showered and put on a fresh pair of khaki pants. He chose a knit golf shirt from the drawer and ran a comb through his thinning gray hair. He climbed in his pickup and drove down highway 23 to Pine Brook. He wound a few blocks off the highway to Mary Junger's house and sat in the driveway with a smile on his face. Mary waved at him from the window and motioned that she'd be right out.

"How was your day?" he asked as they pulled onto the highway.

"There's a funeral Wednesday and we got a half dozen orders for flower arrangements. Pete Watson chose a plant for his wife's birthday, and a cute high school kid came in looking for a dozen roses for his girlfriend. When he found out how expensive roses are, he opted for red carnations with some baby's breath."

Mary chatted about the flower business, the heat, and when it was expected to break, and the sorry baseball season the Twins were having. Floyd smiled and nodded agreement at appropriate times. They pulled into the parking lot at Cassidy's White Pine

Restaurant. Floyd opened the door for Mary and the hostess showed them to a booth overlooking the parking lot. Floyd slid into the booth opposite Mary.

As they looked at menus, Mary said, "You haven't said a word."

Floyd continued to smile. "I'd rather listen to you."

After they ordered, Mary asked about Floyd's day.

"I spent the day chasing ghosts."

"Ghosts?"

"We've got this old picture of six people. One person died the next day and another hasn't been seen since the night the picture was taken. So I've been talking to the other four, trying to understand what happened that night."

"Did you find any of the ghosts?"

"Not yet, but one person told me a secret, another person hung up on me when I called her, and I think a third lied to me."

"People lied to you?"

"Don't be surprised. People lie to cops all the time. The trick is to know when you're being lied to and then use that to your advantage." Changing the topic, Floyd asked about the remodeling project at the flower shop.

"I talked to Robbie Peterson, and he's booked up right now, but he estimated it would take him about three weeks and he put me on the schedule for September. I'll need to give him twenty percent down when he starts, and the balance is due when he's done."

"Just let me know when I need to write him a check," Floyd said, buttering a roll.

Mary reached across the table and took his hand. "Are you sure you want to pay for the remodeling? I can talk to the banker about taking out a loan."

"It's OK," Floyd said, gently squeezing her hand. "I like the idea of being your partner."

Their food came and they talked about mutual friends and whether Mary's shop should have a booth at the winter home show. Floyd picked up the bill and was reaching for his wallet when he felt Mary's toe sliding up his calf. The under-table move was so unexpected that he recoiled.

"I'm sorry," Mary said, giving him a silly grin. "I didn't mean to surprise you." Her toe slid up his other calf.

"It's OK. It's just that. . ."

Mary slipped onto Floyd's side of the table and put her hand on his thigh. "We can go back to my house and have some dessert."

Floyd felt a blush rising from his neck. He gently picked up her hand from his thigh and kissed it gently. "I think we have to eat dessert here."

Mary gave him a quizzical look. "Why?"

Floyd leaned close and whispered, "Because I can't stand up right now."

Mary glanced at his lap and smiled. "Oh dear, I think I've caused a problem."

After sharing a serving of bread pudding with rum sauce, Floyd and Mary drove in the late summer twilight. The sun had set when he pulled into Mary's driveway and the wispy high clouds were crimson and yellow above the western horizon.

Mary slid her hand into Floyd's and squeezed. "We haven't talked about this, but I feel something special when I'm with you. I have butterflies when I see your car in the driveway and I feel like a part of me is missing when you're on night shift and I sit alone watching television."

Floyd was staring at the clouds. He took a deep breath and nodded.

Mary mistook his silence for discomfort and said, "If this is too fast, I'm sorry, but I thought you should know. . ."

Floyd shook his head. "It's not that. It's just that I haven't got my head around what's happening. I can handle going out for dinner with a friend, but my stomach clenches when I hear the word, 'date.'"

"You're more than my friend."

"Yup," Floyd replied, not trusting his voice with a longer answer.

"Come in," she said.

"As much as I'd like to," Floyd replied, "I've got a dead body to search for in the morning. I'd like to take a rain check on that offer."

Mary slid next to him and they kissed. "It's your loss."

"I know."

Floyd walked her to the door and they kissed again. "Don't wait too long to collect that rain check," Mary said from the doorway.

CHAPTER 13

Floyd was awake before the alarm clock rang and after showering, feeding the dog, and making a cup of coffee he was out the door with a lilt in his step. At the courthouse he scanned through the files and reports of criminal activity from the December and January after Ken Solstad's death. He wasn't sure just what he hoped to find, but he had a nagging feeling that the picture of Aaron Roberts might have been linked to something else that happened. The stack of files was sitting on his desk chair, the only clear spot in his corner of the bullpen. Mid-morning he decided to call Melissa Schotten at the Redwood Falls hospital again rather than digging into more of the files. When she answered, he tried a different tack.

"Melissa, please listen to me a few moments. This is Floyd Swenson calling from the Pine County Sheriff's Department and this is not a crank call. If you don't believe me, please write down this number and have the dispatcher page me."

"I can't make a long distance call from this phone," Melissa replied in an irritated voice.

"Call collect if you like. I'll tell the dispatcher to accept the charges."

"Tell me something only a Pine County cop would know."

"I graduated from Pine City high school with your mother, Dolores, whose nickname is Dottie and maiden name was Bradshaw. She was a cheerleader and dated my best friend. She met your dad when he moved here after graduating from the University of Minnesota."

"That's not cop stuff. You could've gotten that information from Facebook or any local gossip."

Floyd took a deep breath. "Your mother trusts me so much she told me something terrible happened to you the night before Ken Solstad died in the car accident. Do you want me to tell you what it was?" It was a big gamble, but it was the only thing he could come up with that might demonstrate Dottie's trust.

"No," she said. "What do you want? And make it quick, I'm on duty and we're busy."

"Would it be better if I called back when you go on break?"

"No, it's bad enough to ruin work time with this topic; I would really hate to waste a break, too."

"Would it be better if I drove there and we spoke?"

There was a pause before she answered. "Redwood Falls is about a four-hour one-way drive. Are your questions that important?"

"My questions aren't but your answers may be."

Floyd heard a deep breath. "Give me your number. I'll call you from home this afternoon."

"Tell the dispatcher to reach me wherever I am. It's that important."

"It must be, otherwise my mother would never have broken her promise not to tell another soul." She hung up.

"I wonder if it's that important?" Floyd asked himself. He picked up half of the files from his chair and put them in front of Pam Ryan who had been writing an accident report.

"What's this?" she asked.

"I've got to assume Aaron Roberts is the person sliced up in the photo. He didn't drop off the face of the earth after he was attacked. I may be reaching for straws, but I think that he may have survived the attack and was stranded in the middle of nowhere. If it were me, I'd try to find a house with someone home, or I'd try to break into a cabin to warm up and then maybe steal a snowmobile or ATV to get to safety."

"So," Pam said, looking at the pile, "we're going through these files to find a reported break-in or stolen snowmobile with the hope it will do what?"

"Maybe we'll find a trail to follow. We weren't looking for an injured guy who was trying to get warm and safe when we investigated these cases. If we focus on the ones that weren't solved, we might be able to find a thread."

Pam looked at the pile and said, "I think I'll make a fresh pot of coffee before I start. This could take awhile."

After lunch, Floyd walked down the courthouse hallway and spent half an hour with the sheriff and Dan Williams, the undersheriff, trying to justify spending time on an old mystery that no one cared about two days ago. Dan agreed that they had to follow up on evidence of an obvious assault and possible kidnapping. The sheriff was less excited and asked them to spend no more than a couple days on it before reviewing the progress with him and reassessing the need for further effort. When he got back to Pam's desk, she held up three files.

"There was a burglary ring busted the winter that Aaron disappeared," Pam explained, "and they broke into dozens of seasonal cabins, stealing electronics, snowmobiles, and ATVs. When they were caught in the act, up in Carlton County, one of the guys turned state's evidence and we cleared almost every burglary from that winter. These three files weren't attributed to that crime spree."

Floyd took the file and read as Pam explained, "That first one appears to be a couple kids who broke into a garage and went joy riding on two snowmobiles. The snowmobiles were found less than a quarter-mile from where they were stolen, which tells me that the kids went on a joy ride but had a car they looped back to."

Pam handed Floyd a second file. "This one looks like someone loaded a couple of ATVs onto a trailer and hauled them away. They've never been found and are probably out of state or in Canada."

"This one is closer to what we hoped to find," Pam said as she handed the third file to Floyd. "An ATV was found abandoned by Round Lake the day Ken Solstad died. There wasn't any report of a theft, so we put it in the impound lot. In the spring," Pam said, pulling out another file and handing it to Floyd, "we got a call from a seasonal cabin owner whose ATV had been stolen from his garage on Passenger Lake. The registration and serial numbers matched, and he claimed it from the impound lot. It hadn't been damaged and there was still gas in the tank."

Floyd walked to the county map posted on the wall and put a finger on Passenger Lake in the northern end of Pine County. He put a second finger on Round Lake. "Someone rode about 20 miles, and walked away from the ATV. That's interesting."

"What's interesting?" Sandy Maki asked, walking into the bullpen, ready for his afternoon shift.

"Someone stole an ATV from Passenger Lake the day Aaron Roberts disappeared." Pam explained. "We were just wondering if he broke into a garage, stole an ATV, and maybe drove it somewhere safe, or maybe to where his car was parked."

"So," Sandy said, looking at the map. "That's a pretty remote location without anything but summer cabins. The high school kids like to have bonfires out there in the winter because it's so remote and quiet. I suppose it'd be a good place to slice somebody up without worrying about witnesses in the depth of winter. Lots of swamp around there to dump a body, too."

CHAPTER 14

Barb Dupre was behind the photo counter when Floyd came through the pharmacy door. She gave him a discreet wave and went back to proofing a pile of photos.

"When I got in this morning there was a note asking me to call you," Floyd said, leaning over the counter.

Barb's outfit was a little more conservative, a navy T-shirt over tan slacks. Her straight bleached-blonde hair was backlit in the photo booth, giving the illusion she had an aura. By all accounts, Barb's life had been anything but angelic. Sandy Maki met her when he was questioning her about a patron who'd been murdered after leaving the bar where Barb waited tables. Her boyfriend had been a biker with several outstanding warrants. He'd physically and psychologically abused Barb before Sandy "liberated" her from the relationship. She had a second job at the time as an exotic dancer who showcased her array of tattoos, including one that said, "Property of Butch," in a very provocative location. Floyd was glad she could use her

Dean L. Hovey

brains in her new job instead of relying on her physical assets.

"Okay," she said stripping off the white gloves, "that's the last data card. I can slip out for a while to show you the tree."

"The tree?" Floyd asked.

"Sandy told me that you think that maybe the guy in the picture was cut up out by Passenger Lake. So, when I was out taking duck pictures last night I drove all the roads around Passenger Lake and I found the tree in the picture."

"Do you really think that you found *the* tree?" Floyd said, straightening up and following Barb to the front door.

Barb took a large manila envelope off the end of the counter and waved it at Floyd. "I made an eight-by-ten reprint so we can compare when we get there." She waved at the pharmacist. "I'll be back in an hour or so, Gordy."

"What happens if someone wants a one-hour photo?" The pharmacist asked with a smile, knowing it was rare that anyone ever wanted one-hour developing service.

"Give them the two-hour price," Barb replied as she and Floyd walked out the door. She smiled and said, "There is no two-hour price."

The coolness of the pharmacy was a stark contrast to the muggy heat outside. It quickly dampened their clothing and by the time Floyd's cruiser pulled away from the curb they were both already sweaty.

"There's a red cabin on the north shore of Passenger Lake where the road turns to follow the shore," Barb explained. "The tree is in that yard."

"I hate the cold and snow," Floyd said, waiting for the air conditioning to overcome the accumulated heat inside the car. He turned toward the interstate. "But I hate this miserable hot weather more."

"I don't know. We keep the apartment kind of cool in the winter and I have to wear so many clothes to keep warm. I like the summer better because I can walk around the house in panties and bare feet." Barb checked to see if Floyd was startled. When her comments didn't elicit a response she added, "Sandy makes me wear clothes when I answer the door."

"You know, we run across a lot of situations when we get called to people's houses. Having someone naked answer the door wouldn't be the strangest thing I've experienced."

"Has Sandy told you about my tattoos?" Barb asked with a twinkle in her eyes. She had fun shocking and embarrassing people with stories about her lurid past and her tattoos.

"There are rumors," Floyd said, but quickly added, "but I don't need confirmation."

"You guys are so straight. Don't you ever let your hair down? Sandy always seems to be so . . . modulated. He's never really high and he's never really low. He just plods along in second gear all the time. Are you like that, too?"

"We pretty much have to be like that on the job, and that carries over into our personal lives, too. If we lose control, people could get hurt or killed."

"I know! And that's what makes life exciting. If you live on the edge once in a while you let off steam."

"If you live on the edge, you sometimes fall off," Floyd replied. "I like Sandy. He's a nice guy and a good deputy. His head and his heart are in the right places."

"We're getting married," Barb said without emotion.

"Really!"

"Sandy asked me a long time ago, but I wasn't ready. We've been together for a couple of years now and I guess it'll be okay. I can't see myself with anyone else and he's the first guy I've really been able to trust."

"That's exciting," Floyd said. "You guys will be making all sorts of wedding plans. Have you made any decision about a date yet?"

"Not yet. But the wedding won't be anything too fancy. I think we'll find a secluded spot and have a sunrise wedding. I've been checking out a lot of places when I've been taking wildlife pictures and there are some spots where the summer sunrises are spectacular. I think I'd like to do that."

They discussed wedding options for the half-hour drive to the Sturgeon Lake exit from I-35. Floyd took the south road around Sturgeon Lake and turned south at Marge's Resort where hand-painted signs advertised pizza and boat rentals. As they got further from the lake the clutter of lakeshore cabins gave way to open expanses of woods with mailboxes at irregular intervals interspersed with driveways blocked with large farm-style metal gates or chains.

"This seems like an unlikely spot to bring someone," Floyd said. "The picture of the five friends looks like it was taken in the Beroun bar, and the people all lived between Pine City and Hinckley. I can't come up with a good reason to drive way the heck up here in December after the bars close to tie Aaron Roberts to a tree so someone could carve up his chest."

"I didn't think about it," Barb said with a shrug. "I just started driving the roads around Passenger Lake that looked like good secluded spots to torture someone. Nobody lives out here in the winter, but the roads are plowed. I thought it seemed like a perfect spot."

Floyd turned off the blacktop and onto a gravel road. "I guess we're looking at it from different directions. I'm thinking that this was a crime of opportunity, and you're thinking it was premeditated. But, even if it was premeditated, this seems like a strange place to drive to in the middle of the winter."

Floyd turned onto a one-lane gravel road and drove slowly through the narrow lane. The opening through underbrush was barely wider than the Crown Victoria for a hundred yards until it suddenly opened into a park-like glade with large oaks and neatly groomed grass. Directly ahead of them was a red summer cottage, and beyond that the sparkling waters of Passenger Lake. The road turned to the right, and a string of eight cottages in various colors and similar architecture came into view.

"There!" Barb said, pointing to a large oak with an unusually low branch on the east side of the road. "Park here and I'll show you."

"I hate to get out of the car now that the air conditioning has finally cooled it off." Barb was out of the car and walking before Floyd finished the sentence. He gave the dispatcher their location and reported that he would be out of service. Barb had the picture out of the envelope and was walking around the tree.

"Here," she said, aligning the picture with the tree. "You can see from this angle how that one low branch is unique and it's right here in the picture." She held the picture out for Floyd to examine. "Oak trees almost never have branches this low. Most people trim them or they get broken off."

"You're right, that does look like the tree, and there can't be many that look like this in all northern Minnesota."

"See," Barb said, "even the birch tree in the background lines up. This has to be the spot."

A screen door slammed, diverting their attention from the photo. A lanky gray-haired man walked slowly toward them as Floyd slipped the photo into the envelope.

"That girl said she'd be back with the cops," the man said. "I thought she was kidding. I'm Ron Birkholz." The man extended his hand.

"Floyd Swenson. Are you the owner?"

"For more than fifty years. This girl said there may have been a murder here back in '98. Is that so?"

"It appears that this tree shows up in an incriminating picture. Do you know anything about a guy who disappeared back then? He was a local guy named Aaron Roberts."

"I can't remember what I had for breakfast much less what happened when those A-rabs were having their tiff."

Floyd grinned at the political incorrectness. "Are you a year-round resident?"

"Nah, I'm what you locals call a 'Cidiot.' That's short for City Idiot. I live down in the Twin Cities and come up here summers. The locals tell me we're all too demanding. I guess it's just that we get used to the pace of the Cities and it used to be kind of infuriating to see how slow things moved here sometimes. Now that I'm retired it's not such a big deal." As he spoke, a gray three-legged cat came hopping around the corner of the cabin and approached them.

"Do you remember finding a rope lying by this tree when you came up one spring?" Barb asked, garnering a skeptical look from Floyd.

Birkholz's eyes narrowed. "You know, we might've." He started walking toward a storage shed behind the cottage with Floyd, Barb, and the cat following.

The inside of the small shed was unlit and cluttered with a lawnmower, tools, a chainsaw, gas cans, and assorted gardening implements. Birkholz pulled an extension cord off a peg on the wall, then removed a hank of dirty cotton clothesline, handing the dusty rope to Floyd. Floyd inspected the rope and noted a knot away from the cut ends as the cat rubbed against his leg.

"Uncle Tripod," Birkholz said, "stop pestering the cop."

"You found it like this?" Floyd asked, holding up the cut ends of the six-foot rope.

"I guess. Seems to me there was that knot in it with the ends cut. It looked like someone had tied some rusty metal with it, or left it on some metal. You can see the rust spots on it still."

"Why'd you save it?" Barb asked.

Birkholz shrugged. "I don't know. My wife used to say I saved everything. I guess I thought that a man could never have too much spare rope. I think the boys used it to hang the deer they got back in '99 and '05."

Floyd smiled, amused that Birkholz couldn't remember breakfast, but knew exactly the years his sons shot deer. He wiped away some dust and examined the spots. To him they looked more like blood than rust. "Can I keep this?" he asked, wondering if the spots were blood from the '99 buck or other deer over the years.

"Makes me no nevermind. It's just been collecting dust in the shed since the last deer."

"I'd like to bring some deputies up to check around the ground if it's all right with you. We'll probably bring in a couple metal detectors and check for buttons and things like that."

"It's okay with me. Since my wife passed on it's pretty lonely around here. I'd be happy to have the company. If you let me know when you're coming I'll even put on some coffee and pick up a dozen rolls."

Floyd smiled and reached down, rubbing the now purring cat behind the ears. "If you do that, you may never get rid of the deputies."

Floyd put the rope into an evidence bag in the trunk.

"You don't seem very happy about finding the tree and the rope," Barb said, reacting to Floyd's silence. "Didn't you want to find the tree?"

"Yes and no. Life would've been so much easier if we asked a few questions and came up with the same inconclusive answers we'd had back when the ATV was stolen. On the other hand, it's amazing that we can come up with new leads years after Aaron Roberts disappeared."

"Do you think that's really the rope in the picture, and that the rust on the rope is actually blood?"

"Who knows if this is really *the* rope. The stains look more like blood than rust," Floyd observed as they got back to the blacktop. "I'll have to send it in for testing, but my guess is that it's more likely from the deer than human."

"Will they test to see if it's Aaron Roberts' blood?"

"That would take DNA testing, and we'd have to get samples from Aaron's parents or siblings. I'm not sure that would buy us anything more than just assuming it's his."

"There could be someone else's blood on it with Aaron's, and that might tell you who else was there, maybe even who cut him." When Floyd didn't answer immediately Barb added, "Is that another one of the questions that you hoped you wouldn't have to answer?"

"To test, we would have to get blood samples from the suspects. To do that, we would have to convince a judge that we had probable cause that someone had committed a crime, and I can't say I'd be doing anything other than fishing right now. Judges won't go for that."

Barb sat in silence, thinking. "Isn't there a DNA database?"

The state only tracks DNA from felons and sex offenders and it's only been active for a couple years. There's a military database too, but I'm sure Aaron's DNA wouldn't be there."

"What *are* you going to do?" Barb asked.

"We'll get a couple deputies out to the tree with metal detectors to see if we can find a button, knife, or something. Then, I suppose I'll talk to a bunch more people about what happened that night."

"Who haven't you talked to yet?"

"There are friends, neighbors, relatives, and old lovers who we haven't interviewed. Any of them might have a nugget of information they didn't remember or didn't want to share back then."

CHAPTER 15

"Hi, Babe," Sandy Maki said, pecking Barb on the cheek. "How did it go with Floyd at Passenger Lake?" Sandy asked as he scraped the remnants of his cereal bowl into the garbage disposal. He set the bowl in the dishwasher and wiped off the counter.

"I showed him the tree and the guy who owns the cabin had a bloody rope he found one spring by the tree. Floyd said he's going to have it tested to see if the stains are really blood."

"Good job! I'll bet Floyd was happy."

"He didn't seem happy," Barb said, leaning against the doorjamb. "He said he would send some deputies out with metal detectors to search the area around the tree. Is that what you'll be doing this afternoon?" Barb asked as she followed him to the bathroom.

"I don't know. I haven't checked in for my shift yet."

Barb reached out and touched Sandy's straight dark hair. "Volunteer to do it. I'll stay up until you get home because I want to hear what you find."

"Chances are we won't find anything. That's usually what happens. But I always appreciate you being up when I get home."

Floyd was waiting for the afternoon deputies in the bullpen when the dispatcher paged him with an urgent call.

"Deputy Swenson, this is Melissa Schotten. I'm calling from home."

"I appreciate you calling back. Some things have come up regarding the night Aaron Roberts disappeared and I wanted to talk to you about your memories." The line was silent so long Floyd asked, "Are you still there?"

"Yes, but I don't see the point in having any discussion. What happened that night is ancient history best forgotten. I didn't want to talk about it then, and now that everyone involved is dead or gone, I don't see any point in talking about it now."

"Humor me. I have to write a report and I'd like to have the best, most complete information possible. Tell me what happened." Floyd slipped the pictures out of the envelope and spread them atop the assorted piles of papers on his desk.

"I talked to Mom, and she said you showed her a picture of five of us in a bar. I vaguely remember Kenny taking a picture when we were sitting in the Beroun bar. I haven't seen it, but I can't imagine there's a smile on my face. I had broken up with Kenny when he was in Korea. When he came back he wanted to get back together and he begged and cajoled me until I agreed to go out with him. He tried to be a gentleman and make a good impression, but I kept waiting for him to revert to the jerk that I'd seen too often. It only took a couple nights of drinking with his friends and he had that old-Kenny attitude, but there was something more. It was like he had to keep proving that he was the toughest guy wherever we went.

"After like two nights of that, I told him to take me home. I was done. He apologized and said it would be different, but I demanded to be taken home. When he refused, I had one of my girlfriends drive me home."

"So, you broke up with him, but somehow you ended up together the last night before he was to report in Missouri."

"It was a mess. He called and begged. He told me it was his last night in Minnesota and that he would be shipping out for Saudi Arabia and might never come home. I told him that didn't matter because we were through even if it was his last night on earth. Finally, he said we'd go out just as friends — no romance — just a bunch of old friends going out for drinks together. He promised there would be at least six of us going out together. I called Kathy to make sure he was telling the truth, and she said that she and Aaron were riding along with us, and that everything would be okay."

"So, you talked to Kathy Tucker and she said that you'd be double dating?"

"Right. I explained to her that Kenny and I were done, and she promised we wouldn't be left alone."

"I've got the picture of the five of you in front of me. Tell me what happened after the picture."

"Well, everyone was drinking heavily and inhibitions seemed to be slipping. I held back a little because I didn't want things to get out of control. Mike and Betsy were necking inside the bar and Mike announced that they were leaving. That left just four of us. I told Kenny and Aaron it was time to call it a night, and that I wanted to go home. Aaron was okay with that, but Kenny was saying things like we were short hitters, and we were party poopers. I threatened to get someone else to drive me home and then Aaron and Kathy said they would drive me home, so Kenny relented.

"Aaron was driving, and Kenny and I were in the backseat of Aaron's Buick. As soon as the doors were closed Kenny was all over me. He was kissing me and giving me this line about this being his last night and how I owed him a special send-off. I remember Kathy in the front seat kind of egging him on and telling me to ease up. You know, saying things like I was no virgin anyway and what harm would it do to give Kenny a special memory. Kenny was really drunk and obnoxious. It was just a terrible scene, even worse than usual.

"Aaron was driving and arguing with Kathy. She stopped talking to me and started coming on to him while I'm fighting off Kenny in the backseat. All of a sudden, Aaron stopped the car and told Kathy to back off. They got out of the car and started having a big fight on the side of the road with the car doors open. I'm finally fed up with Kenny and I screamed at him to stop." The intake of a deep breath filled the phone line, followed by silence.

"But he didn't stop."

"Sorry," Melissa said, composing herself. "When I yelled, Kenny got mad and hit me with his fist. The next thing I know, he's ripping my clothes off and . . ." The conversation was replaced with sobs.

"All that happened with Kathy and Aaron right outside the car?"

"I don't know where they were. All I could see were Kenny's wild eyes, his hands ripping at my clothes, and the smell of his beer breath. At that point I was out of it. I shut down and everything that happened was happening to someone else. I squirmed and resisted, but he was so strong I had no chance. When he was done he pushed away from me like I was some whore he'd bought on the street. He didn't apologize or act like he was sorry. It was like he'd taken what he thought he deserved. He pushed away from me and told me to put my clothes on. I think he got out of the car while

I was trying to find my clothes. I remember a blast of cold air when the door opened. And I think I heard someone arguing, too."

"And they drove you right home?"

"It was really odd. I'd always thought Kathy was my best friend, but something had happened outside the car. When I got dressed as best I could, Aaron got in the backseat with me. He could see what had happened and he told me how sorry he was. Then Kenny drove back to my house with Kathy in the front seat.

It got even stranger when we got to my house. Kenny talked to Kathy and then he dragged Aaron out of the car. Kenny was yelling and swearing at him. I think he may have even punched him. Then he grabbed me and dragged me out of the backseat. He pushed me toward the house and called me a bitch. I said I wanted my jacket, and I'd lost one shoe, but he told me to run to the house, then Kenny threw my jacket out of the car, he grabbed Aaron and pushed him toward the car. I remember looking back, and it looked like Kenny was kicking and punching Aaron when he was in the backseat."

"Where was Kathy? Didn't she try to stop Kenny?"

"I. . .I don't know. She'd been in the front seat with Kenny. I remember them talking while Aaron helped me get my clothes together, but when we got to my house Kathy was crying."

"You have no idea what happened after Kenny, Aaron, and Kathy left your house that night?"

"No. I got in the house somehow and my mom found me crying. She helped clean me up and asked what had happened. When I went into the bathroom she picked up my clothes. When I got out of the bathroom Mom was crying. I asked her what was wrong and she said she found bloody stains in my jeans and understood what had happened. I think she apologized for making me go out with Kenny. Dad came down and we shut up. We were afraid he'd do something crazy."

"It didn't occur to anyone that you should've called the sheriff's department?"

"Why? I'd been on a date with my boyfriend and things got carried away."

"Melissa, you were raped," Floyd said softly. "That's all there is to it. Kenny raped you and he should've been prosecuted."

"It doesn't happen that way. Everyone in town would've called me a whore and Kenny's friends wouldn't have let it rest. No judge is going to convict a guy going off to war."

"It's not the judge's choice. A jury hears the trial and they vote based on the evidence."

Melissa gave a bitter laugh. "How many date rapes have been prosecuted in Pine County?" When Floyd didn't reply immediately she went on, ""And I know why, because some girl would have to sit in a courtroom with a jury of her neighbors and tell them the dirty details of her assault. Then would come the questions about if she'd ever had sex before, and with whom. The defense tries to make you look like the city bicycle — the one everyone's ridden around the block once. I couldn't stand the thought of twelve people I knew sitting in the jury box listening to the details of my sex life. There aren't many girls who can in a small town like Pine City."

"I don't think it's that bad, but I see where you're coming from. Did Ken or Kathy call the next day to apologize?"

"I didn't hear a thing until a deputy came to the door and told us that Kenny had been killed in a car accident. He thought I was crying because Kenny died. They were really tears of relief. If he hadn't died, I would've dreaded his return."

"When did you next hear from Kathy?"

"We've never spoken again. I saw her in the grocery store and I walked the other way. I started nursing school, then I got married, and moved away. I visit my parents on some holidays. I don't look for Kathy, Mike, or any of that old crowd. I'll never attend a high school reunion, and when my parents are gone, I'll never go north of the Twin Cities again."

"There are still a lot of fine people in Pine County."

"They weren't the ones I hung around with."

"So, you never heard about what happened after you were dropped off that night. No one ever said what happened to Aaron after you got out of the car?"

"No, and why is that a big issue after all these years? You said you found a picture that was taken at the bar. Why would that raise all these questions now?"

"Some other evidence came to light and we think that Aaron may have been assaulted later that night. It's probably related to his disappearance."

"I saw Kenny assault him."

"Aaron was cut with a knife."

There was a long pause. "Kenny had a knife. It was a big one with like teeth on the back edge. He showed it to a bunch of people when he first came back. He was really proud of it. He said it was sharp enough to shave with and that he was planning to collect some war souvenirs with it."

"That's an interesting tidbit," Floyd said making a mental note to call the Solstads. "I'll check on it. Is there anything else you can remember about that night?"

"I'm sorry, I've worked hard to put that night out of my memory."

Floyd was dialing Solstad's when the dispatcher paged him. He punched the blinking button.

"Floyd," Mary said, "I went to your house to let the dog out and put some leftovers in the refrigerator. Someone left a note on your door. It says, 'Let dead dogs lie.'"

"Shit!" he uttered. "Where are you now?"

"I'm in the house talking on the phone," Mary replied in confusion. "Is this a big deal?"

"The house was secure? There wasn't anyone around?"

"The door was locked and everything seems in its place. The dog met me in the kitchen and everything's normal."

"Stay on the phone." Floyd got the dispatcher on the intercom. "Get a cruiser over to my house right now. Tell them someone left a threatening note and I want them to check the house."

Trying to keep the concern out of his voice, Floyd clicked back to the other line. "I asked dispatch to send someone over to pick up the note. You haven't handled it too much, have you?"

"I thought maybe one of the neighbors left it. I opened the envelope and unfolded the note to read it. You sound concerned. Is this a big deal?"

"I don't know. It's too coincidental that it shows up when we're in the middle of investigating Aaron Roberts' disappearance."

"Should I get out of the house?" Mary asked, a tinge of fear creeping into her voice.

"Yes. Go to your car, lock the doors, and wait in the driveway. As soon as you've locked the car, call the dispatcher."

Floyd jogged to the dispatcher's cubicle and asked, "Who's closest to my house?"

"Pam Ryan is in Royalton Township. She should be there in a few minutes."

"Mary Jungers is at my house. I told her to go her car, then call you on her cellphone. Keep her on the line until Pam arrives. I'm leaving now."

The afternoon sun was still high in the sky as Floyd peeled out of the Pine County Courthouse parking lot with his lights flashing. He turned up the radio's volume, waiting to hear the conversation between the dispatcher and Pam Ryan. He was passing McDonald's golden arches when the dispatcher called him to announce that the call he was expecting had come through.

Within seconds Pam Ryan responded. "Please advise the homeowner I'm within one minute of the residence."

Floyd took a deep breath knowing that Mary was still on the phone with the dispatcher and that a deputy was within a few seconds of arriving. Deputy Kermit Rajacich radioed he was a few minutes behind. By the time Floyd arrived, there were two county cruisers in his driveway with lights flashing.

Floyd ran up the sidewalk with the dog nipping at his cuffs. He found Mary and the two deputies standing at the kitchen table.

Pam looked up from the table, where she'd been examining the note. "The house is clear. It doesn't look like anyone attempted entry."

The note appeared to be a plain sheet of typing paper that had been tucked inside a plain white envelope. The outside of the envelope was unmarked and hadn't been sealed. Floyd read the neat printed letters of the short message.

"This sounds familiar," Floyd said, wracking his brain, trying to remember the interviews of the previous days. "It must have come from someone we've interviewed about Aaron Roberts' disappearance. Someone told me to let sleeping dogs lie."

"There are a lot more people than the ones we've interviewed who know about the investigation" Pam said. "I heard the sheriff mention Aaron Roberts' disappearance on his Friday radio show and he said you were leading the investigation. That afternoon I was talking to the dispatcher when one of the Twin Cities radio stations called for the sheriff. They wanted an interview too. It's not a quiet little cold case investigation anymore."

"Several people were in the flower shop gossiping about this case," Mary said, nodding her head. "I acted as if I was hearing about it for the first time. This is big news."

The phone rang, jarring everyone. Floyd grabbed the receiver quickly and had a muffled discussion as he shook his head.

He hung up the phone and said, "The neighbors are checking to see if everyone's okay. They're not used to having sheriff's cars race down the road."

"Mary handled both the note and the envelope and she'd already put the envelope in the trash," Pam said, slipping on a pair of plastic gloves. "I'll put them into an evidence bag."

"These investigations eat at me enough without them getting personal," Floyd said as he watched Pam carefully fold the note, then put it in a clear bag with the envelope. "If this escalates I'll be ready to take off someone's head."

"Kerm and I were over at Passenger Lake this morning with metal detectors," Pam said. "We found a brass button from someone's Levi jeans. But that's about it. The guy who owns the cabin served us coffee and muffins. He's quite a character. He's owned that place since it was a one-room shack with a hand pump and an outhouse. He's done a clever job of expanding and adding bedrooms. I think he did most of the work himself. The wiring didn't look like an inspector ever checked it out."

"Did he have any other memories of the year he found the rope?" Floyd asked.

"I think he's been trying to remember and he had a couple other thoughts, but I'm suspicious that he's melding a bunch of memories together. He thought that might've been the year he found a broken a window latch when he came up in the spring. He said there wasn't much missing. He said it looked like someone had unlatched a window, eaten a can of Spam, and slept in the bed. To be perfectly honest, he couldn't remember which year it was and he didn't report the break-in. He said he and his boys just fixed the window latch and threw out the empty can."

"Wouldn't that be interesting," Kerm said. "Suppose Aaron broke in after he got loose from the tree and spent a day or two there while he pondered what to do?"

"Suppose," Pam said, "whoever beat him up broke in and had a sandwich, slept for a couple hours while they came up with a plan, and then took the body somewhere for disposal."

Floyd shook his head. "Suppose the break-in occurred one of the other fifteen years."

"It's like the brass button," Pam said. "Mr. Birkholz was all excited that we'd found a clue. I'm thinking someone in the last hundred years lost the button off their jeans, and only God knows when it happened."

The phone rang again and Mary picked up.

"That was Esther, next door," Mary said, hanging up the phone. "She's bringing over some chicken salad. She saw all the activity and said that you wouldn't have time to fix supper. She's so thoughtful." Before Mary could add another thought the phone rang again and she answered a call from another curious neighbor.

Floyd leaned close to her ear. "Ask if they saw any strange cars on the road today."

"Shush," Mary said, "it's Beverly, from down the road."

Floyd motioned the deputies outside where Spot ran around their feet. "Thanks for the quick response."

"I'm on days," Pam said. "I'll make an extra trip past the house when I can the next couple of days."

"I'll pass that along to the afternoon deputies, too," Floyd added. "I think it's probably some kook and it won't happen again, but we can play it safe."

CHAPTER 16

It was almost midnight when Sandy Maki got back to his apartment. True to her word, Barb was waiting for him while watching an old Humphrey Bogart movie. She was curled at the end of the couch dressed in a white T-shirt and she was so engrossed in the movie she hardly looked up.

"Pam and Kerm checked around the tree where the guy had been tied," he said, locking the door behind him. "All they found was a brass button. I went back and talked to the rest of the neighbors and poked around the rest of the nearby cabins, including the one where the ATV was stolen."

Barb reached for the remote control and turned off the television. "A brass button? That's all?"

Sandy peeled off his sweaty shirt. "Yup, that's it unless you count the billion mosquitoes that tried to suck my blood while I was searching." He held out his arms so she could see the numerous red welts from the bites.

"I've got to take a shower," he said, stripping off his shirt. "The temperature didn't break until long after sunset. I could wring out my shorts they're so sweaty."

Barb followed him into the bedroom and watched him peel off the rest of his clothes and drape them over the wicker hamper to dry. She followed to the bathroom and watched him test the water and step into the shower.

"I told Floyd that we're getting married," she said to the shower curtain. "He was okay with it."

"What did you expect?" Sandy asked over the sound of the water.

"I don't know. I expected maybe he'd ask why, or that he'd laugh. He seemed happy for me. It was so weird. I guess I don't know how to react to nice people. I expect everyone to be mean or sarcastic; that's the way people are."

Sandy stepped out of the shower and wiped his face. "I'm not that way, am I?"

"No, but you're the only one."

"Isn't Gordy nice, too?"

"To my face, but I know everyone talks behind my back."

Sandy draped the towel on the rack and pulled her against his naked body. "There's a whole world of people out there who will accept you for what you are and they won't make fun of you or talk behind your back." He kissed her. "Really. It's true. All the people in the department will be happy for us and they'll come to our wedding. They'll cry tears of joy and they'll celebrate with us."

Barb searched his eyes for a sign of mirth. "You're serious. People who know what I was will come to our wedding?"

"They'll accept you for what you are now, and they'll invite us to Fourth of July picnics and Christmas parties." Sandy took both her hands in his. "This is what it means to be part of a community and to have a family. The department is my family and they'll like you as much as they like me."

"I might not cry at the wedding," Barb said. "I'm not much into crying anymore."

"I'm okay with that, but I think that seeing all those wet hankies will do you in."

"Do you really want kids?" Barb asked.

"Someday. Have you thought any more about a wedding date?"

"I want to have it in the summer, so we can have it at sunrise by a lake."

"So, you're thinking about next summer?" Sandy asked.

"Why wait 'til then?" Barb asked, pressing her body against his.

"It takes time to find a minister and plan a reception." He said softly into her ear. "I'm guessing we couldn't even get announcements printed in less than three weeks. That puts us into August."

"I have connections at the drugstore. I could print invitations in two days" she said, pushing her pelvis against his. "Let's do it next week," she said, nipping his earlobe.

"I don't know if I can get any time off on short notice."

"Which days are you off?"

Sandy pushed her to arm's length. "Don't you want a honeymoon?"

"We can have a one-night honeymoon now and take a trip up to Grand Marais when you get a week off."

CHAPTER 17

Floyd didn't sleep well and he was feeling out of sorts when he got to the courthouse. Pam Ryan was making a fresh pot of coffee in the bullpen when he brought his cup over.

"You look like hell," she said, filling the water reservoir.

"I always appreciate words of encouragement when I'm functioning on three hours of sleep," Floyd said as he watched the coffee dribble into the carafe. "I jumped out of bed every time the house creaked or the wind shifted. I probably wore out my holster pulling out the Smith & Wesson every fifteen minutes."

"The note freaked you out a little?" Pam asked.

"When it gets personal I lose my perspective." Floyd said, looking at the ceiling. "This whole investigation is nothing. Everyone who was involved was drunk and can't remember what happened. It's going nowhere. I was ready to give it up and then someone leaves a note at my house. Now my curiosity is piqued. Somebody has something to hide and I feel compelled to find the secret."

"They may have been drunk," Pam said, "but one couple remembered leaving the bar to neck on some back road and another woman remembered she'd been assaulted. Then there are the parents. Maybe they remember something that happened or was said."

The coffee pot gurgled, signaling the end of the brew process and Floyd poured himself a cup. He took a sip and grimaced. "How can this pot consistently make the worst cup of coffee in the county? It always tastes like it was brewed with manure instead of ground coffee."

"You're welcome to make coffee any time you like," Pam said a little too sharply. "I'll write the directions out for you."

"Sorry," Floyd said. "I didn't mean it as a personal comment. It's just that it seems to taste bad no matter who makes it."

"I think you need to go home and get a few more hours of sleep," Pam suggested. "You're too grumpy to be much good around here."

"Actually, I thought I'd drive down to the Bureau of Criminal Apprehension's St. Paul office to see if they can raise any prints off the envelope and note. They can fume the paper with superglue and may be able to pick up some latent prints. I'll have them test the rope, too. Maybe they'll be able to get DNA off it, or even a hair. Who knows?"

"We're grasping at straws?" Pam asked.

"There's not much else to go on after all these years." Floyd paused. "When were you last in Redwood Falls?" Floyd asked, remembering that Pam had grown up in Blue Earth in southern Minnesota.

"It's not on the way to Blue Earth, if that's what you're asking. I've been there a couple times. Why do you ask?"

Floyd set his coffee on a desk and sat on the desk chair. "I spoke with Melissa Schotten, Ken Solstad's girlfriend at the time. She remembered the night Ken, Aaron, and Kathy Tucker dropped her off, but claimed she didn't know what happened to the others." Floyd paused, then added, "I think she was having some problems relating to me. She'd been raped by Ken Solstad that night and never reported it. I guess it would be fair to say that she didn't want to talk to me about that night, Ken, Aaron, or what happened."

"Imagine that. A woman was raped long ago, didn't report it then, and isn't happy when a cop calls her out of the blue to talk about it." Pam said, rolling her eyes. "Let me guess. She lives in Redwood Falls and you were hoping I'd drive down and talk to her in hopes of gleaning some information she wouldn't reveal to you."

"That's it in a nutshell," Floyd said. Then he recounted the discussion with Melissa, including the argument between Kathy and Aaron that kept them distracted from the attack on Melissa.

Pam listened with sadness. "That's terrible. But rather than rehashing that night with Melissa, don't you think we'd do better talking to Kathy Tucker? After all, she was the one person out of the three remaining who is close by and who was with Ken and Aaron after Melissa was delivered home."

"I talked to her," Floyd said. "She was too drunk to remember what happened that night. I thought I might talk to her parents to see what they remembered, but I think Kathy's a lost cause. She used to have a serious drinking problem, and I'm sure there are a lot of nights she doesn't remember over several years."

"I think that might be a cop-out so to speak. I'd like to talk to Kathy before torturing Melissa further. If it's okay with you, I'll interview her while you run the evidence to the BCA office. Maybe I'll ask her parents a few questions too."

"I'm too tired to argue," Floyd said, getting up and pouring another cup of coffee. "I'll talk to you this afternoon if I don't fall asleep first."

"Are you safe to drive to the Cities?" Pam asked.

"Sure. I'll bring a cup of coffee along so I have something to chew as I drive."

"Ha, ha. That's so funny I almost forgot to laugh," Pam said. "Where can I find Kathy Tucker?"

"She works for her parents at Tucker's Garden Center in Hinckley. I think she's there most all the time."

CHAPTER 18

Dust devils swirled on the shoulder of the road as Pam Ryan pulled onto the interstate frontage road leading to Hinckley. The weeks of hot dry weather had turned the grass a dusty yellow. A small dust storm followed Pam's cruiser across the gravel parking lot, the wind quickly carrying it toward the interstate. Sprinklers sent sprays of water across the rows of potted flowers, shrubs, and trees arrayed around the front of the nursery, adding to the miserable humidity of the morning.

The inside of the building was still full of annual flowers in full bloom, filling the air with a million scents. Through shelves of potted marigolds Pam spotted a middle-aged woman keyboarding on a computer.

"You should charge people just to come in and enjoy the fragrances of the flowers," Pam said with a smile.

The woman was startled by Pam's voice. She turned so quickly that she almost fell from the swivel chair. "Lord, you scared me. I was so wrapped up in the bookkeeping that I didn't hear the bell when you came in."

"Is Kathy Tucker here?" Pam asked.

"No," the woman replied. "It's her day off." The woman stood and said, "I'm Ginny, Kathy's mother. Can I help you?"

"I'd like to talk to you if you've got a moment."

"I've got lots of moments if you will let me get out of this computer program." Ginny sat down, saved her work, and shut down the computer. While waiting for the screens to close she added, "I was just going to pour myself a cup of coffee. Would you care for one too?"

"I'd love a cup. I'm Pam Ryan," she said, offering her hand.

The woman led Pam to a small office in the corner of the building. There was a coffee pot in the corner and mugs hung from pegs on the wall. Ginny filled two mugs from a carafe. "It's pretty strange that two deputies show up the same week wanting to talk with Kathy."

"It's not strange at all." Pam accepted the cup and sat on a metal folding chair. "I take it that Floyd didn't explain the pictures to you? We got some pictures from an old camera that belonged to Ken Solstad. The film in the camera hadn't been developed for years. It was developed this week and the photos show five people, including Aaron Roberts and Kathy, sitting in a bar the night before Ken died in a car accident. Coincidentally, that was also the last night anyone saw Aaron."

"The police talked to us back then," Ginny said. "Kathy had a drinking problem and she didn't remember what happened that night. I guess she wasn't much help."

"What do you remember about that night, Mrs. Tucker?"

"Please call me Ginny. As for the time Aaron disappeared, I can't say I remember much."

"How close were Kathy, Ken, and Aaron?"

"Ken was a stinker and I don't think Kathy had much to do with him except as a drinking buddy. Kathy and Aaron were dating so they were very close."

"Kathy must've been devastated when Aaron disappeared."

Ginny fidgeted, swirling the coffee in her cup. "Something happened between Kathy and Aaron that night. She never said exactly what, but I think they broke up. She's never talked about it but she took it hard. I think she'd been drinking some before that but she really went off the deep end afterwards. I was afraid she'd be killed in a car accident but she was an adult and I guess it was too awkward for me to confront her. After she got her second DWI up in Carlton County her dad talked her into working with us and she dove into the work. I think she's compulsive and she sublimated the work here for her drinking."

"That's not a bad swap," Pam noted.

"It's bad if you want to be a grandmother and you hear your unmarried daughter's biological clock ticking away," Ginny said with a slight grin.

"Do you know what precipitated the breakup with Aaron?"

"Hah! Is that the kind of topic you could discuss with *your* mother?" Ginny asked. "We've been content to let that topic sit on the shelf."

"Where does Kathy live?" Pam asked, sensing that there was little else to be gleaned from Ginny Tucker.

"She's got a little house in town. Turn toward the water tower and go two blocks past. You'll know it as soon as you see it."

"How will I know it?" Pam asked.

"If you can't tell which one it is, you come back here and I'll buy you lunch."

Kathy Tucker's house was tiny by any standard, by far the smallest on the block. What made it distinctive were the thousands of flowers that filled the yard. There were so many flowering plants in the yard that there was literally no grass at all. Kathy was on her knees pulling weeds and throwing them into a pile on the sidewalk. A middle-aged man with a scraggly beard sat on the steps drinking a Coke, watching, and apparently carrying on a conversation as the weeds flew.

Kathy looked up when Pam stopped the cruiser in front of the house. By the time Pam called her location and got out of the car, Kathy was standing and removing her gardening gloves. The man never got up from the steps.

"Kathy, I'm Pam Ryan, from the Pine County Sheriff's Department." Pam offered her hand, and was surprised that Kathy was nearly a foot taller than she was, with an athletic build and hands calloused from hard work. Kathy was dressed in a tank top, dark shorts, and dirty white tennis shoes. The outfit showed off the deeply tanned skin from years of working in the nursery. The first sign of wrinkles showed at the corners of her eyes and mouth.

"What's up?" Kathy asked.

"I was wondering if you had time to talk?"

"It's my day off. I didn't have much planned except pulling weeds." Kathy pointed toward the house. "Why don't we sit out back. Would you like some iced tea or a Coke?"

"I'm Walt," the man said, stubbing out a cigarette butt then tipping his red cap with its Toro logo, "and I've got to get back to the church." He offered his calloused hand to Pam. "I'm the janitor at the Methodist Church and I like to walk down here to enjoy the flowers." He was dressed in a threadbare short-sleeved shirt and jeans. His graying hair was tied back in a loose ponytail.

"Hey!" Kathy said in mock protest, "I thought you came down for the conversation." Pam could see the comfortable chemistry between the two friends.

"Nah," Walt said jokingly, "I can't afford Coke on my salary." His forty-something face had a million creases from years of smoking and working in the sun.

It struck Pam that the repartee between the two was like two old friends. "If this is a bad time, I can come back later."

Walt waved her off. "Nah, my break is over. I've got to get everything cleaned up before the funeral this afternoon." He waved and walked off toward the brick church at the end of the block.

The two women walked the narrow sidewalk around the house. In the backyard Kathy waved Pam to the small patio where a pair of Adirondack chairs shone with a clear finish that made them look wet. The yard was alive with perennial flowers arranged around the small concrete patio. Kathy went into the house and Pam admired the flowers closest to her chair. Tiny tea roses in red and pink dominated the edge of the patio.

"Do you like roses?" Kathy asked, handing a glass of iced tea to Pam.

"What woman doesn't like roses?"

"They're over-hyped," Kathy replied. "The only reason roses are a popular men's gift is that they're the only flower most men can recognize. There are so many other plants with a nicer bouquet that hold up better." The conversation lagged, and she added, "But roses aren't the reason you're here. I suppose you want to talk about Ken and Aaron."

"What happened that night?"

"Don't you guys talk to each other?" Kathy asked as she twisted in her chair and tucked a leg under herself. "I told Floyd Swenson everything I remembered. Six of us went out drinking and I got drunk. I don't remember much of what happened until the next day when the cops came to tell me Kenny was dead and asked if I knew what happened to Aaron."

"Start at the beginning of the night, and talk me through all the things you can remember."

Kathy sighed and stared at the stucco house across the alley. "Aaron picked me up and said we were driving Ken and Melissa to the bar. We met Mike and Betsy there, and we drank a lot. At some point Mike and Betsy left and the next thing I remember is waking up at home."

"You glossed over breaking up with Aaron."

Kathy stared at her iced tea. "Yeah, we broke up. It wasn't the highlight of the evening."

"Didn't you think it might have some bearing on his disappearance?"

"Not really," Kathy shrugged. "People break up all the time and they move on with their lives."

"It was pretty bad, huh?" Without a response, Pam added, "The first one is always the worst." She let the comment dangle.

"I guess."

When Kathy didn't expand on her comment, Pam asked, "Did Aaron say anything about what he was going to do or where he was going?"

"I don't think so. I must've zoned out after he said we were done."

"Tell me about what happened with Ken and Melissa in the car while you were arguing with Aaron."

"I don't know. Like I said, I was drunk and bummed out. Aaron and I were talking outside his car. The conversation inside the car was like listening to Charlie Brown's teacher; you know, there were sounds but you can't make out any of the words. Maybe Ken and Melissa were fighting. I'm not sure. They'd been edgy all night. Ken was trying to pick a fight and Melissa didn't want to be with him."

"Ken raped Melissa in the backseat while you and Aaron were standing outside the car. She also said Ken was really mad at Aaron and after they dumped her at home, Ken punched and kicked Aaron then threw him in the backseat. She said you rode with Ken in the front seat."

"I don't remember anything about that," Kathy said, her face betraying no sadness. "I'm sorry to waste your time."

"Why did Aaron break up with you?"

Kathy swirled the glass, clinking the ice against the side. "I wanted to get married and he wasn't ready."

The answer seemed plausible to Pam, but not heartfelt. "Why did Kenny beat up Aaron?"

"I don't remember Aaron getting beaten up."

"Why did you ride home in the front seat with Ken after you dropped off Melissa?"

"I told you, I don't even remember dropping Melissa off. I don't even know how I got home that night."

"I know how painful this is," Pam said. "I've been through messy breakups and I know how much it hurts."

"I've been over it for a long time." Kathy's voice was flat, like she'd lost the ability to express emotion over the breakup.

"I've never gotten over the first one, at least not entirely." Pam paused and then asked, "Is Walt someone special in your life?"

"Walt's not special," Kathy said, her voice without emotion. "He's just a friend. I do a lot with the church and he's there a lot." She paused, then added, "We're in AA together."

Pam handed Kathy a business card. "Please call me if you remember anything else. We've got something in common — I was burned by my first love too."

"I bet you weren't stupid enough to think that crawling into a bottle was a solution."

"That doesn't mean that I wasn't emotionally strung out. A lot of people are suicidal after a break-up. Did you ever consider hurting yourself?"

Kathy took a deep breath and blew it out as she looked at the sky. "When you get deep into a bottle and there doesn't seem to be any future, a lot of stupid ideas go through your head."

"Do you think that Aaron might've hurt himself?"

Kathy shook her head. "Aaron had moved on. It was me who was messed up."

"Aaron had a new girlfriend?"

Kathy shook her head. "He just moved on with his life."

CHAPTER 19

The drive to St. Paul cleared Floyd's head and once he hit I-694 the morning traffic provided enough stimulation to keep him awake. He wove through the mid-morning I-94 traffic and turned off at the Maryland Avenue exit. A few blocks from the highway a group of Asian boys stepped in front of his brown police car and leered at him with contempt. The drooping shorts hanging to their knees, the expensive athletic shirts with a team logo he didn't recognize, and their half-backward-facing caps amused him. They crossed slowly in front of him studying the car. The last one in line gave him what was meant to be an intimidating stare. Floyd rolled his eyes. In return he got flipped the bird.

"What a bunch of idiots," he said to himself. "They think they're tough until the day they meet someone who really is tough."

He turned on Arcade and drove to Wheelock Parkway where he wound through a neighborhood of prosperous homes on what had once been the outskirts of St. Paul along Phalen Lake. The homes weren't large, by twenty-first-century standards, but had been posh and stately during prohibition, when most had been built. At the time, many of them had been owned by mobsters and bootleggers who had migrated to St. Paul because of the local policy of not arresting criminals who moved there to spend their stolen cash, as long as they didn't break any local laws.

The Bureau of Criminal Apprehension building was a newer brick building on the border between a shopping area and a middle-class neighborhood. At the reception desk Floyd paged Laurie Lone Eagle, his former trainee when she'd been with the Pine County Sheriff's Department in her first law enforcement job. She was now an agent with the BCA specializing in the investigation of child abductions. In addition to her regular duties she served as an informal liaison with Pine County.

"What's up, Floyd?" Laurie asked, shaking his hand. Her straight black hair was cut short and she wore conservative plum-colored wool slacks and an ivory silk blouse that complimented her Native American skin tone. Her stylish outfit made the badge clipped to her waistband and the pistol on her hip seem incongruous.

"The BCA must pay better than the sheriff's department," Floyd joked. "We can't afford pretty clothes like this."

"If you spent your money on clothes instead of courting some attractive widow at all the restaurants in Pine County, you could afford more."

"Someone blabbed about my dinner dates?" Floyd asked, as a blush crept up his neck.

Laurie shook her head. "There are no secrets in Pine County and I still have friends up there. Now, what can I do for you?"

"Someone left a note at my house," Floyd said, holding up the plastic evidence bag with the envelope and note. "I was hoping that your lab techs could raise a print we could trace." Holding up two other bags, he went on, "And we have this rope that may have been used to tie up a man who's been missing for a few years. Also, I have a pair of tennis shoes that appear to have some blood spatter on them."

Laurie turned the bag in her hand and inspected the rope. "You're thinking the rusty stains on this rope may be blood?"

"That's what I'd like to know," Floyd replied.

"What's the link to the shoes?"

"They belonged to a guy who died. It would be really interesting to know if the blood on these match the rope," Floyd said.

"Do you have anything we can use for a DNA comparison?"

"Not right now. I'm not even sure the rope is connected to the disappearance."

Laurie took the bags and motioned for Floyd to follow her. At the reception desk she had him sign into a log and clip a visitor's badge to his shirt. Then she led him into the bowels of the building. She stopped at a desk and filled out a request form from a tray, placed the bags and the completed form in a second tray, then signed a chain of evidence tag.

"Are you interested in lunch?" she asked, checking her watch.

"I guess I've been up for ten hours now, so I suppose it must be lunch time."

Laurie led him out a back door to a parking lot surrounded by a high fence topped with razor wire. Floyd noted the security cameras mounted on the corners of the two-story building. The inside of the car was stifling in the ninety-degree heat. The seat belt buckle was so hot Floyd could barely touch it long enough to secure it.

As they drove out of the lot, Floyd asked, "If the Bureau of Criminal Apprehension has to have that kind of security around their parking lot, what do the local businesses need?"

"Maybe they pay better protection money than the state," Laurie joked.

"Will my car be safe until we get back?"

"If you locked it, I expect it'll still be there." Laurie hesitated then added, "You did lock it, didn't you?"

"I did, but I think it's sad that you have to lock up a police car to keep it from being stolen when it's parked in front of BCA headquarters."

"I don't think we're in Kansas anymore, Toto," Laurie said with a laugh. "You are so spoiled living up in the wilderness. People all over the real world lock their cars and houses all the time. It's prudent."

"It's sad to live where you have to worry that someone's going to steal your car from a major street in broad daylight."

The conversation drifted to crime in Pine City, and they spent an hour eating Greek food at a restaurant on Grand Avenue while Floyd explained about the garage sale camera, the pictures, Aaron Roberts' disappearance, Melissa Schotten's rape, and Ken Solstad's car accident.

Laurie listened intently, and then mused, "It sounds like Ken Solstad killed Aaron Roberts and dumped the body somewhere before he drove off for Missouri. I wonder if he was feeling so much regret when he got to Iowa that he drove his car into the truck intentionally."

"I suppose we'll never know. Ken hadn't slept so it's entirely plausible that he fell asleep at the wheel. On the other hand, if he killed Aaron he'd had time for the adrenaline to wear off and plenty of time to brood over his actions. Maybe he felt some remorse."

"Do you think they were only drinking?" Laurie asked. "Every little town had a meth lab back then, and meth makes people do stupid things. Maybe Ken Solstad's anger and lack of self-control were enhanced by drugs."

"Interesting thought. I suppose some dabbling in meth might fit with the events. I'll have to give that some thought when I'm awake," Floyd said, yawning and feeling the after-effects of the large meal.

Laurie insisted on picking up the bill. They left the restaurant and walked down the block to buy ice cream at the Grand Creamery.

"You know the one thing I like about coming to the Cities?" Floyd asked as he tried to catch the drips of melting ice cream before they ran down his waffle cone. "You have more than three restaurants to choose from."

"That's the *one* highlight of your trip? Eating somewhere new?"

"Well, that and not having to worry that someone I arrested will walk up behind me to stick a knife in my back." Floyd paused, "It might be a complete stranger who stabs me here."

"What do you think happened to Aaron Roberts?" Laurie asked as they walked down Grand Avenue in the light early afternoon crowd.

"A week ago I would've guessed that he'd been picked up by a trucker and caught a ride to some big city after abandoning his car at a rest stop. Then, later he got cross-ways with someone and ended up dead in a dumpster to never be seen again."

"You said Aaron's car was found in a rest stop on the interstate. Do you remember if it still had gas?"

"I'm not sure. We spent a lot of hours searching the area around the rest stop for a body. At the time we suspected foul play."

"I assume you checked out the interior for blood."

"Yeah. We didn't find any. But the state-of-the-art in crime scene investigation has advanced so far since then. We didn't even pick up on possible semen stains in the backseat from the rape of the Smith girl. Now I'd be checking with Luminol and we might pick up all kinds of bodily fluids."

"Let's back it up to that night, knowing what you do now," Laurie said. "If Aaron was left somewhere to die, how would the car get to the rest stop?"

"After dumping Aaron's body, Ken drove away in Aaron's car, then someone drove it to the rest area and left it," Floyd said. "Assuming that the only ones involved were the six people at the bar together, that probably means one of them picked Ken up and drove him home."

"You said that Mike Nelson and Betsy Ring left the others earlier in the evening. So that leaves three others. Melissa Smith's story seems tight, and I can't imagine her participating in anything else after being raped. So the remaining culprits are Ken Solstad and Kathy Tucker. Ken drives Aaron's car to the rest stop and Kathy picks him up. He's home in time to catch a nap before leaving for Missouri."

"There's one hole in that," Floyd said after considering the scenario. "Kathy was so drunk that she couldn't remember what happened. That would leave her incapable of driving."

"She *claimed* to be too drunk to remember what happened. That doesn't mean she was too drunk to remember or participate." Laurie thought for a second and then added, "Who's to say that Mike and Betsy's alibis are solid? They said they were together, but there's no one else to corroborate the story. Maybe Ken called one of them to pick him up."

"Well," Floyd said, "there's still the possibility that someone other than the five others had something to do with Aaron's disappearance. There were another two and a half million people in Minnesota that night and I'll bet half of them don't have alibis."

Laurie shook her head. "It's someone local and someone who was with Ken Solstad because the picture was in his camera. It has to be someone who knows the case has been reopened. Who else would leave the note at your house?"

Floyd stopped and took off his cap. "There's something nagging at me. The wording in the note is so close to something said by another person. I just can't remember who it was."

"Let's focus on something else for a second," Laurie suggested. "Assuming Aaron is dead, someone's got a dead body to deal with. It's December, so the ground is usually frozen. What do you do with it?"

"You can't bury it or drop it in a lake," Floyd said, "but the standard, 'drop it in the swamp' works as long as there are cattails or long swamp grass. What bothers me more is why Ken would take a picture of Aaron cut up and tied to a tree."

"People take pictures," Laurie said, "of things they want to remember, or they take them for someone else to see. I can't imagine that Ken wanted to remember Aaron tied to a tree. So, why would he want to show someone else that picture?"

"To brag, to scare them, to show them how tough he is." Floyd paused. "I'm way too sleepy to be doing this. Take me back to my car so I can weave my way back home."

"What if we're looking way too deeply at this," Laurie said as she drove back to the BCA headquarters. "Were any of the parents being evasive? Would any of them have motive to eliminate Aaron?"

"Good question," Floyd said as Laurie pulled next to his car on the street and turned on the four-way flashers. "I'm just too tired to think it through right now."

"I'll give you a call tomorrow when you're awake. Maybe I can call in a favor and get some preliminary testing on your letter and rope completed by then."

"No need to call in favors to rush testing on a decade-old case."

"Don't worry about it, I have more owed than owing and it's about time I called in a few IOUs."

Floyd was reaching for the door handle when Laurie said, "Tell me about Mary."

"Mary, as in my friend Mary Jungers?"

"Do you have any other significant Marys in your life?"

"What's to tell? We've had coffee and dinner together a few times."

"Is Mary the reason you're so tired today? Maybe you had a sleepover?" Laurie asked with a smile.

Floyd's face colored. "No. We're not friends like that."

"Why not? You're both adults and maybe a little lonely. It's OK."

Floyd felt a sudden dryness in his mouth and his collar felt a little tight. Words escaped him.

"Floyd, I know that you're still grieving over the loss of your wife," Laurie said, putting her hand on his arm. "That's OK. But if you have a chance for a deep friendship that may grow to something else, don't let it slip away."

"It's just that. . ." He paused, unable to articulate the reason.

"Listen to me. I've been there. I've been too tied up in my job, or too busy, or too worried about how a Caucasian boyfriend would look to my family. I've been afraid to open myself up to someone. Now I'm at a point where I'm not meeting eligible bachelors and I'd really like to have someone I love on the other half of my bed."

"You're young. You'll have more chances."

Laurie smiled. "I heard that Mary is very sweet and a little sassy. She sounds like a delight."

Floyd stared through the windshield. "She's good company, but I need to take my time."

Floyd turned to face her and she saw the tears in his eyes. She picked up his hand and kissed it. "Have you kissed her?"

"Yes."

"Floyd, I mean have you really kissed her?"

Floyd stared out the front window. "I'm not ready for this discussion."

"Take her out to supper and give her a real, passionate kiss when you walk her to the front door. Sweep her off her feet."

"I'm afraid she'll ask me to stay for breakfast."

"That would be one of those rare times I'd advise you to think with you heart and not your head."

Floyd shook his head. "What if. . ." He paused. "Sex changes things. I don't want to screw up what we have."

"God knows that I'm not the relationship expert, but it seems to me that falling in love with your friend is about the best thing that could happen. After all, you're probably quite a catch."

Floyd smiled. "I think that you're patronizing an old man who needs to get some sleep," he said, getting out of Laurie's car and unlocking the county car.

Laurie watched him drive away and said to herself, "If you weren't like a father to me, I'd be competing with Mary for the other half of your bed."

CHAPTER 20

Sandy Maki was sitting on a desk in the bullpen talking to Pam Ryan when Floyd returned from his trip to the BCA. "Don't tell me that it's shift change already," Floyd said, pouring the dregs from the coffeepot into his Pine City Dragons cup.

"We're comparing notes on the Roberts' case," Sandy said. "It's going to be quiet this afternoon so I thought I could pick up some interviews or something. Pam was telling me about her conversation with Kathy Tucker."

Pam picked up on the conversation and joined them.

"Kathy claims she can't remember anything about the night, but every once in a while she lets something slip that says she remembers more than she's letting on. She told me about breaking up with Aaron that night while Ken Solstad was in the backseat of the car with Melissa. Kathy said she wanted to get married but Aaron said, no, that Aaron had moved on with his life." Pam paused, re-running the conversation through her mind.

"There's something else that didn't ring true. Kathy's way too subdued when she talks. It's like she's totally numb from the experience or that her reply is over-rehearsed."

"Maybe she's overmedicated," Sandy suggested. "I've talked to a few people who've been on heavy doses of anti-depressants and they can't get excited about anything."

"I doubt that she's taking any mind-altering drugs," Floyd said. "Most recovering alcoholics tend to avoid drugs. After going through all the hell of recovery they don't want to jeopardize their balance."

"You won't believe Kathy's house," Pam said. "She has no grass in her yard at all. It's all flowers and bushes. It's like walking through a garden, and there isn't a weed anywhere. She has to be compulsive to keep it that neat and weed-free."

"Do you think she could have a body buried among the daisies?" Sandy asked.

Pam's eyes grew wide. "I never thought of that."

"Aaron disappeared in December when the ground was frozen," Floyd said. "Besides that, Kathy was living with her parents then. I don't think she bought the house until several years later.

"Here's a question," Floyd said. "Would any of the parents have a motive to kill Aaron? We don't seem to be getting anywhere with the friends, so let's talk through one layer further up."

"I guess I'll check property abstracts," Sandy offered. "We can nail down the date Kathy bought the house."

"I talked to Kathy's mother," Pam said. "She didn't think much of Ken and the others. I think she called them a bunch of drunks."

"I talked to Ken Solstad's mother, Karen," Floyd said. "She was much more positive about the friends. Of course, Ken was the bully so his mother might have different picture of the group. Melissa Smith's mother, Dottie, was very bitter. From her perspective, Ken was a rapist and the others allowed it to happen."

"It sounds like Mrs. Smith might have motive to harm Ken," Pam said, "but I don't know why she would want to hurt Aaron. I'd like to talk to Mike Nelson and Betsy Ring. Something about their alibi of spending the night together on a dead end road is too pat."

"Hey!" Sandy said, "I just had a blinding flash of the obvious. This took place in December, and that couple said they fell asleep in the car until sunrise. It doesn't work! They said they slept from the time they left the bar until the sun came up. Sunup in early December is like seven-thirty so they would've been in the car for probably seven hours.

"Think about it for a second — it's probably below freezing, maybe close to zero. If they leave the car running they get carbon monoxide poisoning or run the gas tank dry. If they run the tank dry they have to walk somewhere to get gas. If they turn the car off, it gets cold and they die of hypothermia. I don't think it happened that way."

"Well," Floyd offered, "they didn't sleep the whole time. Both of them claim Betsy got pregnant that night, so they were generating body heat for a while."

"You're way old, Floyd," Sandy said. "That's about five minutes of heat when you're twenty-one. Right, Pam?"

Pam's answer was a red face.

"Enough of that," Floyd said. "I want Pam to do follow-up interviews with Mike and Betsy. I can give you the phone numbers and addresses. Sandy, I think you should talk to the parents. Start with the Solstads, and then talk to the Nelsons and Rings. We'll catch up with the parents at the same time we're getting their children."

"What are you going to do?" Sandy asked Floyd.

"I've got to sleep. I slept three hours last night. Every noise woke me up."

"Sleep easy," Sandy said. "I'll drive by every chance I get. I'll tell the dispatcher to remind the guys on night shift too."

The dispatcher paged Floyd and he picked up the line on the nearest desk. After a short conversation he hung up. "That was Kathy Tucker's neighbor. She saw Pam's cruiser car at Kathy's house this morning and she was wondering if there was some problem."

"Don't you love life in a small town?" Pam said with a laugh.

"She was genuinely concerned. She assumed there was a problem because of the guy who hangs around Kathy's house a lot and the neighbor thinks that he's some sort of felon or sex offender on work release."

"Her friend, Walt, and Kathy are in AA together. He is a little grizzled," Pam said. "I could see that someone might think that he was a criminal. He got really nervous when I showed up and left immediately."

"See if you can get his full name, Pam, and run a background check. I doubt that he was around that many years ago, but who knows what slime you find when you start turning rocks?"

CHAPTER 21

Mary was asleep on the couch when Floyd got home. The sound of the dog scurrying around Floyd's feet stirred her to look up. "You look tired," she said as he hung his key ring on a peg.

"And so do you, Mrs. Jungers. I hope you got more sleep than I did last night."

"Are you kidding? You tell me to lock myself in my car and call the dispatcher. Then you send deputies with sirens blaring to see if there's a burglar in the house. You ask if I got any sleep?"

"Do you have any plans for supper?" Floyd asked.

"I thought a big spender like you would take his girl out for supper after she slaved away all day at the flower shop." Mary slipped her shoes on and stretched. "I'm not terribly hungry, but I could eat a bowl of soup and a burger."

Floyd took a deep breath. "I'd be happy with a sandwich at home and a hot shower."

"Luckily, you can get the sandwich at Gamper's and a shower at home after I've been fed." Mary plucked the keys from the peg and threw them to Floyd. "This way you can tell me about all the crimes you solved today, making the county safe for all the good citizens."

"I can tell you about all the crimes I solved on the walk to the car," Floyd said as he locked the door behind them. "There's no need to drive all the way to Moose Lake."

"Humor me. The computers were down all day and everyone was on edge. The air conditioning quit mid-afternoon and the flowers started to wilt. It hasn't been one of my better days."

"Let me try a question out on you," Floyd said as he turned onto the county road. "Why would a parent want to kill one of their adult children's friends?"

"Is this a hypothetical question, or are we solving a crime?"

"It doesn't matter."

"Well," Mary paused and thought, "if the friend had done something really bad to my child, I would be really mad and I could see some parents taking that too far. I read about a father who killed a boy who sexually assaulted his daughter. There have been revenge killings like people who've killed their dead child's drug dealer after an overdose. I suppose people find all kinds of reasons."

"Rape, murder, drug overdose," Floyd said. "Those are all really high-level felonies. Those are the kinds of things that would take a parent to the boiling point. Throw in someone who's a little unstable or intoxicated and I could see someone boiling over. The problem with that is, those are crimes of passion and we routinely see terribly violent outbursts with a dead body that's pretty messed up and a crime scene painted in blood.

"In Aaron Roberts' case, we have a crime scene in a picture where the damage is controlled and almost ritualistic. Barb Dupre said the body appeared to have been tortured. I agree with her. Aaron was stripped to his underwear, tied to a tree, and then someone made shallow cuts on his chest."

"That's more information than I needed, dear."

"Sorry. I was talking to myself."

"But I was listening. Let's stick with philosophy until after I eat."

"So," Floyd said, "if this wasn't a revenge killing by one of the parents, who would want to hurt Aaron like that? And, why would someone take a picture of him after they'd done it? It had to be Ken Solstad, because the picture was in his camera."

"If it was a stranger, they might've wanted something Aaron had. I hear about people getting tortured and killed over drugs. Was he into drugs?"

"It doesn't sound like it," Floyd said. A flicker of Laurie Lone Eagle's comments teased his conscious mind, but wouldn't come forward. "The whole group was more into alcohol than drugs and they'd spent the entire evening drinking. The one person who's still alive and who was with him all that evening was so drunk she can't remember what happened."

"I guess my mind doesn't run in those kind of tracks. I can't come up with a motive."

"Let me try a different question on you."

"You know," Mary interrupted, "if I'd realized this was the price I was going to pay for getting supper, I might've been able to find a pot pie in my freezer."

"Too late, I've got you trapped for another ten miles unless you want to walk home. Anyway, you've just killed Aaron Roberts and it's the middle of December. I'm a tidy killer, and I decide that I can't just leave his body lying around. I drive his car to the rest area by Sandstone and leave it there. What do I do with the body?"

"I'd bury it or dump it in a swamp."

"The ground is frozen, so I can't bury it. I can leave it in a swamp and hope it sinks in when spring comes, but there's a risk that some snowmobile rider will come across it before then."

"Well," Mary thought for a second and said, "I guess I'd start a big fire and throw the body in so there's nothing left but ashes."

"That's interesting. But an open fire doesn't totally destroy a corpse. Someone would find bone fragments or teeth and call the cops."

"Smear honey all over the body and feed it to the bears."

"The bears are hibernating in December."

"Here's Gamper's. Don't miss the turn."

"I take it that you're out of ideas?"

"I'm hungry. I'm cranky because my blood sugar is crashing, and you're shooting down all my ideas. It's time to eat."

"I enjoy bouncing ideas off you," Floyd said as he opened Gamper's front door.

"Well, I'm glad one of us is having a good time."

Floyd waved to two highway patrol officers who were sitting in a booth near the windows. Greg, the owner, met them with menus.

"Greg, how's your golf game?" Floyd asked.

"It sucks," Greg, a barrel-chested man with a quick smile and hearty handshake replied. "I lost ten bucks to Father Mike yesterday. It got too hot and I petered out on the last five holes. Did you guys want to sit with the troopers?"

Mary pointed at the back dining room. "If I have to talk shop on the drive, I refuse to eat with two more cops. God only knows what grisly stories they might have."

A young couple in a corner booth craned their heads around the edge and quickly pulled their heads back after identifying Floyd. Mary noticed the move and when they got seated in the dining room she asked, "I suppose you noticed the couple in the corner. Have you arrested them at some point?"

Floyd picked up the menu and spoke without looking up. "Yup, I busted them a couple weeks ago for possession of marijuana."

"I'd like to go out sometime and not run across a cop you know or someone you busted," Mary said, trying to read the soup choices listed with the daily special on a board near the kitchen.

"You're awfully cranky tonight."

"I was awake half the night checking the locks after you spooked me with your panic over the note on the door, I had a crummy day at work, you tell me graphic details about some guy who's been tortured, and you expect me to be in good humor? If you're going to scare me, the least you could do is let me spend the night curled up in your arms so the bogey man won't get me."

A smiling, trim, brown-haired waitress arrived with a carafe of coffee. "Would you like coffee, too, Mary?" the waitress asked as she poured for Floyd.

"I'd better stick with something decaffeinated tonight. Bring me a large glass of milk, a bowl of bean soup, and a California burger."

"Just cherry pie for me, Noelle" Floyd said. Seeing Mary's glare he asked, "What? You've been telling me to eat more fruits and vegetables."

"Cherry pie is not a good source of vitamins or minerals," Mary whispered, "and how does the waitress know my name?"

Floyd smiled. "I may have mentioned your name when I was having lunch here the other day."

"You're telling strange waitresses about me? I suppose I should be flattered."

"She asked why she hadn't seen me for a while and I told her that you'd been feeding me supper so I haven't been eating out as much."

"And she said?"

Floyd shrugged. "She said that you must be a good cook because it looked like I'd put on a couple of pounds."

Noelle set the soup, milk, and pie in front of them. "I also told him that he's been smiling a lot more lately. The burger should be up in a minute. Is there anything else I can get for you?" she asked as she set a squeeze bottle of ketchup on the table.

Mike Nelson's parents lived on a small hobby farm halfway between Pine City and Beroun. Sandy drove down the short driveway and parked between a freshly painted red barn with white trim and the tan farmhouse. The Nelson farm was a nice contrast to the numerous old farms that were falling into disrepair as the owners could no longer make a living off the forty or eighty acres around them, and their town jobs didn't provide the income to keep the buildings in repair.

A red Farmall tractor was pulling a baler through the nearest field, and two foals frolicked in a white-fenced paddock next to the barn. Sandy waved at the farmer before knocking on the screen door of the house. Through the open door he smelled something frying and heard a television game show.

Mildred Nelson answered the door in an orange tank top and green shorts. Her body was stocky and her brown hair was tied back, exposing a scar under her left ear where a tumor had been removed a few years earlier. Sandy recognized her as the cook from the high school, where he'd had numerous meetings with parents or administrators when he was the sponsor for the *DARE* drug awareness program. Millie always had a pot of coffee brewed and a hidden package of sandwich cookies in the back of the school kitchen for the DARE cop.

"Sandy Maki," she said, pushing the screen door open. "C'mon in. I've got pork chops frying and I need to turn them over before they burn. What brings you out in the country?" she asked as she hustled back to the kitchen with Sandy following.

Millie Nelson's kitchen was immaculately clean, with countertops bare of clutter and a neat arrangement of fresh-cut flowers on a small table in front of the window. Someone had painted the cupboards a bright yellow, and then done intricate Norwegian painting on the margins in blue. If ever there was a floor that could be eaten from, it was Millie Nelson's.

"We opened the old Aaron Roberts missing person case," Sandy explained, "and I wanted to ask a few questions." The kitchen table was set for two, and several pots simmered on the stove. Sandy sat in a kitchen chair and watched Millie flip chops in the cast-iron frying pan, and then stir all the other pots.

"Fire away," Millie said after wiping her hands on a towel. She sat across the table.

"We found an old picture taken the night before Aaron disappeared. It was of Mike, Betsy, Kathy Tucker, Melissa Smith and Aaron Roberts. We talked to most of them, but no one seems to remember much about that night, and no one knows what happened to Aaron."

"I sure don't know anything," Millie said. "They were a pretty wild bunch and they did a lot of drinking before and after they turned twenty-one." She got up from the chair and turned the burners off under all the pans. "Mike ran around with them some, but I don't remember that particular night. That was a long time ago. Mike's been married twice since then."

"It was the night before Kenny was killed in the car accident in December of '98. Mike said he and Betsy fell asleep in the car and didn't wake up until the sun came up."

The sound of the tractor grew louder and Millie looked out the window. "I was wondering if Larry had lost track of time. I told him supper would be ready at six." She walked to the cupboard and took out another plate. "You'll stay and have a pork chop, won't you?" She took out silverware and set a place in front of Sandy without waiting for an answer.

"That's kind of you, but I didn't mean to barge in on your supper."

"Oh hell, you didn't barge in; you're doing your job, and you stopped at just the right time. If you don't eat the extra I'll just have to feed it to the dog."

The screen door opened with a creak and Millie said, "Larry, wash your hands and get in here before your supper gets cold. Sandy Maki's over for dinner so behave yourself."

Larry Nelson came around the corner dressed in an olive short-sleeved work shirt stained dark with sweat. He was a big man and his ample belly hung over the waist of the pants worn low on his hips. He went to the kitchen sink and washed his hands while Millie served up heaping portions of mashed potatoes, fresh green beans, and pork chops with steaming brown gravy.

"You sure timed that right," Larry said with a huge smile. He offered his clean hand to Sandy. "I hope you realize that you're saving me from having to eat way too much of this good stuff Millie whips up. All four kids are gone and she still makes the same amount of food, then she gets mad at me when I don't eat half of what she's made."

"I feel awfully guilty dropping in on your supper, but it smells so good I'm sure not going to say no."

"So," Larry asked, "what brings you out here?"

"I was explaining to Millie," Sandy said as he cut his pork chop, "we reopened the Aaron Roberts disappearance and Mike was with him the night he disappeared. I thought you might remember something."

"I don't remember what today's last customer bought," Larry said, referring to his saddle shop in Pine City, "much less what happened the night Aaron disappeared."

"It was the night before Kenny Solstad was killed in that terrible car accident," Millie explained. "Sandy reminded me that Mike had been drinking with them and he didn't come home until after sunrise."

Larry Nelson shook his head. "Mike didn't come home until sunrise too many times. That bunch had too many bad apples. I can't say I was sad when Kenny went in the Army. They settled down some then. But when Kenny came home he sure thought they should raise some hell and Mike was right there alongside him."

"Do you remember anything special about that particular night? Sandy asked. "It was in December and Kenny was headed to an Army base in Missouri the next day. Mike said he and Betsy spent the whole night asleep in his car after they left the party early."

"I suppose," Larry said, "it was one of those days when Mike showed up with bloodshot eyes as I was going out to feed the horses. I probably dragged him with me and made him work awhile just to make him a little more miserable." His words were tinged with obvious disdain.

"He'd been sleeping in the car all night. I'll bet he was nearly frozen," Sandy said, hoping to dredge up a buried memory.

"Sorry," Larry said. "Everything Mike did for a few years ticked me off. Even if he was frozen to the bone, I would've dragged him out to shovel manure."

"Mike had a way of getting under Larry's skin," Millie explained. "It got to the point that Mike would argue that black was white if he thought it would make Larry mad."

"How did you feel about Mike getting Betsy pregnant?" Sandy asked. "She thought it happened that night."

Millie and Larry exchanged a glance before Larry replied. "You guys have done some investigating." He took another bite of pork chop, chewed, and swallowed before answering. "We weren't happy about it, if that's what you're asking. Betsy was a nice enough girl and, frankly, I thought she deserved better than Mike. When we found out, he was trying to get her to see a doctor about an abortion I put my foot down and told him they were getting married."

"We knew something happened that night," Millie said. "I guess maybe it was just me who knew. Anyway, Mike had been out all night a few times and he always came home and went right to bed. That morning he came home and got right on the phone. I don't know who he was calling, because he tried to keep it quiet, but he was upset about something. I always assumed that he was talking to Betsy and that he was trying to patch something up that had happened during the night."

"Do you remember him being really cold, or sick?"

Millie shook her head. "Not really. He was just upset about something. He talked on the phone for a while and then left. I remember that now because his boss called and wanted to know why he was late for work. I told him Mike was too sick to work, but I wasn't sure where he was. I suspected he was at Betsy's."

"When did you see him next?"

"Supper time I suppose. It really doesn't stick in my mind." Millie replied.

Larry shook his head. "I remember a deputy stopping by the saddle shop to ask about Mike. He told me Aaron was missing and he wanted to ask Mike if he knew where Aaron was. I suppose I told him to check where Mike worked. I can't remember for sure. Later that day a customer told me Kenny had been killed in a car accident."

"Do you remember talking about those events with Mike?"

Both parents shook their heads. "There were a lot of things we didn't discuss with Mike," Larry said. "If the topic was distasteful to him he'd just walk off. I suppose I asked him about Aaron and Ken but I don't remember what he said."

"I remember hearing about Aaron and Kenny," Millie said, "but I can't remember discussing it with Mike either." Can I get you a piece of cake, Sandy? I apologize because it's store-bought, but I have some ice cream."

"Thanks, but no," Sandy said. "If I eat any more I'll burst. And thanks for letting me have supper while we talked. I don't get many home-cooked meals unless I cook them."

"That pretty girl at the camera shop doesn't cook suppers for you?" Millie asked with a smile.

"She's not much of a cook," Maki said as he got up from his chair. "If we're eating in, it's me who does the cooking."

"I hired her to take some pictures for my advertising brochure," Larry said. "Her photography skills make up for whatever she lacks in the kitchen. She put together a fine brochure and had ideas to improve the market appeal I'd never considered. Truth is that she really impressed me."

"I should get back on the road, but I feel bad that I can't help with the dishes."

"Forget the dishes," Millie said. "Larry will be on the tractor until dark and the dishes are the only project I have until bedtime."

Floyd was surprised to see a county cruiser parked next to his house when they returned from the restaurant. His immediate fear was that someone had reported a break-in or someone snooping around the yard. The dog hadn't come running to the sound of the car and that added to his anxiety.

"Stay in the car for a minute," he said to Mary. "Let me see what's up."

He closed the car door and within seconds Spot rounded the corner of the house at a full run. She danced around his feet as he walked toward the back door.

"Hey, Spot, what's all the excitement?" The sound of Floyd's voice added to her animation. A second later Sandy Maki rounded the house corner and Spot ran to him.

"What's up, Sandy?"

"The car was gone so I decided to make sure there wasn't anyone snooping around. The house is secure and I didn't see anyone lurking in the shadows."

"I was afraid someone had called in a burglary," Floyd said as they walked back to the cars.

Mary saw the smiling faces and got out of the car. "Is it safe for women and small dogs?" she asked.

"So far," Sandy replied. "I can't guarantee what the future will bring."

"Is there anything else going on around the county?" Floyd asked.

"If there was any excitement, I wouldn't be here. I even had time to eat supper."

"Floyd told me that you're getting married," Mary said. "Have you set a date?"

"Not officially. I was thinking about a year, and Barb's thinking next month."

"Next month?" Mary asked. "You can't get anything arranged in a month!" Mary froze and put her hand to her mouth. "Oh, my. Did I stick my foot in my mouth?"

"No, she's not pregnant," Sandy said, quickly seeing Mary's embarrassment.

"I'm sorry to be so impolite," Mary said.

"Hey, don't sweat it. I've suffered a lot worse comments than that in the time Barb and I have been together. For a while, every place we went brought looks like I was out with a hooker."

"I think Barb likes to cultivate that image," Floyd observed.

"Yeah, but as people get to know her they see through the façade. Lately she's wearing clothes that leave a little more to the imagination."

"If Barb needs any help with wedding plans, have her give me a call," Mary offered.

"I'm sure she won't make that call. She doesn't understand that people will really be okay with our wedding and that she'll be accepted in the community. She isn't close to her family so she's not getting any support from them either."

"Oh, Sandy," Mary said, putting a hand on his shoulder. "If she doesn't know that we're excited for you two, I'll call her right now."

Barb Dupre answered the phone on the second ring. "Hello."

"Barb, this is Mary Jungers, Floyd Swenson's friend. Floyd just told me about your wedding plans and I wanted to tell you how happy we are for you."

"That's nice of you to say," Barb said in her usual slow manner.

"I'd really like to help with any of the planning. I know your family isn't nearby, but I can give you a hand."

"Um, thanks. I don't know what date it will be, but there will be some things to do. I can probably handle it though."

"Planning for a wedding is fun, Barb. Will you let me help?"

"Okay, but I don't know what needs to be done."

"Are you working at the drugstore tomorrow? I can drive down from Pine Brook, meet you at noon, and we can talk over lunch."

Barb was skeptical of the sudden friendliness. "That's nice, but things are under control."

"Barb, I want to help. It would be my pleasure. What time would you like to meet?"

"Um, I don't start work until one, so I can meet you for lunch and then go to work. Where would you like to meet?"

"How about the Dairy Queen?"

"Okay." Barb paused, then asked. "Did Sandy ask you to call me?"

"Barb, I think you and Sandy getting married is a wonderful thing. I love weddings, and I'm really excited that you're going to let me be part of the planning."

"You're a shit," Barb said as Sandy walked into their apartment after his shift.

"I love you, too," Sandy replied as he locked the door. "So, what did I do to earn that greeting?"

"You told Floyd to have his girlfriend call me, didn't you?"

"Mary called you?"

"You know damned well that she called me. I don't like being manipulated."

"I told Floyd and Mary that we were getting married and that you wanted to do it soon. She said that you'd need help because there are so many things to plan, and I left it at that. If she called you, it was because she wanted to help."

Barb's eyes narrowed. "I've met her, and she's a nice, professional lady, and I'm hardly a lady. Why would she offer to help me?"

"Because she's nice and she likes to do nice things. What did she tell you?"

"She said that weddings were fun and she asked if she could be part of it. She said something about me not having any family around to help and that she would like to help if I'd let her."

"She asked permission?"

"Isn't that weird?" Barb asked.

Pam Ryan was turning off the television when the phone rang. Her mother knew that the only sure time to catch her home was just before bed, so Pam picked up the phone expecting her mother's voice.

"Pam, this is Mary Jungers. Do you have a minute to talk?"

"Sure, what's up?" Her mind searched for a reason Floyd would be calling at 9:00 in the evening and came up blank.

"Floyd just told me that Sandy Maki and Barb are getting married. I talked to Barb a few minutes ago and we're getting together tomorrow over lunch to start wedding plans. Sandy said that Barb wants to get married in the next few weeks, and she doesn't have any family in the area, so I thought it might be fun to have a wedding shower for her."

Of all the possible reasons for Mary to call, a wedding shower for Barb Dupre didn't even make the list. "I hadn't even thought of that," Pam said. "But I think that would be really nice. Barb doesn't have many friends here and she might be pleased if we could get some women together to throw a shower."

"Great! Start putting together a list of people we should invite. I'll start looking through some cookbooks for recipes. We can have it at Floyd's house. Since the wedding may be coming up fast, we'd better think about a day next week for the party."

Spot growled as she lay next to the bed. Floyd's eyes popped open and he listened to the wind blowing through the pine trees. Something unheard by Floyd made the dog's ears perk as she let out another low growl. Floyd sat on the edge of the bed. The display on the clock said 2:34.

"What did you hear, girl? You think we've got another raccoon raiding the bird feeder?" he asked as he eased out of bed. He pulled open the nightstand drawer and took out his pistol. He quietly walked through the dark house with the dog at his side, her toenails clicking on the hardwood floor and her ears perked.

The night breeze caused the living room drapes to stir. Floyd gently spread the curtains and peeked out the window toward the bird feeder. Fireflies made irregular loops in the backyard, their eerie neon glow flicking on and off, and tree frogs peeped in the darkness. The frogs stopped abruptly.

"Something scared the frogs," Floyd said to the dog.

A clicking sound emanated from beyond the living room and Spot launched herself toward the kitchen, barking and snarling, the ten-pound terrier mix acting like she was a hundred-pound attack dog. Floyd followed behind, cocking the pistol as he walked.

Spot scratched at the door and whined. The clicking noise repeated itself as a gust of wind caught the storm door. After a quick look through the window, he opened the door and Spot pushed through the unlatched screen door and raced into the night barking.

"It's the wind," Floyd said to the air where Spot had been standing. "The screen door wasn't latched." He stepped onto the patio and whistled. Spot stopped barking, and came trotting back from the darkness, strutting like she'd just driven off a threat.

As he turned back he saw the business-sized white envelope that dangled from a strip of Scotch tape on the screen door.

Floyd stepped to the phone and dialed the dispatcher. "This is Floyd. Send the nearest cruiser to my house."

Spot pushed past him and lay in the corner of the kitchen, licking the dew from her feet. "I guess there mustn't be any imminent threat," Floyd observed. The dog curled into a corner and closed her eyes, content that the house was safe.

After a few minutes, a car engine slowed on the road. The dog stood up at the engine sound and started barking at the sound of crunching gravel.

Floyd stepped out the door in his boxers and waved at the cruiser. "Bring in your evidence kit," he told Kerm Rajacich.

Floyd carefully pulled the envelope from the door with forceps, and pulled the folded paper from inside the envelope. It fell open enough so he could read the carefully printed words inside.

Let him rest in peace

Floyd called dispatch. "Get someone over to Kathy Tucker's and Mike Nelson's houses," Floyd said to the dispatcher. "I want to know if their cars have been driven recently."

"It has to be someone connected who wants us to drop the investigation," Floyd said to Rajacich.

"I'll play the devil's advocate," Said Kerm. "I think it's someone who's reconciled themselves to whatever happened and doesn't want us to reopen the wound. I'm thinking it's either Aaron Roberts' or Ken Solstad's parents. They took the emotional brunt of the disappearance and death. I think they don't want to relive it now."

"I can understand Solstad's," Floyd said. "They buried their son and that case is closed. I think the Roberts will be pleased to have the case reopened so they might get closure on Aaron's disappearance."

"It's got to be terrible losing a child and not knowing what happened," Kerm said. "Remember the Jacob Wetterling case in Stearns County? He disappeared more than twenty years ago and his mother is still a national advocate for missing children. It's one of those things that's never forgotten."

The kitchen phone startled everyone when it rang. Floyd picked it up and spoke to Sergeant Tom Trent. From the one-sided conversation Floyd understood that Tom was in Kathy Tucker's driveway and that neither of the two cars in her driveway were warm.

"Drive over to Solstad's and check their cars, too." Floyd listened for a few more seconds and then hung up.

Floyd took a cream container out of the refrigerator and retrieved two spoons from the drawer. "Let's assume someone is pleading with us to stop investigating because of the pain it's causing. Other than the Solstads and the Roberts, who else is feeling pain?"

"It'd be good to know who else Ken Solstad and Aaron Roberts were close to," Kerm suggested. "It sounds like the six people together the night before Aaron disappeared were close, but was there someone else? Did one of their buddies have to work that night, or was someone out of town?"

"I looked through my notes from the original investigation and those six were a pretty tight group. But, that's probably a good question to ask again," Floyd said, making a note. "I asked all those questions at the time, but sometimes people's memories are clouded by the overwhelming events of the moment."

"That," Kerm added, "and there may have been people being protected. Allegiances change over time. There are so many instances where a crime is solved after a couple break up and the scorned girlfriend calls to turn in the guy who she's been providing an alibi for, sometimes for years."

"Melissa Smith had broken up with Ken while he was in Korea," Floyd said. "I wonder if she'd been seeing someone else. If she was, and Ken found out about it, he might've gone on the warpath."

"What if it was Aaron?" Kerm asked.

"Well," Floyd said, "that would explain a lot of things. Ken might have taken it out on both Melissa and Aaron. If Ken found out that last night, he might have beat up Aaron and the attack on Melissa would make more sense."

"I don't buy it," Kerm said. "Aaron and Kathy Tucker were an item."

"You're being naïve. Teen-aged guys and girls are in constant turmoil—dating one person this week and the next week dating a different one. There can be lots of hard feelings and best friends can quickly become worst enemies. We get calls to the high school a couple times a month about some guy mad because his ex-girlfriend is dating one of his buddies."

"I guess I'll talk to Kathy Tucker again," Floyd said. "She seems to be at the center of all the circles I draw."

Tones for a fire call sounded on Kerm's radio. "I guess it's time to get back on the road." The dispatcher called the Pine City volunteer fire department for a barn fire in Chengwatana Township near the opposite corner of Pine County. "It'll take me more than half an hour to get there at a-hundred-miles-an-hour. I hope someone else is closer."

"I hope the firemen are closer," Floyd said.

CHAPTER 22

Floyd was sitting in his office when Pam Ryan came in early for the day shift. "Couldn't sleep?" she asked.

"Someone left me another note in the middle of the night," he said, getting up with his coffee cup. "I need another cup of coffee."

"I ran a background check on Kathy Tucker's friend," Pam said as they walked out of the bullpen. "His name is Walter Flaherty and he's been through the jail turnstile a couple times. No violent crimes, just shoplifting, burglary, and petty theft. He's been in and out of most of the county jails around the Twin Cities. It seems that winter was a bigger problem for him than the summer. Kathy told me that they shared a problem with alcohol, so I'm guessing that's he was a vagrant in Minneapolis who used the jails for a warm bed and a breakfast."

Pam poured coffee for both of them and took a sip. "Yuck! This is even worse than usual," she said after spitting into the sink. "It must be left over from the afternoon shift?"

"I made it a couple hours ago," Floyd said, looking sheepish. "There weren't any directions so I put in twelve scoops of coffee to make twelve cups of coffee."

"Twelve scoops? I usually use four scoops to a pot if I want it extra strong." Pam dumped the remaining coffee into the sink and measured fresh ground coffee for a new pot.

"Kathy Tucker's friend, Walt, has been working as a janitor and handyman at the Hinckley Methodist Church," she said as she measured out water. "I spoke with the pastor and he said Walt's been a good worker and they have an agreement that keeps him on the wagon. One of the parishioners puts Walt up in an apartment over her garage. He lives on his own. It sounds like Kathy is his only friend in town. Walt looks a little grizzled and that puts people off. The funny thing is that the church has been providing new clothes and they bought him an electric razor, but Walt seems to prefer his grizzled look."

"I don't recall any recent problems with petty theft around Hinckley," Floyd said as they returned to the bullpen, "so I assume Walt is keeping his nose clean. Maybe he was only stealing to buy booze. With a regular job, a place to sleep, and no booze, he doesn't need the cash. Or maybe Kathy Tucker is his support group and together they keep each other on the wagon."

"Any news from the BCA," Pam asked.

"Laurie Lone Eagle left a message yesterday afternoon," Floyd said. "They raised some prints off the first note and the envelope and they put them into AFIS. We should hear back today if they found a match. They also had results from the rope. There were traces of both human and deer blood on it. They said the blood is old and degraded, but they might be able to test for DNA if we ever want to attempt a match. The most interesting thing is that the blood type on the rope matches the blood on Ken Solstad's shoes. That's not the same as a DNA match, but it's likely they're the same considering the picture."

"That was quick," Pam said.

"Laurie said she was going to pull in an IOU to get the envelope and rope examined. The response was so quick I wonder if she has compromising pictures of someone," Floyd said, grinning.

"What should we do today?" Pam asked.

"You should get some work done," the Sheriff's bass voice came from the hallway. He walked into the bullpen with an unlit cigar clenched between his teeth and a coffee cup in his hand. His dark hair was in the same slicked-back cut he'd worn for forty years.

"You're in early, John," Floyd said.

"You can't all spend your time chasing ghosts in an old picture," Sheriff John Sepanen said as he poured himself a cup of fresh coffee. "There are modern crimes to investigate."

"Someone left another note on my door in the middle of the night," Floyd said. "This one said, 'Let him rest in peace.' Someone doesn't want this case examined."

"In every case we investigate there is someone who doesn't want us snooping around," the sheriff said. He took a sip of coffee and looked surprised. "This isn't half bad! We should give a commendation to whoever made this pot and make them the official coffee brewer."

"I think someone from the night shift made it," Pam blurted out, not wanting permanent coffee duty.

"Let's not make this Ken Solstad thing the only case we're working on," Sepanen said, looking directly at Floyd.

"Actually," Floyd said, "the focus is on determining what happened to Aaron Roberts and why he disappeared. I'm convinced that he's dead."

"He's not dead until we have a body," Sepanen said. "When we have a body, we have a murder investigation. The department did a missing person's investigation at the time and came up empty. I don't need everyone in the department repeating that investigation now because we found a murky picture that might be Aaron Roberts on the night he might've disappeared."

"We found the place the picture was taken," Pam said. "The man who owns the property found a rope next to the tree in the picture and the BCA found human blood on the rope."

"The rope was found right after the Roberts kid was missed? I don't remember anything about a rope," Sepanen asked.

"No," Floyd replied. "We identified the site where the picture of Aaron Roberts was taken. When we questioned the property owner he remembered finding a rope by the tree. He went to his storage shed and gave it to us."

"The guy found this rope right after the Roberts kid was kidnapped and stored it in his shed until now?"

"He didn't find it until spring, and he's not absolutely sure it was the year that Aaron Roberts disappeared. That's why we had the BCA test it. I thought that if there was human blood on it, we might have a link to the Roberts disappearance."

"Please tell me," the sheriff said, "we didn't pay taxpayer money to do DNA testing on a rope that might have been used to tie up a missing man that might've been found six months after the crime and stored in a shed for maybe fifteen years."

"No," Pam replied. "The BCA did an exam of the blood stains just to determine whether they were human or something else."

"How many more hours are you planning to dump into this rat hole?" The sheriff asked Floyd, his voice a little sharp.

"We have a few more leads to follow but we should be able to wrap it up in a few more days. Of course that assumes no more notes are left on my door in the middle of the night. I won't drop anything this personal."

Sepanen shook his head. "What idiot leaves notes taped to a cop's door in the middle of the night?"

"Maybe it's a plea for help," Pam said. "You know, like a suicide. They call and ask for help, or report that they've taken pills. It's an irrational way to ask for attention."

"The notes sounded more pleading than threatening," Floyd said. "It's hard to convince Mary that any note taped to my door in the middle of the night is anything but threatening."

"Mary?" the sheriff asked.

"Floyd's girlfriend found the first note," Pam said as Floyd turned red.

"You have a girlfriend?" Sepanen asked, suddenly curious.

"She's just a friend. I met her when we were investigating the girl missing from the summer camp and we've had coffee together a few times."

The sheriff gave a brief glimpse of a rare smile. He said, "Just wrap it up so we can move onto some of the other crimes."

After she was sure the sheriff was out of earshot Pam asked, "What other crimes is he talking about? I'm not aware of anything close to the magnitude of a kidnapping. And, if this isn't important, why is he talking about it on his radio show?"

"There isn't anything else," Floyd said. "The sheriff has a problem with us working on anything that doesn't have political value. Working on an old missing person case doesn't get many votes."

"I'd think that solving an old missing person case would get votes."

"True," Floyd said, "but the odds of solving this case are slim and none. The sheriff knows that as well as anyone. He's also the one who has to explain where the budget gets spent. If the story doesn't sell well with the county board, they'll cut our funding."

"I never thought that politics and budgets determined priorities when I decided to go into law enforcement."

"Really? You don't think that we patrol the county board members' roads more often than the others? Every time any city faces spending cuts the first thing they threaten to cut is police coverage. I can't think of anything more political than law enforcement."

"Have you ever considered running for sheriff?"

"No way! The sheriff loves the limelight and I hate it. When we solve a crime he gets to stand in front of the cameras and explain how the department did a great job of solving the crime. He shares the credit, but he gets a share of the glory because it's his department. For me, the only thing more painful than talking to the media is being nice to lawyers."

Pam smiled. "Okay, what do you want me to do today?"

"Interview Aaron Roberts' parents and see what they remember about the night Aaron disappeared. I'd really like to have their perspective on the relationships between Aaron, Kathy Tucker, and Ken Solstad."

"Can I admit that's what I'm doing if the sheriff asks?"

"Sure," Floyd said with a smile. "Just don't tell him I directed you to do it."

"Maybe I'll just avoid him," Pam said as she walked out the door.

CHAPTER 23

Pam Ryan and Mary Jungers were eating burgers at the Pine City Dairy Queen when Barb Dupre rushed in. She sat down at their table breathlessly.

"I'm sorry to be late," she said with her usual slow speech. "The alarm didn't go off and I'm not a morning person."

"It's okay, Barb," Mary said, smiling that Barb thought of a noon meeting as morning. "Go get something to eat. Then we'll talk."

Barb came back with a chocolate malt and a package of fries. "I'm not a breakfast person either."

"Barb, this is so exciting! Mary said you are thinking about a wedding in the next couple weeks. Have you picked the date?" Pam asked enthusiastically.

"Sandy thought we should wait, but I think we should have the wedding soon. Sandy's off the weekend after next, so I thought that's when we'd do it. I want to have a ceremony at sunrise by a lake with a few friends."

"That's really soon," Mary said. "It doesn't give you a lot of time to make plans and get out invitations."

"It's not a big deal. I don't think many people will want to come."

"Pam and I were putting together a list of people who'd enjoy coming to a bridal shower. We've got ten people. Who would you like to add?"

"I don't know," Barb replied, looking stunned. "Who should I invite?"

"You must have some girlfriends you'd like to invite," Mary said. Sensing that Barb wasn't sure what she meant, she added, "Are you close to any of the clerks at the drugstore, or maybe someone from your previous jobs?"

"Dale at the drugstore and I get along okay, and Harvey, from the Pine Brook Inn, was a nice guy."

Pam smiled and Mary leaned close. "Wedding showers are usually girl-only events. What about girlfriends?"

"Not really. I get along better with men."

"Well," Mary said, "here's the list of people we've put together so far." She read off the names of women from the sheriff's department who'd known Sandy for years plus the pharmacist's wife, and sheriff's wife. "We should add Sandy's mother and his sister. I don't know who you've chosen for your maid of honor, but we should invite her, too."

"I haven't got one yet," Barb said. "Who should that be?"

"Usually it's your best friend," Mary suggested, "or your sister."

"Sandy's my best friend, and I don't have any sisters." Barb hesitated. "I've been to some weddings and they usually have two or three women. Isn't that right?"

"Sure," Pam replied. "My sister had four attendants."

"Can I have the two of you as bridesmaids?"

Mary and Pam exchanged a quick look of surprise. "I'd be proud to do that," Mary said, "and I'm sure Pam would be honored, too. But are you sure we're the right people?"

"I don't know," Barb said as she dunked a few fries into a puddle of ketchup. "You're both nice to me and Sandy thinks you're both great. I think you'd be the right people."

"I don't know what to say," Pam said, reaching out and putting her hand on top of Barb's. "It's a really big deal to be in someone's wedding. If you want me, I would be honored."

Barb looked at the tears in Pam's eyes. "You must be the right people. I don't know anyone who'd cry if I asked them."

"I'm sorry to say this," Mary said, "but I have to get back to the flower shop." She pushed the list of names toward Barb. "Look through our list and tell me if you have anyone to add."

Barb read through the short list quickly. "I guess it's good."

"Would you like us to invite your mother or other relatives?"

"I'd rather not. We haven't been close for a few years."

"I don't mean to tell you what to do," Pam said, "but my mother wouldn't forgive me if I didn't invite her to my wedding shower."

"I don't think she'll care," Barb said. "I wasn't planning to invite her to the wedding either."

"What day will work for the shower?" Mary asked, sensing the need to change the topic. "Sunday afternoon I can throw Floyd out and we can take over his house in Willow River."

"I work until three," Barb said. "I can come over right after work."

"Great!" Pam said. "Mary and I will whip up invitations and plan some silly games. We'll have fun."

As they walked out the door Mary took Barb's hand and led her to a picnic table in the shade. 'Come over to the flower shop tomorrow. I want to show you some flowers that might be nice for a lakeside wedding."

"I'll have to talk to Sandy. This is all really fast and I don't have much saved up for flowers, a cake, or things like that."

"Barb, Floyd and I are giving you the flowers as a wedding gift. Just pick out the ones you want and we'll have them at the wedding."

Barb searched Mary's face for a moment, trying to find some reason she might be playing a cruel joke or evidence she thought Barb was suddenly a charity case.

"What's the matter, Barb?"

"I've heard that wedding flowers cost a lot of money."

"Forget about the money. They're a gift."

"I don't know what to pick," Barb said, seeing Pam waving goodbye as she left the parking lot.

"Come to the flower shop and I'll show you some ideas that I think would work for an outdoor wedding with the flowers that are available this time of year. Besides, Floyd told me that you're a photographer. I'll bet that you have a great eye for color and composition. We'll dream up something together." Mary handed her a business card.

"I'll look at the schedule when I get to the photo lab and I'll give you a call. Okay?"

"That'll be great. I should be back at the shop in half an hour or so."

Pam called Mary at the flower shop shortly after lunch. "Mary, I can't believe that Barb doesn't want her mother at the shower."

"I suspect there's some bad blood between them. I'm guessing her mom might not have approved of Barb's former life."

"It's really sad that she doesn't have anyone close to be her maid of honor. I'm really pleased that she asked us, but I've never been close to her."

"Look at it from Barb's standpoint," Mary said. "Most women don't relate to her very well. She's led a tough life, and she's finally at a point where she has something solid and reliable. You and I may be the only female support group she's ever had. We may be her best friends right now, and the most important thing we can do is to be by her side at the wedding."

"She needs unconditional love."

"Exactly," Mary said. "Even is she doesn't understand it right now."

A few minutes later, Barb called the flower shop to set up an appointment for the next day.

CHAPTER 24

"Is Melissa Schotten on duty?"

"Who should I say is calling?" the receptionist asked.

"Tell her it's Floyd Swenson, from the Pine County Sheriff's Department."

It took several minutes for Melissa to answer. "Please don't call me anymore."

"I'm sorry to disturb you again, but I need one more answer."

"I'm sorry, too. I have to work." Melissa's words were followed by the dial tone.

Floyd drove to the credit union and walked to Dolores Smith at the teller's counter. "Can I steal a few minutes of your time, Dottie?"

"It's pretty slow," she replied. "Maybe Brad will cover for a bit."

Floyd closed the manager's office door. "We're still muddling around in the Aaron Roberts disappearance."

"I know. Melissa called and said you'd been harassing her. She was particularly angry that I'd told you about Kenny attacking her."

"I understand that Ken and Melissa were an item before he left for Korea. At some point they broke up while he was still overseas. Was it because Aaron starting dating Melissa?"

"I'm sure Aaron had nothing to do with it. Kenny was being a jerk, suspecting Melissa of cheating on him with every other guy in town. Melissa had been so supportive, writing letters daily, even sending boxes of cookies and treats. When Ken got this crazy idea she was seeing someone else she got fed up and told him they were through. He wrote back and apologized, but within a week he was back with the paranoia about her dating other guys. Melissa and I talked about it a lot and we guessed he was being fed this information by someone who wanted to needle him. But Melissa couldn't forgive his lack of trust and she wrote him that it was over again."

"There wasn't anyone else?"

"I think Melissa and I were pretty close, and she told me there was no one else. I know she wasn't dating anyone regularly."

"Did you ever find out who was feeding Ken the false information that she was cheating?"

"No. I didn't spend much time pursuing it, but I know Melissa asked a lot of people who all denied it. The strange part was that none of them were communicating with Ken at all. The group they hung with weren't the type to be pen pals. They seemed more the hard drinking, hard living, meet-me-at-the-bar-but-don't-expect-me-to-write type. I got to the point where I just decided that Ken was paranoid, and that maybe the guys in his unit were feeding his paranoia."

"What happened when Ken came home?"

"He called Melissa and wanted to get back together. She said no but he kept after her. The last days he was in town he called and begged her to go out, and she agreed only if they were part of a group. You know the rest."

"You're sure there was nothing between Melissa and Aaron?"

"The only reason Melissa hung o ut with Aaron was because he was Ken's friend. She said he was nice, but really immature, and she didn't like the way he treated Kathy."

"So much for that theory," Floyd said. "Thanks for your time."

He turned to leave, but hesitated. "Dottie, the last time I was here you said to let sleeping dogs lie."

"Maybe. I don't recall."

"Have you been past my house recently?" he asked.

"I don't know exactly where you live," she replied. "Why would I have been past your house?"

"Someone left notes taped to my door asking me to let sleeping dogs lie. That was exactly what you said last time I was here asking about Aaron's disappearance."

Dottie's eyes hardened. "Maybe you should take the hint."

"I think Aaron Roberts' parents would like to know where he is. I owe it to them to do all I can to solve the mystery."

"I can't imagine your investigation is going to do anything but scratch scabs off old wounds. That's probably why I told you to leave things alone." Dottie closed her eyes and took a deep breath. "Melissa and I have no interest in discussing this again. Karen Solstad was here, and she asked if I knew why you were digging into Kenny's past. Millie Nelson called and asked why Sandy Maki showed up at their farm asking about Mike getting Betsy pregnant. What good can come from any of this?"

The streak of hot weather had left everyone with short fuses and boiling tempers and the deputies were responding to domestic disputes daily.

Pam could hear the Roberts shouting at each other from the driveway as she parked her cruiser behind the MACK white semi-tractor with its bulldog hood ornament. The house windows were all open and Pam assumed the voices could be heard by the neighbors a quarter mile to the west. She called the dispatcher, announced she was at a domestic dispute and asked for backup. She knocked on the screen door. When her first knock failed to gain acknowledgment she knocked with her flashlight.

"Sheriff's department!"

"Go away!" a male voice yelled from inside the house.

"Sheriff's Department! Open up!" Pam yelled in her best command voice. At the same time Floyd announced to the dispatcher that he was en route to back up Pam. He was still more than ten minutes away from the Roberts' rural home east of Pine City.

The argument stopped and footsteps pounded across the floor. Somewhere deeper inside the house a door slammed. A burly man with graying blonde hair tied in a ponytail came to the door. His face was red and drenched in sweat; his dark blue tank top was stained around the armholes and in the middle of his barrel chest.

"Who called?" Mark Roberts growled. "I s'pose it was the Eastlunds again." In the background Pam heard sobbing and another door slammed.

"No one called. I could hear you arguing from the road."

"Bullshit!" he snorted, the smell of beer heavy on his breath. "Someone called to turn us in. What's going on here is no one's business. You can leave."

"I want to talk to your wife. Either let me in or ask her to come to the door."

"She doesn't want to talk to anyone right now," Roberts said, barring Pam's view of the entryway behind him. "You might as well leave."

"I'm talking to her before I leave. Ask her to come to the door."

Roberts' eyes narrowed as he studied Pam. He was obviously sizing her up, trying to determine what a tiny deputy would do if he refused her entry to the house. "She's not coming out, and you're not coming in."

"Okay, we'll do it the hard way," Pam said. "We'll get all the available deputies here. We'll arrest you for interfering with a deputy. Then, I'll spend the rest of the shift filling out reports while you sit in the county jail waiting for a bail hearing. Nobody wins."

"Fuck you, Blondie."

Pam took the radio from her belt. "Every available Pine County unit, please respond to a domestic." She relayed the fire number and gave the county road and the nearest crossroad.

It took less than five seconds for the dispatcher to relay the message over the airwaves and three units, including Floyd and a state patrol trooper, responded with their estimated arrival times.

"Why don't you just come in here and see if she wants to talk," Roberts said, pushing the screen door open. The smile on his face was an obvious challenge.

"Step away from the door, and back down the hallway," Pam said with her hand on the butt of her pistol.

"What's the matter, Blondie?" Roberts said, stepping into the doorframe so his height and weight advantage over Pam were more intimidating. "Are you afraid I might play grab-ass if you try to walk past me?" He gestured as if he were squeezing buttocks with his hands.

A siren whined in the distance and Pam took a deep breath. "Give it up before you make a bigger fool of yourself. So far, all you've been is obnoxious. I'd hate to see you arrested for assaulting an officer."

"Ooh, I think you'd love it," Roberts said, licking his lips lasciviously. "Maybe I could get a peek at whatever you've got hidden behind that bulletproof vest. I bet you've got some interesting bikini lines, or do you tan in the buff?"

Another door slammed inside the house as the first siren turned off at the end of the gravel driveway. Footsteps padded across the linoleum floor and a petite woman peered around the corner. Pam's first impression was that the woman's complexion was ashen until she realized that she'd applied heavy makeup, probably to cover bruises. She pulled a flowered housecoat tight at her neck and chest.

"Mrs. Roberts," Pam said, looking past the man, "please come to the door."

"Get back in there!" Mark Roberts commanded the woman. "I got this under control."

Floyd's unmarked cruiser pulled next to the sidewalk and he trotted to the door. Two more sirens wailed nearby.

"Jesus, Mark," Floyd said, "what the hell do you think you're doing?"

The sour look on Roberts' face said he and Floyd had a history. "I was talking to this sweet young deputy of yours about her bikini lines. I was just holding the door so she could come in and show them to me."

Floyd looked at Pam's stance, with her feet set wide and her hand on the butt of her gun. "I think you'd better step back, Mark. Walk ahead of Deputy Ryan into the house and keep your hands where she can see them so she doesn't have to shoot you."

"She ain't shooting no one. I haven't threatened her life or anything."

"You're twice her size, and you're drunk. If you tried to lay a hand on her there isn't a grand jury in the state who wouldn't agree that she'd have shot you in self defense." When Roberts didn't move Floyd added, "Look at her. She's got her hand on her gun and if you take one step toward her she'll have the gun pointed between your eyes with her finger on the trigger."

Roberts looked at Floyd and then looked at Pam's gun. A highway patrol cruiser rolled to a stop behind Floyd's car and the trooper sprinted to Pam's other side. Seeing Pam's stance, the trooper drew a can of Mace from his belt and held it at his side.

"You guys got no right to come and threaten me in my own home."

"There was a domestic assault going on when I arrived," Pam said. "The law says we have to make sure both parties are safe before we can leave the scene. You won't let your wife come out, so we have to do whatever is required to enter the house to assess her safety."

"Who made you a fucking lawyer?" Roberts said, spraying spittle as he became more agitated. "This is my fucking house and you have no right to come in here."

"Settle down, Mark," Floyd said, trying to drain some tension from the situation. "We don't need to come in the house. We need to talk to Sue. If she's okay we get back in our cars and drive away quietly."

Another Pine County cruiser raced down the driveway and parked behind the highway patrol car as a cloud of gravel dust engulfed it. Sergeant Tom Thompson sprinted to the group and stepped behind Pam.

The afternoon sun pounded down on them in the ninety-degree heat. The armpits of Pam's tan uniform were soaked and a trickle of sweat ran down her temple and into her shirt collar. Floyd mopped his forehead with his arm before sweat ran into his eyes.

"Tom," Floyd said, "see if the other door is open and if Mrs. Roberts will come to the door."

"Sue!" Roberts shouted over his shoulder. "You lock yourself into the bedroom! Don't you come out for anyone but me!"

Thompson eased away from the group and walked around the corner of the house.

"You listen to me," Roberts said, "Sue and I were having something out that doesn't concern the county. You can all go away and everything will be fine."

The sound of Thompson knocking on the door echoed through the house. "Mrs. Roberts, this is Sergeant Thompson. It's safe to come to the door."

Mark Roberts spun and ran into the house with amazing speed, lurching toward the steps leading into the kitchen.

Floyd yelled, "Look out, Tom, he's coming through!"

Pam was first through the outer door, and was a few steps behind Roberts when he stumbled on the top step of the entryway. She grabbed his belt, but was brushed off with the sweep of one huge hand. As she lost her balance, the trooper, who was following her, stepped on her heel and the two fell to the floor. Tom Thompson rushed through the other door holding a can of Mace, spraying Mark Roberts full in the face before being bowled over.

In the haze of pepper spray Roberts misjudged the corner to the hallway, stumbling into the wall and staggering just enough to allow Floyd to throw his shoulder into Roberts' kidneys, propelling him face-first into the wall. Roberts let out a roar of pain as his knees buckled and he clawed at his burning eyes. The four officers pounced on his back and struggled to pull his muscular arms into a position where they could be handcuffed. By the time they were done, all the officers' eyes were burning from the pepper spray and their clothes were soaked with sweat.

"Jesus, Tom," Pam said, "did you have to spray the whole house?"

"Do me a favor next time," the trooper said as he brushed off his burgundy pants. "Don't call me for backup," he said, gasping to catch his breath. "Either that, or shoot the sonofabitch. I'll swear it was self-defense." He wiped at his eyes with a handkerchief.

Floyd and Tom helped Mark Roberts from the floor. In their rush to subdue him, they hadn't noticed that the interior of the house was a shambles.

"What a mess," Pam said, looking around, "I wonder if they were trashing the place when I got here." She then remembered Sue Roberts and limped to the closed door down the hallway. "Mrs. Roberts, are you okay? Everything is under control out here. You can come out now."

After a few seconds the doorknob turned and the door opened a crack. A blue eye appeared. "Is it safe? Is Mark gone?" Sue's breath also smelled of beer. Pam looked at her watch. It was barely two o'clock in the afternoon.

"He's under control. Are you okay?"

The door opened slowly and Sue Roberts emerged. Her heavy makeup was streaked with trails left by her tears. A trickle of blood flowed from her nose and over her bruised and swollen top lip. She stepped into the hallway, her left arm wrapped across the housecoat that was pasted to her body with sweat. Her breath came in short, shallow rasps.

"Are you okay?" Pam asked. "Does your chest hurt?"

"Yes," Sue whispered. "I hurt it when I fell against a table." Her words came in short gasps.

Pam reached for her radio, only to discover that it had been ripped free at some point in the struggle with Mark Roberts. "I'll call an ambulance," she said. "Wait here."

"No!" Sue gasped. "We don't have insurance."

Pam ignored the plea and limped back through the house, looking for her radio. She reached under the table and felt a twinge in her back that caused a spasm. "Ow!"

Floyd was leaning on the doorframe smiling like a Cheshire cat. "It's hell to get old."

"I think I fell into a chair when the trooper stepped on my ankle." Pam held a hand to her low back. "I bet that'll be a hell of a bruise tomorrow. Maybe it'll match my ankle."

"Sue Roberts looks like she's been beaten," Floyd said. "I called an ambulance."

"I thought so, too. She's holding her ribs like one or more might be broken." Pam rolled her shoulders and grimaced.

"Greg, the highway patrolman, rolled his ankle when he fell over you."

"Maybe it was his knee in my back that's killing me and not the chair."

"Ride the ambulance with Sue," Floyd suggested, "and have the ER doc check you out. I'll have someone drive your cruiser over to the hospital."

"Where's Mark Roberts?" Pam asked.

"He's already on his way to the jail in Tom's car."

CHAPTER 25

Pam was sitting with Sue Roberts in an ER exam room when Floyd arrived. Both women were wearing hospital gowns. Pam's uniform shirt and bulletproof vest were hanging over the back of a chair in the corner of the room.

"How are you two doing?" Floyd asked, closing the door as he entered.

Sue's eyes flew to Pam, who answered, "The doctor says I'm only bruised, but Sue has cracked ribs." She paused while she composed her thoughts. "Sue says Mark was upset because she hadn't cleaned the house while he was on the road. He got back early this morning and started drinking. He forced her to have a few beers with him and then got mad and started throwing his weight around."

"You know it's not your fault," Floyd said to Sue, sitting on the edge of the closest chair. "Mark has to be able to talk to you without hitting. There's no excuse for a man who hits a woman. None."

"I can't get going sometimes," Sue explained, her head hung in shame. "The house gets to be a mess and the dishes pile up. I know it makes him mad when he comes home to a mess. It's my fault. I just can't help it."

"No matter what the house looks like, he shouldn't hit you," Pam said.

Doctor Ken Swanson knocked lightly on the door-frame and stepped into the exam room. He was only a few years past his residency and was considered one of the most eligible bachelors in the county. He wore blue surgical scrubs with a matching blue cover over his brown hair.

"Sue, I want you to wear a sling for two weeks until your ribs don't hurt anymore. I ordered Tylenol with codeine for the pain. Take one every four hours when the pain is bad."

He flipped the charts and addressed Pam. "Based on where you indicated the chair struck you, I'd say your bulletproof vest took the brunt of the impact. You're going to have some sore muscles, but there are no broken bones and no cracked ribs.

"Keep your ankle iced and wrapped in the Ace bandage tonight and maybe it won't swell up like a basketball. Take a couple of Aleve with your next meal and take them every twelve hours for the next few days."

Kristie Naber, the ER nurse, came in carrying a pill bottle and a styrofoam cup of water. She handed Sue a pill and the water. "Take this, and you should get some pain relief in a few minutes. The rest of the bottle goes home with you."

"Can someone take me home?" Sue whispered, the effort to speak made her cringe with pain.

"I think you should go to a shelter for a few days," Floyd suggested. "Mark's in jail and it'd probably be best for you to be somewhere you can have some other people around."

Doctor Swanson set the charts on a table and sat on a small stool. "Mrs. Roberts, this isn't the first time you've been here with bruises. Your chart lists at least a dozen visits in the past ten years. Every time you come in there's a story about how you fell down the stairs or ran into a door. Each time you come in, the injuries are a little more severe. I can believe an accidental fall story once, but this is out of control. If we don't intervene I'm afraid we'll have you in the intensive care unit."

"Mark would never do that. He gets mad because I get blue and he has to snap me out of it. It's really my fault."

"Tell me about your blues," Swanson said, gently.

"I just get tired. You know how it goes; some days things get overwhelming and I just can't get myself out of bed. Just the thoughts of all the things I have to get done are too much."

"Is your family doctor treating you for depression?"

"Mark doesn't believe in that stuff. I have to do what he does — just suck up and work my way through it."

"How often do you have bouts of the blues, Mrs. Roberts?"

"It runs in streaks," Sue replied. "Sometimes I'm just overwhelmed for a couple weeks. Sometimes it's just for a couple days. It's been worse lately. Mark's gone a lot lately so I'm home by myself. That seems to make it worse."

"I think you need to see your family doctor and have a talk about depression," Swanson said. "Do it today. He can prescribe something that will make it easier to cope with your blues. You don't need to let it become overwhelming."

"Mark won't let me take any 'happy' pills. I have to cope on my own."

Doctor Swanson looked at Floyd, waiting for him to jump in.

"Mark will be in jail for a while, Sue," Floyd explained. "He assaulted you, and he also assaulted four police officers. A judge will set bail and I expect that he won't be able to pay it, so he'll be in jail until there's a hearing and maybe even until a trial."

"What will I do?" she asked. "I don't work and there isn't much in our savings. We'll have to sell the farm." A few tears rolled down her cheeks.

Pam put a hand on Sue's shoulder. "The county has a safe house for battered women and children. I can drive you there. You'll be safe and there will be women there who have the same problems."

"I think the shelter would be a good idea," the doctor said. "I think you should see your family doctor while you're there, too. I've got his name and I'll give him a call." He gathered the charts and left.

"I'll drive Sue to the shelter," Pam said to Floyd, "if you'll make the call to get it set up."

"Sure," Floyd said, digging the cellphone out of his pocket.

"Um, Floyd," Pam said. "Could you call from the waiting room? We need to put our blouses back on."

"I'll call from the car," Floyd said, shaking his head at missing the obvious awkwardness of the situation.

"When did you start having problems with the blues?" Pam asked as she and Sue pulled out of the hospital parking lot. "Did Aaron's disappearance have anything to do with it?"

Sue nodded, tears welling in her eyes.

"Do you remember if anything special happened the night he disappeared?"

"He didn't want to go out with Ken. I remember that clearly. Aaron eased off his drinking after Ken left for basic training and he started spending time with his sister, who lives in the Cities, and hanging around with a different bunch of people. Then Ken showed up on leave from Korea and he expects the old gang to be the same as before: drinking and carousing all night, then coming home at daybreak to crash. Aaron had a job, a nice car, some clean-cut friends, and he was saving money. He wasn't interested in risking what he had on a night of drinking. The night he disappeared Ken called and badgered Aaron to go out. Ken told Aaron he was having problems with Melissa and the only way she'd go out was if Aaron and Kathy went along. Aaron resisted, but Ken always got his way."

"It's interesting that Aaron had been cutting back on his drinking," Pam said. "I talked to Kathy Tucker and she said she was a heavy drinker until a couple years later. It seems odd that they were dating seriously with such different ideas about drinking."

"We thought Aaron and Kathy were going to get married the summer before. . ." Sue paused. "I think the pain pill is working. I'm a little lightheaded.

"Anyway, they'd been dating for two years and we were waiting for them to set a wedding date. Kathy was making wedding plans and the harder she pushed the more reluctant Aaron got. They'd agreed to cool things off for a while that fall and Aaron started doing things with friends he'd made in the Cities. When Ken came back he tried really hard to push them back together, but Aaron told me that he and Kathy had grown apart."

"Kathy told me that she and Aaron had a big fight that night," Pam said. "They argued, then afterward

Aaron and Ken got in a fistfight. She was so drunk she can't remember what happened after that."

"Something happened between them that night," Sue said. "Kathy and I were close before then and we'd even done some wedding planning together. After Aaron disappeared she didn't return my calls and she couldn't even look me in the eye when we met in town."

"Interesting. I read through the old files," Pam said. "I don't recall seeing any interviews with Aaron's sister or his friends in the Cities. Did you give the deputies names and phone numbers for his friends?"

"I told them about my daughter and I'm sure they talked to her. Aaron had friends in the Cities, but I didn't have their names or phone numbers. When I met them Aaron only told me their first names and I never found any phone numbers when we went through his stuff. I'm sure they weren't involved. They were all really nice, clean-cut boys with nice cars. The ones I met were really polite and pleasant, not at all like Ken and that bunch."

"How did you feel about Aaron's migration from hard drinker to clean-cut kid?"

"I thought it was great that he was thinking about college and hanging around with a better crowd. Mark didn't like Aaron drinking and running around, but I think he knew how to deal with that. When Aaron started buying shirts with collars and khaki slacks instead of rock band T-shirts and worn-out jeans Mark accused him of turning into a geek. Aaron applied to the University of Minnesota, in Minneapolis, and registered to start classes in January. Mark thought that was about the stupidest thing he'd ever heard. I remember Mark taunting him and asking if he was going to be a frat boy, too. In Mark's mind, that was about the lowest thing you could be." Sue blinked a couple times. "My head feels funny, and I'm talking too much."

"How's your pain?"

"It's pretty dull; more of an ache than the sharp pain I had at the hospital." Sue stared out the side window, watching the farms along old highway 61. "Is Mark really in jail?"

"Yes, he was booked on assault charges."

"You know, he wasn't hitting me when you came to the door. We were just yelling."

"When did he hurt your ribs?"

"Last night, right after he got home."

"You must've been in terrible pain all night. Why didn't you go to the doctor?"

"Mark wouldn't let me. He was afraid the doctor would report him to the police. He told me to 'suck it up' so I took a some aspirin and tried to sleep in the recliner."

"Haven't you ever been tempted to leave him?"

"I haven't got anywhere to go. Besides, Mark would kill me. He told me that."

"The place we're going is a secret," Pam explained. "You can't tell anyone where it is. You're safety, and the safety of the other residents, depends on no one knowing where it is. You'll be able to call people and assure them that you're safe. You can give them the phone number, but under no circumstances can you tell *anyone* the location. Do you understand?"

"I'll be able to call my daughter?"

"Yes, call her so she knows that you're safe." Pam paused. "Is she older or younger than Aaron?"

"She's five years older than Aaron. She's married and living down in the Cities. I have three grandchildren: the two girls are in high school and my grandson's in sixth grade."

"Were she and Aaron close?"

"Not really. Five years is a big spread in years when you're a kid. She got married when Aaron was a teen, so she'd been out of the house for almost ten years when Aaron disappeared."

Thoughts flashed through Pam's head about Sue's earlier comments. The question that flirted with her brain finally gelled. "Did your daughter have any influence on Aaron's decision to quit drinking and start college classes?"

"I don't know. He always talked to Jen, but they were in different worlds. He was wild and she was quiet. He stayed single and caroused, while she had a husband, a house, and family."

"It sounds like a stereotypical oldest child and youngest child," Pam said. "The old one is stable and does what mom and dad want, while the baby gets easier rules and goofs off."

"I always thought we treated them the same, but it's sure funny how two kids from the same parents can be so different. I guess part of it was growing up. It seems like Jen was grown up when she was in junior high. Aaron didn't seem to get past the juvenile stage. Toward the end, it seemed like maybe he did figure it out and I was kind of hopeful that he'd be something other than a drunk who lived with his parents for the rest of his life."

"I'd like to talk to Jen," Pam said. "I think she might have some insight we haven't had before."

"Go ahead. Her name's Jennifer, and she's married to Keith Zollner. I can't remember their phone number, but they live in Cottage Grove, down in the south part of the Cities. I talk to her once a week or so, when Mark's on the road. He doesn't like me talking to her because Jen's told me to leave him and move in with her."

"Have you considered her offer?" Pam asked.

"Mark needs someone to take care of the house, and we're married," Sue said. "I took a vow to stick with him through better or worse."

"There is no reason for you to stay in an abusive relationship," Pam said. "Go talk to your pastor or priest and he'll tell you the same thing."

"We're not really church people," Sue said. "I don't know that I've been in church for anything but weddings and funerals since I married Mark."

"Mark violated your marriage vows the first time he struck you. There is no reason you have to stick with him."

Sue considered Pam's words in silence.

Pam turned off Highway 23 when she reached Pine Brook. She drove past a few blocks of businesses and homes. A quarter mile further down a township road she turned into a gravel driveway leading to a plain, two-story white house.

"It's so hot the cattails in the ditch are drying up," Sue noted. "I haven't hung clothes out this week because they get coated from the cars raising dust on the road."

As they stepped out of the car the compressor for the house's central air conditioning hummed to life. "This place has air conditioning?" Sue asked.

Pam took Sue by the elbow and led her to the door. "They have air conditioning and all kinds of appliances." Pam pushed the doorbell button.

"I can't afford to stay here," Sue said, her voice wavering.

"The county is treating you for the time being," Pam said. "Don't worry about the cost."

A matronly woman with a broad smile opened the door. "You must be Sue. Come in, we've been expecting you."

CHAPTER 26

The next morning Floyd drove directly from home to the Pine City Library. Brenda Engelbrekt, the librarian, was busily restocking the shelves when he approached the counter. Brenda, who was in her 20s, was smart, perky, pretty, and always smiling. Floyd often described her as the most eligible bachelorette in Pine County. She had stepped into big shoes, when she was hired after an expansion and the retirement of Christy Cook, who many people felt was unreplaceable. Brenda had quickly won the admiration and support of the library board and community.

"Hello, Floyd. We don't see you in here very often."

"I don't have a lot of time to read, and you know that old saying about life being stranger than fiction. I have all the excitement I can stand."

"Then what brings you to the library?"

"I want to read back issues of *The Pine City Pioneer* from December of '98."

"We don't actually have the paper newspapers from then, but we have all the old issues on microfilm." Brenda led Floyd to the microfilm reader and sat down. "All the recent issues are on the Internet, but most newspapers can't afford the time or money to convert microfilm files to the electronic format. I don't have many requests to see old issues of the newspaper, so when this microfilm reader dies, I'm not sure I'll be able to find the parts or money to repair it."

"Do many people come here doing research anymore?"

"Most of our customers are here for the books but we still get some requests for assistance with research. The role of the librarian has been reinvented with the advent of the Internet and that's really shifted our jobs from scouring resource books to assisting people who are unfamiliar with computers.

Brenda took out a box of microfilm and sorted through the small spools, looking for the December '98 reels. "There are a lot of people who come in here to access the Internet. The high school is requiring students to use Internet sources for their history papers so the kids are getting proficient at using computer resources. No one wants to use microfilm to search for anything anymore. Everything is sequential and you have to look at every page to search for your information. With the Internet, every database is searchable by keywords and so much easier to navigate. I have one gentleman who is in here three or four days a week doing genealogy research. He's convinced that he's related to the Queen of Denmark and he spends hours tracing his family tree.

Brenda loaded the microfilm into the reader and stood. "Here you go! Just roll through the film until you reach the day you want and then you can look at each page."

"I use the computers at the courthouse, so I'm not a total idiot. But this microfilm search is a whole new animal to me."

"It's not a new animal, Floyd. No one has used microfilm since I was in kindergarten."

"I'd been with the sheriff's department ten years when you started kindergarten. I'm not sure what that makes me."

"Dinosaur is the term the kids use to describe older people struggling with the Internet," Brenda said with a smile. "Not that you're that much older than my parents."

After dismissing Brenda with a deep sigh, Floyd flipped through days of newspaper headlines, slowly feeding the pages across the screen. "I didn't remember that the Duluth National Guard had been called up for service in Iraq," he said to himself. He read through the lead article about all the local National Guard and Air Force Reserve units who had been called to active duty for the troop surge. One local businessman was quoted as saying he'd lost half his workforce to the call-up. His production of electrical cords for a St. Cloud refrigerator plant was slumping even with the hiring of temporary employees and his remaining employees working overtime.

A headline on the third page caught his attention. "Local man missing." Floyd read through the story about Aaron Roberts' disappearance and the lack of leads reported by the sheriff's department. It mentioned his evening with friends, and quoted the Beroun bartender, who said the group had left before closing time.

He stopped at a fourth page story. "Local Soldier Dies in Iowa Accident." The details of the accident were thin except for the location, on I-35 near Des Moines.

> *A spokesperson for the Iowa State Patrol reported that Kenneth Solstad's car lost control, crossed the median and struck a north-bound semi on I-35 near Des Moines. Solstad was declared dead at the scene of the accident, and the truck driver was taken to the hospital where he was treated for minor injuries.*

> *Solstad, a resident of Pine City, and the son of Karen and Theodore Solstad, had been home on leave from the Army. He was returning to his station at Fort Leonard Wood, Missouri, at the time of the accident. The funeral arrangements will be through the Johnson-Bradshaw Funeral Chapel on Monday at 3:00 PM. The American Legion Auxiliary will serve a luncheon after the funeral service.*

Floyd looked through a few more articles, but saw nothing else of interest. He moved to the following week, and found a follow-up article about the Roberts disappearance. It stated briefly that Aaron Roberts' disappearance was still unsolved and the sheriff's department was asking the public's assistance in providing any leads or related information. With his mind wandering, Floyd fed the microfilm ahead until another article caught his eye. A lutefisk, rutabaga, and mashed potato dinner was being served by the Lutheran Church. They were taking a free-will offering to cover the cost of the dinner. Swedish meatballs were offered as an alternative entrée for those who didn't like lutefisk. Floyd tried to remember if he and his wife had attended the dinner.

"I made a fresh pot of coffee," Brenda said, holding out a mug of steaming brew.

"Thanks."

"Did you find what you were looking for?" Brenda asked as she rolled a chair beside Floyd's.

"I guess," Floyd replied. "I hoped to find something we overlooked in an investigation. He took a sip of coffee and added, "but there's nothing here I didn't already know."

Brenda looked over his shoulder at the microfilm reader. "You thought you'd find a lead in the story about the lutefisk dinner?"

"Nah, I got bored."

"If you go to the following week, I'll bet you can find an article with the headcount from the dinner and an accounting of the free-will offering. They probably reported how many pounds of Lutefisk were eaten, too."

"As odd as it seems, the sheriff's department doesn't arrest people for serving lutefisk. That's more of a crime against humanity than a statutory crime."

"Hey!" Brenda complained, "I like lutefisk."

"How can you like something that has the texture of gelatin and the flavor of . . . Well it doesn't have any flavor after the lye soak."

"You put butter or white sauce over it and it tastes like the sauce. What's not to like about butter?" She asked playfully.

"I don't know. It just seems like a terrible thing to do to perfectly totally innocent butter." Floyd paused to take another swallow of coffee. "The coffee is great. I appreciate you bringing me a cup."

"It's pretty quiet here weekday mornings. I appreciate getting a break from sorting book returns. What were you looking for?"

"We reopened an old missing person case this week hoping something new would come out, but so far we've been spinning our wheels."

"If you give me the name of the missing person I'll do a search on some databases to see if there is anything more than *The Pioneer* reported."

"I appreciate the help," Floyd said, "but don't knock yourself out. I think we're winding down to the end of this investigation."

CHAPTER 27

Pam called directory assistance and got the number for Keith Zollner in Cottage Grove, a St. Paul suburb. The phone rang three times and rolled over to an answering machine. She left a message for Jennifer, then picked up the stack of subpoenas from her box. She went to one of the twelve metal desks arranged in open cubicles around the bullpen and pulled over a desk chair with squeaking wheels.

"I guess I've got my work cut out for today," she said to herself, as she sorted the paperwork geographically to plan the route she'd take to serve the papers.

The sheriff walked into the bullpen as Pam was gathering up the sorted stacks of subpoenas. "How's life?" he asked, sitting in the guest chair next to her desk.

"Things are okay," Pam said, taken aback by the sheriff's casual demeanor. He tended to be all business and dealt primarily with the undersheriff, and the sergeants.

"I mentioned the Aaron Roberts case on my weekly radio show," the sheriff said as he sat in the guest chair next to Pam's desk. "I know a few people listen because I've caught some flak about issues I've mentioned, but this Aaron Roberts thing is ancient history and I doubt anything new will arise."

"You reached someone, because two notes have been left at Floyd's house."

"I'm more inclined to think they're a result of you and Floyd asking questions around town," the sheriff replied. "On the other hand, both the *Duluth News Tribune* and the *Minneapolis Star Tribune* picked up the story after the radio show.

"Maybe it was the newspaper articles," Pam said, then suddenly blushed. "Not that your radio show doesn't reach a lot of people."

The sheriff smiled. "Have you adapted to life in the north woods?"

"Pretty much. I still miss the open farmland at home, but it's really beautiful here a lot of the year. The fall colors were never as pretty in Blue Earth as they are in some of the maple stands up here."

"It's a different life being a cop no matter where you live. You can't run around getting drunk and doing stupid stuff that makes the newspapers. You're constantly vigilant, and you look for the seamy side of everyone."

Pam's mind raced trying to decide if they were having a friendly discussion or whether she was getting a lecture. "It's really hard to date here," she said. "I don't feel right going to a bar to meet guys, and I'm tempted to run a background check on every guy who says 'Hello.'"

"That's why I wanted to talk to you. You've been with the department for almost three years and Floyd thinks you're doing a great job. He told me how you stood down Mark Roberts yesterday and probably defused a situation that could've been bloody if some macho deputy had played cowboy and tried to take Mark down alone. You used judgment by calling for backup instead of trying to be a hero. You stood your ground until Floyd and Tom arrived. We all think that you're part of the future of this department, and I was wondering if you felt the same."

"Wow, I've never thought about my distant future," Pam said, pulling her foot onto the chair and sitting on it, grimacing as she got a shot of pain from her bruised back. "I like the people in the department, and Pine City is a nice enough place to live. I can see myself staying here."

"Good," the sheriff said. "It's really odd that I have no problem talking to the press, but I have a heck of a time talking to my deputies." He took a cigar from his pocket and put it in his mouth. He rolled it around with his tongue until it was in the corner of his mouth. "What I wanted to say is that I really want you to consider staying with us for a long time. We. . .I like your work ethic, and you handle yourself well. You're a good deputy."

Pam watched the sheriff walk out of the bullpen, thinking she'd had the strangest conversation she could imagine. After a few minutes of thought she felt smug, and then pleased as she picked up the pile of paperwork and headed for the door.

"Mary," Debbie yelled from the flower arranging bench, "pick up the phone."

"Hello, this is Mary Jungers."

"Um. . .hi, this is Barb. I was thinking about the shower and I decided I didn't know what to wear. Is this a fancy thing, or can I wear shorts?"

Mary smiled at the sound of Barb's voice. "You can come in shorts if you'd like. I think everyone will be casual in this hot weather."

"Should I bring anything?"

"Absolutely not. This is your shower. All you need to do is show up tomorrow."

"I feel really strange about this," Barb said in her halting style. "I'm not used to this treatment. You helped me pick out flowers that you and Floyd are buying and tomorrow you're throwing a party for me. It's embarrassing."

Mary was surprised by Barb's candid talk about her feelings. Floyd had told her about Barb's lifestyle when she and Sandy Maki first met. Barb had been a lingerie model, an exotic dancer, and a bar waitress who wore skimpy outfits, when she realized it resulted in better tips. The concept of Barb suddenly admitting embarrassment over anything was almost incomprehensible.

"It'll be fun, trust me. We're getting together to help you celebrate a new phase of your life and we're all really happy for you and Sandy. Are you okay with that?"

"I guess so, but it'll still be strange."

"Don't worry about it," Mary said in her most reassuring tone. "We'll all have a great time."

"I have to call Floyd, now," Barb said. "I'm at work and I have a picture to show him."

"Not another dead body, I hope," Mary said.

"No, just a better version of the other dead body. The blood is a lot more. . ."

"Please, don't tell me anymore," Mary interrupted. "I'll see you tomorrow."

Barb was dialing the sheriff's department number from Floyd's business card when Pam Ryan walked into the store and waved. "Hi, Barb. Have you picked out a wedding dress yet?" Pam was in uniform. Her bullet-proof vest, pressed against the inside of her tan uniform blouse, made it appear that she was wearing a back brace. Her short, blonde hair was damp at her neck and sweat stained her blouse around the edges of the vest.

Barb shook her head. "Not yet. I thought I'd look around town this weekend. Sandy's on days and I don't have much else to do except go to the shower."

"You won't find a wedding dress in this town," Pam said. "I'm off this weekend, too. I think you and I should drive to Duluth and see what we can find. Most places won't have anything off the rack because brides usually have their dresses custom made, but I once went with a friend to a place in the Miller Hill Mall where they had a dozen or so choices in stock."

"I don't think I want a frilly wedding dress," Barb replied, obviously shying from the whole concept of dress shopping. "I thought I might just get a dress from a nice store, like Herbergers."

"That's okay, too. I think it would be fun to go along if you don't mind. That way we can get lunch and get to know each other better. I really love to shop, especially when someone else is doing the buying."

"I guess that'd be okay."

"Have you picked out a ring for Sandy yet?"

Barb looked startled. "I hadn't even thought about it. Most guys don't wear wedding rings, do they?"

"Sandy will wear a ring. He loves you a lot, and I think he'll be proud to wear a ring that shows he's married to you."

"Really?"

"Really," Pam said. "I'll pick you up at 9:00 tomorrow morning." As she walked out of the pharmacy Pam thought how sad Barb's life must've been to have never felt she was loved before, and to not have girlfriends to go shopping with.

Floyd picked up the blinking phone line in the bullpen. "Sergeant Swenson. How can I help you?"

"Floyd, this is Barb, at the drugstore. Remember the picture of the dead guy? The one with his chest all cut up."

"I can't get it out of my mind. I have a copy in front of me"

"A guy at the Rocky Mountain Photo Lab told me I shouldn't have developed the film myself because they use special techniques to bring the colors out better. Since it was too late to do anything about that, he suggested I send him the image to see if he could bring out any of the detail better with the photo-shop programs he uses. I just got his version of the picture back. You've got to see it."

Floyd pushed aside the county auditor's report he'd been reading. "I have nothing going on right now. I'll be there in a few minutes."

Floyd was locking the envelope with the photo and CD in his desk when the dispatcher paged him. He walked to the dispatcher's cubicle and said, "I was heading out. What's up?"

"There's a call for Pam Ryan on line one, and she's out of service right now and not answering her cell-phone. Do you want to take it?"

"This is Floyd Swenson. Deputy Ryan is out of the office right now. Can I help you?"

"I don't know," the female voice said. "Pam Ryan left a message on my home voicemail, asking me to call her back. She mentioned that she was investigating my brother's disappearance."

"Are you Aaron Roberts' sister?"

"Yes, my name is Jennifer Zollner."

Floyd's mind raced as he tried to remember references to Aaron Roberts' family in the old reports. He knew about the parents, but had only a fleeting memory of a reference to Aaron's sister. "Deputy Ryan and I are working on the re-opened investigation. Were you living in Pine City when Aaron disappeared?"

"I've lived in Cottage Grove, south of St. Paul, since high school. I met my husband right after I graduated, and he works for the refinery on highway 61, so we bought a house here when we got married."

"Do you remember anything special about the night Aaron disappeared?"

"I talked to a deputy right after Aaron disappeared. I told him Aaron was at our house the weekend before, but I never saw him again." Jennifer paused, and then asked, "Why are you asking all these questions now? Is it because of my parents? I called home after

I got Deputy Ryan's message and no one answered, which is unusual. Has something happened to them?"

"Well, your father's in jail. We've placed your mother in a women's shelter. I can pass a message to her and ask that she call you."

"Dad beat her up again." It was a statement and not a question.

"She was treated at the emergency room and released," Floyd said. "You don't sound surprised by the fact that your father was arrested for domestic battery."

"He's mean, especially when he's been drinking. Since Aaron disappeared Mom's been terribly depressed and he can't deal with her dark moods. I've suspected that he's been abusing her, but she always denies it." A teenage girl's voice yelled in the background and Jennifer put her hand over the phone. "Sorry, the kids are arguing."

"What was going on in Aaron's life right before he disappeared?" Floyd asked. "Was there anything that would lead you to believe he was either in danger or on the verge of running away?"

"Actually, he had turned his life around. Aaron and my husband talked a lot the summer before Aaron disappeared and Keith convinced Aaron that he might be good enough at math to be an engineer. Aaron took the SAT test and scored very high in math aptitude. He applied to the University of Minnesota and was accepted into a chemical engineering program. He would've started that following the spring semester." Jennifer paused, then asked, "But why are you re-opening the investigation now? That all happened like fifteen years ago."

"We found a picture of the group that were together the night he disappeared. He was with Ken Solstad, Kathy Tucker, Melissa Smith, Mike Nelson, and Betsy Ring. Do any of those names sound familiar?"

"I don't know any of the last names, but I remember Ken and Kathy. Aaron and Ken were really close all through high school. I think they got in trouble several times for drinking or smoking dope. Aaron mentioned that Ken was home from the Army when he was here. It sounded like Ken had turned into a bully. Aaron was actually looking forward to Ken returning to the Army so life would settle down."

"Tell me what you remember about Kathy."

"Wow, that's some ancient history. Aaron and Kathy had dated since high school. Mom told me she really liked Kathy, and I think there was pressure being put on them to get married. I remember Kathy being the star of the basketball and volleyball teams and, when I met her, thinking she was such a tomboy. She'd shoot baskets with Aaron at the high school and she'd always embarrass him."

"Kathy says they had a fight the night Aaron disappeared, but she was too drunk to remember what happened after they fought."

There was a long pause before Jennifer answered. "I don't think that's right. Kathy was an athlete — she didn't drink. She always took great pride in her athleticism and I remember her lecturing Aaron about his drinking and smoking."

Floyd froze. Kathy had been arrested for a DWI after Aaron's disappearance, but he couldn't recall any violations before. Why would she lie about drinking that night unless she needed a convenient and reasonable excuse for not revealing what she'd seen? He made a mental note.

"I suppose that could've been what Aaron and Kathy argued about the night he disappeared," Floyd suggested.

"I doubt it. Aaron quit smoking and had cut way back on his drinking before he was accepted at the University. He and Kathy had been growing apart for a while, and I think their relationship was over. Now that I think about it, maybe he told her they were through that night. Aaron told my husband that his life was on a new track, or something like that. He said Kathy was a part of the old life."

"I wonder if Kathy was terribly unhappy about Aaron's new path."

"I know at least two people were unhappy about Aaron's choices; My father didn't like the idea of his son as a college kid, and Ken Solstad told Aaron that spending money on school was about as stupid as throwing it out the window. I suppose you might add Kathy to that list if Aaron dumped her."

"Was it just Aaron registering at the university that caused all the commotion?"

"It was his whole lifestyle change. Aaron started coming to the Cities for concerts and Twins games. He stayed with us and met new friends. They were clean cut and not into spending every night killing brain cells in a bar. He saved some money and bought a car that ran all the time and he started wearing clothes without holes and grease. He got a job at a coffee shop near the University and moved into an apartment with some other students."

"Have you heard from Aaron since then?"

There was a long pause.

"I don't understand what you mean. Do you think he might be alive?" Jennifer asked.

"We can always hope."

"I gave up hope," she sighed. "He's never called. He's never stopped by. The only way I'll ever hear from Aaron is if I hire a clairvoyant."

"Did you ever call his roommates to ask if they'd seen him?" Floyd asked.

"Aaron was very protective of his new life. I didn't have his address or phone number. When he called, and that was rarely, it was from the coffee shop."

"Please call either Deputy Ryan or me if you think of anything else."

"Wait! Before you hang up, tell me where Mom is."

"I can't because she's in a safe house. I promise that I'll have her call."

"What's going to happen to my father?"

"The county attorney filed charges of domestic battery and assaulting an officer against him today, and bail was set. I don't think that he's posted bail."

"They'll let him out. Mom won't admit that he hit her."

"A deputy overheard a fight and witnessed your mother's injuries. That's all that's required to file domestic battery charges. He also assaulted three deputies and a state trooper during the arrest."

"Will you do something for me?" Jennifer asked.

"I can try."

"Don't let Mom go back to him. One of these times he's going to kill her."

Floyd paused, then asked, "Has your father ever assaulted you?"

There was silence until she whispered, "He hit everyone in the house when he got drunk."

"Did you ever tell a teacher or counselor about it?"

"I was afraid to, and he was always careful not to leave bruises where my teachers would see them."

"Is he capable of killing someone?" Floyd asked.

"When he's drinking, I think he's capable of anything."

"Do you think he could've hurt Aaron?"

"When he's drinking, he's capable of anything."

The line went dead.

CHAPTER 28

Floyd parked in downtown Pine City and walked the few blocks to Gordy's Drugstore past old brick buildings built with apartments on their second floors. He waved to Mrs. Slinkard, his fourth grade teacher, who was sitting by her window fan watching people passing by. The afternoon heat radiated through Floyd's shoes and his lungs struggled to draw oxygen from the hot, humid air. When he stepped into the drugstore his shirt was streaked with sweat. The air conditioning quickly turned his damp shirt clammy.

"Everyone in town will have pneumonia by the time this hot weather breaks," Gordy said. He was taking inventory of the card rack near the cash register when he saw Floyd.

"Isn't that good for business?" Floyd asked.

"It makes no difference. The bulk of our business comes from people who are on maintenance medications for chronic illnesses. The cold supplies aren't a high-margin item and I've always got too many when I don't need them and too few when I do need them.

Now that we're required to keep the cold remedies behind the counter so that people don't make them into methamphetamine, it's even more of a bother."

"As much as that's a bother for you, controlling the cold medicines really put a dent in the meth labs. For a while we had to watch every abandoned house to make sure someone wasn't cooking meth in it. That, and the number of arrests we're making for meth distribution and use has dropped off. It was terrible to see those messed up people with their teeth falling out, robbing houses to pay for their next hit."

"I don't know, Floyd," Gordy said. "It seems like drug use is like a big balloon; when you squeeze out one drug, a different drug takes its place. Meth use goes down and Ecstasy goes up. We control Oxycontin and Vicodin use and heroin shows up. I don't think there's a solution."

"Barb's been doing a great job for me on the picture investigation," Floyd said, changing the topic and hoping to create some goodwill between Barb and her employer. Floyd assumed that most of Barb's effort was at the expense of the drugstore, but he didn't want to open a sore topic.

"She's a good worker," Gordy replied. "The women were put off by her some at first, but once people get to know her they see how hard she works for them and what good work she does. My sales of photographic equipment and supplies have more than doubled since I hired Barb. People used to bring their film and

SD cards to Walmart for cheap photographic prints, but now they're bringing them here and Barb sometimes spends half an hour with a customer to help them crop photos and order enlargements."

"I sense there's a, 'but' lurking behind your words."

"Well, she's a little flaky sometimes, and I wish she'd show up on time more often." Gordy smiled. "But I'll put up with it as long as she keeps people happy. By the way, I understand Mary is throwing a wedding shower for Barb tomorrow at your house. My wife said she was surprised when Mary called, but she couldn't be more pleased that she's been invited."

"I hope you told that to Barb. Mary says she's very insecure and really doesn't feel comfortable as the center of attention."

"She doesn't feel comfortable at a party with women. I'd bet she would eat up the attention if the attendees were all men. You should see her work the old guys who come in with pictures and camera repairs. I swear she could sell books to a blind man."

"I doubt that a blind man would appreciate the view," Floyd said. He nodded toward the camera counter where Barb was leaning over the counter showing a middle-aged man how to operate a demo camera. His eyes spent equal time on the camera and Barb's cleavage.

"I'll bet you a dollar he buys that camera," Floyd said.

"His wife is buying groceries," Gordy said. "If she gets back before Barb closes the sale she'll drag him out by his ear."

As they drank coffee and watched, the man reached for his wallet and Barb went to the cabinet behind the counter to get a boxed camera. "You win this time," Gordy said, pulling out his wallet and handing Floyd a dollar bill.

"It's hard to believe someone like Sandy Maki would have anything to do with a woman like Barb," Gordy said as the man accepted his new camera and thanked Barb. "She seems like such an unlikely match for a deputy."

"I think Sandy saw the softness under Barb's brash exterior. They were thrown together when she left her biker boyfriend. She needed someone like Sandy and he found that he liked someone smart with a hard exterior. It's not easy being a cop's wife, and I think Barb can tolerate his strange hours and the chilly response he gets from some people when they're out together, especially those he's arrested."

"Excuse me, I've got someone at the pharmacy counter," Gordy said, setting down his coffee cup and ducking behind the counter.

"Excuse me, ma'am, I came to see some pictures," Floyd said playfully.

"I just happen to have some here for you to see." Barb took a manila envelope from under the counter.

"Like I explained, this photo lab specializes in recovering old film and pictures." She spread four eight-by-ten-inch enlargements on the counter alongside a CD in a plastic case. "They sent me an electronic file after they enhanced the development. I made two prints of each picture with different color balance and downloaded their file onto a CD for you."

Floyd stared down at two pictures of the man's bare chest. In both pictures the blood was more vividly colored than in the first pictures Barb had printed. The contrast was sharper and it left Floyd even more convinced the person in the picture was indeed Aaron Roberts.

The other picture was of the five friends sitting at a table. He could make out details of the Beroun bar in the background that hadn't been visible in the original picture. The color and length of Aaron Roberts' hair was consistent between the pictures. Betsy Ring and Mike Nelson looked drunk and happy. Melissa Smith looked unhappy. Aaron and Kathy looked sober and pained. Jennifer Zollner's comments about Kathy not drinking came to mind and he looked at the glasses on the table. The glass in front of Kathy contained dark liquid in a distinctive tulip-shaped Pepsi glass while all the others had clear amber liquid he assumed were beer.

"Look at the cuts on his chest," Barb said, diverting Floyd's attention from the bar photo. "It looks like they were cut in a crosshatch pattern."

"Some are like that," Floyd agreed, "but these others are loops and arches." The blood trickling down from each cut obscured the pattern. The bloody image was almost too much to stare at.

Floyd slipped the pictures and CD into the envelope and tucked it under his arm. "I assume the drugstore will bill the department for this."

Barb shrugged. "I can't. I paid for them myself."

"Have Gordy pay you back, and then bill us."

"He'll shit a brick. The work cost fifty bucks."

"They're worth that," Floyd said. "You used good judgment and found a way to improve our evidence. We'll pay for it."

Floyd held up the envelope and waved to Gordy, who was talking to a customer at the pharmacy counter. "These are great! Barb did a wonderful job on them."

The pharmacist waved like he understood.

Barb was watching William Powell and Myrna Loy in *The Thin Man* when Sandy got home from his shift. She jumped up from the couch and met him at the door with a kiss.

"What got into you?" he asked.

"People are being really nice to me, and I'm learning to like it."

"Who's being nice?"

"Everyone!"

"Give me an example."

"Pam Ryan is picking me up tomorrow morning. We're going to Duluth to pick out a wedding dress and a ring for you."

"That's cool," Sandy said as he peeled off his shirt and walked to the bedroom. "Pam's fun. You should have a great time."

Sandy spread his sweaty clothes over the back of a chair and the laundry hamper. "I'll be really happy when this heat breaks. I hate going back and forth between the air-conditioned cruiser and the hot air all afternoon."

"I watched the news. They said there's a cool front coming through tomorrow. We might get some thunderstorms in the afternoon and evening. Barb watched as Sandy chose fresh underwear from a drawer.

"You never watch the news," Sandy said as he walked to the shower. "You told me it was too depressing."

"People at the store want to talk about stupid meaningless stuff like the weather and terrorism in the Far East. When I watch the news I can talk to them."

"You're really turning a new leaf," Sandy said as he started the shower and stepped into the tub. "Will I still recognize you when you're fully evolved?"

"Of course," Barb said to the shower curtain. "I'm going to be a more refined version of what I've always been." She thought for a second and then said, "Mary said you and Floyd are doing something during the shower tomorrow. What've you got planned?"

"Floyd said he was taking me out for lunch. I think we're going to Hinckley."

"You're not planning a stag party, are you?" Barb's voice held a rare tinge of concern.

"The groom doesn't plan the stag party; his friends do."

"I know what happens at stag parties. Remember, I used to be the entertainment."

"It's traditional," Sandy said, teasing.

A smile spread over Barb's face and she slipped out of her T-shirt. She slid the shower curtain back and stepped into the tub. "This is the only stag party you're going to need," she purred.

CHAPTER 29

The following day Pam arrived at Barb and Sandy's apartment at 9:00 and didn't get a response to the knock on the door. She was about to knock again when Sandy pulled the door open.

"C'mon in. Barb's trying to wake up under the pounding water in the shower and it'll take her a few minutes more to get ready. Would you like a cup of good coffee?"

"Sure. Thanks." She followed Sandy to the kitchen where he took out a second cup and poured coffee. "Do you have any input on what you'd like to see in a wedding dress or ring?" She asked.

"I suppose something subdued and white in a dress, and something round and gold in a ring."

"Smart ass," Pam said with a smile.

"Use your own judgment. I think your tastes will. . .um. . .buffer Barb's. My only request is that you keep the spending under one paycheck."

The sound of the shower stopped and Barb hummed as she dressed. "She's the happiest I've ever seen her," Sandy said. "I think most of her life has been a toilet and she's finally realized what we have is real and permanent." He paused. "Pam's here!" he shouted.

"I'll be another minute or two," Barb replied. "Give her some coffee."

"What are you doing about a ring for Barb?"

Sandy shook his head. "My lips are sealed."

"So," Pam said with sparkling eyes, "you do have plans."

Sandy nodded.

Barb emerged from the bathroom with damp hair, wearing a conservative dark blue blouse and tan shorts. "I'm sorry I'm running a little late."

"Not to worry. There's no schedule or rush," Pam said. "We're going to have a relaxed, fun day."

"Let's go!" Barb said as she slipped on a pair of sandals and fluffed her damp hair with her fingers.

At noon, Sandy met Floyd at the apartment door. "So, where are we headed?" Sandy asked.

"I need to make a stop at the garden center in Hinckley, then I thought we'd have lunch at Tobies."

"We're buying plants?" Sandy asked as they walked to Floyd's pickup.

"I need to talk to Kathy Tucker again."

"Isn't this about the fifth time someone's questioned her?"

"I think it's the third," Floyd said. "She's not coming clean with us and I'll keep asking questions until I get straight answers."

The sky was clear and the heat shimmered off the pavement as they drove the interstate north to Hinckley. Dark clouds colored the western horizon as they turned off the interstate at the Highway 23 exit.

"It looks like we might get a break in the weather," Sandy said. "It's too bad we're in this cycle where the only time we get cool breezes is when they blow in with thunderstorms."

"I'll take a thunderstorm," Floyd said as he turned onto the frontage road. "If we don't get some moisture soon, my grass will blow away."

"I guess that's the advantage of renting. I don't have to worry about the grass."

Kathy Tucker stood in the gravel parking lot with a hose, spraying the bushes and trees with water. She wore a white tank top and denim shorts that showed off her athletic build. Floyd parked near the door to the building, but Kathy didn't acknowledge them.

"Hi," Floyd said. "Have you got a second?" Sandy followed behind.

"Are you buying, or asking more questions?"

"More questions," Floyd replied.

Kathy made no effort to turn off the hose. "Ask away," she said, continuing to water the trees.

"You weren't drunk the night Aaron disappeared. You didn't start drinking until after Aaron disappeared." When Kathy didn't respond he went on. "You were an athlete, and you didn't smoke or drink at all. During Ken Solstad's last night in town you guys were at the bar in Beroun. You drank soda pop all night and were sober when you left the bar."

"What's your point?"

"You've been telling us for years that you were too drunk to remember what happened that night. Why?"

Kathy released her grip on the spray nozzle and let it fall to the ground. She turned slowly and stared at Floyd with contempt. "Because it was the worst fucking night of my life. I've never wanted to remember a second of it." She stomped across the parking lot with determination and threw the door open with Floyd and Sandy close behind.

"That's not the only answer I need," Floyd said as he walked briskly to keep up with her long purposeful strides. "I need to know what happened."

Kathy stopped at the back door and spun around to face Floyd. "All right. If you *have* to know what happened, here it is. Aaron dumped me. I thought we were going to get married and he told me that he had new friends in the Cities and we didn't have anything in common anymore." Tears welled in her eyes and her hands shook. "Aaron was the only person I've ever dated. Ever! I was devastated. I argued with him and then I swore at him. I asked him if he'd been cheating on me and told him that I hated him. I yelled and screamed and he just stood there and took it all. That's why I never realized what happened to Melissa in the car; I was too mad at Aaron and I was yelling at the top of my lungs.

"Ken got out of the car, and I thought he came to see what was wrong. So, I told him that Aaron was a shit and that he'd cheated on me. Ken took my side and he punched Aaron, but Aaron still didn't fight back. Ken threw Aaron in the backseat with Melissa. I didn't realize it at the time, but he probably did that so I wouldn't see what he'd done to her. When he dropped Melissa off, Aaron tried to confront Ken about Melissa. Ken went ballistic and started pounding Aaron. He knocked Aaron down then dragged and pushed him into the backseat of the car, then drove me home. I never saw either of them alive after that."

Tears welled up in Kathy's eyes and she looked around for a tissue or napkin. Finding neither she wiped her nose on the back of her dirty glove, leaving a smear of mud across her face. "Damn you. I hope that you've finally got the answers you needed so bad. Can I go back to my fucked-up miserable life now?"

"What happened to Aaron after Melissa was dropped off?"

"I told you! Ken threw him in the backseat of the car. He was still there when Ken dropped me at home."

"Do you remember Ken's knife, the one with the saw blade on the back edge?"

Kathy hesitated for a fraction of a second. "He showed it off that night. Yes, I remember it."

"Ken took a picture of Aaron tied to a tree with cuts all over his chest."

Kathy pulled off her gardening gloves and wadded them tightly in her hand. With her eyes clenched shut she said, "God, why did you have to tell me that? I have enough terrible visions in my mind without that being the last image I'll have of Aaron." Standing a few inches taller than Floyd she looked down at him. "Did you think I needed a larger helping of guilt?"

Kathy threw her gloves at Floyd's chest, swung the garden shop door open, and stalked through it. It slammed, almost breaking the glass.

"I think you touched a nerve," Sandy said quietly as Floyd brushed bits of dirt off his shirt.

"I'm sure I'm still not getting the whole truth and nothing but the truth. Did you notice how she hesitated a bit before answering my question about the knife? She didn't want to admit something there, but knew I had more information than she thought I had."

They walked back to Floyd's pickup in silence. "If that wasn't the truth, what do you think she's holding back?" Sandy asked.

"I wish I knew."

CHAPTER 30

Thunder rumbled as Pam and Barb pulled into Floyd's driveway. The horseshoe loop was lined with cars and pickups, and the sound of women's laughter carried through an open door. Spot raced to them like a brown streak and slapped their calves with her tail as she circled their feet.

"Good puppy," Barb said, kneeling down and petting Spot, who ate up the attention.

Mary met them at the door and gave Barb a hug. "Did you find a dress?"

Barb was surprised by the show of affection and stammered more than usual. "I. . .I tried on a couple and found one that we both liked."

"Tell us about it," Mary said as she ushered Barb into the room of women. The women quickly flocked around her and listened intently to all the details of the simple ivory dress. Thunder rumbled more closely as they lined up at the kitchen table for coffee, and a buffet of tiny sandwiches and cake.

Barb was opening the last gift when the doorbell rang. Mary was surprised to find a gaunt man, probably in his thirties, standing on the doorstep. He was dressed in a bright floral shirt and linen pants with sandals on his feet. His hair had frosted tips and was carefully styled to look random and messy. His face had red marks that looked like he'd had deep acne in his youth. Although he looked determined, there was an air of discomfort about him.

"May I help you?" Mary asked, noting how tired his sunken eyes looked.

"I'd like to talk to Floyd Swenson," the man said, shifting nervously. "Is he home?"

"I'm sorry, he's not here right now. If you leave a message I'll have him contact you when he returns."

Pam Ryan stepped to the door. "Is something wrong?"

The man shook his head. "I was trying to get in contact with Floyd Swenson. I'll catch him later." The man turned to leave.

"What's your name, so I can tell Floyd who was here."

"Tell him a friend of Aaron Roberts stopped by," the man said over his shoulder as he approached his car.

Pam dashed out the door as lightning flashed, followed quickly by thunder. Mary watched out the open door as Pam sprinted after the man. The other women ran to their cars to roll up windows and then ran back to the house. They watched Pam as she talked to the man standing next to his car. Large raindrops splatted on the cement sidewalk as the wind picked up. Pam's dress flapped in the wind as she put a hand on her thigh to keep it in place.

"Who's the gay guy?" Barb asked.

"I don't know," Mary replied, then paused and asked. "What makes you think he's gay?"

"He's gay," Barb replied. "Did you see how he walked? And look at that outfit. Would any of your husbands be caught dead in a flowered shirt like that and sandals?"

The rain came with fury and Pam ran back to the house. By the time she got to the door she was drenched and her hair was plastered to her head. Mary ran to the linen closet for towels. Pam wrapped a towel around her hair and tried to dry her dress with the other.

"Where are Floyd and Sandy?" Pam asked.

"I think they were going to Tobies for a late lunch," Mary said. "Why?"

"I know why Aaron was attacked." Pam got her purse from the bedroom and took the keys out. "I'm also sure there won't be any more notes left on Floyd's door."

"If you're going out, take this slicker." Mary handed Pam a bright yellow raincoat. Pam wrapped it around herself and dashed for her car.

"Can someone take Barb home if I'm not back in time?"

There was a chorus of affirmative responses.

CHAPTER 31

Pam looked like a drowned rat wandering through Tobies Restaurant with a dripping yellow slicker hanging from one hand. Despite the protection of the slicker, her short blonde hair was plastered to her head like a helmet, and her dress sagged under the weight of the water. She spotted Sandy and Floyd drinking coffee at a table in the corner near the kitchen.

Geez, what happened to you?" Floyd asked. "I thought you were at the wedding shower."

"It's a long story," she said, signaling the waitress for coffee and draping the raincoat over the back of the empty chair.

The waitress brought Pam coffee and topped off Floyd and Sandy's cups while the three sat silently.

"A guy showed up at your house during the shower," Pam said after the waitress left. "He asked for you and Mary explained that you weren't home. She offered to take his name and phone number, but he said he'd get in touch with you later, but added that he was a friend of Aaron's. I followed him to his car. I identified myself as a deputy and asked if he wanted to contact you regarding official business. He was hesitant. I told him that I was working on Aaron Roberts' disappearance but his body language said he wasn't comfortable. He said he really wanted to talk directly to you because he's seen your name in the newspaper. I asked where you could call or meet him and he really didn't want to share that information. What he did say was that he wanted us to leave the investigation alone. His exact words were, 'Enough damage has been done.' I asked him what that meant and he said continuing the investigation would only cause more pain."

"More pain for whom?" Floyd asked.

"He didn't say, but he offered to meet you somewhere discreet. I suggested a restaurant, but he balked."

"So we're not meeting him?" Floyd asked.

"He's parked in the back row of the casino parking lot. I told him you'd be there at 3:30."

Floyd looked at his watch. "That's about five minutes." He stood and threw a ten-dollar bill on the table. "Aren't you coming along?" he asked Pam.

"He made it clear that he wants to talk to you alone."

"How will I know which car he's in?"

"It's a purple Chevy Corsica."

"Purple?" Floyd asked.

"Purple. The guy is very slender and is wearing a flowered yellow silk shirt. We'll wait for you here."

"Is it still raining?"

"Pouring," Pam replied. "Take the raincoat. Mary gave it to me when I left. I think it's yours."

"What do you think this guy wants?" Sandy asked Pam as they watched Floyd walk to the door.

"I think he's going to tell Floyd he was Aaron Roberts' lover."

"No way! Aaron was close to getting married to Kathy Tucker."

"Think about it," Pam said. "Aaron starts drifting away from his drinking buddies here and finds new friends in the Cities. There weren't many openly gay men in Pine County now, much less back then. It's easier to meet like-minded people in Minneapolis. He and Kathy start drifting apart because he realized not only wasn't he in love with Kathy, he really wasn't interested in girls."

"That's an interesting theory," Sandy said. "When I think about Kathy Tucker I think of a tomboy. I heard she was a jock and very competitive, like male jocks. She's tall, slender, and has a more athletic than matronly build. He may have found her more attractive than other women."

"She's close to Aaron's ideal woman until he found someone who showed him that he's not into women at all." Pam stood up. "I've got to visit the lady's room. I'll take a warm-up to my coffee if the waitress comes by."

"Take a comb along just in case you look in the mirror."

Pam reached for her purse. "Is my hair that bad?"

"Don't walk past any children; they might think you're the wicked witch of the west."

Sandy and Pam were sharing an enormous caramel roll when Floyd returned a half-hour later. Pam licked caramel from her fingers and said, "We're betting that guy was Aaron's boyfriend."

Floyd was wet and looked defeated when he sat down. He threw the raincoat over the back of a chair. "It's more complicated than that. Aaron was HIV positive and his friend has full blown AIDS."

Pam drew a deep breath. "I'd guessed that Aaron had come back to tell Kathy that he was gay and to break up permanently. So, what really happened was that Aaron came home to tell Kathy he was HIV positive and that she needed to be tested?"

Floyd nodded. "That's part of it. The other part was Aaron decided it was time to come out of the closet. He was going to tell his family and then drop the bombshell about his blood test."

"Mark Roberts would not handle that well," Pam predicted.

"I don't imagine," Sandy said, "that his drinking buddies would be very supportive either."

"If I were casting a vote," Pam said. "I think that Mark Roberts is the most violent person on the list of people we've interviewed and the most likely to do someone bodily harm." She unconsciously rubbed the ankle injured in the scuffle with Mark Roberts.

Floyd stared out the window, deep in thought. "I don't know. Mark's demeanor when he's drinking is certainly a problem. I'm not sure Aaron ever dropped the news on his parents. I think it was Ken Solstad's knife that did the damage we saw in the photo and it was probably Ken who wielded it."

"Everyone keeps talking about how bitchy Ken was that night," said Sandy. "I think I have to go with Floyd and put Ken Solstad at the stop of the list of suspects."

Floyd continued to stare out the window. "Something else is nagging at me. When I talked with Ken's mother, she mentioned how gentlemanly he was when he came home from Korea, but within a few days he was back to being the old Kenny again. I have a hard time seeing someone make a personality turn-around like that in the span of a few days. I wonder if he picked up something mood-altering. I've seen a lot of cases where people snort or shoot-up some drug and they either lose all inhibitions or get angry."

"I don't know that he needed anything other than alcohol and his old buddies," Pam replied. "Look at Mark Roberts; he holds down a job and lives a semi-normal life until he drinks himself into a rage."

Floyd let out a deep sigh and sipped his coffee. He said, "Aaron's friend didn't want to tell me his name but I got his license number and I'm sure we'll be able to track him down again. Let's call him Mr. G for the time being. Mr. G wants us to drop the investigation. He thinks that Aaron never got to tell his parents or

Kathy and it's better to let things lie than to air dirty laundry in the community."

"I'm guessing it's too late for Kathy Tucker," Pam said. "I'll bet a week's pay that was the topic of the fight she and Aaron had the night before he disappeared. Maybe she was so upset she lost control. She'd have a pretty strong motive in a second-degree murder case if we had corroborating evidence."

"Nah," Sandy said. "She loved him, and even if she were really upset, I don't see her cutting him up like that. A knife is a man's weapon, especially when you consider the sadistic way Aaron was tortured. Kathy couldn't do that. My money's on macho Army guy, Ken Solstad. I can see him getting drunk, learning that his drinking buddy is gay, and going ape-shit. The pictures are in his camera, and I think he did the deed."

"I can't argue," Floyd replied. "Either of them might've been driven crazy by the announcement. I can even see Ken pulling out his K-Bar knife and slashing Aaron, but I don't know why he'd take a picture of Aaron."

"What we're missing," Pam explained, "is that Aaron wasn't found tied to the tree the next day, or the next spring. The bottom line is that we don't know what happened *after* Aaron was tied to the tree. Where is he, or where is his body?"

Floyd stood and gathered the raincoat. "It's time to talk to Kathy Tucker again. Anyone want to ride along?"

"I'm with you," Pam said, snatching the raincoat from Floyd's hand. "Sandy has to go home to ooh and aah over the shower presents."

"Did Barb choose a dress?" Sandy asked.

"Yes," Pam replied, "and it's not the backless one with a neckline that plunged to her navel or the sheer one she planned to wear without underwear. You owe me big time."

"Tell me it didn't cost a paycheck," Sandy said to their backs.

"It didn't cost a paycheck," Pam said over her shoulder. She leaned close to Floyd and whispered, "It cost two paychecks."

Floyd shook his head and held the door against the strong winds driving the huge raindrops. Pam's hair was plastered to her head again and, despite the raincoat, rivulets of water ran down her neck soaking the front of her dress.

Kathy's car was parked in the driveway at her home, which was only a quarter-mile from the restaurant. The pounding rain had flattened the greenery and stripped the blossoms from the flowers in her yard. Water spilled over the retaining walls separating the carefully tended plots. Marigold, geranium, and dahlia leaves floated in the puddles and six-foot hollyhocks struggled to stand against the house.

Floyd led the run to the front of the house and pushed the doorbell. Pam followed and stood downwind from him where he blocked some of the pelting rain.

The inside door opened and Kathy stared at them blankly, making no effort to invite them in out of the rain. "Haven't you bothered me enough?" she demanded.

"Could we come in?" Pam asked.

Kathy pushed the screen door open and backed up far enough so they could enter, but didn't invite them any further. "What do you want this time?" she asked as water dripped onto her tile floor.

"We need you to come clean with us." Floyd said. "You've given me at least four versions of the night Aaron disappeared. I also had a conversation with a man from Minneapolis who claims he knew why Aaron was coming home that weekend. It doesn't match your version of events. Before we get into that, I'd like to give you one more chance to set the story straight."

"I have nothing to add." Kathy reached for the door.

"We know Aaron was HIV positive," Pam said softly.

Tears sprang from Kathy's eyes and a shudder ran through her body, but she didn't speak.

"We know he was gay," Floyd said. "He told his Minneapolis friends he was coming home to come out of the closet and let everyone know about his HIV. How many people did he tell?"

Kathy hung her head, unable to speak.

"Did he tell you before you left the bar?"

Kathy shook her head. "No," she croaked, staring at the floor.

"That's why you had the big fight?"

Kathy nodded as tears rolled down her cheeks. She patted her pockets, and pulled out a tissue to wipe her nose. Pam started to say something but Floyd put his hand on her arm and shook his head. They let the silence work on Kathy.

After several seconds Kathy said, "Do you have any idea how hard it is? Aaron's the only guy who ever asked me out. I've always been an outcast because I'm strong and tall. Other guys thought I was too competitive or too much of a tomboy and they couldn't deal with a self-confident female jock. Aaron was gentle and sweet. He never tried to compete with me. He let me be who I was and I never wanted to be with anyone else.

"When he told me he was gay, I lost it. I thought he was lying and then I thought he was playing a joke. Do you have any idea how hard it is on your femininity to have the guy you love tell you he's decided he likes men better? Do you?" She shouted. Kathy started to pace in the small entryway.

"Let me tell you how hard it was. All the other girls in high school talked about how they held their boyfriends off, then how they gave in to sex until after they'd been petting for weeks or months. Aaron never tried to be sexual with me. Never. I had to put his hand on my breast so I could tell the other girls we'd been to second base. I had to seduce *him!*" We went out one night and I talked him into parking by McCormick Lake. We went for a walk and I dragged him into the bushes and I made love to him while he lay on his back dumbfounded. It wasn't fun, exciting, or sexy. He never mentioned it afterwards and he never made an attempt to have sex again."

"So, Aaron being HIV positive didn't affect you?"

She looked down as tears flowed down her cheeks and dripped onto the tile. "I'm positive, too. The drugs cost me five-hundred bucks a month." Kathy paused and wiped her nose again. "One time! We had crappy sex one time and I get HIV! Damn him!"

"What happened after the fight?" Pam asked.

Kathy shrugged.

"Let me try a scenario on you," Floyd said. "Then, you tell me which parts are correct.

"Aaron was sitting in the front seat of the car with you, and whispers to you that he needs to talk. You walk outside and he tells you that he's gay, he's HIV positive and you need to get a blood test. You freak out and tell him just what you think. Ken gets out of the car and asks what happened. You're so mad that you blurt it out in the worst terms and Ken goes crazy, punching and kicking Aaron. Ken dumps Aaron in the backseat and drives Melissa home." Floyd paused. "Am I getting it?"

"Pretty much," Kathy replied quietly.

"Once Melissa is in her house, Ken starts talking wildly about teaching Aaron a lesson. He pulls him from the car, punching him and shoving him into a snowbank before jamming him back into the car. He's probably talking about how they take care of gays in the Army. He maybe even makes some comments about his K-bar Army knife. At this point, you're in shock and you've shut out most of what's happening. Ken's driving around, ranting with Aaron unconscious in the backseat.

"Ken stops the car in the middle of nowhere. He climbs out of the car and drags Aaron out while you watch in terror. Before you can stop what's going on, Ken strips off Aaron's clothes and ties him to a tree."

Floyd stops at that point and looks at Kathy, who's staring at the floor. "What happened after that?" he asked.

Still looking at the floor Kathy said, "Aaron started to come around, and Ken threatened him with that terrible knife. He cut off Aaron's shirt and pants, then told Aaron to change his mind, to admit he wasn't queer. Aaron just sat there is his underwear shivering. He didn't say a thing, and that made Ken even madder." Kathy choked up and stopped to blow her nose.

"What happened to Aaron's chest?" Pam asked.

"When Aaron didn't respond, Ken sliced him. I shrieked and Aaron screamed in pain, but Ken just glared at me." Kathy broke into sobs. "I tried to stop him, but he pushed me away. He tied Aaron to a tree then cut and cut. There was so much blood but Ken kept screaming at him. I think Aaron passed out from the pain at some point. When Ken was done he jammed the knife into my hand and told me to teach Aaron a lesson. He said Aaron had more than cheated on me; he'd cheated on me with a man."

Kathy stopped, looked up, hoping for a sign that she'd shared enough. The silence ate at her and she went on, "I was trapped. Ken was drunk, screaming at me to use the knife. I'm sure he thought I was so mad that I was going to kill Aaron, but I saw this pathetic man I'd loved and nurtured for five years. He was half frozen and bleeding from cuts all over his chest and all I wanted was for the madness to stop.

"I was going to cut Aaron loose when Ken told me to wait. He went for the camera and I stood by Aaron, not sure of what to do next. I knelt down behind Aaron. I must've been crying at that point. All I remember was whispering in his ear that I was sorry and that I'd come back for him as soon as I could get rid of Ken. I cut the rope behind Aaron's back, and then I thrust the knife into the tree behind him so it looked to Ken like I'd buried it into Aaron's ribs. When I stood up, Ken took a picture and said he wanted to show his Army buddies how people in Pine County dealt with homos.

"Ken drove me home and told me we'd done the right thing by ridding the world of another homo. I was a basket case. I ran into the house. As soon as Ken pulled away I got the car keys and drove back to Aaron. He'd come around and had crawled on his hands and knees to a cabin where he was leaning against the siding. He was nearly blue when I put him into the car with the heater blasting. His teeth started to chatter and we held each other for the longest time. He never seemed to warm up and his chest started to bleed again, so I said I'd drive him home or to the hospital. He refused saying he needed somewhere safe to go for the night. We'd been sitting in the car next to the cabin for a couple hours. Aaron said we should break into the cabin and start the furnace. He said it was the only place he'd be safe. We couldn't get the cabin door open so I went back to the tree and got Ken's knife and pried a window latch loose. I crawled in and started the furnace while Aaron stayed in the car. When it started to get warm inside I helped him into the cabin and put him into a bed with some electric blankets I found. I fed him some Spam we from the cupboard and a cup of hot chocolate mix from a package, and then promised that I'd be back in the morning with clothes and some bandages for his chest." Kathy took a deep breath and let it out, stopping the narrative.

"What happened in the morning?" Floyd asked.

"Aaron was gone. The door was unlocked and the furnace was off. Even the bloody sheets were gone from the bed. I thought maybe Aaron had called someone to pick him up, but there wasn't a phone. My next thought was that Ken had gone back, so I drove to Solstad's. Ken was driving away. I stopped him before he got to the interstate and I asked him what had happened to Aaron. He looked confused and reminded me that we'd left him dead, tied to a tree. He also told me not to go there, to just let someone find the body in the spring and to act surprised when I was asked about it."

"So," Floyd summarized, "you don't think Ken went back?"

"I don't know. I've asked myself the same question a thousand times."

"Why didn't you tell us this story before?" Pam asked.

"Because. . .because it's crazy. I didn't want to talk about Aaron dumping me. I didn't want to tell anyone he was gay. I sure as hell didn't want anyone to know that I'm HIV positive. And, I was always afraid that I'd committed some crime and would go to jail."

"If you'd told the original investigators this story," Floyd said, "they might've been able to find Aaron."

Kathy shrugged. "I was confused and afraid."

"Ken's rage was fueled by more than alcohol and his homophobia," Floyd said.

Kathy was about to answer when she hesitated and bit her lower lip. "Ken had scored some Ecstasy that night and he was pushing it on all of us. I don't do drugs, period, and Aaron refused. Mike and Betsy were happy, high and they were all over each other. The Ecstasy had the opposite effect on Kenny. Instead of getting mellow and funny, he got edgy and mean. He was on a bad trip and I'm sure the drugs fueled his reaction to Aaron's announcement."

Kathy leaned against the wall, covered her face with her hands and slid to the floor. "It's my fault," she sobbed. "I was mad at Aaron and I told Kenny that he was gay hoping to . . . I don't know, maybe get even or get revenge. I killed him. I used Ken as the weapon and I killed Aaron. I should never have left him alone."

Pam knelt next to Kathy and put a hand on her arm. "You didn't kill Aaron. You had no control over Ken's rage or his frenzied knife attack. There's no way to know how Ken might've reacted if you'd stepped in to stop him."

"I'm just a shit," Kathy said, wiping her cheeks with the back of her hand, then pushing herself up from the floor. "I've replayed that night in my mind a million times and every time there was something I could've done to stop Kenny."

"Kathy," Floyd said, "we're not sure what happened after you left Aaron at the cabin, but we've uncovered some clues to what happened, and Aaron may have left the cabin under his own power, which would say he survived Ken's attack."

"We think Aaron might've stolen an ATV from one of the cabins and then drove it to Round Lake. Do you have any idea why he'd go there?" Pam asked.

Kathy hesitated a fraction of a second, then shook her head.

A gust of wind slammed the house and the sound of hail hitting the windows diverted Kathy. "Oh, hell.

I've got to run to the garden center and cover the hostas. This hail will rip them to shreds." She sprinted for the back door and grabbed a ring of keys off a hook near the door. "Close the door behind you!" she yelled as she sprinted for her car. They watched Kathy back out of the driveway and speed down the street.

"Do you believe her?" Pam asked.

"I believe at least ninety percent of it. The guy who owns the cabin reported someone broke in and ate a can of Spam. There's no way she would know that unless she'd been there."

"She said Aaron didn't have any clothes, so I doubt he would've walked any further than the garage with the ATV."

"Most cabin owners leave some clothes and old jackets around, so I don't think a lack of clothing would have kept him there. On the other hand, Passenger Lake is a long way from anything, especially in the winter. There aren't any permanent homes for miles in any direction. Why would he pick Round Lake as his destination?"

"Without a phone," Pam said, "he couldn't have called for a ride. So maybe he knew someone there or knew where he could find a phone. I wonder who he would have called?"

"They pay us the big bucks to figure out mysteries like that," Floyd said with a smile.

"What big bucks?" Pam asked.

CHAPTER 32

By the time Pam and Floyd retrieved her car and got back to his house the guests were gone and Mary was washing dishes. Spot, looking like a muddy drowned rat, raced to meet them as they pulled into the driveway. The heavy rain had given way to a steady sprinkle, providing the slow saturation the ground needed to recover from the searing heat and strong winds. Cooler air accompanied the rain and Mary had opened the windows to take advantage of the fresh air.

Floyd pecked Mary on the cheek while Pam called the dispatcher and gave them the license plate number to identify the owner of the purple car.

"How'd the party go?" Floyd asked.

"I think everyone had a good time. Barb got some nice gifts and we laughed a lot. Most of the women had met Barb, but had never really had a chance to talk with her or get to know her."

"Don't you mean that most had avoided her?"

"Let's not go there right now," Mary said, glancing at Pam who was talking to the dispatcher. "Barb was like a little kid at Christmas and her excitement was contagious."

Pam hung up the phone as she made notes on a pad mounted on the wall. "Mary, I'm really sorry I ran out on you. Did I miss much?"

"We had coffee and everyone went home after that. You were here for the games and gifts. That was the biggest part."

"And I'm here for the cleanup," Pam said. "Hand me the dishrag."

"You don't need to."

"Why don't you start putting away the clean dishes," Pam said. "I'm washing." She spoke with kindness, but also with authority. Floyd smiled as the two women dove into the stacks of dirty dishes while he retreated to the living room.

"Floyd, I made a note of the car owner's name on the pad next to the phone," Pam said. "He's Steven Parker, with an apartment on Groveland Avenue in Minneapolis. You had a message at the courthouse from the BCA. They got a match on the prints from the envelope. It seems Mr. Parker has a record in Minneapolis for soliciting a male prostitution decoy."

"Too bad we didn't talk to him a couple days ago so we could've saved the time and money of tracking down his prints on the note and envelope," Floyd grumbled.

"I wonder where the K-bar knife is?" Pam asked, handing a glass platter to Mary. "Kathy said she used it to break into the Passenger Lake cabin. If it's not there, I suppose it's wherever Aaron is."

"Unless," Floyd added, "it's still wherever Aaron stopped at Round Lake."

Floyd took the phone book out of the drawer and flipped through the pages until he located the name he was seeking. He dialed the number and waited.

"Who are you calling?" Mary asked.

Floyd put a finger into the air. "Hi, Alex, this is Floyd Swenson. I talked to Karen a couple days ago about some pictures we found on Ken's camera — the one she sold at the garage sale. It's caused us to re-open the investigation into Aaron Roberts' disappearance, and I'm trying to track down some loose ends. Several people have mentioned Ken's military knife and I was wondering if it was among Ken's gear when you went through it?"

Floyd put his hand over the receiver and said, "He doesn't remember it, but he's asking Karen."

"Yeah, Alex, it was the long knife with saw teeth on the backside." Floyd listened again, and then said, "Thanks for checking. I'll let you know if we turn up anything."

"There wasn't a knife in either the stuff Ken left behind, or in the gear the Army shipped back to them after the accident so that matches Kathy's story about Ken not returning to the scene."

"Kathy told us," Pam explained to Mary, "that she'd used the knife to break into the Passenger Lake cabin, so whoever has the knife was with Aaron after Kathy left."

"Unless it was left at the cabin," Mary suggested.

"I'll talk to the old guy who owns the cabin again," Floyd said. "You ask Kathy if she's got the knife."

"Are you kidding?" Pam asked. "There's no way I'm talking to Kathy again after the scene at her house. I'll talk to the old guy and you talk to Kathy."

"I've got seniority," Floyd said as he ducked out of the house and sprinted to his cruiser.

"Dammit!" Pam said. "I always get the crappy jobs no one else wants."

Mary smiled and took a plate from Pam's hand and wiped it. "Floyd says you're a pretty good investigator. I suppose that finding the key clues in the crappy jobs is what solves the crimes."

"You sound like Floyd," Pam said with irritation. "He always recites some philosophy when I get mad."

"Does it work?"

"Sometimes I get a gem out of his words. Most times I think he just likes to talk and I'm more polite than the guys."

"What do the guys do?"

"They ask him if he's been smoking evidence out of the property room."

Mary smiled and said, "There was one thing you missed. Barb was packing up her presents and she tipped over the box with the sheer black nightgown.

When she picked it up Joanne made some comment about putting spice into their wedding night. Barb told her she might have to try it out before then. That gave the women quite a laugh."

"Poor Sandy. He's going to get so much grief when I tell the other deputies."

"That would be cruel."

"Yes, it *will* be." Pam punctuated the comment with a sly smile.

Floyd pulled into the driveway of the red cabin on Passenger Lake. Before he got out of the cruiser Ron Birkholz had the front door open and the three-legged cat came hopping out.

"I haven't had this much company in the last ten years." The owner held out his hand and said, "Glad you're back. You were here the other day with that blonde with the goofy tattoos."

"Hello, Mr. Birkholz."

"C'mon in and please call me Ron." Birkholz walked back to the cabin before Floyd could answer. "I've got coffee on if you'd like a cup."

Ron poured two cups of coffee and set one in front of Floyd. "What crime we solving today?" He pushed a well-worn vinyl-covered chair back for Floyd and sat on the other side of a scarred drop-leaf table.

The inside of the cabin was Spartan. A row of pegs near the back door held a variety of jackets, rain gear, and caps. The kitchen area was small with appliances that appeared to date from the 1940s. The red linoleum floor matched the counter tops, and the open area beyond the kitchen morphed into a living room that probably had once been a porch. The threadbare furniture looked like it had been rejected from a garage sale. Large windows and French doors looked out over a deck with Adirondack chairs, and Passenger Lake beyond.

"It's the same question," Floyd said. "I have more information and that may lead to answers."

"Fire away," Birkholz said, taking apparent pleasure from the company and being the center of attention.

"We checked the rope you gave us, and it has human blood stains. After talking to a lot of folks we got someone to admit they broke in here the night the kid was tied to the tree. Was there much damage?"

"Not really. If they hadn't left the front door unlocked and eaten a can of Spam I might never have noticed. I never even called it in because it wasn't like I was out a lot of money or had any damage to speak of. I kinda figured some kids had been ice fishing and needed a place to warm up."

"The girlfriend opened a window with a knife and let the injured guy in to warm up. She apparently started the furnace and put the guy into bed with an electric blanket going. When she came back the next day with bandages, the guy was gone and so were the sheets from the bed. We're looking at a couple of possibilities: One is that the guy got warmed up and was afraid someone might come back to get him, so he stole some clothes from the cabin and walked down to your neighbor's garage where he stole their ATV. The other is that someone other than the girlfriend came back and took the guy and the sheets with him. Can you help us nail down one or the other of those possibilities?"

"If sheets were missing, I didn't notice. My wife used to strip the beds most times when we left for the winter, but sometimes she didn't. By spring, I doubt that either of us would've noticed the missing sheets. I sure don't remember her complaining about a set of missing sheets. As for missing clothes," Ron pointed to the row of pegs by the door. "We keep an assortment of Goodwill-quality stuff around for the kids and grandkids when they're here fishing. Sometimes it stays and sometimes it gets carried away. I don't notice and care even less. He could've cleaned the rack off and I wouldn't have cared a bit. I'd just go to the Goodwill store and pick up some cheap replacements."

"How about pants and shoes? We think he was wearing only underwear when he arrived and it was December."

Ron shrugged. "I guess I haven't noticed any missing, but there's lots of cast off shoes, slippers and wool pants too. If my boys were up deer hunting that year they may have left something that later disappeared, but I don't recall anyone asking about missing boots or pants."

"The girl said she used a K-Bar knife to open the window latch. You know the kind, with a long blade and saw teeth on the backside. Did you find one of them lying around the next spring?"

"Now that," Ron said, "I would remember! They cost thirty bucks at the outlet store. Sad news is that wasn't left here." He thought for a second and shook his head. "On the other hand, the cabin was unlocked all winter after they broke in and if they left it here it might've been stolen. It was probably the most valuable thing here." He thought for a second, then added, "You might want to check the garage where the ATV was stolen. I suppose he might've used the knife to pry open the hasp on their garage door."

Floyd finished his coffee. "When you talk to your sons, please ask them if they're missing any hunting clothes."

"I sure will," Ron said as he walked Floyd to the door, "but I doubt any of them care. That's ancient history and their waists are probably too big to fit in any pants that disappeared that long ago."

Floyd looked at the lake where the rain had slowed to sporadic drops. Each raindrop was making its own little ring on the surface as it struck. "The lake's sure pretty. How's the fishing?"

"Slow. The grandkids get a few pan fish but we go over to Sturgeon Lake to catch walleye and bigger crappies."

"Thanks for the coffee."

"I appreciate the company. Coffee's a cheap way to make sure visitors know they're always welcome. The pot is always on. Stop anytime. You don't have to wait until you have questions."

Kathy Tucker's car was alone in the muddy gravel lot at the garden center. Pam parked and stepped around the puddles even through her dress and shoes were already soggy and mud-spattered. A bell tinkled above the door when she stepped in.

Kathy was sitting on a stool stocking the bottom shelf with weed killer. Her shoes were muddy and her calves were splattered with mud halfway to her knees.

"Got time for one more question?" Pam asked.

Kathy looked up with sad eyes. "Can't you guys write them down and come once a week with a whole list of questions?" Kathy stood, her full height towering over Pam by nearly a foot. "What is it this time?"

Pam followed her to the cash register counter. "The knife you used to break into the cabin on Passenger Lake. What happened to it?"

"What do you mean?"

"Did you leave it at the cabin, or did you take it when you left?"

"I don't remember. What difference does it make after all these years?"

"If you left it at the cabin, it wasn't there after Aaron disappeared."

"I didn't take it with me. I must've left it on the table where I cut up the Spam."

"You're absolutely sure you don't have it?"

"Absolutely."

Pam hesitated. "I'm really sorry about your HIV situation. I wish we could get through this investigation without dredging up things like that."

"I'm really sorry you dredged that up too. Being the 'Amazon woman' in this little town is hard enough without everyone avoiding me because I'll be coming down with AIDS someday."

"We don't need to publicize that discovery. It's part of our private notes and it doesn't need to come out unless it's germane to the prosecution of a crime and I can't imagine any scenario where it would be."

"I've lived in this little town my whole life and there are no secrets. You let a word slip to one person some night over a beer and the next day I lose a customer who overheard you say it. Hinckley is the definition of a small town. Everyone knows everyone else's business and secrets are scarce."

"Tell me about Walt," Pam said.

"I'm sure you've already run a background check on him," Kathy said curtly. "He's a former addict who used to steal to support his habit. So, yes, I know about him and his problems — no need to warn me off, if that's what you had in mind."

"I don't like to see people get hurt."

"Yeah, right. Like finding out about Walt's criminal record would've been more painful than the discussion we had this afternoon at my house."

"I'm sorry, but we need to know the truth and you've been less than candid."

"Well, I had my reasons, and the dredging you've done isn't going to bring Aaron back. I doubt it'll yield anything but more pain for those of us who've been trying to forget it for years."

CHAPTER 33

Sandy Maki met Barb during his supper break. When he arrived at the Rock Creek Café, Barb was sitting at the counter talking to the waitress. He took the stool next to her and pecked her on the cheek as every person in the restaurant looked up to check out the cop coming in to eat.

"Hi, babe. How was the party?"

"I was telling Sharon how great it was. Everyone was really nice and I got a pile of gifts."

Sandy smiled. He'd rarely seen Barb get excited about anything, and certainly not about a gathering of women. "So, tell me what was best." He said, picking up a plastic laminated menu that was wedged between the sugar and napkin dispensers.

"What was best? I mean it was all great. We ate fancy sandwiches without crusts that Mary spent all day preparing. Then we all sat down and played silly games, then everyone gave me gifts. I mean we got some really neat stuff, like new towels and flowered pillowcases." Barb's usual slow speech rattled off at a speed that was nearly normal for most people.

Sandy ordered a cheeseburger with fries and asked the question again. "That all sounds great, but what was really special?"

"This sounds corny even to me, but just having the party. Mary invited all these women who I'd met, but didn't really know. They all hugged me and were really nice. We got to know each other and I thought they'd all be stuffy and act like they were too good. But none of that happened. They were nice and asked about my job and what I did for fun. They really cared and treated me like a friend. It was so much more than I expected. I didn't think I could ever be friends with a woman and I was wrong."

"That's fantastic. I heard you and Pam found a wedding dress, too."

"I was looking at some I thought were pretty, but Pam steered me to some that were more. . .conservative. I tried them on and she had me stand in front of the mirror with the saleswoman. They told me the secret was to buy a dress every woman would remember and every man would forget."

"I guess Pam's pretty smart. If you bought one every man would remember, every woman would hate you."

"She didn't say it like that, but that's what she meant. The sales lady agreed with her and we found one that we all liked. Then I had to buy some special underwear that goes with the dress. It. . ."

"I really don't need to know any more than that. Surprise me."

"Everyone asked what we're doing for our honeymoon. Have you made any plans?"

The waitress set Sandy's order on the counter and asked, "Yeah, have you made any plans, big spender?"

"I take it the honeymoon's been discussed beyond the shower."

A retired farmer sitting two stools down from Barb set his newspaper aside and leaned over Barb's shoulder. "Barb had us take a vote on Alaska or the Canadian Rockies. I think Alaska won."

"Alaska? I was thinking we'd go to the North Shore of Lake Superior. There's a lodge in Grand Marias with hot tub rooms that look out over the lake."

An old man and his wife brought their check to the cash register a few feet down the counter from Sandy. The man paid the bill and the woman tapped Sandy on the shoulder. "You know," the woman said, "you're both in your 30s and neither of you have been married. I think you should try an Alaskan cruise to celebrate finding the right person this late in your life."

"I can't believe this! You really did take a vote," Sandy said as he looked around at the patrons who were all smiling at him.

"Oh, settle down," the old woman said. "She's happy and she's sharing it with us. We all had fun. You know, she's really proud of you, too. You're the nicest guy she's ever dated."

Sandy started to laugh. "You really told all these people all that?"

"Yes," Barb said. "I'm really excited. Is that bad?"

Sandy took her face in his hands and kissed her. "It's okay."

"So, we're going to Alaska?"

"I'll see if I can make arrangements Monday, but this is really short notice. If I can't arrange Alaska right now, will Grand Marais be acceptable until we can plan a cruise at our leisure?"

"I haven't been to either place, so they're both okay."

Someone behind Sandy uttered, "Cheapskate," just loud enough for Sandy to hear.

Floyd drove home and found Mary curled up on the couch with a romance novel. "If you let me put dry clothes on," Floyd said, "I'll take you out to supper."

"I don't really need supper. We ate so much at the shower that I'm still full. There are some sandwiches in the refrigerator if you'd like them for supper. I wrapped them up so they wouldn't dry out."

Floyd disappeared down the hallway. "Are you talking about those tiny ones without crust with lettuce hanging out the edges?" he asked from the bedroom.

"Those would be the ones."

"I think I saw Spot eating them in the yard."

"Floyd Swenson! You didn't feed them to the dog!" Mary yelped as she jumped up from the couch and looked out the window, searching for the dog.

Floyd emerged from the bedroom in a dry shirt and pants. "No, but I was just about to if I was going to be forced to eat them for supper." Floyd pulled a golf umbrella from a peg on the basement stairway. "I thought I'd drive down to the Kaffe Stuga for a burger and a piece of homemade pie."

"You're driving all the way to Harris for pie?" Mary asked as she set her book on the end table and slipped on her shoes.

"I'm going mostly for the ride. I've got a bunch of things inside my head that need to get discussed."

"You wait one second, Floyd Swenson" Mary said, standing akimbo. "Let me make this perfectly clear. We are not driving all the way to Harris with you talking about grisly murder pictures and bouncing around ideas about blood. . .and cop stuff. . .and other things that give me nightmares."

Floyd pulled her close and kissed the top of her head. "I'm sorry if I give you nightmares. It's just that you're so easy to talk to, and when we talk things get clearer for me."

Mary gently pushed him back and held him at arm's length. "You sure can come up with a great line sometimes. You know what Pam told me? She told me that the other deputies ask if you've been smoking pot out of the evidence room when you start philosophizing to them."

Floyd gently took her elbow and steered her to the door. "That's only Kerm Rajacich, and he's more of a knock-'em-down-and-drag-'em-off guy, rather than a philosophy guy."

Mary planted her feet when they reached Floyd's truck, and wouldn't move. "I'll go, but there will be no discussion involving blood or bodily fluids. Is that understood?"

"No bodily fluids discussion. That's fine," he said as he held the door for her.

As they pulled out of the driveway, Floyd explained, "I'm sure Aaron Roberts was left for dead outside a cabin on Passenger Lake after Ken Solstad. . ." Mary glared at him in anticipation of the next words. Floyd hesitated. "After Ken hurt him, he left Aaron for dead. Aaron's girlfriend went back and found Aaron huddled against the side of a cabin. She broke into the cabin, got Aaron warmed up and fed him some Spam. When she went back the next day Aaron is gone. We have a report of an ATV stolen from a neighboring cabin. It was abandoned near Round Lake."

"Wow, Ken was pretty calloused about the whole thing," Mary said. "I can't imagine many people would hurt a friend and then leave his body for someone to find in the spring."

"Ken was a piece of work," Floyd said. "He manipulated everyone into going drinking with him, raped his girlfriend, assaulted his buddy and left him for dead. I don't know if he grew up that way or if the Army affected him. At this point, I guess it doesn't make a lot of difference."

"Okay," Mary said, "so you've got Aaron warming up in a cabin. His girlfriend goes back the next day expecting to find him and she finds the place empty. The question is: Did Aaron steal the ATV and if he did, why did he ride it to Round Lake? Maybe it wasn't Aaron who stole the ATV. Maybe he tried to walk to a main road. Maybe his body is in a ditch along the way, or maybe he got disoriented, wandered the wrong direction and got lost in a swamp."

"Those are real possibilities, but most of those bodies show up during hunting season or when someone's dog brings a bone home." Floyd drove a few miles in deep thought.

After his silent contemplation, Floyd said, "There has to be something at Round Lake that drew him there."

"Is there a way to find out?"

"There's always a way to find out. All it takes is patience and looking under the right stone." Floyd said, pulling off the interstate at the Harris exit, "That means asking a lot of people a lot of questions they don't want to answer."

"Pam was injured in a standoff with some drunk yesterday. Is she better?"

"That drunk was Aaron Roberts' father and it turned into more than a standoff. Pam had reason to believe that his wife had been injured and he wouldn't let his wife talk, so Pam called in reinforcements and there was a scuffle in the house. Pam got knocked down and has a sore back and twisted ankle."

"Was his wife injured?"

"She had a couple of cracked ribs. Pam took her to a safe house for battered women. She's blaming herself for being depressed and causing her husband's anger that led to her beating."

Mary was going to ask another question as Floyd pulled into the gravel parking lot alongside the restaurant, but hesitated. "I just realized something," she said.

"What's that?" Floyd asked as he locked the truck.

"You just fed me the juiciest gossip in the county and I can't tell a soul about it, can I?"

"Nope. It's just like when we were talking about the creepy guys who lived behind your mother's house when you were a kid. It's all confidential."

"Well, that stinks. Can I at least admit that I know it when someone else tells me about it?"

Floyd opened and held the door for her and replied. "No. You'll have to act surprised and interested, and whatever you do, don't correct the facts during the discussion."

"Being around you can be a real downer. One night you tell me horrific stories about bloody pictures and rape evidence that leaves me with nightmares. The next night you feed me hot gossip and tell me not to share it." Mary slid into a booth and leaned forward to ask, "What if I forget that I'm not supposed to know and something slips out?"

"You can't pull off the dumb blonde act with me. You're a businesswoman who's kept a struggling business alive in a little town that really shouldn't be able to support it. I think you could match wits with Donald Trump and win."

Mary picked up a laminated menu and smiled. "I think that was a compliment."

"I only speak facts."

"That's right. I forgot that you're Sergeant Friday. 'Just the facts, ma'am,'" she said in her best Jack Webb imitation.

"If you don't stop talking and decide what you're going to order, that last piece of lemon meringue pie will be gone."

The Kaffe Stuga was rustic, with pictures of school children from the past and baseball teams from the era when each little town had a backstop built in a pasture and fielded its own team.

After ordering the burger platter, Mary asked, "Can we move to a topic that doesn't have a plot?"

"Sure."

"I invited Barb to the shop and we looked through the wedding books and chose a nice bouquet for her to carry, corsages for the bridesmaids and boutonnieres for the groom and best man. We're going with a yellow theme to complement her ivory colored wedding dress."

"That sounds nice," Floyd replied as the waitress set cups of coffee on the table and slid a stainless steel container of cream next to them.

"We're paying for the flowers."

He looked up from the cream he was pouring into his coffee. "Who's 'we?'"

"You and I are we."

Floyd nodded. "No father of the bride to pick up the wedding tab and I don't imagine that Sandy and Barb have a lot of savings to cover things either. I can live with that."

Mary reached across the table and took his hand. "We're not 'just living with it,' we're proud to be able to do it. That's what I told Barb."

"She's got no one but Sandy," Floyd said. "I guess that buying the flowers would be a very nice thing to do. I'm glad you made the offer."

"There's one other thing."

"Oh?"

"In all the excitement of the wedding planning and the shower planning, and having the shower at your house, I think I forgot to mention that Barb asked Pam and me to be her attendants."

Floyd saw the sparkle in Mary's eyes and smiled. "That's great."

"I've never been a bridesmaid before. I have to buy a dress. We'll go shopping some evening and pick one out together. Maybe we'll get you a suit at the same time."

"My suit is at the cleaners and I don't need a second one. Maybe one of the girls from the shop would go with you."

"I'd rather have you come along and help me pick it out."

"I'm not really a dress-picking kind of guy. I can appreciate a pretty dress, but I'd be way out of my comfort zone sitting in Herberger's rendering opinions about dresses. Way out."

Mary smiled. "My big, strong deputy sheriff who faces down bad guys with guns, doesn't want to shop for dresses?"

"No."

As dinner arrived she said, "I suppose your presence on a trip to Victoria's Secret to choose some suitable underwear would be out of the question."

"Hey!" Floyd said, pointing to the newspaper box by the entrance. "The Twins won yesterday. That Joe Mauer is really doing a job for them. I'm really glad they moved him from catcher to first base."

"Nice try," Mary said, "but Mauer's been out with an injury." She hesitated, then added, "The shopping trip would be less expensive if you came along."

"I'm sure it would cost me in ways I don't care to consider."

CHAPTER 34

The coincidence of the stolen ATV being found near Round Lake nagged at Floyd, keeping him from sleep. He drove to the courthouse Sunday morning and pulled out a book of property abstracts, looking at the names of the property owners around Round Lake. None of the names seemed familiar, nor did they connect with any of the sextet of partiers. He stood by the county map and traced the roads around Round Lake, trying to find anything that would attract an injured guy on an ATV. There was nothing but seasonal cabins and farmhouses, and there were plenty of them closer to Passenger Lake. If Aaron had stolen the ATV he'd driven past a dozen warm farmhouses with telephones on his way to Round Lake. There had to be a reason he chose Round Lake but the reason wasn't obvious.

The dispatcher paged him as he was making another pot of coffee. "This is Sergeant Swenson, how may I help you?"

"Floyd, this is Kerry in the jail. Mark Roberts has been making a stink for two days. Could you come over and talk to him about where you have his wife stashed. He keeps complaining that you've kidnapped her."

"He hasn't posted bail yet?"

The jailer chuckled. "That's part of the problem. The bail bondsman says the only way he'll put up bond for him is to get a second mortgage on the house. Mark can't find his wife to sign the mortgage papers."

Floyd stared at his steaming cup of coffee, deciding whether to dump it out and go quickly to the jail, or to drink it at a leisurely pace and go to the jail when it was convenient. "Tell Mark I'll be over when I'm through with my coffee."

An hour later, the jailer moved Mark Roberts to an interview room and Floyd met him outside the room.

"He's really hot," Kerry explained. "I think you want me in the room with you while you talk."

"C'mon in," Floyd said, pushing the door open.

Mark Roberts was in a pair of orange jail coveralls with flip-flops on his feet. His belly strained at the coverall zipper and his cuffed hands were resting on the metal table. He looked up with fire in his eyes when Floyd entered the room.

"This is a bunch of bullshit," Roberts said. "You can't hold me. My wife won't press charges."

Floyd took a chair across the table from Roberts while the jailer stood with his back to the only door. "We don't need Sue to press charges anymore. The legislature changed the law a couple years ago and now all we need is to witness the abuse or evidence of the abuse and we can press charges on behalf of the state. I'm surprised your lawyer didn't explain that to you."

Roberts looked past Floyd into the corner. "That snot-nosed bitch had all kinds of stupid ideas. I didn't believe any of her bullshit."

"You didn't like the public defender?" Floyd asked. He pictured the young female lawyer, the newest member of the public defender's office.

"Where's my wife? I've been calling the house every day and she doesn't answer."

"We have her at a safe location."

"Safe from what?"

"Safe from you, mostly," Floyd said. "If you give me a message, I can pass it along."

Roberts' eyes narrowed. "Tell her to get her butt in here to bail me out."

"Hasn't your lawyer contacted Sue already?" Floyd asked.

"She's about as worthless as teats on a boar pig," Roberts replied. "I think she's mad at me anyway. I might've said something that upset her."

Floyd smiled. "She's a little sensitive about people calling her names and swearing at her. I guess she hasn't been a lawyer long enough to develop a thick skin."

"That bitch is too big for her britches," Roberts said, shaking his head. "She thinks she can tell me what to do, and I don't take shit from women."

"I'll tell Sue you want to see her. Is there anything else I can tell her, like maybe you're sorry?"

"I'm sorry your bitch deputy showed up when we were arguing, but I'm not sorry I was fighting with Sue. She needs to be straightened out. All she does is mope around the house feeling sorry for herself. I work my butt off to keep the house together and she sits around crying over sad TV crap."

"She might need treatment for depression," Floyd suggested. "It sounds like she hasn't been dealing well with things since Aaron disappeared."

"Who made you a psychiatrist?"

"I see a lot of people with lots of problems. Sue acts like a person who is dealing with depression. Lots of them get treatment or drugs and are able to cope. Without treatment they stay withdrawn and sometimes end up suicidal. I do know that beatings don't improve depression."

"Fuck you," Roberts muttered.

"I suppose hitting Sue makes you a big man."

"I've never hit her unless she deserved it. You can ask her yourself."

"Tell me about your daughter? Did you hit her too? Is that why she married a guy in the Cities and moved out of the county?"

"Listen, Swenson, you're starting to piss me off. This is a free country and how I discipline my kids is my own business. I can tell you one thing — my kids respected authority and weren't a problem at school.

They knew that if they got in trouble with their teachers they'd be in bigger trouble when I got home. That's the trouble with the country these days, people don't respect their parents."

"How did you and Aaron get along?"

"I kept him in line. He tried to give me lip a couple times, but I set him straight."

"I heard he was thinking about going to the University and you weren't too happy about that?"

"What a fucking waste of money that would've been," Roberts said, sliding back in his chair and crossing his legs. "Aaron could've had a job with the trucking company making twice what any smart-assed college kid was making. It wouldn't take him four years, and it wouldn't cost ten thousand dollars. I blame his sister and her shit-head husband for that. They put all kinds of crazy ideas into his head."

"They didn't convince Aaron that he was gay."

Mark Roberts flew out of the chair and lunged across the table for Floyd. The jailer, caught totally by surprise, watched in a stupor as Floyd twisted to miss the momentum of Roberts' lunge. In one swift motion Floyd pushed Roberts past and onto the floor before the jailer took two steps. Floyd put his knee into the small of Roberts' back as the jailer pushed his face against the floor.

"Aaron wasn't no sissy," Roberts spat at Floyd over his shoulder. "My boy was as tough as any kid in the county. I taught him to fight and drink and he wasn't a queer."

"Sexual orientation has nothing to do with fighting or drinking," Floyd said. "Some people are just wired differently. It's not a choice they make; it's just the way they are."

"Not my boy, and don't you go 'round spreading rumors like that. I'll. . ."

"You'll what?" Floyd asked, keeping the pressure on Roberts' back. "You'll beat me up like you beat your wife? Give it up, Mark. We know that Aaron came home the last weekend he was here to tell everyone he was gay and that he was HIV positive."

"He wasn't queer and he didn't have AIDS!" Roberts screamed. Spittle ran from the corner of his mouth as he flailed and kicked. One heel caught Floyd in the ribs. He grabbed Roberts' ankle and pulled it until the knee popped. Roberts grunted and the resistance ended.

"I'll let go if you stop struggling," Floyd said. "If you keep fighting me, you're going to need knee surgery."

"Let go," Roberts said with a gasp.

Floyd released the pressure on Roberts' knee, but he and the jailer pinned the prisoner to the floor, then fastened the handcuffs behind his back. Floyd helped him stand up.

"My boy wasn't a queer. Who told you lies like that?"

"Several people have told us the same story," Floyd said, setting Roberts back on the chair. "As consistent as they are, it seems like they're telling the truth."

"That's bullshit. He was going with that Tucker girl and they were talking about getting married. I suppose she told you that to get even with him for breaking up with her." Roberts twisted his head and wiped the spittle smeared around his mouth on the shoulder of the jail coveralls.

"I heard it from enough people to know that it's probably the truth," Floyd said, straightening his pants and tucking his shirt in. "I imagine he never told you because he feared your reaction would be just as it was here."

"Well, they're lying to you. If he had a problem like that, I would've taken care of it. No son of mine is going to be a sissy."

"Is that what happened to Aaron?" Floyd asked. "Did you find out he wasn't what you thought he should be and you took care of it?"

Roberts opened his mouth, but for the first time thought about his words and held his tongue. "You're putting words in my mouth."

"What happened between you and Aaron that last night before he disappeared?"

"Nothing. I was on the road."

"When did you hear Aaron had disappeared?"

"I delivered a load in North Dakota and when I talked to dispatch they told me to call home. Sue told me he was missing and that people were looking for him. I think it was like two days after."

"Where in North Dakota were you when you called?" Floyd asked.

"Grand Forks. I had a load of parts for the Air Force base."

"Grand Forks isn't a two-day drive."

"I dropped a load in Minneapolis and then spent a day waiting at the foundry for the Air Force load."

"Your memory of a delivery years ago is awfully good. Most innocent people can't remember where they were last Friday night."

"Could you forget where you were when someone told you your kid was missing?" Roberts asked.

"Probably not," Floyd conceded.

Floyd made calls from his office, first to identify the trucking company Mark Roberts drove for in '98, then to get copies of his logbooks from December. After half an hour he had someone at Consolidated Express promise to fax the pertinent logs that afternoon. He reached for his coffee cup, but decided that his hands were already shaking and more caffeine wouldn't be a good idea.

He stared at the piles on his desk. "I was doing something before all this broke loose."

Floyd read through the December '98 report again, which said a homeowner near Sandstone had found an ATV abandoned in a ditch on his farm. The man said that it had been in the ditch for several days and he hadn't called, assuming the owners would return for it. When no one came back for it he pulled the ATV to his yard and called dispatch to report the abandoned vehicle. The responding deputy found the vehicle and called a tow truck to haul the ATV to the county impound lot. He noted that the state-required license was missing, so he had no way to check ownership. At that time, there were no reports of stolen ATVs so the county held it pending a call from the owner.

Floyd took a box of colored pushpins from his drawer to the bullpen. He started putting pins in the wall map of Pine County to identify all the locations involved in the Aaron Roberts case. He put red pins on the homes of the six friends; yellow pins at Passenger Lake, where the break-ins occurred, the interstate rest area where Aaron's car was abandoned, and Round Lake, where the ATV was found; and blue pins at the bar where the friends were drinking, where the fight between Aaron and Kathy occurred, and where Betsy and Mike claimed to have been necking near Minke Lake.

When he stood back, only two pins were close to each other. Betsy and Mike claimed to be necking within a quarter mile of where the ATV was recovered. "Isn't that interesting?" Floyd said to himself.

"Isn't what interesting?" Pam asked as she walked up behind him.

"It appears that Aaron may have stolen an ATV from a Passenger Lake cabin to make his escape. The

ATV was reported abandoned right here." He pointed to the yellow pin. "Betsy and Mike were necking here," Floyd said, pointing to the blue pin nearest.

The sheriff walked in with an unlit cigar clamped between his teeth and an empty coffee cup in his hand. "What's so interesting?"

"I'm putting up pins representing all the locations involved in the Aaron Roberts disappearance," Floyd explained. "It looks like Aaron may have stolen an ATV the night he disappeared. It was recovered where this yellow pin is stuck."

The sheriff leaned close to the map and looked at the arrangement of pins. "You couldn't have made this arrangement any more random if you'd used a shotgun to pick the locations." He stepped back. "I didn't know we picked up Aaron Roberts' fingerprints from a stolen ATV."

"We didn't know to look for them. The ATV wasn't reported stolen until the next spring."

The sheriff pulled the cigar out of his mouth and pointed at the map. "You mean to tell me that you're conjuring up crazy scenarios trying to tie this Aaron Roberts thing to some old burglaries, too? Tell me we're not spending a lot of the taxpayers' money on this."

"It's costing the taxpayers almost nothing. From here on, Pam and I will work on it on our own time and we won't even charge mileage on our personal cars," Floyd said with a smile.

"Don't use your own cars and you don't need to use personal time, but if the county board finds out we spent one dollar of overtime on this, someone's goose will be cooked." The sheriff jammed the cigar back in his mouth and poured coffee. "Furthermore, if we ignore some other crime because of this, I'll be the one cooking the geese."

The sheriff started for his office, but stopped short of the hallway. "Pam, my wife said the wedding shower you and Mary threw for Sandy's fiancee was great. I guess Sandy's girl, Barb, is quite a character. My wife says she hasn't laughed so hard in years."

Pam watched the sheriff leave. "Is he really mad about the Roberts investigation?"

"You've got to remember," Floyd explained, "the sheriff's job is to run this place within the budget, to keep fifty-one percent of the voters happy, and to keep a majority of the county board members happy. If that happens, he gets re-elected and our budget doesn't get cut."

"He said someone's goose would be cooked."

"Don't worry," Floyd said, waving off the comment. "If he gets too upset I'll tell him that I'm going to retire and he'll cool off."

"How does his compare with our jobs? I thought we were *supposed* to find missing people and arrest bad guys."

"Oh, that's our job. That, and making the sheriff look good enough so that those fifty-one percent of the people will want to vote for him in the next election. You see, there are several things at odds here. The county board wants us on the road 100% of the time and driving past their houses at least once a shift. They want all felonies solved within twenty-four hours and all court papers served the day they're issued.

"We need to do those things, but we also need to do the invisible things that make Pine County a safe and wonderful place to live and raise a family. Part of that is tracking down unsolved crimes and not giving the sheriff too much information that would make him culpable in case something goes very wrong with an investigation."

"He needs deniability," Pam summarized.

"That, and he needs to know enough so he can leverage outside resources for us, like the BCA. He needs enough information to make the press happy and to make it look like we're being competent and diligent. Sometimes, though, I need to plow ahead with something that's not glorious just to make sure we're pursuing our jobs diligently. Those things I do quietly until it's obvious that they're going nowhere, when I drop them, or until they break. Then I feed the information to the sheriff so he can take it to the press and the county board."

"Seems stupid."

"Get used to it, Pam."

CHAPTER 35

The fax machine came to life with a whirr. The tones signified the sound of another machine attempting to complete a connection. Floyd poured a cup of coffee while the sheets slowly fed into the tray.

"You're expecting something?" Pam asked.

"I had a discussion with Mark Roberts today. He left me a little uneasy about his relationship with Aaron, so I called his employer to see where he was when Aaron disappeared."

"He made you uneasy in what way?"

"He's extremely homophobic," Floyd explained. "When I asked about Aaron coming out of the closet just before he disappeared Mark flew over the table at me screaming that his son was no queer."

"Oh, great. Not only is he a misogynist, he's a bigot, too."

"Would you have expected anything less?" Floyd asked as he picked up the fax sheets from the bin. "He said he found out about Aaron's disappearance when he called his dispatcher from Grand Forks two days later." Floyd studied the sheets, and then said, Here he is on Monday, picking up a load in Minneapolis, which means he could have been in Pine City Sunday morning. So much for his alibi."

"Do you think he'd hurt his own son?"

"He told me if he had a son who was gay that he'd straighten him out," Floyd said. "I'm betting that a gay son would be 'way bad' on Mark's list of bad."

The dispatcher's voice crackled over the intercom directing Floyd to pick up line three. He was surprised to hear the librarian's voice.

"Hey, Floyd, it's Brenda Engelbrekt. You piqued my interest the other day, so I did some more searching in the newspapers about Aaron Roberts and Ken Solstad. I have a few pages printed out if you'd like to look at them."

"Is there anything special?" Floyd asked.

"Well, the most interesting thing is an article about Ken Solstad's funeral. I guess I hadn't thought about it much, but his family brought the body back from Iowa to have him buried here. The article says the funeral ceremony was a couple days before Christmas and it must've been a slow news week because it lists the people who attended. Right after that article is news about the lutefisk dinner. I thought that'd give you a chuckle because the church served over two hundred pounds of lutefisk and one hundred fifty pounds of meatballs."

"I never thought you'd find enough crazy Scandinavians to eat two hundred pounds of lutefisk," Floyd said with a chuckle. "I'll swing by and pick up the article about the funeral. That might be interesting." Floyd paused, wracking his brain for the idea that had passed through before he'd been diverted by the Lutefisk data. "Say, Brenda, I assume the funeral article mentions where Ken Solstad's accident occurred. Do you have a database where you could check a local newspaper and get a follow-up article about the car accident that killed him?"

"Hang on," Brenda said. Floyd could hear papers rustling. "The accident was outside Des Moines, Iowa. I'll pull up *The Des Moines Register* website again. If you give me an hour I may have something for you."

"Thanks!"

Pam had listened to Floyd's half of the conversation with curiosity. "What do Ken Solstad's car accident and funeral have in common with two-hundred pounds of Lutefisk?" she asked.

"Nothing," Floyd replied. "Brenda and I were talking about a lutefisk dinner when I was at the library. Separate from that she did some research to find Ken Solstad's obituary and funeral article. The funeral and the lutefisk dinner were the same week, right before Christmas. We'd laughed about the lutefisk and she was just passed along the information about the amount of lutefisk eaten."

"Why would the newspaper report who attended the funeral?" Pam asked.

"There wasn't a lot of news that week," Floyd replied, "and this is a small town."

"Why are you interested in the Solstad funeral and accident?"

"I haven't got anything specific other than a nagging feeling in the back of my head," Floyd said. "Having more information is better than not having enough. Sometimes you find a nugget that ties to something else when you put all the pieces together."

"Do you want me to do anything more with Mark Roberts' truck logs?" Pam asked.

"Put them into the file. Knowing that he lied about being out of town when Aaron disappeared is probably enough information for now." Floyd got up and washed his coffee cup. "I'll head over to the library and see what Brenda found."

Floyd parked downtown and walked the few blocks to the library, nodding to people he met on the street. One old man stopped him to ask about the annual sheriff's auction of seized and abandoned goods. The rainwater had evaporated from the street in the afternoon sun and the humidity was nearly 100%. Floyd arrived at the library hot and sweaty.

"Hi, Brenda!" He said to the librarian who was sitting behind the counter studying a computer screen.

"Hi, Floyd," Brenda said when she saw him approach the reference desk. "I sent the *Des Moines Register's* website a request for a search. Their archives are on microfilm and it'll take them awhile to search and send me a copy of the article. A copy of the funeral article from the *Pine City Pioneer* is on the counter."

Floyd picked up a grainy photocopy that had apparently been made from the microfilm machine. He read through the description of the tragic loss of Ken Solstad and a summary of Reverend Johnson's eulogy. He quickly scanned the names of the attendees. Included were Kathy Tucker, Mike Nelson, Betsy Ring, Sue Roberts, and Karen and Alex Solstad. Significantly absent were Melissa Smith and her parents. The arrangements had been made through the Johnson-Bradshaw Mortuary.

"Floyd, Des Moines just e-mailed a copy of the article." Brenda pushed back from her computer and stood so Floyd could read her computer screen.

The copy was also grainy with an article only three inches long on the obituary page of *The Des Moines Register* dated December 12, 1998.

A Minnesota man was killed yesterday in a head-on crash on I-35 south of Des Moines. The Iowa state patrol reported that the driver apparently lost control of his vehicle and crossed the median, striking a semi driven by Nancy Bennett of Charles City, Iowa. The semi driver reported that the victim's car drifted slowly across the median and into her path and she was unable to avoid the collision. The highway patrol reported that the victim was ejected from his vehicle upon impact. The State Patrol spokesman said the driver may have fallen asleep. The identity of the victim is being withheld pending notification of relatives.

"You must've used some tricks to find this," Floyd said. "It doesn't mention Ken's name anywhere."

Brenda's face beamed. "We librarians have ways of digging out information. That's why they keep us around."

"Can you print a copy of this for me?"

Brenda leaned over and clicked a few keys. Within seconds the printer whirred and the page started printing. "Will this help with the investigation?"

"I never know what will help," Floyd replied. "I just know that the things I don't get copies of are the things that I always want later."

Brenda pulled the paper off the printer and handed it to Floyd. "Is there anything else I can do for you?"

"If you can figure out where Aaron Roberts has been for the past fifteen years I'd really appreciate a call."

Brenda shook her head. "I suspect that he's somewhere in the hundred-square-miles of swamp and bog around here. That's what I find creepy about Pine County, a killer could drag a body ten yards off a road and it might never be found."

"Luckily, most killers aren't that smart."

"How would you know, Floyd?" Brenda asked playfully. "You only know about the ones you arrest."

"Oh, I know."

CHAPTER 36

Kathy Tucker registered the sound of the kitchen door somewhere in her subconscious. It wormed its way into her dream, making her sleep restless and light. She squirmed under the sheet and rolled onto her side facing the window. A slight movement in the room caused the thin curtains to move in front of the open window and the movement of air combined with the subconscious recognition of the sound of denim jeans rubbing together brought her fully awake.

"Who's there?" she croaked.

"Time for paybacks."

Kathy reacted too slowly to the strange voice. She turned her head in time to see the motion from the corner of her eye, but not fast enough to bring her arm up to deflect the blow that struck her ribs. The air rushed from her lungs followed by the searing pain of broken ribs. Before she could clutch her ribs and gather her wits a second blow hit the point of her shoulder. Unable to catch her breath enough to whimper, much less cry out in pain, she tucked her head and covered it with her free arm.

A hand ripped the sheet away, exposing her naked body. "Mouthy bitch!" More blows rained on her hips, arms, and legs. The attacker grunted with each swing of the baseball bat. Before he'd spent his anger, Kathy lapsed into oblivion.

Floyd rolled over in bed and picked up the phone on the second ring. "Swenson."

"This is dispatch. We've got an assault in Hinckley. Kathy Tucker is on her way to the Sandstone Hospital. Kerm Rajacich is on the scene and he requested you."

Floyd looked at the glowing numerals on the clock, which indicated 5:12 AM. "Who called it in?"

"Kathy Tucker called for an ambulance. Kerm responded ahead of the ambulance and found Kathy badly beaten, lying on the kitchen floor next to the phone."

"Tell Kerm I'm on my way."

Floyd pulled on a pair of jeans, then slipped on a windbreaker to cover the holster he'd clipped to his belt. He dialed Dan Williams on his cellphone when he reached I-35. "Somebody beat up Kathy Tucker," he reported to the undersheriff and gave him the address.

Hinckley was just starting to awaken as Floyd sped off the interstate and wound the narrow city streets to Kathy Tucker's house. He could see the flashing lights reflecting off house windows and lighting the leaves on the trees from blocks away. When he pulled to a stop there were already a half-dozen neighbors standing on the sidewalk in bathrobes and slippers.

"Did any of you hear anything?" Floyd asked as he walked toward the house.

"Nothing," the man closest replied. "Not till the sirens came."

Floyd ducked under the crime scene tape strung between two trees in the front yard.

Kerm Rajacich was standing at the bedroom door taking pictures when Floyd walked into the small house. Floyd looked over Kerm's broad shoulders at the bedroom. Bloody sheets lay crumpled on the bed and floor, and blood splattered the walls. A smeared trail of blood crossed the small bedroom and led down the hallway.

"My God," Floyd said. "How bad is Kathy?"

Kerm stopped snapping pictures and looked away from the scene of carnage. "Somehow it's easier to look at through the viewfinder. It doesn't seem so enormous or so personal." He took a deep breath. "She's bad. If any normal person had taken a beating like that they would've been dead. Kathy's in great physical shape, so she may have fared better. Even at that, she's got a bunch of broken bones and a lot of contusions. I can't believe she was able to drag herself to the kitchen to call 911."

"Was she coherent?" Floyd asked.

"She was passed out when I got here. Her breathing was shallow and she had blood running out of her mouth."

Floyd looked at the room. "Sexual assault?"

"I don't think so, but she was so badly battered I wouldn't hazard a guess. I haven't seen any evidence of burglary either." Floyd looked into the bedroom and pointed to the pattern of blood droplets sprayed on the walls. "Whoever did this was really angry. I didn't see a cut on her, so all the blood here is from wounds inflicted with a blunt object. If you look at the blood spatter, you'll see the droplets are tiny and spread rather far apart. Someone was swinging a blunt object really hard and fast to make a pattern like that. In my book that means intense anger and the desire to take something out on the victim."

"Any sign of the weapon?"

"Not in the house, but I haven't looked around the yard or driveway. With all the flowers in the yard it might just be laying out there hidden under the leaves."

"Bloody fingerprints or footprints?"

Kerm motioned Floyd into the room and pointed to the doorframe. "One palm print here. It looks like someone cleaned up in the kitchen sink so we may pick up more there. I just haven't dusted the sink yet."

"I wonder where her creepy friend is?" Floyd said to himself.

"Kenny's over talking to the pastor now," Kerm said. "That was the first comment the neighbors made too."

"I'm heading for the hospital," Floyd said. "Dan should be here shortly. Make sure he calls the sheriff so he doesn't get blindsided by the press."

The morning I-35 traffic was starting to pick up when Floyd accelerated down the Hinckley entrance ramp. He turned on the red and blue flashers to get an opening in the traffic, and then he flew past the remaining cars as they eased to the right lane.

"Who would want to hurt Kathy Tucker?" he asked himself. "I can't believe the gay guy from Minneapolis cared one iota about Kathy. No husband, so a boyfriend is the second most likely suspect."

The morning-shift hospital employees dressed in blue and green scrubs were walking from the employee parking lot when Floyd sped to the emergency room entrance. He approached the admissions desk with his badge holder. "Where's Kathy Tucker?"

An aging admissions clerk with red-rimmed eyes looked like he was probably ending his night shift. He pointed down the hallway. "Room two."

Floyd stopped at the empty nurse's station and checked the white board listing the room numbers and occupants. No one had written Kathy's name on the chart. Generally, that was a sign the staff was too busy with the patient to step away.

The rooms were actually dividers with curtains hung across the hallway opening. Under the curtain covering room two Floyd could see several pairs of white shoes and he could hear muffled discussion. He pulled the curtain back enough to peer into the controlled chaos. Kathy's naked body lay on the bed as people rushed around her. A monitor traced the EKG and beeped out a steady rhythm.

"Get that guy out of here!" A man wearing a surgical mask shouted.

A nurse broke away from the group and pushed Floyd back. "I'm sorry sir, you have to wait in the other room."

Floyd pulled back his windbreaker, exposing the badge clipped to the waist of his jeans. "I'm Floyd Swenson with the sheriff's department."

A matronly nurse with graying hair peeking out from under a blue surgical cap gently put her hand on Floyd's arm and walked him back to the nurse's station. "She's got a punctured lung, probably some other internal injuries, and numerous broken bones. We're giving her whole blood to see if we can bring her blood pressure and oxygenation up. If we get her stabilized we'll transfer her to a trauma center in the Cities for intensive care and orthopedic surgery."

"*If* she gets stabilized?" Floyd asked.

"About the only thing going for her is that she doesn't have head injuries," the nurse replied. She hesitated and drew a breath. "I've never seen anyone injured this badly survive."

"Did you do a rape kit?" Floyd asked.

"Not yet, but I'll tell the doctor you made a request, but that won't be a priority right now. Now please go to the waiting room, I'll keep you informed."

"Has anyone notified her parents?"

"Not as far as I know."

Floyd went to the empty waiting room and found the admissions clerk. "Show me where I can find a cup of coffee and a phone."

"Use the phone in the cubicle next to me, and I'll grab a cup for you. Black or otherwise?"

"Black would be great," Floyd said. He dialed the dispatcher and told him to get a deputy over to Tuckers' and tell them to get to the hospital ASAP.

By the time he hung up the phone the clerk was back with coffee in a Styrofoam cup. "Black and on the back burner for half the night. If you want fresh, the cafeteria will open in half an hour."

"Thanks," Floyd said taking the cup and drinking half of it in one gulp. "It's better than we have at the courthouse."

"I pity your stomach."

"The girl in the back is pretty bad, isn't she?" Floyd asked.

The clerk paused. "They usually leave someone at the nurse's station unless they get someone really bad."

The clerk shook his head. "They haven't asked me to call for the LifeLink helicopter yet. They usually have me call right away unless. . ."

"Unless they're afraid they can't save them?" Floyd asked.

"That's pretty much it." The clerk looked at his watch. "I've got to close out the end-of-shift reports. Holler if you want more coffee."

Floyd drank the last of the coffee and walked back to room 2. Through the curtain he could hear the voices of the staff as they worked to save Kathy Tucker's life. More importantly, he could hear the steady beep, beep, beep of the cardiac monitor. Kathy was hanging on.

A hand pushed the curtain back and a man stepped out as he stripped off bloody surgical gloves. He held the gloves in one hand and took the surgical mask off with the other while facing away from Floyd.

"How's she doing, Glenn?"

Glenn Bergstrom, MD, spun around, startled by Floyd's voice. "Christ, Floyd, don't sneak up on me like that." He took a deep breath and pointed toward the nurse's station. "She's starting to stabilize, but I'm really afraid she's got major internal injuries. Do you know what happened? It looks like she's been beaten with a baseball bat."

"She called 911 herself. When my guys arrived she was passed out. All we know is that she was assaulted in her own bedroom, and that whoever assaulted her did it viciously." Floyd paused, and then added, "Most often an attack like this is by a lover or husband. We're not aware she has either, which is why I asked for the rape kit."

"There's no sign of sexual penetration, but we'll take a swab."

"There's one other thing you should know, she told me she's HIV positive."

"To be on the safe side we treat everyone like they've got hepatitis or AIDS, but I appreciate the warning." Bergstrom paused, "Sorry I yelled to have you thrown out. Things weren't going well and I didn't need a spectator. I didn't recognize you peeking around the curtain."

"Not a problem. That girl's life is more important that my feelings."

A woman in a lab coat walked briskly toward them carrying a sheet of paper. "Here are the blood gases."

Bergstrom studied the numbers briefly. "Cross-match two more units of whole blood," he said to the medical technologist. "I've got to get back in with her."

"I had a deputy dispatched to notify her parents," Floyd said.

"Maybe you should dispatch one to light some prayer candles, too."

"I think she's Methodist, Glenn. We don't do prayer candles."

"Cover all the bases, Floyd. I wouldn't refuse a Rabbi right now."

CHAPTER 37

Pam Ryan beat the Tuckers to the hospital. Floyd was standing at the window staring at the shrubbery across the back of the hospital when she rushed into the emergency room waiting area.

"The Tuckers will be here momentarily," she said. "How's Kathy doing?"

"Doc Bergstrom called a surgeon in," Floyd said. When he turned Pam could see the bags under his eyes and the weariness in his face. "They couldn't get her stabilized enough to transport her. Doc Bergstrom said her only chance was immediate surgery to stop her blood loss."

"Kerm found Walt Flaherty, Kathy's friend. Kerm said Walt hadn't been out of his apartment all night. He was very upset that something bad happened to Kathy."

"We should talk to Walt again later," Floyd said, "just to make sure he wasn't putting on an act for Kerm."

"I don't think it was Walt," Pam said quietly. "Mark Roberts made bail last night. He called one of his buddies, who showed up with a check. He was released about eight o'clock."

"Is Sue still at the shelter?"

Pam nodded. "Yes. That was the first call I made when I heard he was out. She was still in bed. I asked the coordinator to dial 911 if he showed up there."

A blue pickup with the garden center logo on the doors pulled into a visitor's spot next to the emergency entrance and the Tuckers walked quickly across the parking area. Ginny Tucker wore a wrinkled windbreaker over jeans. Her brown hair was gathered into a ponytail with stray hairs sticking out around her face so it appeared she had a halo in the early morning sun. Brian Tucker wore a Minnesota Twins T-shirt over jeans. His hair looked like it hadn't seen a comb and his face was covered with gray whiskers and looked like it had aged a decade.

"Floyd, how is she?" Brian Tucker asked. "Can we see her?"

"She's in surgery right now."

Ginny broke into tears and buried her face into Ed's shoulder. Tears welled in his eyes as he patted her back. "How. . .how bad is it?" he asked.

"She's badly injured with several broken bones and some internal bleeding," Floyd replied. He decided it wasn't his place to tell the Tuckers that her injuries were so bad she couldn't be transported to a trauma center.

"Can we talk to Doctor Bergstrom?" Brian asked.

"He's assisting the surgeon. They'll be down as soon as they can."

"What happened?" Ginny asked, wiping her eyes with a tissue. "Deputy Ryan said Kathy had been assaulted. Who would hurt her?"

"We don't know who attacked her. She was in her bedroom and someone entered the house while she was apparently asleep."

"It must've been that creepy Walt," Ginny said to Brian.

Floyd said. "We've already talked with him and he was home all night. Can you think of any other likely suspects? Is there someone who had a beef with Kathy at the nursery? Have you fired anyone lately?"

"There isn't much for people to get upset about at a nursery," Brian replied. "If someone buys something that doesn't grow, we replace it. The three of us are the only employees. I can't think of one person who would want to harm Kathy."

"You don't think it was a stranger?" Ginny asked.

"That'd be really unusual," Pam replied. "We sometimes see an assault when someone surprises a burglar, but nothing seems to be missing. The rest of the house looks fine."

"Was she. . .?" Ginny couldn't bring herself to form the words.

"Doc Bergstrom said there was no evidence of sexual penetration."

"I just can't believe this is happening." Ginny broke into tears again and buried her face in Ed's shoulder.

"Doc Bergstrom will be down when they know something more," Floyd said. "You folks wait here and tell the admissions clerk if you have to go anywhere. Pam and I have to meet with the sheriff."

"We're meeting with the sheriff?" Pam asked as they walked out of the hospital.

"I think he'll want to meet us at Roberts' house when we go to question Mark."

"You think Mark will be sitting there waiting for us?"

"I don't think he's smart enough to realize that we might suspect him of the attack." Floyd opened the car door and asked the dispatcher to have the sheriff call his cellphone.

"What army are you going to call in to arrest Mark Roberts?" Pam asked. "Last time didn't go all that well if you recall."

"It's shift change, we may be able to catch Tom and Kerm going off shift. With the day-shift deputies, Dan Williams, and the sheriff, that should give us about seven people."

"Don't let Sandy help," Pam said. "He's getting married in four days and facial bruises would make for some pretty ugly wedding pictures."

"He's on afternoon shift. He's probably asleep."

Floyd's cellphone rang. "John, I need a warrant to search Mark Roberts' house. We're looking for shoes and clothing with bloodstains and a blunt instrument like a baseball bat. I want to search the house, the vehicles, and the outbuildings."

Floyd listened for a few moments. "Okay, we'll meet you there in half an hour. You'd better grab Tom and Kerm before they finish up reports. We're probably going to need some beef for this arrest."

"I'll meet you in Pine City," Pam said.

"Hey, aren't you the maid of honor?" Floyd asked.

"Yeah."

"I guess we should worry about bruising you, too. It wouldn't look good for the maid of honor to be black and blue in the wedding photos."

"Are you serious? I wouldn't miss this for anything."

The police cars parked along a cattail filled ditch on a gravel crossroad a half-mile from Roberts' house. With one highway patrolman, who happened to be at the café having coffee with the deputies, there were seven uniformed officers plus Dan Williams, all swatting mosquitoes in the sultry morning heat. The sheriff's car approached, and despite the recent rains it raised a plume of dust. He stopped at the end of the line of cars, the dust drifting across the ditch in the light breeze.

"I've got a search warrant. We all know that Mark Roberts can be a royal pain and this probably isn't going to go down easy, so I want a volunteer to run the video camera so there's no question about who did what to whom when this is all over."

"Pam's running the camera," Floyd said. "We can't have her bruised for Sandy's wedding pictures."

A collective groan ran through the male officers and Pam turned bright red. "Bullshit!" Pam said. "Let Floyd run the camera. He's too old and might get broken in a fight."

"Ooh, let me," said Kerm. He weighed in at nearly three hundred pounds and loved few things as much as wading into a bar fight. "I might soil my uniform."

"Enough!" Sepanen said. "Roberts has a problem with women, and I want Pam on the recorder for all of our safety. I don't want the situation to get out of hand just because Pam's in the mix." Once he was sure everyone was clear on Pam's role he went on. "I want Dan and the trooper on the front door. Kerm, Floyd, and I will serve the warrant. The rest of you can search outside the house once we're sure Roberts is controlled. If that's clear to everyone, let's do it!"

The cars rushed down the driveway single-file, raising a huge cloud of dust in their wake. There was no sign of activity outside the house and the drapes were drawn in all the windows. Floyd stopped near the door in an area strewn with beer cans. The deputies bailed out of their cars and rushed to their assigned positions as Pam climbed atop the hood of the car nearest the back door with the video camera in her hand.

The sheriff pounded on the screen door with his fist. "Sheriff's department! Open up!"

The inside door was open although there was no sound coming from the house. The officers stood quietly, waiting for a response. Birds chirped in the trees and a cicada trilled in a grove of trees behind the house.

The sheriff turned to Pam and the camera. "There's no answer to our knock, and it appears no one is home. We'll conduct our search on this warrant." He held up the warrant for the camera. Finding the door unlocked, he announced, "Let's go."

Pam climbed off the car hood and followed the sheriff, Floyd, and Kerm into the mudroom of the farmhouse. Floyd stopped just inside the door. "There are several pairs of shoes here that I'll bag to check for blood or evidence."

Pam followed the others up the few steps to the kitchen. There was a slight smell of rotting food in the kitchen, like someone had forgotten to take the trash out for too long. Dishes cluttered the countertop, although there was no sign anyone had prepared food recently. The kitchen table was covered with empty beer cans and the carton from a twelve-pack of Grain Belt beer, a local favorite.

"Sheriff's department!" the sheriff called out again. He crossed the kitchen and opened the front door for the two officers standing outside. "There doesn't appear to be anyone home."

Pam was standing near the hallway to the bedroom when she heard a rustling noise from behind. She turned toward the bedrooms just in time to catch Mark Roberts on the video camera as he stumbled out of the bedroom with a baseball bat in his hand. Her first impression through the viewfinder was of a clown in striped boxers running from a long way off. Roberts' image was tiny in the viewfinder and Pam's mind failed to register the threat quickly enough.

"Bitch."

Sensing the swing of the oncoming blow, Pam's instinct told her to fall back, but her training sent her into auto-pilot and she lunged forward, to get inside the arc of the bat. She threw herself against Roberts' beer belly, and then rolled to her right, away from the hand with the bat. In the collision the video camera flew against the wall.

Pam spun as she passed Mark Roberts, catching her balance briefly only to be knocked to the floor as Floyd Swenson catapulted himself against the off-balance assailant. The three of them fell to the floor in a heap. Kerm Rajacich was close behind Floyd and he ripped the bat loose, throwing it into the living room.

Pam tried to scream in pain as Roberts landed on top of her, but her face was buried under the big man's abdomen and his weight pressed the air from her lungs as her nose and one cheek were ground into the carpet. Her discomfort was only intensified as Floyd and Kerm struggled with Roberts as they attempted to cuff him. Pam panicked as she struggled to take a breath and she kicked her legs wildly to draw attention. Like suddenly emerging from the depths of a lake after holding her breath too long, Pam was freed when Rajacich yanked Roberts to his knees.

"Thank you, God," Pam gasped as fresh air rushed into her lungs. She pushed herself to hands and knees and tried to get her eyes to focus. Behind her, Kerm, Sepanen, and the state trooper struggled to subdue the handcuffed Mark Roberts as he swore invectives at the officers, kicking, spitting, and biting anyone within reach.

"Are you okay?" Floyd asked, kneeling next to Pam.

Her nose was running and the side of her face burned. When her eyes finally focused Pam wiped her nose with the back of her hand and saw blood. She put her hand to her face and got a shot of pain when she touched her nose.

"I think my nose is broken," she said.

A loud crash shook the house as Mark Roberts was thrown to the living room floor. Floyd reached for the video camera lying on the floor next to Pam. It was still recording, so he pointed it toward the melee in the living room as Pam rolled into a sitting position against the wall. Floyd captured the last few moments of Mark Roberts' resistance, up until the highway patrolman took out a Taser and shocked Roberts into submission by immobilizing his muscles with a high-voltage shock.

The sheriff took one look at Pam and hustled into the bathroom. He was back in a few moments with a wet towel. "Are you okay?" He asked as he wiped the blood from Pam's face and neck with a wet washcloth.

"I think I'm fine other than some bruises and maybe a broken nose." Pam took the towel and held it across and under her nose to stem the flow of blood. Tears flowed from her eyes when the cold compress hit her face.

Kerm Rajacich and Floyd Swenson were dripping with sweat as they stood Roberts up and moved him to the door. All the officers in the house were dirty and had disheveled shirts and pants. Floyd followed Roberts out the door to fully document the care they were using in handling Roberts once he was subdued. He was determined that Rodney King's name wouldn't come up in any defense of Mark Roberts or his arrest.

Pam sat with Floyd in one of the Pine City emergency room bays waiting for their X-rays. Pam's nose was packed with cotton and her right cheek was covered with a white pad where the doctor had treated her carpet abrasion. She was feeling no pain due to the lidocaine administered prior to setting her nose.

The purple bruises were just starting to blossom under both eyes. The only thing looking worse than Pam's puffy, bruised face was her bloodstained uniform shirt.

Floyd's left arm was in a sling. The doctor reset his dislocated shoulder, and said he suspected several broken ribs. Floyd was unable to take a deep breath without experiencing significant discomfort. His uniform shirt and pants were torn and dirty.

"I suppose the television news crew is here," Floyd said. They're probably waiting outside the ER entrance.

"Why?" Pam asked.

"It seems like the kind of thing they like to splash as a teaser on the evening newscast. You know, two of Pine County's finest beaten to a pulp during the execution of a search warrant."

"Oh yeah," Pam said. "I'd love to have my face splashed all over the television the way it is."

Floyd sat next to Pam. "I'm sure it'll be lots better by Saturday. You'll hardly be swollen at all for the wedding pictures."

"Oh, dear God! I'd forgotten about the wedding. Barb will kill me. She won't want me in the wedding pictures."

The emergency room doctor walked toward Pam. "It looks like all you've got is a broken nose, bruises, sprains, and strains. Take Aleve for the discomfort. I'll give you both prescriptions for Tylenol with codeine, but I suggest you not even fill it unless the pain is intolerable." He handed Pam and Floyd each a prescription slip. "If you do take the codeine, don't drive."

The exam room curtain flew back and Mary Jungers peeked around the doctor. Seeing Floyd, she rushed in and gave him a hug, which caused Floyd to gasp in pain.

"Oh, no, Did that hurt? I'm so sorry," she said, stepping back.

Then she looked at the other patient. "Pam! Is that you?"

"Oh God, my face is so bad Mary didn't recognize me!"

"No, no, no, it's all the blood." Suddenly, Mary took in the full picture of Pam's bruised face, the bloody and torn shirt, and the nose packed with cotton. Mary's face turned ashen and her eyes rolled back.

"Catch her, Doc," Floyd said as he reached out with his good arm, trying to get his hand under Mary's armpit as she slumped to the floor.

"I'm so embarrassed," Mary said, for the tenth time. "I was just standing there, and then I woke up on the floor."

Floyd held her hand as they crossed the parking lot. "It happens to lots of people who aren't accustomed to seeing blood." In the background a newscaster was speaking to a camera as they captured Floyd and Pam's exit from the hospital. The logo on the white truck was from one of the Duluth television stations.

"I know, but I'm a grown woman; I shouldn't just pass out like that."

Pam, with an extremely nasal voice, said, "Mary, you've never seen a mess like that. I didn't realize how bad I looked until you didn't recognize me. It must've been a terrible shock."

"It's not like you deal with any blood around the flower shop," Floyd added. "What's the worst injury someone ever had there, a pin-stick from a corsage?"

"We've dealt with some nasty thorns," Mary said trying to regain some dignity.

This might not be the best time to ask, but have you had an update on Kathy Tucker?" Pam asked Floyd as they walked across the hospital parking lot.

"They removed her ruptured spleen here, got her stabilized, then sent her to North Memorial trauma center via helicopter. Last I heard she was still unconscious but her vital signs were still stable." Floyd opened the car door for Pam and added, "We matched the bloody footprints in Kathy's house to the shoes in Mark Roberts' breezeway. The palm print on the door frame also matched Mark Roberts. The sheriff is making a statement to the press in about fifteen minutes to announce the arrest in Kathy's assault."

"Do we know *why* he attacked her?" Mary asked.

"Roberts isn't talking," Floyd said. "But the hostility he showed after I told him Aaron was gay was certainly clear evidence he was angry about Aaron's life choice. He also asked me if it was Kathy who'd told me about Aaron's coming-out. I tried to deflect it by saying I'd heard it from several sources, but he obviously focused on the one person who would've known. For once in his life, he's actually listening to a woman. His female public defender told him to keep his mouth shut."

Floyd closed the car door for Pam and walked Mary to her car.

"Are you really OK?" Mary asked as she unlocked her car.

"I'm sore, but I'll survive," he replied.

Mary bit her lip, then said, "Pam will look like a horse kicked her on Saturday. I'm not sure she'll want to be in any of the wedding pictures."

"There's never a perfect wedding ceremony," Floyd said with a shrug. "This will make everyone laugh in a few months."

Mary kissed him gently and got in her car. Before closing the door she asked, "Can I make you supper?"

"Sure. Just don't make me laugh."

CHAPTER 38

Floyd dropped Pam at her apartment and returned to the courthouse. He studied the map showing the location of significant events related to Aaron Roberts' disappearance. The coincidental location of the recovered ATV and the place where Mike Nelson and Betsy Ring said they'd spent the night nagged at him.

"There are no coincidences in law enforcement," he said to himself. Fifteen minutes later he was at the Pine City lumberyard waiting for Mike Nelson, who was helping a contractor load a hot tub onto his truck.

He checked out the rack of cordless power tools across the aisle from pails of wallboard compound and trowels. The showroom walls were covered with samples of siding and flooring. Rows of shelves featured every variety of tool imaginable. The back of the showroom was lined with bins of nails and screws. The smell of pine and cedar boards filled the air, melding with the aroma of coffee perking in the corner next to a box of pastries.

The coffee pot was like a magnet for Floyd and when Mike walked into the showroom he found Floyd sipping coffee and munching a doughnut.

"I should've known," Mike said as he retrieved a cup from behind the sales counter. "If I put out doughnuts, the cops will show up."

"That's an old wive's tale," Floyd said, shaking his head. "Cops prefer Danish."

"What happened to your arm?" Mike asked, looking at Floyd's sling.

"I lost an arm wrestling match with my girlfriend."

Floyd followed Mike back to the coffee pot where Mike poured himself coffee. "Tell me again where you and Betsy spent the night Aaron Roberts disappeared."

"We were necking in my car, and we fell asleep until daylight," Mike said as he poured coffee into a yellow cup adorned with a logo of a Canadian lumber company.

"It doesn't work for me, Mike. I checked with the National Weather Service, and the low temperature was five degrees that night. You would've had the car running to keep from freezing and if you'd done that, you'd have run out of gas. Try another version of the story on me."

Mike stared at Floyd in disbelief. "You checked to see what the weather was that night?"

"Yup, and you're lying. What's the real story?"

"That's the real story, Floyd."

"Would you like to come to the courthouse and sit around in an interview room while we talk it over?"

"What is the big deal? Betsy and I spent the night together. What difference does it make if it was in the backseat of my car or in a motel room?"

"Were you in a motel room?"

"Sure! We rented a cheap motel room and shacked up there for the night. Does that solve your problem?"

"What motel?"

Mike took a deep breath and rolled his eyes. "The Rock Creek Motel."

"It wasn't built until two years after that. Try again."

"Jesus, Floyd. I don't get it. What's the big deal?"

"You tell me. If it's no big deal, why don't you tell me where you spent the night?"

"It might be a big deal. We might've been some-where we weren't supposed to be."

"You mean like someplace illegal. Did you break into the bank and spend the night having sex on the money bags?"

Mike looked around nervously, and then directed Floyd to the manager's office. "It's about that bad," he said as he closed the door. "We were in a lake cabin that was unoccupied for the winter. We turned the heat on and slept there. Does that satisfy your curios-ity? Are you going to lock me up?"

"Did you break into the cabin?"

"Not exactly. We knew where the owners kept a spare key."

"How did you know about the key?"

"Geez, Floyd. I could get a few people in some hot water over this."

"Spill it."

Mike took a deep breath. "Melissa's uncle has a cabin on Round Lake, near Hinckley. She used to spend the 4th of July with them, and they kept a spare key under the deck in case they ever forgot to bring one along. Melissa took us out there a few times for parties and stuff, so we knew where the key was. She told us never to use it by ourselves, but that night. . . Whew, this gets even worse. Kenny scored a few Mollys from his buddy, Dog, and we decided to use the bedroom at Melissa's uncle's house."

"When you say 'our,' who would that include?"

"I guess it wasn't everyone," Mike said, closing his eyes to visualize that night. "Betsy and I each popped a Molly and Kenny did too."

"Are Mollys the same as Ecstasy?" Floyd asked, already knowing they were.

"Yeah. It's some type of amphetamine that's not as bad as meth, but you get almost the same rush. Mollys are pretty low risk."

Floyd stared at Mike for a second, then asked, "If Mollys are low risk, would you object if your kids took them?"

Mike stared at Floyd for a moment in silence. "I wouldn't want my kids to do much of anything I did as a teenager. Life is different now."

"Tell me about Dog," Floyd said. "I don't remember his name coming up in any of the discussions about your group of friends."

"He was some buddy of Ken's not really part of our group."

Floyd was searching his memory as Mike spoke. "Was Dog that drug dealer who lived outside Finalyson?" he asked.

"You've got some memory," Mike replied. "Yeah, I think he lived by Finlayson. I think they called him Dog because he had a Finnish name that meant dog."

"I think his name was Bryan Santo," Floyd said. "He was arrested a few years ago for cooking methamphetamine in an abandoned house."

"I heard that," Mike replied. "I also heard he got crosswise with an Asian gang in the Cities and they found him dead in an alley.

"So, everyone was high on Ecstasy that night?" Floyd asked.

"Naw. Like I said, Kenny, Betsy, and I took some. Kathy was too straight to do any kind of drugs. She didn't want Aaron to do any either, so he didn't take any. Melissa was getting a lot of pressure from Kenny to drop a Molly, which made her fight Ken even harder. Kenny even dropped one in her beer when she went to the bathroom, but Kathy spilled the beer before she drank any."

"How did Kenny react to Melissa's spilled beer?"

"Instead of making him mellow, the Mollys made Kenny paranoid, which just added to his bitchiness.

He was already being hyper-macho and the Mollys turned him into an ass. When Kathy spilled Melissa's beer, she tried to make it look like an accident, but Kenny was screaming at her. I think if a guy had done it, Kenny might've killed him, but because it was Kathy, he tried to slap her, but she was too quick and she ducked his hand. At that point, Kenny had tipped over a chair and the bartender yelled at us. He threatened to throw us out and Kenny settled down."

"Who owned the house where you crashed."

"I never heard his name other than it was Melissa's uncle's place. It's a big A-frame with a loft and huge windows that look over the Round Lake. It's hard to miss."

"Did Aaron know about that house and where the key was hidden?" Floyd asked.

"I suppose," Mike said, after thinking a bit. "But the night before Kenny died it was just Betsy and me at the house."

"But Aaron had been there and he knew where to find the key," Floyd said.

"We partied there a few times after Kenny went into the Army and Aaron was with us once or twice. He started hanging out in the Cities more in October and November, before Kenny died, but he was with us that summer. Why would it matter?"

"I think Aaron stole an ATV from a cabin on Passenger Lake. A farmer found it in his ditch near Round Lake."

The news shook Mike although he tried to hide it from Floyd. "What makes you think Aaron stole the ATV? After all these years it's hard to say it was him that stole it. It might be a coincidence that it was found near Round Lake."

"You seem awfully interested in debunking my theory. Why?"

"No reason. It just seems like. . .well, like a stretch, that's all."

Floyd took a Kleenex from a box on Mike's desk and wiped some non-existent doughnut residue from his hands, letting the silence work on Mike. "Aaron showed up at the A-frame house while you and Betsy were still there, didn't he?"

"No," Mike said. "We cleaned up and locked the door behind us while it was still dark out. No one else was anywhere near as far as I know."

"You're keeping something back, Mike." Floyd had studied people's behavior for nearly four decades and Mike was sending strong signals he was equivocating. "Something else happened at the house. What was it?"

"Nothing really." Mike acted like he hoped that answer would satisfy Floyd. After several seconds of silence he added, "Melissa found out we'd spent the night there and went ballistic. That's all."

"Why'd she go ballistic?"

"You know. She didn't want us to go there without her. She was mad we'd used the key to let ourselves in. I think she panicked and went back to change the sheets and things like that. That's all. It wasn't that big a deal."

There was more to the issue than Mike was letting on, but a buzzer sounded as the front door opened. A customer walked into the showroom.

"I've got to go," Mike said, looking out the office window and watching a contractor walk through the aisles wearing his paint-stained white coveralls.

"Tell me if you think of anything else about Aaron and maybe seeing him at the Round Lake house," Floyd said as Mike opened the office door and held it open.

"Sure, Floyd."

CHAPTER 39

Floyd knocked on the Brooklyn Center townhouse door at 4 o'clock. Betsy's teenage daughter answered the door with a flourish that quickly died when she saw Floyd standing on the step. Her hair was spiked, each spike a different color. She wore a skintight tank top that clung to her budding breasts and was short enough to leave a lot of exposed skin above her hip-hugging jeans. The gap exposed the ring through the edge of her navel.

"Hello, Alyssa."

"You're the cop, right?"

"Right. Is your mom home?"

"Why's your arm in a sling? Did you get beat up in a bar fight?"

"Something like that. Can you get your mom, please?"

"Mom! There's a cop here to see you!" The girl gave him a sly grin, then walked away swaying her narrow hips provocatively.

Betsy Webb rushed to the door trailing a towel. Her hair was still wet from a shower and wet spots dotted her purple Minnesota Vikings T-shirt. She wore denim shorts without socks or shoes.

"Oh, God. I thought it was a real cop." Betsy shook her head, "I mean I thought it was a local cop. Alyssa's been in a little trouble lately."

"May I come in?" Floyd asked.

Betsy pushed the door open and led Floyd to the kitchen where a batch of chocolate chip cookies was cooling next to the sink. The countertops were littered with bowls, and cookie sheets. She picked up two cookies and set them on a plate on the kitchen table.

"Have a cookie and talk while I load the dishwasher," she said.

"I talked to Mike about the night Aaron disappeared," Floyd said. "He told me about the Ecstasy you took at the bar, the night at the Round Lake house, and Aaron. I'd like to hear your side of it."

The glass mixing bowl fell to the floor and smashed. Betsy stood still, staring at the broken glass around her bare feet with a stunned look on her face.

"Don't move!" Floyd said. "Stay still while I clean up the glass."

"The wastebasket is under the sink and the broom is in the closet next to the refrigerator."

Floyd picked up the largest pieces of glass and dropped them into the wastebasket with his free hand. He was taking out the broom and dustpan when

Alyssa came down the hall. "Stay back while I clean up the broken glass," Floyd told her.

She stood next to the kitchen door and watched Floyd sweep with one hand. "Mom would've been really pissed if I'd dropped that bowl."

"It's spilt milk," Betsy said. "I thought you were waiting for a ride to the mall?"

"Jen's mom wasn't home from work yet and she's giving us a ride. Who broke the bowl, you or the cop?"

"It slipped out of my hands. Deputy Swenson is just helping so I don't cut my feet."

Floyd finished sweeping with one hand and wiped the floor quickly with a damp paper towel. "That should do it."

Betsy had been standing with her arms wrapped across her chest as if she were cold. She took three tentative steps and sat in a kitchen chair. "Thanks." Alyssa walked away once the excitement died. Floyd dumped the glass from the dustpan into the wastebasket.

"You were going to tell me about the Ecstasy, the Round Lake house, and Aaron," Floyd prompted as he picked up a cookie and took a bite. The warm chocolate oozed around his fingers.

"I'm sure there's nothing I can add to whatever Mike said."

"Like I said, I want to hear your side of it."

"The Ecstasy was a stupid idea," Betsy said as she got up and started a pot of coffee. "It seemed daring and fun, but that, combined with the beer was a pretty strong cocktail. Mike and I were flying high." She was about to measure coffee when she paused. "Kenny turned into a nightmare. He got edgy and paranoid. When the bartender threatened to throw us out, Mike whispered that we should leave." She finished measuring the coffee and flipped the brew switch.

"Tell me about the Round Lake house."

"It's not like we broke in. We used the key and we cleaned up before we left."

"What time did Aaron show up?"

Betsy hesitated a fraction of a second, then shook her head. "He didn't show up while we were there."

"He did show up though. When?"

"I don't know what you mean?" Betsy said without looking Floyd in the eye.

"He broke into the cabin on Passenger Lake and stole an ATV. He drove it to Round Lake. Then what happened?"

"We weren't there."

Floyd sat there quietly eating a second cookie. He stared at Betsy, waiting for her to add to her statement. The coffee pot gurgled and he poured coffee into two cups he took off a mug-tree standing on the counter.

"I don't know!" she said, abruptly standing. "I don't know what happened after we left." She walked to the counter and ripped a paper towel off the roll. She held it to her face as tears wet her cheeks.

When the tears stopped she threw the wet paper towel into the wastebasket. "So, what did Mike tell you happened?" Betsy took her coffee to the table.

"I want your statement without guiding you one way or another," Floyd said, returning to the table with his coffee. He sipped the fresh coffee and took another bite of cookie.

"Well, you've got it."

"Tell me about Aaron."

Betsy shook her head. "He's missing."

Floyd suppressed a smile. "Yes, but you know more about what happened than you're telling me."

"Whatever Mike told you is more than you need to know. I'd appreciate it if you'd leave now."

"How bad was Aaron bleeding the last time you saw him?" Floyd asked as he stood.

Betsy froze. "Mike didn't tell you anything, did he? You're lying to me!"

"I have a picture taken of Aaron with cuts all over his chest. Kathy Tucker helped bandage him up and broke into a cabin on Passenger Lake so he'd have a place to warm up. The next day he stole an ATV and drove away before she got back." Floyd reached in his pocket and took out the picture of Aaron tied to the tree. He held it out for Betsy.

"I don't want to see it," she said.

"He rode the ATV to Round Lake. What happened after that?"

"I don't know. We left before he got there."

"Ah, Floyd said. "So you were gone, but he did go there."

Betsy stared at the coffee mug she was clutching in her hands.

"What time did you go back?" Floyd asked, walking down the hallway toward the front door.

Betsy rubbed fresh tears from her cheeks with the backs of her hands. "I didn't go back."

"You never went back to the cabin? That's not what Mike said."

"Just go away." Betsy pulled the door open. The afternoon heat rushed in.

Floyd studied Betsy's irrational reaction to his questions. She was far too overwrought to have only been chastised by Melissa about using the hidden key to spend a night with her boyfriend and she's let it slip that Aaron had shown up at the house, just not when she was there. In her unspoken language Floyd saw extreme distress every time he mentioned Aaron and the Round Lake house.

"How long was Aaron dead before you found him?" Floyd asked, taking a wild guess that he might've struck the heart of Betsy's distress.

Betsy shuddered. "I don't know what you're talking about," she said, pushing Floyd toward the door. "Now go away!"

CHAPTER 40

"Now what?" Floyd asked himself as he walked back to his car. "I suppose I have to talk to Melissa again." The inside of the car was furnace-like and he turned the air conditioner to maximum. The first blast of air to reach him was hotter than the interior of the car, so he stepped outside and turned his cellphone on. It indicated he had two messages.

The first message was from the dispatcher, "Floyd, the sheriff asked me to track you down. He said Mark Roberts wants to talk." Floyd deleted the message and listened to the second. "Floyd, where the hell are you?" The sheriff's deep voice barked at him with annoyance. "Mark Roberts says he wants to talk and dispatch says you're in the Cities tracking down that old Aaron Roberts case. Get your ass up here and work on something that's happened this decade!"

Floyd rolled is eyes and deleted the second message. "The two cases are related," he muttered to himself as he climbed inside the car. The steering wheel had barely cooled enough to touch it when he pulled away from the curb.

When he merged onto I-35W Floyd dialed dispatch. "Tell the sheriff I'm on my way. I'm pushing the speed limit and I should be there in about thirty-five minutes." He wove through the late afternoon traffic, passing cars as he moved between the lanes. When the rush hour traffic came to a complete stop he turned on the flashers and sped down the shoulder. A highway patrolman glared at him as he passed a fender bender.

"You made it in twenty-five minutes," the dispatcher noted as Floyd passed though the outer security door.

Floyd nodded and rushed to the sheriff's office. "Where's Mark Roberts?" he asked the startled sheriff, who was staring at a report while facing away from the door.

"He's still in a cell," Sheriff Sepanen said, getting up from his desk. "Where were you when everything broke loose?"

"What broke loose?" Floyd asked as he followed the sheriff toward the jail.

"Roberts is claiming abuse and screaming at his lawyer. He got fed up with her and told her to take a hike, in so many words. Next thing I know the head jailer is in here telling me that Mark Roberts wants to talk to you and the dispatcher says you're down in the Cities talking to one of Aaron Roberts' old friends."

"What else broke loose?" Floyd asked as they went through the jail security door.

"Kathy Tucker took a turn for the worse."

"Shit," Floyd said, "that was the other thing I was going to do when I was down there. I got side-tracked when I got your threat."

"My threat?"

"You made it sound like my butt was on the line unless I got back here quickly."

"Well, it was. Roberts wants to talk, and you're the man. What are we supposed to do, tell him you're in-disposed and hold the confession until we can find some free time in Floyd's busy schedule?" The sheriff hailed the head jailer, "Kerry, put Mark Roberts in an interview room."

Floyd set up the video recorder while the sheriff unwrapped a cigar and clamped it between his teeth. "You know," Floyd said, "tobacco products aren't al-lowed in the jail."

"So arrest me." The sheriff glared at Floyd, and then put the cigar back in his shirt pocket.

A key rattled in the door and Mark Roberts en-tered the room. Floyd pointed to the chair where Mark would sit and said, "I see they decided to put you in manacles this time instead of just handcuffs."

Roberts held his hands up to waist level where the chain between his hands and feet grew taut. "This sucks."

"Don't try to assault any more officers and we might go back to handcuffs," Floyd suggested.

"I don't think you remember who got beaten up," Roberts said, sticking out his bandaged chin where the ER doctor had taken half a dozen stitches after treating Pam and Floyd. A bruise darkened the right side of his face.

"I watched the video of your arrest with your lawyer," Sepanen said. "I don't think she wanted a jury to see you chasing Deputy Ryan with a baseball bat."

"Bitch didn't believe I'd been provoked. I'll get a new lawyer and we'll nail your butts. All of you will be looking for jobs and filing bankruptcy to cover the judgments."

Floyd took a seat next to the sheriff, across the table from Roberts. The jailer stood with his back against the door. "For the record," Floyd said, "it's July 10th, 2013 at 4:50 in the afternoon. I'm Floyd Swenson, and we're interviewing Mark Roberts. Mark, your lawyer is not here. Do you want to make a statement without the advice of your lawyer?"

"Stupid bitch is worthless."

"I'll take that as a yes. You requested a meeting. What do you want to say?"

"I want to tell you, and your camera, that the Pine County goon crew broke into my house and beat me up while I was defending my home." Roberts sat back smugly after his statement.

"We had a search warrant which we tried to serve. We have a video of the entire incident and the sheriff says that video shows you attempting to assault one of our deputies with a baseball bat. I don't think you have much to stand on, and if that's all you have to say

I think the interview is over." Floyd stood and moved to shut off the camera.

"Hang on a second," Roberts said. "The lawyer said you found evidence at Kathy Tucker's house. You have to tell the lawyer the truth, right?"

"We tell the truth all the time," the sheriff said.

"Don't feed me that bull. I know better because you've lied to me before." Roberts paused. "But the lawyer says you have to tell her the truth. So if you told her you found evidence I was there, it would be the truth?"

"We found your bloody hand print on the doorframe," Floyd said, "and we found Kathy Tucker's blood on shoes at your house. That's pretty incriminating."

"I might have made a mistake about something." Roberts stared at the corner of the table. "The lawyer said that if I was apologetic about a mistake, the court might take it into consideration."

"Go ahead," Floyd said without committing the court to anything.

"I thought the Tucker bitch told you Aaron was a queer and that made me really mad. I stewed about it here in jail, and when I got out I kinda lost it. I didn't mean to hurt her bad, I just wanted to teach her a lesson. I'm sorry. I guess she's hurt pretty bad."

"She had surgery in Sandstone then they flew her to the Cities," Floyd said. "The doctor said she has a bunch of broken bones and some other injuries. The sheriff just told me that she's taken a turn for the worse."

Roberts shook his head. "It was the beer. I had a few too many and I made a stupid decision. That's all. I've got homeowner's insurance and maybe that'll help with the doctor bills."

"Mark," the sheriff said, "she might die."

Roberts' eyes raced between Floyd and the sheriff, trying to find some hint that they were being less than serious. "Die?"

Floyd nodded. "She lost a lot of blood. You did a number on her. You know that Aaron had HIV?"

Mark shook his head in disgust, "I heard that."

"He and Kathy had been intimate," Floyd paused, not able to reveal Kathy Tucker's medical history. "I see you have some cuts on your hands. If you got them when you beat Kathy, you need to get an AIDS test."

Roberts looked at the cuts on his scarred knuckles and his eyes grew wide as the meaning in Floyd's words struck him. "I might've gotten AIDS from Kathy's blood?"

Floyd nodded. "We asked the hospital to take a blood sample when you were stitched up. You'll need to check back to see if you're building antibodies to the AIDS virus in your bloodstream."

"What a fuck-up this has been," Roberts said to himself.

"We checked your log books," Floyd said. "You were still here the night Aaron disappeared and the following day. Why did you lie to us about that? Did you have something to do with Aaron's disappearance?"

"You are one nosy son of a bitch. I told you I wasn't home, and I wasn't."

"You weren't in Pine City?" Floyd asked.

"No. I wasn't."

"You weren't on the road, either."

"I don't remember."

"Let me tell you something interesting I discovered today," Floyd said. "Aaron stole an ATV from a Passenger Lake cabin and drove it to Round Lake the day Sue reported him missing. He went to a house where he and some of his buddies had partied and probably let himself in with a key that was hidden outside the house. Something happened to him there, and I think you might know what. Did he call you from the house?"

"I don't know what you're talking about."

"I think he called you to come and get him, but you were all pissed off because he'd told you he didn't like girls anymore, so you went into a rage, like you did with me and with Kathy Tucker. Maybe you went too far. Is that why you don't want to admit where you were that Sunday?"

"I think you've lost it," Roberts said.

"If that's not where you were, then where were you?"

Roberts lifted his hands, but the shackles wouldn't let him reach his face. "I had a honey down in Harris for a couple years. I'd tell Sue I had to leave a day earlier than I was driving and I'd spend a day in Harris."

"What's her name?" the sheriff asked.

"You're not going to call," Roberts protested. "She's married now and we didn't have what you would call a clean split."

"We need to call," Floyd said. "How else can we verify your story?"

"Joyce Opp." Roberts stared at his hands. "How much trouble am I in?"

"Lots," Floyd said. "If Kathy Tucker dies, or if she doesn't recover her mental capabilities, you're in even more trouble."

"I should quit drinking."

"They have AA groups in prison," the sheriff suggested. "You'll probably have lots of time to dry out."

CHAPTER 41

Floyd smiled when he pulled off the road and saw Mary's car parked next to his garage. Spot met him as he stepped out of the car, racing circles around his legs and whimpering around the tennis ball she carried. He took the ball from her and threw it into the backyard, wincing with pain from his his rib injury. She was back before he made it to the steps.

"I don't think I can throw it again, pup," he said, petting her head and ignoring her attempts to get him to take the ball from her.

Mary met him at the screen door with car keys in her hand. "We're going over to Barb and Sandy's for supper, if you're not in too much pain." She locked the door without waiting for his response and added, "If you'd been five minutes later I would've been gone and you'd either be eating leftovers or driving by yourself."

"What inspired this soirée?" Floyd asked, following Mary to his pickup.

"Barb said she bought a bunch of steaks and she'd talked Sandy into cooking them on the grill behind the apartment building." They got in the truck and as Floyd drove down the gravel road she added. "I think they're worried about Pam Ryan. Barb said they were going to try and cheer her up."

"Steak might be a poor choice for Pam and me," Floyd said as they drove. "I'm not sure I can cut up my own steak one-handed and Pam may have a problem breathing with her nose plugged."

"I'll cut up your steak," Mary said, patting his knee.

They rode a few miles in silence until they came into the town of Sturgeon Lake. "How were things at the flower shop today?" Floyd asked.

"Boring, like usual. I ordered flowers. I got a shipment of vases. No one had anything interesting or controversial. Have you had an update on Kathy Tucker?"

"I heard from the sheriff that she is still critical."

"What were you and your gimpy arm doing today? Mary asked as they turned onto I-35.

"My day was pretty much like yours: same old, same old."

"You're awfully evasive tonight."

"I need to make a trip to Redwood Falls tomorrow. I have to talk with Melissa Schotten face-to-face. I found out Aaron's friends were partying at a house that some relative of hers owns. It looks like Aaron stole an ATV and drove it near there the day he disappeared. No one is willing to say they saw him there and I'm thinking there's a skeleton in the closet."

"Literally?"

"Maybe. I'd sure like to get a straight answer about what happened."

"What do you think happened?"

"Aaron died there, or someone helped him disappear. One or more of the group knows or they wouldn't be evading my questions."

"Can't you press them for the information? I mean, it's been years since the incident and whatever happened is ancient history."

"There's no statute of limitation on murder in Minnesota."

Floyd drove through downtown Pine City on the way to the apartment Barb and Sandy shared. Passing through town he noticed the hearse parked in front of the Johnson-Bradshaw Funeral Home and pulled into their driveway.

"Hang on for one minute. I need to talk to someone," Floyd said.

"Your minutes sometimes get long."

"Listen to the radio."

"You don't like the classical stations I choose."

"I'll change the station when I come back," he said as he climbed out and closed the door.

"That'll be harder when I reset all your stations," she said to herself as she started a scan of the radio stations.

Floyd walked into the lobby of the funeral home and listened for signs of activity. Directly ahead of him was a viewing room and to his right was a lighted office.

"Hi, Floyd. What can I do for you?" Paul Bradshaw walked out of the viewing room. He was nearly fifty, but kept himself trim and neatly groomed. He wore a dark gray suit with a subdued blue tie. His short gray sideburns conveyed an air of maturity. They'd been gray for two decades and Floyd wondered if he'd been coloring them to look more professional.

"Paul, I have a question." Floyd walked to the door and noticed the open casket surrounded by flowers at the north end of the room. "Do you remember Ken Solstad's funeral?"

"A lot of funerals run together in my mind, but it hits even people in the mortuary business when a family loses a young person. Those funerals are hard to forget." Paul gave Floyd a questioning look, "Why do you ask?"

"We've got some new evidence about Aaron Roberts' disappearance. He was out with Ken and their other friends the night before Ken died in the car accident. I don't know that there's any connection, but I wanted to ask if anything unusual happened at Ken Solstad's funeral."

"Nothing unusual. It was a closed casket because of the . . . damaging effects of Ken's accident. It was a very sad ceremony."

"The casket was closed?"

"I retrieved the body from Iowa myself," Paul explained. "They transported his body to a mortuary in Des Moines where I picked it up. Ken died at the accident scene. He'd been struck by several vehicles after being ejected from his car." Paul paused, searching for the correct words. "The Iowa mortuary had attempted to embalm the body, but there was so much damage— I've seen a few who've been in worse shape."

"So, you put him in the casket and closed it."

"I tried to persuade his parents that they didn't want to remember him as he was in death, but Karen demanded to see him as soon as I returned from Iowa. I had to unlatch the casket and open the lid. I'm sure Karen couldn't recognize his face. She broke into tears and nodded. Alex didn't want to look. I think he understood what I was trying to tell them."

"Who identified the body?"

"I don't know. I suppose the Iowa coroner made an identification based on the driver's license and his size and hair color. They usually don't bother to check dental records unless there's some question. . ." Paul stopped mid-sentence. "You don't think. . ."

Floyd shook his head. "Not really. I'm sure Ken was headed back to duty. Kathy Tucker saw him leave and I'm sure his parents did too.

"Was he buried here or at Fort Snelling?"

"Because he was on active duty, he was qualified to be buried in a national cemetery, but the family decided they wanted him interred in the family plot in the Birchwood Cemetery here. I dressed him in a uniform even though the casket was closed."

"So, you had a service at the church and then buried him outside town?"

"Actually, we had a funeral procession to the cemetery, but it's more expensive to dig the grave when the frost is so deep in the ground so we didn't do the actual interment until spring. We had a small family ceremony in May. It's so hard to go through it all again, but deep frost doesn't leave us inexpensive or quick options. We used to have about a dozen interments every spring when we could dig. Now there's better equipment to thaw the ground and bigger excavators so we can dig a grave regardless of the season."

"So, you had a stack of coffins sitting in a warehouse waiting for warm weather?"

Paul smiled. "It's a little more sophisticated than that. We have secure slots in a cemetery building. The caskets are carefully labeled, refrigerated, and stored under lock and key. You would certainly know if we'd ever had a problem, and I can assure you that we haven't."

"Do you open them and check the contents before you bury them?"

"No. The system is flawless. As I said, each slot and each casket is labeled, the caskets are sealed, and the entire facility is under lock and key. There's no risk of a mix up."

"Thanks, Paul. I'm relieved that you've never had a problem. I wouldn't like to run an investigation of a missing casket."

Floyd was back to the pickup in slightly longer than he'd promised. "You were gone for six songs," Mary pointed out. "What was so interesting in the funeral home?"

"Just checking out their security system."

"Security system? Who'd break into a funeral home?"

"Haven't you heard? People are dying to get into them."

"You're a sick man, Floyd Swenson," Mary said with a groan.

Floyd started the engine and pulled away from the curb. As he drove he selected a different radio station and was listening to a Mahler opus. He chose another button and heard Mozart.

"That was really cruel," he said, turning the radio off.

"You need to do a better job of keeping me entertained," Mary said with a mischievous smile.

CHAPTER 42

The cookout at Sandy and Barb's was a glowing success. Sandy kept busy with the preparation of five porterhouse steaks, while Barb kept beer and drinks refreshed. Mary grilled Pam about the events that led to her colorful bruises and cotton-packed nose while they prepared salads.

"Barb's a little keyed up." Floyd said as he watched Sandy flip steaks on the grill.

"She said she's never really entertained before. We've had people hang around and drink a couple beers, but formally inviting people over and preparing a nice meal is a big step for her."

"Welcome to the world of the married and dull, Sandy. No fistfights will break out and I doubt that anyone will even raise their voice."

"It's kind of like a coming out party for Barb. The customers at the drugstore and I have been the extent of her social universe this past year. This opens a whole new realm of people that she and I will be socializing with. It is a big step past the two of us sitting around watching movies and eating pizza."

"Is Barb okay with that?"

"I think that she's approaching it as a jump into the unknown. She's been doing a cocoon thing since we got together, much of that is just recovering from her abusive prior relationship. I think we both know that it's time to move our lives to a new stage, and she's making that jump with both feet."

Barb stepped out on the patio and looked at the steaks. "We're ready to eat, and I like my steak rare. Can we call them done?"

"Sure we can." Floyd held the platter with one hand while Sandy stacked four steaks up. He pulled one from the back corner that was barely browned.

"When Barb says rare," Sandy said as he held the door for Floyd, "she means warm on both sides. I actually put all the other steaks over the heat for a few minutes."

CHAPTER 43

"What's in the plat book?" Pam Ryan asked as she sat in the chair next to Floyd's desk.

"You sound like you've got the world's worst head cold and you look like you've been kicked in the face by a horse," Floyd said as he appraised the broad adhesive strip over Pam's nose and the dark bruises under her eyes. She'd removed the pad over her cheek and it was scabbed over, giving the appearance that someone had scuffed it with sandpaper. "How do you feel?"

"Like I was kicked in the face by a horse."

"Why are you here? You should take the day off."

"I feel worse when I'm sitting at home without distractions. Where's your sling?" she asked. "I thought you were supposed to wear it for a couple weeks."

"It interferes with my driving."

"I thought the doctor told you not to drive."

"That's only if I take the pain pills." Floyd closed the plat book and stood up. "Well, I can't have you on the road scaring people, so I guess you're riding with me to Redwood Falls."

"Remind me what's in Redwood Falls?" Pam asked as she followed him down the hallway. "I'm not firing on all cylinders today."

"Melissa Schotten, who used to be Melissa Smith. She works at the hospital there, and we need to interview her," Floyd said as he walked down the hallway leading to the parking lot.

"You've talked to her like three times already. Do you think that being there in person will yield different answers?" Pam asked as Floyd held the security door open for her.

"I might have a new twist to my questions."

"Does that tie in with the plat map tucked under your arm?" Pam asked as she got into Floyd's car.

"I think so."

"I had a nice time with you guys at Sandy and Barb's apartment yesterday. I felt crappy, but had a nice time anyway. I felt sad leaving early, but I really crashed after supper. Did I miss anything?"

"You missed Barb's stories about her road trips with the motorcycle guys. She had us in stitches."

"It's probably good I missed them. It hurts to smile. Between the broken nose and my bruised ribs, I don't want to think about the pain a laugh would cause."

"I understand. Driving around with my arm in a sling was hardly a treat."

"Every time I hang around with Mary, I like her more. She's really sweet." When Floyd didn't respond she asked, "Are you guys just buddies who go out for meals together, or is your relationship going somewhere?"

"It's comfortable for now."

"Is it comfortable for Mary too? I have the impression that Mary would like your friendship to progress, based on the way she hangs on your arm and fawns over your every word."

Floyd gave her a suspicious glance. "Did someone put you up to this?"

"I like both of you, and I don't want to see either of you hurt." When Floyd didn't respond, she asked, "Are you still going to the cemetery to talk with Ginny like you did before you met Mary?" Pam asked, referring to the conversations Floyd was known to have with with his wife's headstone after her death.

Floyd had consulted with Mary during a murder investigation and her engaging personality had drawn him out of his depression after becoming a widower. He was returning to her flower shop for conversation weeks after she had nothing left to contribute to the investigation. They started having coffee together after that and Mary had slowly talked him into letting her cook dinner. After months of meeting for coffee at the Rock Creek Restaurant he'd given her a key to his house to open the door to let the dog out when he worked long hours.

Floyd shrugged. "I'm not going there as often, but sometimes I like to talk over things with her. We were married a long time and she's still. . ." He stopped, at a loss for words. "I like Mary, but there are still things I can't say to her."

"I bet Mary listens pretty well, and she will even offer an opinion, unlike Ginny."

Pam's words were true, but they stung nonetheless. "Who are you dating these days?" Floyd asked, trying to redirect the discussion.

"I'm not dating anyone lately," she replied, followed by a sharp intake of air. "I should have filled the prescription for the codeine."

"You can't be on duty with codeine in your system. Do you want me to drive you home?"

"How long is the drive to Redwood Falls?" Pam asked as they reached the interstate.

"I'm not exactly sure. There's no interstate once we get to the south edge of the Cities, so I'm guessing we'll be gone about ten hours. Do you have a hot date tonight?"

"Oh sure! The guys are lined up outside my apartment waiting to take out the deputy sheriff with the broken nose and two black eyes. Guys find black eyes very attractive this time of year."

"Are you taking the codeine?"

"No," Pam replied. "Do I sound like I'm out of my mind?"

"Just checking. I wouldn't want to spend a long day in the car with a woman carrying a gun who's on pain meds."

"Let's stop in Rush City for coffee. I'd like to pour a cup on your lap."

"Ooh! A little edgy today?"

"Give me a break, I'm in pain. Okay?" They rode in silence for while, and then Pam said, "You never explained the plat map."

"Mike Nelson and Betsy Ring said they were necking on a dead end road the first time we talked to them. Well, I challenged Mike yesterday and pointed out that if their story were true they would've run out of gas or had frostbite. He broke down and explained that they knew where the key was hidden for a house on Round Lake that belonged to Melissa's uncle, having partied there a few times. The night Aaron disappeared, Mike and Betsy were inside the house, not in the backseat of his car."

"That makes a lot more sense."

"I also told him about the ATV disappearing from a Passenger Lake cabin near where Kathy Tucker left Aaron Roberts and the large coincidence that the missing ATV showed up in a ditch near Round Lake, where Aaron knew how to get into a warm house."

"Too many coincidences," Pam said.

"Exactly. When I talked to Betsy and Mike, they admitted to spending the night at the Round Lake house, but got really strange when I asked about Aaron. They admitted to having partied with him at the Round Lake house. On top of that, Betsy let it slip that Aaron didn't show up while they were there, but she didn't deny he'd shown up later. Since the house belongs to Melissa's relatives, I thought our best chance for getting information was going directly to her."

"Back to the plat map," Pam suggested.

"I was checking to see who owned the Round Lake house. It's the big A-frame you can see from the road. Steven Bradshaw owns it. You showed up before I could check the tax rolls to see where he lives, but Mike thought they lived in the Cities."

"So, what do you expect Melissa Schotten to tell you?"

"I hope she tells us why everyone is nervous about connecting the dots between Aaron and the Round Lake house. I hope she will expand on Betsy's comment that Aaron didn't show up *while* she and Mike were at the house."

"And if she doesn't cooperate?" Pam asked.

"We've spent a long drive for nothing.

After a few miles Floyd asked, "How are Sandy and Barb's wedding plans coming along?"

"As you heard last night, I tried to back out of my gig as the maid of honor. Barb wouldn't hear a word of it. She says my bandages will make the pictures memorable."

"You've got to admit, Barb is no nervous debutante. She's about as laid back about this whole wedding thing as anyone I've ever met."

"What I find really comforting," Pam said, "is that she's so realistic about the whole thing. She doesn't want to squander a pile of money they could better use on other things, and she doesn't have any dreamy notions about married life being all cream and straw-berries. I hope I'm as well grounded as Barb when my day comes."

"I think she's been burned by life a lot, and that keeps you from lofty ideals."

"I know a lot of brides who've been through some busted relationships, divorces, and hard knocks," Pam said, "but when you put them in a frilly gown and walk them down the aisle, all reason is gone."

"We're only a couple days away from the wedding. Are the plans all set?"

"As far as I know," Pam said as she counted off the plans on her fingers: "The guests are invited. The wed-ding gown is purchased. The judge is committed. The flowers are ordered. The park is reserved. Sandy and Barb are both off work. I think that's it."

Floyd's cellphone chimed and he handed it to Pam. "Deputy Ryan." She held the phone away and looked at the screen. "You have a text message."

"What? I've never had a text message before. That must be why the ring tone was different."

"It's from Barb," Pam said as she scrolled through the lines of text. Her fingers started flying across the keyboard.

"What are you doing" Floyd asked.

"I'm replying to her text."

Pam held the phone away and waited for Barb's response. "If you've never received a text before, I assume that you've never sent one, either?"

"How can you send text with only twelve keys, but twenty six letters?"

"Are you serious?" Pam asked.

"Yes."

"You've got three letters on each number, so you punch the number 2 once for A, twice for B and three times for C, and so on."

The phone chimed and Pam read the text. "Barb took the blowup of the Aaron Roberts picture and digitally removed all the drips of blood," Pam explained as she typed in "OK" and handed it back to Floyd. "With drips gone, she said it was easy to see the actual cuts, and they spelled out, 'HOMO.'"

"Barb typed all that in on ten keys, like you did?"

"Barb has a Smartphone with a keypad, so she can type a lot faster." Sensing that Floyd was still confused, she added, "A Smartphone is that flat cellphone she uses sometimes. It also has 4G Internet capability."

"Why do you need to access the Internet on your cellphone?"

Pam shrugged. "You can get maps and driving directions."

Floyd shook his head. "What do you call people like me who don't understand all the Internet and cellphone capabilities?"

"Dinosaur is one term I've heard. But, having access to all that information is only valuable if you use it. I mean, all the technology is great, but it's just giving you a tool. If you don't use the tool, it's just an interesting toy."

Floyd mulled that thought and then said, "What a jerk Ken Solstad turned out to be. He finds out one of his best friends is gay and instead of having empathy, Ken strips him naked, ties him to a tree, and cuts a homophobic message on his chest."

"You quit too soon," Pam said. "In addition to that, he took a picture of it, probably so he could show his macho Army buddies." Pam paused. "It's hard to live an alternative lifestyle in a small town. In Minneapolis it's easier to be anonymous and to find others with a similar lifestyle. Out in the boonies it's hard to find acceptance."

"Not accepting someone's sexual orientation is one thing," Floyd said. "Tying someone to a tree and cutting them up is a leap. Aaron could only thank God that Kathy Tucker came back and got him into a cabin before he died of hypothermia." Floyd thought for a second, then added. "Maybe Kathy didn't do him any favor. Who knows what happened after he got warmed up. He might've been better off with hypothermia."

CHAPTER 44

The Redwood Falls Hospital receptionist was seated at a desk just inside the entrance. She was a petite blonde and the photo ID hanging from her neck said her name was Anne Flagg. She smiled and didn't seem rattled to see two uniformed officers show up at the desk. "May I help you?" she asked, obviously intrigued by Pam's bruised face.

"We need to speak with Melissa Schotten," Floyd said.

"Please have a seat in the ER for a moment," she said, directing them past the reception desk to the waiting area where they seemed to be surrounded by sick children with runny noses and coughs. A little blonde girl, with a pale face and a bright red nose, stared at them. Pam smiled, only to have it turn into a grimace as pain hit from making a smile. The girl continued to stare, then suddenly looked around frantically. A second later, she spewed vomit across the narrow aisle. Pam pulled up her feet just in time to save her shoes, then swung them onto Floyd's lap.

The girl's mom was mortified, but springing into action she ran to the bathroom for paper towels. The blonde receptionist was also in motion, bringing a container of antiseptic wipes, then paging a janitor.

As Pam carefully slipped off her chair, avoiding the cleaning efforts, a trim thirty-something nurse wearing blue surgical scrubs, stopped at the reception desk. The receptionist nodded toward Floyd and Pam.

She smiled at the sight of Pam's bruises and bandages. "When the receptionist called she said that I'd be able to tell which deputy wanted to see me. She wasn't sure if you needed treatment or if you were making a social call."

"Actually," Floyd said, "we're here for other reasons. We've spoken on the phone a few times. I'm Floyd Swenson and this is Deputy Pam Ryan. We're from Pine County."

The smile slid off Melissa's face as if it had melted. "You drove to Redwood Falls to talk to me?"

"Is there somewhere we could have a private discussion?" Pam asked.

"I don't think we need a room. There's nothing to discuss." Melissa turned and started walking back toward the desk.

"Bradshaw's house on Round Lake," Floyd said loud enough to be heard over the emergency room commotion. Most of the people stopped talking and looked at the two deputies and the now-frozen nurse.

Melissa turned red and started walking back. "There's a consultation room behind the reception desk." She motioned them toward the hallway.

Inside the room she closed the door and stood with her back against it. Floyd and Pam sat in two of the five chairs. A box of tissues sitting next to the phone hinted at the serious, and sometimes sad discussions held there.

"What's this all about?" Melissa asked sharply.

"You tell me," Floyd said. "You've been giving me the same runaround I'm getting from Mike Nelson and Betsy Webb. I know about the hidden key for Bradshaw's Round Lake house and I know that Mike and Betsy spent the night there the night before Ken Solstad died in a car accident and Aaron Roberts disappeared. They said that's where Betsy got pregnant."

Melissa rolled her eyes. "That's it? You want to verify that Mike and Betsy broke into a house and she got pregnant?"

"Take a seat," Pam said. "There's a lot more to it, and you're attitude isn't making it any easier."

Melissa looked at her watch. "Look, I'm on duty and I have patients who need me. I don't have time for a game of twenty questions. Cut to the chase or I'm out of here."

Floyd gave her a withering glare. "Melissa, take the chip off your shoulder and sit down. We can ask you questions here politely, or we can arrest you for obstruction of justice and take you to Pine City for questioning. Which would you prefer?"

"You've got nothing to arrest me for. Nothing. Now ask your questions and let me get back to work."

"Are you related to the Bradshaws who own the Round Lake house?" Floyd asked.

"Rick Bradshaw is my mother's brother."

"You used to spend time with them on the lake, and that's how you knew about the hidden key?" Pam asked.

"They *told* me about the spare key and *told* me to use it anytime I wanted to. There is no crime involved if I used something that was offered to me."

"However," Floyd said, "you got upset when your friends used it after you took them there for a party. Correct?"

"Wouldn't you get upset? I mean, they go out there without me and leave a mess. After I found out I had to go back and spend a day cleaning up."

"What happened after Aaron showed up at the house?" Floyd asked.

Melissa froze. "I don't know what you mean. When did Aaron show up?"

"Cut the crap. Ken Solstad left Aaron tied to a tree by Passenger Lake. Kathy went back and cut him loose. They broke into a cabin and turned on the furnace so he could warm up. He stole an ATV and rode it to Bradshaw's Round Lake house the day he disappeared." Floyd paused to let the words sink in. "What happened after he got to Round Lake?"

"I. . .I don't know." The starch was coming out of Melissa's resolve as she spoke.

"You do know, and we need to get to the bottom of it," Pam said. "Were you the last person to see him alive?"

Tears welled in Melissa's eyes and she shook her head. "No. I don't know. Can't you just let it be?" She reached for a tissue on the small table in the corner. "Aaron's gone. Ken's gone. It's all ancient history."

"What happened to Aaron at the Round Lake house?" Floyd asked softly.

"Don't you understand? It doesn't matter."

"It matters to Aaron's mother," Pam said. "She's suffering from major depression and still holding out hope that he'll call some day."

Melissa closed her eyes, gripped the table edge, and let out a sigh. "Ken killed Aaron and left his body in the house." She broke into tears.

There was a light knock on the door and it opened a crack. A woman in paisley scrubs stuck her head in and saw Melissa crying. Floyd leaned forward so she could see his uniform. "We need a few more minutes."

The woman stepped in and knelt next to Melissa. "Are you okay?" she asked, gently putting her hand on Melissa's arm. "Did something happen to your parents?"

Melissa shook her head. "I'll be back on the floor in a few minutes. See if Gina can cover for me a little while longer."

When the door closed Floyd asked, "Were you there when it happened?"

"No," she said, blowing her nose and shaking her head. "After I yelled at her, Betsy and Mike went back to clean up the house. Aaron showed up first, and then Ken. I guess they got in a big fight and Mike told Betsy they'd better leave. All three of them had taken the Ecstasy Kenny brought to the bar and they were crashing. I went out later and found Aaron slumped on the table, dead. So, you see, there's no crime left to pursue. Aaron's dead, and so is Ken."

"How did Ken kill him?" Pam asked, reflecting on Ken's handiwork with the knife the previous night.

"I think maybe Ken strangled him," Melissa said. "I'm not a medical examiner, and I didn't know much about death then, but he was. . .dead."

"Why didn't you call 911?"

"It didn't seem to matter anymore, especially when we found out Ken was dead too."

"What happened to Aaron's body?"

Melissa opened her mouth to speak, but stopped. "I think I need to talk to a lawyer."

CHAPTER 45

Floyd called the county attorney's office from his cell-phone while Melissa called a lawyer from the phone in the consultation room. The county attorney's secretary answered the phone.

"Jenny, this is Floyd Swenson. I need to talk to anyone who's in the office."

"I'm sorry, Floyd, but it's noon and everyone's out to lunch or in court."

Floyd looked at his watch, having lost track of time. "Leave a message for Tom to call me on my cellphone."

"He's in court all day. He's personally prosecuting the Haglund case with Rick assisting."

"Who is in the office this afternoon?"

"Me. Everyone else is out."

"Can you get a message to Tom? Tell him I've had a break in the Aaron Roberts disappearance. We know Aaron is dead, and I think I can get a witness to tell us where his body is located if Tom will agree not to press charges."

"I'll page him, but he usually doesn't like to be interrupted during lunch. He can't have the phone turned on in the courtroom, so he may not get your message until they break this afternoon."

"Can you hand carry the message to him?"

"Not a chance. Like I said, I'm the only one in the office this afternoon."

"Okay. Put the message on his cellphone and we'll hope for the best. Thanks for helping."

Floyd folded the cellphone and looked at Pam with exasperation. "There's nobody in the county attorney's office with the authority to offer immunity to Melissa. They may get a message this afternoon."

"So," Pam summarized, "if Melissa's attorney tells her not to talk to us, we're screwed."

"*When* he tells her not to talk to us," Floyd corrected. "No attorney is going to tell her to talk to us without some sort of immunity from prosecution. We're so close I hate to walk away without closure."

Floyd's cellphone chirped and he fumbled with it before answering on the second ring.

"Floyd, what in hell are you doing in Redwood Falls?" The sheriff's deep voice asked.

"I take it you got a call from Jenny in the county attorney's office," Floyd said. "Anyway, I'm here talking to Melissa Schotten, who used to be Melissa Smith. I had a hunch that she knew more about Aaron Roberts' disappearance than she let on. I presented what we knew to her and she admitted that Aaron Roberts died in a house on Round Lake. When I asked her what happened to the body she asked to talk to her attorney."

"Does she know who the killer is?"

"According to what she was told, Ken confronted Aaron at the house on Round Lake. Betsy and Mike Nelson left during the argument and Melissa went over later and found Aaron's body. She didn't witness the murder. She assumed Ken was the murderer based on Betsy's comments and what she saw."

"Then Melissa could be the murderer."

"I doubt that. She had no motive. If Ken had been killed, I'd be looking at Melissa as a suspect."

"But you really have no substantive evidence Ken was the murderer either," the sheriff said, mulling the information in his mind. "For all we know, Aaron and Ken had a fight, and Ken may have left Aaron alive. Anyone in the county could be a suspect. I might even throw out a guess that Aaron called home and when his father found out where Aaron was holed up, he might've gone over and killed him."

"Ken Solstad had taken Ecstasy the night before and all the friends agreed that it made him paranoid and angry. By morning he would've been coming down hard, which may have made his paranoia worse. Melissa said Aaron's body was slumped over a table. She thought Ken had strangled Aaron. I could see Mark physically assaulting Aaron and accidentally beating him to death, which probably would've trashed the house, but not strangling him. On the other hand, I know now that Ken carved the word HOMO into Aaron's chest earlier that evening, and then took the picture. That shows extreme contempt and the need to make a show of his contempt. I'd say choking Aaron might be consistent with that type of hatred and the need to demonstrate his contempt."

Floyd thought for a second, and then added, "I might even hazard a guess that Ken acted this all out in the heat of the moment. With the Ecstasy metabolizing out of his system, he may have had an extreme fit of remorse and the Iowa car accident may have been his suicide. Either that, or his system just crashed when the Ecstasy was gone and he couldn't keep his eyes open anymore."

"I doubt that. People don't have deep enough hatred to carve up a friend's chest, and then have a change of conscience a few hours later. Anyway, the county attorney called and asked if this was important enough that he should ask the judge for a recess. Based on what you're telling me, I don't think we can yank him out of court. This is a fifteen year-old murder and waiting until next week to find the body isn't going to make one iota of difference since the probable killer is dead anyway."

"John," Floyd said, his voice rising, "I've got Melissa in the middle of a confession. I don't want to walk away and have her recant her statement. If I can offer her immunity I'm ninety-nine percent sure she'll tell us where Aaron's body is hidden this afternoon."

"There is no way I'm pulling Tom out of the courtroom over this, and he won't authorize immunity without a full briefing on the case. Get her to tell you where Aaron's body is, or come back and talk to one of the attorneys next week."

Floyd folded the cellphone and jammed it into his pocket. "I assume that you could hear the sheriff's booming voice." Floyd said. "Get a statement without immunity, or come back another day." He paced for a second and then asked, "I wonder if they have a coffee machine around here somewhere?"

"Let me try something," Pam said. "Stay here." She walked to the consulting room and knocked gently on the door.

"Did you reach your attorney?" Pam asked.

Melissa was sitting next to the phone staring at her clasped hands. "The office is closed for lunch."

"We're having the same problem on our end," Pam said, taking the chair next to Melissa. "I assume you had nothing to do with Aaron's death."

"Of course I didn't kill Aaron!" Melissa said sharply. "I don't know how you could even think that."

"We don't think that," Pam said quietly, trying to defuse the situation. "I was stating the obvious. I understand that you want to protect Ken's parents, but you've already told us he was the murderer. It's time to do the right thing for Aaron's family. They want to know what happened to Aaron and they deserve to have the closure they need, especially Aaron's mom."

Melissa shook her head. "You don't understand. Karen Solstad and I were really close. She expected Kenny and me to get married. We talked all the time and made plans, especially when Kenny first went into the Army. We cried with each other and we shared the letters Kenny sent us. She was like a big sister and we got closer than I ever was to my own mother. I can't do this to her."

Pam reached out and patted Melissa's hand. "The lawyer is just a diversion. You really aren't going to tell us anything no matter what he says."

Melissa wiped her eyes with a tissue. "No."

"Go back to work," Pam said as she stood. "Floyd and I have a long drive back to Pine City."

CHAPTER 46

They drove in silence on the two-lane highways lined with the new corn crop. The only breaks were driveways leading to big farmhouses with metal barns, blue silos, and grain storage bins.

"Does this look like home?" Floyd asked, after a while.

"It's pretty much like this. Blue Earth is a little further south and west, but every farm grows corn and they plow right to the driveway and the ditches. The fields turn into a beehive of activity in the fall when everyone is out combining their corn and rushing it into the dryers. Everyone in the family get involved. I drove a tractor hauling grain wagons as soon as I was tall enough to reach the pedals. Mom drove a semi and my dad and brothers would take four-hour shifts in the combine. Our combine even had headlights so the guys would work until midnight, then start up again at daylight."

"You sound like you miss it."

"Not really. It was an intense couple of weeks, and that was kind of fun. We had an uncle who'd come home for two weeks each fall to help, and it turned into a big family reunion. The rest of the year was pretty bleak and the winter months were pretty isolated in the middle of nowhere. You know, once the corn is down, there isn't much to stop the wind so it's like living on an island in a sea of snow. I like the trees in Pine County; they break the wind and it doesn't seem so desolate in January and February. Pine County looks more like a Christmas card, with the snow hanging from the boughs of the pine trees."

A billboard advertising "The Pie Lady" drew Floyd to a small restaurant in Winthrop. He pulled into the gravel parking lot and turned off the car.

"Are you sure you want to eat here?" Pam asked. "It looks like an old house with about five additions and four of them look like their roofs are sagging."

"C'mon. If they've got good enough pie to brag about on a billboard it must be an okay place. Look," Floyd said, pointing to a police cruiser parked in an alley, "the local cop is even eating here."

"That might mean they have good doughnuts."

"Right. Ha ha," Floyd said sarcastically. "All cops eat doughnuts."

They walked in and found the Winthrop cop eating a piece of pie, drinking coffee, and talking to the waitress who was leaning on the counter. Floyd took a stool next to him at the Formica counter, with Pam sitting at his other side.

"Well, Beth," the local officer said, "it looks like we're in deep trouble. There haven't been three cops in this town at the same time since Elmer Quist shot his wife." The officer put his hand out to Floyd and then to Pam, "Ray Brock. I'm the chief of police, day shift officer, and dispatcher for Winthrop." Ray looked about sixty, and other than a slight paunch that fell over his belt, he appeared to be in good shape for his age. He wore a blue uniform and he had the ugliest comb-over Pam had ever seen, bringing blonde hair from just above one ear, over the top of his head, and touching the ear on the other side of his head.

"We figured the food must be good if the local cop is eating here," Pam said after introducing herself.

"Well, it's either that, or the cop's cousin owns the place and he gets free coffee," Ray replied. "And in this case, it's the relationship that counts."

"Hey," the waitress, who's nametag said "Beth" protested. "We make the best pies in the county, and anybody who wants more than the Dairy Queen offers has to eat here." Beth was in her mid-fifties and her figure told a lot about her love for the food she prepared, or maybe the pies.

"What's my best choice for lunch?" Floyd asked. "Of course you have to keep in mind that I have to save room for a piece of pie."

"Hot turkey sandwich with mashed potatoes and gravy," Beth suggested. "If you want to go lighter than that, I suggest a bowl of hamburger sauerkraut soup."

"I'll have the hot turkey sandwich," Floyd said, looking over a hand-written list of pies marked on a chalkboard behind the counter. "Then a piece of sour cream raisin pie."

"I'll take a bowl of soup and lemon meringue pie," Pam said.

Beth poured coffee for Floyd and Pam without asking, and then topped off Ray's coffee. "Coffee is always on the house for law enforcement," she explained.

"So, what brings two Pine County deputies to Winthrop?" the chief asked, glancing at their shoulder patches.

"We're on our way back home," Floyd explained. "We had to interview someone in Redwood Falls this morning."

"Where's Pine County?"

Halfway between the Twin Cities and Duluth," Pam said. "Highway 35 cuts it almost in half with the east edge up against Wisconsin along the St. Croix."

"Drove through a couple times, but I guess I never paid attention to what county I was in. Did Redwood Falls arrest somebody for you?"

"No, just talking to someone connected with an old missing person's case. We picked up some new leads in a case and some of the people involved have moved on."

"Yup," Ray agreed. "It's tough to keep people in these dying little farm towns anymore. The farms keep getting bigger with fewer people working on them and even fewer people able to actually make a living off the land anymore. I think half the people in this county are retired and the other half are living off welfare."

"So what kind of criminal excitement is there in Winthrop these days?" Pam asked.

"Not much on the day shift. We get a few drunken drivers after the bars close and a few break-ins to steal the copper wire from abandoned houses, but that's about it for excitement. How about Pine County?"

"Pretty much the same," Floyd said. "We're spread out over almost twelve hundred square miles, so we spend a lot of time just driving the back roads. Some nights I've seen more deer than cars."

"I used to be a county deputy, so I hear what you're saying. I remember serving papers on folks, and sometimes I'd spent half a shift looking at plat books, just trying to locate their houses."

"I was doing the same thing just this morning," Floyd said. "We had a guy murdered in a seasonal lake home, and I was trying to figure out who owned the house and what connection they had with the people involved."

"That was the Bradshaw house?" Pam asked.

The waitress showed up with their orders. Floyd's plate was mounded with mashed potatoes and gravy dripped off the edges of the plate. Pam's portion of soup was only slightly smaller.

"How am I going to have room for pie after all this?" Floyd protested in jest.

"Eat dessert first," the waitress said. "Life's uncertain. You're pie will be up momentarily."

"Are the owners of the house the same Bradshaws who own the funeral home?" Pam asked. To the police chief she said, "Floyd always claims that there are no coincidences in police work."

Floyd stopped mid-bite and set the fork back on the plate. He took out the cellphone and dialed information. "Please connect me to the Johnson-Bradshaw Funeral Home in Pine City."

"Paul Bradshaw, please," Floyd said to the person who answered.

A few seconds later Floyd said, "Paul, this is Floyd Swenson. I need your help with a couple quick questions. First, are you related to the Bradshaws who own a house on Round Lake?"

"My brother owns a house on Round Lake. They usually come up for two weeks over the 4th of July, so they're probably still around. Is there some problem?"

"No problem. Just trying to nail down some loose ends we've got in the Aaron Roberts disappearance," Floyd said. "So, you're related to Melissa Smith?"

"Sure, she's my niece. Dottie Smith is my oldest sister. What's up, Floyd? Why the questions?"

"Bear with me for one more," Floyd said, "and then I'll try to explain. Has Melissa ever worked for you?"

"She was my receptionist one summer during high school, and she took night calls for a whole year while she was in the nursing program at the technical college. Now, please explain your questioning."

"I'm in Winthrop right now, on my way back from Redwood Falls. I just spoke with Melissa and she gave me a lead on Aaron Roberts. This has to be kept in complete confidence, but Aaron may have been killed in your brother's house."

"Melissa told you that?"

"Again, I have to ask you to keep this in confidence. I need to talk to you about some other aspects of the case. Can I meet with you when I get back to Pine City? I'm probably four driving-hours from there now."

"We have a wake tonight, so I'll be here. But please, remember to honor the solemnity of our service, too."

"I need you to do one more thing for me," Floyd said. "Pull out the records of the caskets you held for spring interment over the winter Ken Solstad died."

"I don't like the sound of this."

"It's not going to get better," Floyd said. "Trust me."

"What was that all about?" Pam asked as she started her pie.

Floyd wolfed down a bite of turkey sandwich and said, "I went to the funeral home last night on the way to Sandy's cookout. I'd read an article in the newspaper about Ken Solstad's death, and something was nagging at me. Paul Bradshaw told me that Ken had been badly injured in the accident, and I was toying with the thought that maybe it was Aaron who had been killed in the accident instead of Ken. Anyway, he said that they'd held a closed-casket service because Ken's body was so badly injured, and because the ground was frozen they didn't actually bury the casket until spring."

"This is great!" the police chief said, allowing Floyd to get a few more bites of sandwich eaten. "The most interesting mystery I've investigated in the past ten years is what caused the food poisoning at the Lutheran Church hot-dish contest. Turned out that Mrs. Olson had left her mayonnaise-tuna casserole on the counter too long before taking it to church. We had eighty folks doing the two-step trot for days." He paused to sip his coffee. "So, you're thinking your boy, Aaron, is double-bunked in a casket with another guy?"

"I didn't need that image in my mind while I'm eating," Pam said with a grimace.

"Assuming Aaron's actually dead and the group of friends isn't trying to throw us a red herring so we leave him alone in whatever new life he may have," Floyd said, pushing aside half his sandwich and starting to eat his pie. "We haven't had any sign of a body in over a decade. He could've easily been dumped in a swamp but two bodies in one casket seems so much more logical, especially if Melissa had access to the mortuary and maybe even the storage facility at the cemetery."

Pam almost choked on her pie. She covered her mouth with a napkin and then took a drink of water. "It's what Melissa said. That's where the body is! Double-bunked."

She took another swallow of water. "Melissa said twice that it would be too painful for Ken's mother. It would be painful because it would prove that Ken was the murderer, it'd be painful because we'd have to exhume Ken's coffin to find Aaron!"

Floyd pushed the pie aside and dialed the sheriff's private office number on the cellphone. "John, I think we've got it! Aaron Roberts is most likely buried in Ken Solstad's coffin."

"Where's Ken Solstad?"

"We think he's in the coffin, too," Floyd said as he pulled his wallet and threw a twenty-dollar bill on the counter. "I'll explain when I get back. We're still four hours from the office, and I'm going directly to the funeral home when I get back. Please talk to a judge about getting an order to exhume Ken Solstad's casket to look for a missing body."

"Judges don't like to dig up graves. It's harder to get an exhumation order than a search warrant."

"I think you should approach Judge Farris. Ask him what probable cause he'd require to order the exhumation. Then, I'll try to come up with the answers."

Floyd shook hands with the police chief. "Nice to meet you."

"Call me when you find the body," the chief said, handing Floyd a business card.

"With any luck," Pam said, "you'll read about it in the papers."

"I want the gritty details," the chief said as they walked out the door.

"Hang on a second!" The waitress yelled as she walked briskly across the parking lot carrying two plastic containers with plastic forks taped to the lids. "You didn't finish your pie!"

CHAPTER 47

"Have you got any plans for the evening?" Floyd asked as they reached the Pine City exit.

"Women with broken noses and black eyes don't get many dates. I thought I'd go home, pack my face in ice, maybe watch some television, and fall asleep early."

"I'm sorry. I bet you're in a lot of pain. Do you want me to drop you at the courthouse so you can drive home, or would you like to come along to the mortuary?"

"I'm sore, but I took a couple Aleves at the restaurant. I'd like to come along and hear what Paul Bradshaw has to say. By the way, shouldn't you call Mary and tell her where you are?"

"She's making supper tonight. If I don't show up she just puts my supper in the refrigerator."

"You know, she's a gem. I'd feed it to the dog."

"There have been occasions. . ."

"Take out your cellphone and call her. Paul Bradshaw can wait."

Floyd parked across from the funeral home and called Mary. Pam stood on the sidewalk for the short conversation and watched the few cars driving into the funeral home parking lot.

"Don't worry," Floyd said, leading the way to the front door, "she's not going to disown me today." He held the door open for Pam, then led her to the office, past the family gathering for the wake near the front door.

Paul Bradshaw was in his office reviewing a stack of papers. His suitcoat hung neatly on a hanger on the wall. When Floyd knocked on the doorjamb Paul took off his reading glasses and stood.

"I can't say I'm happy to see you," Paul said, gesturing toward guest chairs and closing the office door. "Please tell me what this is all about."

"Would it have been possible for Melissa to put Aaron into a casket without anyone knowing about it?"

"I don't think so," Paul said. "Melissa isn't a big person and it's not easy for one person to get a body into a casket. Also, the casket lids are secured each night with a special tool, and the building has an alarm system. If someone were snooping around they'd set off the alarm."

"That's a lot of security," Pam said. "Is there a problem with break-ins at mortuaries?"

"We store a lot of chemicals, and a number of them are subject to misuse. Then there are always vandals who don't have any objective other than causing damage. They could cause a lot of pain if they damaged a deceased client."

"You were going to get the records of funerals for the winter Ken Solstad died," Floyd said. "Were you able to pull them together?"

"Here's a list of the deceased who we weren't immediately interred, followed by the date of the memorial service and the date of interment," Paul said, handing a neat three-column list to Floyd and Pam. "There were eleven in total."

Floyd scanned the list quickly. "Most of these were after January first, leaving only Ken Solstad, Ted Munson, and April Luverne in December. Do you recall anything unusual about any of the caskets when you buried them?"

"Nothing comes to mind. As I told you before, we kept them in locked storage at the cemetery until the ground thawed in the spring. You can see by the dates of interment that they were all buried within a couple of weeks of each other. The dates are determined by when we could make arrangements with the families who wanted to be present at the interments."

"Is there room in a casket for two bodies?" Pam asked.

"I've never tried. In general, I'd have to say if the two bodies weren't too large they could fit in a single casket."

"Would you notice if there were two bodies when you handled the casket?"

"It depends," Bradshaw said, obviously uncomfortable with the direction of the conversation. "I suppose we might not notice the weight, depending on the size of the deceased. But we'd notice damage if someone pried open a latched casket."

"How do you latch a casket?" Floyd asked.

"I'll show you the work area," Paul said, retrieving a blue smock from a hook behind the door. He took them into a large well-lit room with a table in the center. Bradshaw led them to the wall where two caskets were stacked on a rack. He took a small metal tool with an ornate handle from a drawer.

"The end of each casket has a small hole," Paul said, pointing to a pencil-sized hole just below the lid on the end of a casket. "I insert this wrench and it engages an internal screw mechanism." Paul lifted the lid, exposing the Rayon lining. He turned the wrench and hooks emerged from the lower part of the casket as he turned the wrench. "The hooks catch pins in the lid and lock it closed. When I remove the wrench the lid is sealed and locked down."

He reversed the direction he was winding and the hooks retracted into the base. "So, you see that if someone tried to open the casket lid without the wrench, they'd do a great deal of obvious damage."

"Unless they had a wrench," Floyd noted. "You told me Melissa worked for you. Would she know where to find a wrench?"

"I don't think she ever spent any time back here."

"Do you remember any missing wrenches from that time period?"

"We get a wrench with every casket, so we throw most of them away." Paul looked at his watch, "I'm sorry, but I really need to get ready for tonight's wake. Do you have any other pressing questions?"

"You embalm the bodies before you bury them," Pam said, noticing the large containers of chemicals in the room. "If someone put a body in a casket without embalming it, wouldn't you notice the smell?"

"Probably not. Latching the lid also seals it pretty well."

"Is it possible that Melissa managed to put another body in Ken Solstad's casket if she had friends to help her?" Pam asked, restating Floyd's earlier question.

"I suppose it's *possible*. If you'd asked me if it was probable, I'd say no." Bradshaw said. "Where are you going with this?"

"As you've probably surmised," Floyd said, "we think it's likely that Aaron Roberts died the same day as Ken Solstad. Based on comments by your niece, we believe she knows that Aaron is dead and helped with the disposal of his body."

Bradshaw straightened his tie while he considered Floyd's comments. "I don't appreciate having my business dragged into this mess based on your interpretation of something Melissa inferred. If you'll excuse me, I have to get back to the visitation."

"Thanks for your time," Floyd said.

"How are you doing?" Floyd asked Pam as they walked back to the car.

"I'm getting sore," Pam admitted. "I should head home and put some ice on my face." After she got in the car she asked, "So what will we do tomorrow?"

"I think it's time to corner Mike Nelson with Melissa's information. If Melissa couldn't put Aaron into a coffin by herself, we should be able to find her helpers. My guesses are Mike Nelson and Betsy Ring."

CHAPTER 48

It was twilight by the time Floyd got to Mary's house. She met him at the door with a hug. "You look bushed. I think you need another day or two before you're ready to be out there chasing bad guys."

He nodded and sat in a kitchen chair. "Maybe I'm getting too old to do this."

Mary took plastic wrap off a sandwich and slid it in front of him. "You're not too old; you're banged up and haven't let yourself heal."

"I feel old."

"That's because you hung out with spunky Pam Ryan all day. She's got all the energy of youth spilling out."

"She got a text message from Barb today. Her fingers flew over the keypad, then she sent off a response. I'm a dinosaur."

"Feeling a little sorry for yourself tonight, tough guy?" Mary asked as she pulled a chair close and sat down. "Did something bad happen that made you so glum?"

"No. We actually found out what happened to Aaron Roberts."

"Really? You found out what happened to Aaron after all these years?" Mary leaned close, waiting to hear the story.

Floyd stopped with the sandwich halfway to his mouth. "What?"

"You can't tell me that you solved the case you've been quizzing me about and then just stop talking."

Floyd took a bite of the sandwich and chewed, staring at her, unsure how much he could share.

Mary leaned back and asked, "Did you discuss cases with Ginny when she was alive?"

"She didn't want to know. . .police stuff."

"Ah, but the flower lady does want to know some of the police stuff, just not the blood and gore parts." She pulled the plate away playfully. "So, cough up some details, or the sandwich dies."

"You wouldn't hold an innocent sandwich hostage, would you?"

"Try me, county boy. I get details or you'll hear the sound of the disposal."

Floyd cracked a smile. "It appears that Ken Solstad killed Aaron at the house on Round Lake. We have a lead on where we can find Aaron's body."

Mary slid the plate back on the table. "Did you eat lunch?"

"Hot turkey sandwich with a mountain of mashed potatoes, followed by a slice of pie." Floyd's eyes lit up. "Half the pie is still in my car!"

He jumped up from the table and almost ran to the car. In a minute he was back with the two pie containers. "Do you want the lemon or the sour cream raisin?" he asked.

Mary scrunched up her face. "Who eats sour cream and raisins in a pie?"

"Good choice," he replied, slipping the container with the lemon pie to her.

Mary opened the container and paused. "It looked like there are a couple of bites missing," she said suspiciously.

"Pam ordered it, but lost her appetite when we started talking about Aaron's dead body."

"Mmm, good pie," she said after a small bite. "But it's a little warm. How long has it been in the car?

Floyd shrugged. "Since Winthrop. I guess it's been a few hours."

Mary stopped eating and pushed the pie away. "A lemon pudding sitting unrefrigerated in a car in July is a recipe for food poisoning."

Floyd pulled the lemon pie in front of him. "I have a cast iron stomach."

Mary watched him eat the second piece of pie, shaking her head. "Let me be perfectly clear, I will *not* be the one holding your head when you retch into the toilet tomorrow."

"I won't get sympathy?"

Mary gathered up the plate and the pie containers, still shaking her head. "I give no sympathy for self-inflicted wounds."

"Then, I suppose I should go home and retch in silence," Floyd said, getting up from his chair.

"You don't have to," Mary said, pulling him into a hug.

Floyd suddenly turned somber.

"What's the matter?" Mary asked.

"This sounds stupid, but I can't. . .I can't lie with you in the same bed where you made love with your husband. I'm sorry."

Mary smiled. "I thought it was something about me that was keeping you away."

"You're. . .perfect. It's just my baggage that's getting in the way."

"I'll bet you'd have an even bigger problem with the thought of us in the bed where you and Ginny. . ."

"I can't get my head around that either."

Mary reached up and touched his cheek. "You're sweet," she said, giving him a gentle kiss.

"I hope you're patient," he replied, returning the kiss before walking out the door.

CHAPTER 49

The ringing phone woke Pam from a fitful sleep. "Hey, Pam, are you feeling any better?" Pam looked at the clock, which said ten o'clock.

"I'm kinda sore, Barb, but I'm getting by. How are the wedding plans going?"

"We're pretty well set. I mean, I can't think of anything else that needs to be done. We just need to show up and then we'll be married."

"It's hard to believe it's only a day-and-a-half away. You must be excited."

"Actually, I've got this strange feeling. It's like I'm nauseated every time I think about it."

"Barb! You're scared. You're feeling butterflies. It's normal."

"I'm not scared. I can ride a motorcycle a-hundred-miles-an-hour on a gravel road without being scared."

"It's a different kind of scared. This isn't the kind that gets your adrenaline flowing. This kind settles in the pit of your stomach and twists it around. In case you hadn't noticed, it's a lot like love, either that, or you're pregnant and you're having morning sickness."

"I'm not pregnant," Barb laughed, "so, I guess it must be love."

Changing the subject, "I texted you on the drive to Redwood Falls. Did that help you make any headway in your investigation?"

"We know Aaron is dead and we think we know where his body is hidden. But that's all I can say right now."

"So how much pain are you really in?" Barb asked. "Will you be able to be my maid of honor?"

"It's not the pain, Barb. It's the bandage across my nose and the black rings under my eyes. By Saturday they should be turning green. You'll have the world's ugliest wedding pictures."

"You and Mary have taught me a lot. This wedding's not about the pictures or the way we look, it's about friends and people who care enough to take you as you are. That's why you talk to me even though I've got ugly tattoos and I talk slow. Isn't that right, or did I miss something?"

"You've got it exactly right," Pam said as her eyes moistened. "It's just that so many people are hung up about having perfect weddings. I don't want to mess that up by showing up looking like I'm dressed for a Halloween party."

"Mary called, too. She thought I wouldn't want a fifty-year-old woman in the wedding party. I told her that I wanted her, and I didn't care how old she is."

"I think that's what love and friendship are all about," Pam said. "I think you're helping all of us learn that again."

"So, you'll still be my maid of honor?"

"Sure, black and green eyes, ugly bandage and all."

CHAPTER 50

At 8:00 the next morning Pam was telling Floyd about Barb's old boyfriend burying drug dealers in occupied caskets when the sheriff walked into the bullpen. "The judges are reluctant to let us dig up dead bodies without someone making a statement stating definitively that they put an extra body in a casket." He poured a cup of coffee and took a sip, followed by a sour expression. "Did we brew this batch with turpentine? It tastes even worse than usual."

"Pam and I were just talking, and we think Melissa couldn't have done anything with Aaron's body alone," Floyd said, ignoring the sheriff's comments about the freshly brewed coffee. "He probably outweighed her by fifty pounds and there's no way she could've handled the dead weight. Mike Nelson was at the Round Lake house when Aaron arrived, and Melissa was really pissed that she had to go clean up after their tryst at the house, so I'm guessing that Melissa dragged the two of them back to help her deal with Aaron's body. Leaning on Mike with this new information could break him."

"The county attorney had a call from Melissa Smith's lawyer last night. The lawyer made it very clear there was no way his client was going to make a statement with or without immunity. So, if you're going to get a statement from someone, it's got to be from someone else."

"Did Tom authorize us to offer immunity to get this resolved?" Floyd asked.

"He thinks it'd be great to close an old case, so we can dangle the immunity offer, but he wants to authorize the offer before it's formally made." Sepanen looked closely at Pam and asked, "Are the bruises under your eyes turning green?"

"Yes, and they're spreading down my cheeks. I should look great in Barb and Sandy's wedding pictures."

"They'll be memorable," the sheriff said.

"C'mon, Pam," Floyd said getting up. "We've got to corner Mike Nelson."

"Before you go," the sheriff said, "I heard from North Memorial Hospital. Kathy Tucker is stable but still unconscious."

"Thank God for that anyway," Pam said. "Did they give you any prognosis for her recovery?"

"They haven't even started to repair her broken bones yet, because she's been so critical. They're doing an EEG to check her brain function and that'll determine a lot of their path forward."

"But Kathy didn't have any head injuries," Pam said.

"The doctor said she had a setback yesterday. They had to put her on a respirator."

"You know," Floyd said, "Kathy is another person who could've helped Melissa. She's been less than candid with her answers."

"I don't think a woman could help stuff the body of someone she loved into a coffin with or without the help of another person," Pam said. "It's just not going to happen. Kathy may look tough and strong, but I sense that she was really shattered by Aaron's announcement and the revelation she'd been exposed to HIV. My intuition says she wasn't part of what happened at, or after, Aaron arrived at Round Lake."

The sheriff pulled a cigar from his pocket and clenched it between his teeth. "I'm going to bet on you guys, so I'm calling public works to see if they can bring a backhoe out to the cemetery this afternoon."

"When did you turn into an optimist?" Floyd asked.

"I'm optimistic about every election, otherwise I wouldn't do all the campaigning."

Dan Williams walked in as the sheriff left. "I read your reports about the Melissa Schotten interview. That was good work. Too bad she decided to lawyer up."

"She worked at the funeral home when she was in high school and nursing school. I'm convinced that she knew how to disable the alarm and open a latched casket," Floyd explained.

"She was very close to Karen Solstad, and Melissa didn't want Karen to know that Kenny's last act on earth was killing Aaron. So, we think that was why they put Aaron in the casket," Pam added

"What's next?" Dan asked.

"I think Betsy will cave in. I think she's more likely that Mike to admit to the scheme."

Floyd and Pam were parked in front of the lumberyard when Mike Nelson showed up to open for the day. They met him at the front door.

"I'm getting double-teamed today. Did we have a break-in last night?" he asked as he unlocked the door and disarmed the alarm.

"We need to talk about Aaron," Floyd said, following Mike into the showroom. "We had a long talk with Melissa yesterday and now we need to know your side of the story."

"I told it all to you the last time we talked," Mike said as he walked around the store unlocking doors and turning on the lights.

"Actually," Pam said, "you quit before you got to the most important part."

"What would that part be?" Mike asked as he drew water for a pot of coffee.

"The part about Aaron being killed in the Round Lake house, and you and Melissa disposing of his body."

"I didn't skip it. That never happened," Mike said calmly.

"So," Floyd said, "when we dig up Ken Solstad's casket this afternoon we won't find your fingerprints?"

"What?" Mike asked as he set the pot on the coffee machine. "I don't know what you're talking about."

"It's too late, Mike," Pam said. "We know what happened to Aaron and your involvement amounts to being an accessory to murder by disposing of the body. The county attorney is willing to offer immunity to close this case. Do you want to talk to us about it here, or shall we have you come down to the courthouse?"

"I can't believe this," Mike said, trying to steady his hand while he measured coffee and dumped it into the filter. "The whole thing is ancient history. Just because you guys find an old picture you have to go plowing up all this old stuff. What does it accomplish? I'll tell you what: it got Kathy beaten nearly to death. It dredged up all kinds of sadness for the Solstads. It got Mark Roberts thrown in jail, maybe for the rest of his life. It's going to make three of us look like ghouls. All over what, a stupid picture?" Mike shook his head and put his hands flat on the counter.

"All right. Here's the deal. Betsy and I were still at the house when Aaron showed up. He was half frozen and dressed in Salvation Army clothcs. His chest was covered with bloody bandages he said Kathy had put on him. He said Kenny had cut him up and he was afraid Kenny would find out Kathy had set him free. We got him cleaned up some, and put fresh bandages on his chest. Betsy gave him some pain killers she found in the bathroom. We were going to take Aaron to the hospital, but Kenny knew where Betsy and I had gone from the bar, so he showed up. When he saw Aaron he started screaming at all of us. Betsy freaked and demanded that I take her home. While Betsy went to the car I tried to calm Kenny down, but he was still high. I made him go outside to the car and he promised that he wouldn't go back in.

"Anyway, I called Melissa from Betsy's house, thinking that she might be able to calm Kenny down. She told me about Kenny attacking her, too, and then she freaked about Betsy and me using her uncle's house. I told her I'd go back and check on Aaron, but she said I'd done enough damage and that she'd check on Aaron, then clean up after she was sure Kenny had left for Missouri."

The coffee stopped perking and Mike poured himself a cup and set the carafe on the counter so Floyd and Pam could help themselves. "Melissa was mad about us spending the night at the Round Lake house, but I thought it was all over. Then I got this frantic call from Melissa about mid-morning. She told me that she went to the house to make sure we'd cleaned up and found Aaron dead. She said Kenny had killed him and left him there. I called Betsy, then I rushed over and it was bad. I mean. . .well, it was bad. Aaron was slumped on the table and there was no sign of Melissa. I was going to call the cops, but Melissa showed up and was freaked out about Aaron. After she thought a while, she gave me this sad story about how we couldn't do that to Ken's parents. They're nice people and it would tear them up if they knew that Ken had killed Aaron. I was totally out of it. I've never seen a dead body before, and Aaron didn't look like himself."

"Was there a lot of blood?" Floyd asked.

Mike shook his head. "There wasn't any blood or even a chair out of place. It was like Aaron had fallen asleep."

"There wasn't any sign of a struggle?"

"No, there wasn't anything out of place. Like I said, it was eerie. Everything was just as we'd left it, except that Aaron was still at the table with the bottle of pain pills Betsy had given him."

"Okay, so tell me what happened next."

"All of a sudden, Betsy pulls up to the house and comes in screaming that Kenny's dead. Someone called her house and told her that Ken had been killed in a car accident in Iowa. At that point, Melissa goes totally berserk. She's crying and swearing, and Betsy freaks when she sees Aaron."

"You left him sitting in a chair?" Pam asked.

"Yeah, I guess so. No one would touch him, so he just sat there. We went to Melissa's house and talked about what to do. She was adamant that Ken's mom would be totally berserk if she found out Ken had killed Aaron. . .well, she was sure it would kill Ken's mom. We finally decided to do nothing. It was a secret, and we split up until someone came up with a plan."

"What made you think that Kenny had killed Aaron?" Pam asked.

"Well, they'd been arguing and then the next time we saw Aaron he was dead. I guess we just assumed. . ."

"Didn't you wonder how Kenny had killed him if there was no blood or evidence of a struggle?" Floyd asked.

"Not really," Mike replied. "Kenny had been bragging about how he'd been trained to kill with his bare hands. I just assumed that Kenny had somehow. . .somehow killed him in a way that I couldn't see. Maybe he broke his neck or strangled him, or something." Mike gripped the table edge and drew a deep breath.

"The next day we wrapped Aaron in a blanket and loaded him into my parent's minivan. Melissa opened the back door of the funeral home at like five in the morning. She and I carried him in through the back door and she used some sort of fancy Allen wrench to unlatch Kenny's coffin. That was the worst part; Kenny was in there and he was a mess. They'd put a uniform on him but his head was wrapped up in gauze like a mummy."

"So," Floyd summarized, "you loaded Aaron on top of Ken and locked the casket again. When they had the memorial service the next day both Ken and Aaron were in the casket."

Mike nodded and looked sheepish.

"You said Aaron was still alive when you and Betsy left," Pam said. "So there's really no witness to Aaron's death."

"I guess not," Mike said, "but who other than Ken would've killed him?"

CHAPTER 51

Floyd was part of a small crowd watching the back-hoe drive across the baked gravel driveway leading through the Birchwood Cemetery. Bradshaw's hearse was near Ken Solstad's grave, and the groundskeeper was busily arranging a tarp to protect the grass from the dirt that would be removed.

"What's a corpse that's not embalmed going to look like after years in a coffin?" Floyd asked Tony Oresek, the St. Louis County Medical Examiner. Oresek had a dark complexion and hair consistent with his eastern European heritage. He was a few inches taller than Floyd and was known for being totally wrapped up in his job to the point of forgetting meals or dealing with his personal appearance. Although his office was in Duluth and he was an employee of St. Louis County, he served as the medical examiner for many northern Minnesota counties.

Oresek's assistant, Eddie Paulson, stood next to the medical examiner in his blue smock. He was a Viet Nam vet who chose to wear his graying hair in a ponytail. His weathered face watched the activity without emotion.

"Depends," Eddie Paulson replied. "If the casket was watertight and in a vault, it may be pretty well decomposed, but still articulated at the joints. Sometimes we get a collapsed casket and there are crushed bones with no tissue left at all."

"Will having another embalmed body with it have an effect on the other body?" Floyd asked.

"Not much." Oresek was a man of few words.

"This isn't going to be pretty," Pam said from behind Floyd.

"Depends," Eddie replied. "You'll probably find it less offensive than a postmortem on a fresh corpse. It'll be less. . .odiferous."

"Like I can smell anything with all the cotton jammed up my nose," Pam said.

"What happened to your nose?" Eddie asked.

"A bungled arrest. I ended up on the bottom of the pile when everyone jumped on the bad guy."

"You should try some green eye shadow," Floyd suggested. "It'll go nicely with the fading bruises under your eyes."

Eddie chuckled. "I think she should go with black and try for the Goth look."

"Shh," Sepanen said, nodding toward the Solstads and Sue Roberts, who were standing side by side on the opposite side of the excavation.

It only took five minutes for the backhoe to dig down to the concrete lid of the burial vault. The cemetery groundskeeper jumped into the hole with a spade and chain, and a few moments later the shovel on the backhoe raised the lid. Ten minutes later a copper-colored casket, dusty, but looking unscathed from its two decades in the vault, emerged from the ground. Three men moved quickly to align it on a cart sitting on the driveway before detaching the chain and rolling it into the hearse.

"Showtime," Oresek said.

Karen Solstad was standing on the edge of the driveway hugging Sue Roberts as the hearse rolled by.

The short procession of the hearse, the medical examiner's Suburban, and several sheriff's cars stopped at the mortuary's rear entrance. Floyd, Pam, and John Sepanen were at the end of the procession of people following the casket into the workroom.

Paul Bradshaw cranked the latch mechanism and then stepped back. "Do you want me to open it?"

"I'll do it," Eddie, the medical examiner's assistant, said as he pulled on a pair of latex gloves and donned a surgical mask. Paul Bradshaw moved a bank of adjustable overhead lights over the casket and turned them on, brightening the area like daylight.

"Here," Oresek said as he handed out surgical masks to the others in the room. "At a minimum there will be lots of mold spores you don't want to breathe."

Eddie slid his fingers under the edge of the lid and lifted the smaller lid segment with apparent ease. He took a brief look inside and then opened the larger section. "It appears we have two sets of remains," he said.

Pam let out her breath, not realizing that she'd been holding it. "Thank God," she whispered.

They watched Tony Oresek step beside Eddie and engage in a muted conversation. "Mister Bradshaw, can you help us?" Oresek asked.

"If we had a sheet or blanket," Oresek said, "I think we could roll the corpse back and forth to get fabric under it. Then, we could remove it intact."

Paul moved quickly to a cabinet and returned with a white sheet. The three men worked in concert and after a few moments they carefully lifted the top set of remains free of the casket.

"Let's set him on the stainless steel table," Paul said.

Oresek took out a small tape recorder. "The remains have been resting on top of a second set of remains in a single casket.

"The upper set of remains is arranged head-to-toe with the lower remains. The upper corpse has not been embalmed and the tissue is decomposed. The resulting decomposition has stained the clothing beneath the body. The upper corpse is dressed in a blue and white plaid flannel shirt and denim bib overalls. The lower set of remains have been embalmed and the tissue is intact, although desiccated. The lower corpse is clothed in a military uniform and much of the material is badly stained."

Oresek turned off the recorder and motioned for Floyd to join him next to the table. "You said the victim may have been strangled. There's so much decomposition that I really can't tell. There's a chance that the Hyoid bone will be intact and if that's crushed, there's a good chance he was strangled."

Oresek gently slid his fingers under the bones of the hand. "There's not a single broken nail. When I find a victim who fought off a vicious attack I usually find broken nails and sometimes even broken fingers. This person might've just come from a manicure as neatly as these nails are trimmed."

"What are you saying?" Sepanen asked.

"I'm not sure yet," Oresek replied.

Eddie and Floyd helped Oresek wrap the sheet over the remains, and then they gently turned the whole bundle. Pam stepped to the end of the table. She watched apprehensively as the leathery skin and empty eye sockets were uncovered. The clothing on the front of the body was stained a deep brown.

"I thought he'd look a lot worse," she said. "This is kind of anticlimactic."

After half an hour, Oresek stepped back. "There isn't any trauma that I would point to as a fatal injury. We'll take the remains to Duluth and do a full postmortem and a toxicology screen on his stomach contents. We may have something more definitive in a few days."

Oresek stepped back to the casket and ran his gloved hands over the other set of remains. He turned to Bradshaw and said, "I don't see any evidence that this set of remains has been disturbed. I think you can close the casket and return it to the cemetery."

CHAPTER 52

Floyd and Pam drove to the Smith's. Dolores met them at the door in a gray blouse and dark slacks. She'd taken time to make sure her makeup and hair were done carefully but her makeup failed to hide the dark bags under her eyes.

"Floyd," she said, "I'm so sorry about this. I feel so sorry for Karen Solstad and Sue Roberts. I had no idea. Please come in." She stepped aside and let them enter the air-conditioned comfort of their living room. "Oh my, Deputy Ryan, what happened to you?"

"I got caught in the wrong spot."

"I would certainly say so. I had a friend who had a nose job and she looked like that for several weeks."

"Great," Pam said glumly. "I'm in a wedding party tomorrow."

"So, here are my inquisitors," Melissa said as she walked in the room. Her face was pale and lined like she hadn't slept enough. She wore a plain gray sweatshirt over her jeans. She sat on the couch across from Pam.

"I'll be in the kitchen if you need me for anything," Dolores said to Floyd as she left the room.

"I hear you've already told Karen Solstad. I suppose she's taking it hard," Melissa said quietly.

"She was happy for Sue Roberts," Pam said, "but sad that we had to exhume Ken's body. We haven't told her that Ken was probably a killer."

"Who else could've killed Aaron?"

"How long was it between Mike Nelson leaving the house and your return?" Floyd asked.

"I don't know. Mike called me the day it happened, but I didn't go over until the next day. I suppose it was at least twenty-four hours."

"In that period of time any number of people could've come and gone. Since we weren't called," Floyd left that jab dangle, "we weren't able to determine the time of death. Aaron may have been dead that whole time, or maybe only a few minutes."

"It wasn't minutes."

"How were Aaron's hands bound when you found him?" Floyd asked.

Melissa looked puzzled. "I don't remember that they were. No, his arms were on the table."

"So you didn't untie them?" Pam asked.

"No. I remember. . ." Melissa stopped and put a hand over her eyes. She waved her other hand. "They definitely weren't tied."

"Bad image?" Pam asked.

Melissa only nodded.

"How much blood did you have to clean up?" Floyd asked.

"There wasn't any blood. Why are you asking these questions? You already believe I was there, or you wouldn't have bullied me into coming back to Pine City.

"He wasn't bleeding. His face was. . ." Melissa took a deep breath. "There wasn't any blood."

"Do you remember anything that might've indicated someone else had been in the house other than Mike, Betsy, Aaron, and Ken?" Pam asked. Not seeing recognition in Melissa, she added, "Like a jacket that looked out of place or muddy footprints on the floor?"

"I don't remember anything special. I dragged Betsy and Mike back that next day and we cleaned the whole house. Even then I don't remember anything out of place. Of course, it wasn't really my house and I might not have noticed something had been moved or was missing."

"Betsy gave Aaron something for pain when he showed up," Pam said. "Was the bottle still out?"

"I don't know," Melissa replied sharply. "My God! It was nearly twenty years ago. How the hell should I remember a pill bottle?"

"Talk us through the events after you got the call from Mike."

"Well, I yelled at him and told him he was a jerk for using my uncle's house for his private party with Betsy. Then I think I slammed the phone down. Later that night I realized that someone probably had to go over to clean up the place and I decided to do it the next day after work."

"When I got to the house there were lots of tire tracks in the snow, but no cars around. I had to get the hidden key to unlock the door, and then I walked in on Aaron. He was almost straight across from the door and I remember thinking that he was sleeping."

"Where did you place the call to Mike?" Pam asked.

"I didn't want to be alone at the house with Aaron's body so I called from a pay phone in the gas station parking lot on I-35. I had him meet me there and I followed his car back to the house. Mike wanted to call the cops, but I told him we couldn't do that to Ken's mom, especially since we were both pretty sure Ken had killed Aaron."

"Whose idea was it to put Aaron in Ken's casket?"

"Well, Mike was worthless. He said we should just leave him at my uncle's house. When I vetoed that, he said we should dump him in a swamp. I insisted that we owed him better than that. I'd worked at Uncle Paul's funeral home and still had a key and knew the alarm code. The next day I heard they wouldn't have an open casket because of Ken's injuries, so I knew we could hide him there and no one would figure it out. So we left him at Round Lake until the night before the funeral."

"Wasn't it hard for you to open Ken's casket?" Pam asked.

"I was on automatic pilot and it went okay until we actually lifted the lid. I tried not to look, and it helped that he didn't look like. . .well, you know, his face was wrapped. . ."

"What did you do after you closed and latched the casket?" Floyd asked.

"I reset the alarm, locked the door, and we all went home. I cried all night and couldn't make myself go to the funeral."

"I don't think we have any other questions," Floyd said as he stood. "I wish you'd been candid with us immediately instead of dragging this whole thing out."

"Well, I wish a lot of things were different," Melissa said. "I wish I'd never met Ken Solstad. I wish Ken hadn't taken Ecstasy that night. I wish I'd called the cops as soon as I found Aaron's body. I wish I'd told Aaron what a great guy he was when he was alive. I wish. . ."

"Anyone want a cup of coffee," Dolores Smith asked, popping her head around the corner.

"We're finishing up," Floyd said, "so don't bother brewing any. I did have one question for you, Dottie. Since your brother owns the house on Round Lake, would you call and ask his permission to get inside and look around?"

"You don't need his permission. I have a key and I can let you in."

"I'd prefer to have verbal permission from the owner."

"Hang on," Dolores said. She disappeared around the corner.

"What do you expect to find there after all these years?" Melissa asked.

"I don't know," Floyd replied. "But sometimes I get a surprise."

Dolores walked back into the living room with a cordless phone in her hand. "You're lucky. Randy is home and he says I can let you in." She handed the phone to Floyd.

"Hello, Randy, I assume Dolores explained the situation and that I'd like to look inside your house."

There was a pause, then Randy's subdued voice said, "Dolores told me, and frankly I'm shocked. I had no idea a murder happened there. You have my permission to search. Dolores will let you in."

"Thanks," Floyd said. "I have another question. Did you notice anything missing from the house when you went back the next spring?"

The line was quiet for so long Floyd thought Randy had hung up. "Um, I can't say. I didn't go up right away in the spring and a few relatives had been up already by the time I got there." He paused. "It had been a tough year. My wife was losing a fight with lung cancer and she passed away that winter. I wasn't dealing with her death well, and I was in no rush to go back to the house. It seemed empty. . . Everything seemed empty."

"Did you spend time there when she was sick?"

"We spent much of the fall there watching the leaves turn. She had a lot of pain and it finally got so bad that she let me take her to the hospital in late October. She never came home."

"What was she taking for the pain?" Floyd asked.

"The doctor prescribed oxycontin. But at the end, even that wasn't enough which was why we left for the Cities. We left everything at the house, even our clothes and a refrigerator full of food."

After hanging up the phone, Floyd turned to Melissa. "What did you do when you cleaned up?"

Melissa cocked her head. "I threw the sheets into the washer. Like Uncle Randy said, the refrigerator was still full of food and that had all molded. I just scooped it into a bag and tied it."

Pam and Floyd followed Dolores and Melissa to Round Lake and parked in the driveway leading to the A-frame house. "This place looks like a ski chalet," Pam said as they exited the car. "I'd swear that the cedar siding and big windows could've been cut right out of the Swiss Alps and dropped here."

"I can't believe this is the place Aaron died," Dolores said as she unlocked the door and stood aside. Melissa stood silently by the door looking ill.

"The inside is as picturesque as the exterior," Pam said. "I love the open feel and all the cedar wall coverings." She walked over to look through the tall windows.

"Where was Aaron?" Floyd asked.

"Um, right about there," Melissa said, pointing to a round table in the kitchen. "He was slumped over the table, kinda like he'd fallen asleep there with his head resting on his arms."

Floyd bent down. "This seems to corroborate your statement about no blood," Floyd said, kneeling down to look at the hardwood flooring. "If there had been blood we would see dark stains in the cracks between the boards even after all these years." Floyd stood again.

"It seems odd that Ken Solstad would kill Aaron, then seat him at the table." Pam said. "Did you see any evidence that Aaron resisted Ken's attack?"

"I didn't look that closely," Melissa whispered. "I didn't want to look at him at all when I realized he was dead."

Pam and Floyd walked out the door and Dolores was closing the screen door when Melissa said, "Wait a minute." She pushed past her mother and looked around the inside of the house. "There was an empty prescription pill bottle on the table. I threw it in the trash when I cleaned."

The obvious hit Floyd just as he opened the car door. "C'mon, we're going back to the funeral home!"

CHAPTER 53

"What's the rush?" Pam asked as Floyd pushed past the speed limit with lights flashing and siren blaring.

"It's so simple," Floyd said. "No one killed Aaron. He either overdosed on the pain killers or committed suicide."

"Why are we rushing back to the mortuary?"

"He didn't leave a note at the Bradshaw's house or Melissa would've known Ken hadn't killed him. I'm guessing there's a note on his body."

They parked behind the mortuary and rushed in. Tony Oresek was making notes on a desk in the corner while Eddie Paulson was wrapping Aaron's naked remains in a sheet.

"There was an empty bottle of oxycontin on the table next to Aaron's body," Floyd said. "Where are his clothes?"

"In the garbage bag here by my foot." Eddie said. "We cut them off so Tony could do a surface exam of the body."

"By the way," Oresek said as Floyd dove into the bag of clothing, "his chest was all sliced up. The cuts weren't deep enough to penetrate the chest cavity, but I'm sure they inflicted a lot of pain before he died."

"Did you find anything in his pockets?" Pam asked.

"Like what," Oresek asked, his curiosity piqued.

"Like a suicide note," Pam said

"I checked the pockets," Eddie said. "I didn't find anything but lint. The front pockets are all crusty from the decomposition so they were a little harder to check."

Floyd spread the clothing, now cut into long strips. He dug his fingers into the back pockets of the over-alls and came out with nothing. He moved to the front pockets, starched rigid by dried fluids when the body decomposed, and came up empty there, too.

"Last chance," he said, reaching into the breast pocket of the flannel shirt. "Nada."

"You obviously weren't a farmer," Pam said. After pulling on a pair of gloves, she picked up the overalls Floyd had set aside. "Every farmer who wants to keep his papers clean and dry knows you keep them in the bib pocket, here between the brass suspender buttons."

She dug her hand into the pocket slowly, cracking the dried blood that was sticking the layers of denim together. Once the pocket was completely open she slid her fingers around until she felt the corner of something.

"There's a piece of paper here, but it's kind of glued to the fabric and I don't dare try to pull it loose. Can we wet the fabric to get it loose?"

"No," Floyd said. "Cut the fabric free around the paper and let's have a look at it while it's still stuck on."

After a few moments the three of them were staring at what appeared to be a piece of paper stained almost black with the faintest hint of blue ink showing.

"You said these clothes were some he'd stolen from someone's cabin," Eddie said. "It might be an old shopping list."

Floyd stripped off the gloves and took out his cellphone, dialing ten digits from memory while the others tried to make sense of the faint markings on the paper.

"Laurie, I need another favor," Floyd said to Laurie Lone Eagle when she answered.

"I know," Laurie said. "You never call unless you need a favor you don't have coming. What is it this time?"

"We recovered a note when we exhumed a body, but the paper is stained and adhered to fabric. Is there anyone at the BCA who could recover the writing for us?"

"We have a woman who's great at paper projects. She used to be a book conservationist at the historical society."

"I'll have a deputy run it down this afternoon."

"I take it this is a rush or you'd go through normal channels. I haven't read about any new murders up there."

"Well, this is part of the case we met about last week." Floyd chose his words carefully, "We're trying to decide if we're solving a murder or whether we've got a suicide. The note may answer that question."

"You have guts, Floyd Swenson," Laurie said with a laugh. "I'm sure you want your twenty-year-old case solved tomorrow. Tell you what, you get your stained note down here and I'll see if I can throw myself on someone's good graces to get it analyzed within this decade."

"Super!"

Eddie Oresek had listened to the conversation and nodded. "I'll see what we can do about rushing a toxicology scan. Lacking any surface trauma, that may be our best chance of finding a cause of death. Do you know what pain killer was in the bottle?"

"Oxycontin," Pam and Floyd said in unison.

CHAPTER 54

Floyd drove the back roads toward Dago Lake as the early morning twilight created a pink glow across the eastern sky. "I can't believe I'm up before dawn on a Saturday morning, dressed in a suit, and driving to a wedding."

"Quit griping," Mary said. "You're as happy about this wedding as I am." She sat carefully, trying not to wrinkle the long pink dress she was wearing. "You know, I've never been a bridesmaid before."

They pulled into the small park on the east end of the lake where another dozen cars were already gathered. Floyd was barely out of the car when the first mosquito buzzed around his head.

"Hell of a place for a wedding," he muttered. "I can already smell the roses and insect repellent."

"Shut up, dear, or I'll tell everyone what a spoilsport you are." Mary smiled and waved to Barb, who looked radiant in her ivory wedding dress and long gloves.

"People!" Judge Larson said. "People, can we gather together here and start the ceremony?"

The judge, dressed in her black robe, stood with her back to the lake. The wedding party lined up in front of her with the twenty guests behind them. Mary and Pam Ryan stood next to Barb and Sandy's two brothers stood beside him. The judge started the ceremony as the sound of tires crunching on the gravel caught Floyd's attention. He stepped away from the crowd and quickly jogged up the short trail to the parking lot where he approached the driver's door of a blue Cadillac.

"Mr. and Mrs. Dupre, you're just in time." He led Barb's parents down the path and to the back of the small crowd.

"Do you Sandford Maki, take this woman. . ."

The sheriff leaned close to Floyd's shoulder. "Sandy is short for Sandford?" he asked. "I'll bet the bullpen will have some fun with that."

The mosquitoes started to swarm around the small gathering as the bride and groom read their vows. A loon wailed its eerie call on the lake, causing the judge to pause and making everyone smile.

"Now, by the powers vested in me by the State of Minnesota, I declare you husband and wife." The judge smiled broadly and nodded to Sandy. "You may kiss your bride."

After the lingering kiss, Floyd took Barb's mother's elbow and led her past Mary and Pam, who were hugging Sandy. "Barb, we found some people who wanted to be here, but were afraid they might not be welcome."

Barb turned away from Gordy's hug. "Mom? And Dad?"

Tim Dupre grabbed Barb and pulled her close. "I can't believe we almost missed your wedding," he said with halting words as tears streamed down his face.

His wife pushed him aside and gave her own hug. "Things are different, honey. I'm so glad Mary Jungers called to let us know about the wedding."

Tears streaming down her face, Barb leaned away from the hug. "God, I can't believe I'm crying. Mary! Get your butt over here!"

"I see you found the secret guests," Mary said. "I called to feel them out a little and decided that maybe some of the history was far enough past that you might be happy to see them."

"Why didn't you tell me?" Barb asked as she wiped tears with her right glove while holding the bouquet in her left.

"I was afraid you'd say no."

Barb lurched forward and pulled Floyd and Mary into a group hug. "You guys."

CHAPTER 55

As more hugs were dispensed the guests drifted to a long table set up near the lake. A brown thermal urn dispensing coffee quickly drew a crowd. Pam, Floyd, and Mary carried white bakery boxes from the parking lot. They held a huge assortment of doughnuts, Danish, caramel rolls, and muffins, still a little warm from the ovens at Tobies bakery. The remaining guests carried lawn chairs and folding picnic tables to a grassy area next to the parking lot.

Mary steered Sandy and Barb to the picnic area so they could lead the guests through the impromptu buffet line.

"Really?" Sandy said, shaking his head. "The groom is a cop so someone thought there should be doughnuts and coffee at the wedding reception?"

Barb grabbed his arm and pulled him over for a kiss. "I asked for the doughnuts," she said, pulling a chocolate frosted doughnut from the nearest box and taking a big bite as everyone laughed.

Pam made a second trip to her car and returned with a small, square bakery box which she set on the end of the table. With Mary's assistance she removed a two-tier wedding cake and set it next to a stack of paper plates and plastic forks.

"Ladies and Gentlemen," Pam shouted. "It's time for the bride and groom to cut the wedding cake!"

Arm in arm, Sandy and Barb moved through the crowd to the cake. Mary passed a large knife to Barb and stepped back. Barb looked at the cake, then looked at the smiling faces circled around them.

"I guess..." Barb stammered. "I never..." she stopped with her mouth open, but unable to find any words.

"Cut the cake!" The sheriff's voice boomed, breaking the tension.

Sandy steadied Barb's shaking hand and guided the knife through the cake, carving out a small piece that he picked up with his fingers. "Open wide," he said playfully as camera's flashed around them.

Sandy pulled Mary, Floyd and Pam next to them, posing for a picture.

With her face still a palette of colors from deep purple to yellow and her nose still bandaged, Pam tried to duck away from Sandy's grasp. Barb gently grasped Pam's arm and pulled her gently into the group pose.

"But I look..."

Barb shushed her. "You look fine. This is just the way I want to remember this moment." Pam drew a deep breath and smiled, ignoring the pain caused by her smiling.

Floyd heard tires crunching across the gravel. He spotted a blue Crown Victoria parking next to the sheriff's car. After a minute, he saw Laurie Lone Eagle walking down the path to the picnic area. She bent down and picked a wood tick off her slacks and threw it into the grass as she stopped short of the celebrants and waited for Floyd.

"Laurie! What are you doing here?" he asked, steering her away from the celebration and hugs.

"Damned ticks. I hate ticks." Laurie looked like she hadn't slept. "You gave me a rush job, and I rushed it. I was going to catch you at the courthouse, but the dispatcher said the whole department was out here for Sandy's wedding.

Laurie handed Floyd a manila envelope. "The original note is in a zip-lock bag. The transcription is typed on a separate sheet."

Pam pushed up beside Floyd. "What is it, Inspector?"

"A suicide note," Laurie replied.

Floyd slipped the transcription from the envelope and read.

Mom, I'm sorry but my life isn't worth living anymore. I went to my old friends and they rejected me. Dad will never accept what my life is. I really do still love you, Kathy, even though it's not in the way you thought it would be.

Aaron

"Who are Kathy and Aaron?" Laurie asked.

"High school sweethearts who grew apart," Floyd explained.

"He committed suicide," Laurie said. "What happened to her?"

"She never entirely got over him. But, they're together again." Floyd slipped the note into the envelope.

"Together?" Pam asked with a frown.

"Kathy's parents had her disconnected from the respirator yesterday about the time we exhumed Aaron's body."

Floyd held Mary's hand as they walked the narrow trail to the parking lot. "You and Pam did a great job. I can't believe that you pulled all this together in such a short time."

"It seemed like the right thing to do," she replied. "Barb deserves a little happiness and I'm glad I could help her find it."

They stopped next to Floyd's car and he stared at the ground, his hands jammed in his pockets like an embarrassed teenager. "All the pieces finally came together in the Aaron Roberts investigation."

"Is that why the black-haired woman showed up at the end of the wedding?"

"She's an investigator from the BCA. We found a piece of paper in Aaron's pocket and her analysis brought out the writing. It was a suicide note."

"Oh," she said, waiting for Floyd to speak again.

"I also heard from the medical examiner," he said, looking at the ground. "They found lethal levels of oxycontin in Aaron's body."

When Floyd looked up, he had tears in his eyes. He pulled his hands from his pants pockets and took Mary's face into his hands. He kissed her gently.

"Life's too short to live in the past," he said.

Mary searched his eyes and then pulled him close. She gently returned the kiss and they stood silently holding each other close.

"I know," she said, whispering in his ear. "So, what comes next?"

"Since we're all dressed up, let's go to the top of the Duluth Radisson," he suggested, leading her to the pickup and unlocking the door. "We can have dinner and share a bottle of wine."

Mary climbed into the pickup cab and buckled her seatbelt. "That would be lovely, but you never drink and drive."

Floyd got in and started the engine. "I think we might find a bed there that doesn't hold any personal history for either of us."

ACKNOWLEGDEMENTS

I offer special thanks to the many people who helped make this book possible. Pat Morris did her usual fabulous job of fact checking and editing. Frannie Brozo and Nancy Mohr read, commented, and kept me honest on many levels. Dennis Arnold helped me make sure the "cop stuff" was right (although I didn't exactly follow his advice about every detail). My wife, Julie, offers medical advice, support and keeps me humble.

Thanks to my many friends and readers who keep me motivated and focused. Among them, Lynn Hovey, Russ Birkholz, Mike Mercer, Maria Westfall, Vida Meland, Kurt Hegland, Nancy Helmbrecht, Brian Johnson, Sarah Hawkins, Jeanne Coffey, Deb Shaw, and many, many other readers who have been reminding me that they're awaiting this next Pine County mystery.

And finally, thanks to Brenda (Engelbrekt) Bonney, who bid for the chance to have her name in this book during a fundraising auction at the Eagle Bluff Environmental Center. I am humbled, and the children who will be able to attend camp this year because of your generosity thank you.